REBOOT

AFTERLIFE ONLINE
BOOK ONE

Domino Finn

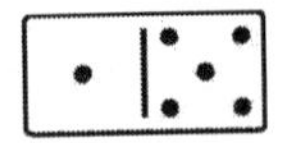

Published by Blood & Treasure, Los Angeles
First Edition

Cover Typography by James T. Egan of Bookfly Design LLC.

Print ISBN: 978-1-946-00881-7

DominoFinn.com

Also by Domino Finn

BLACK MAGIC OUTLAW
(http://dominofinn.com/black-magic-outlaw)
Dead Man
Shadow Play
Heart Strings
Powder Trade
Fire Water

SHADE CITY
(http://dominofinn.com/shade-city)

SYCAMORE MOON
(http://dominofinn.com/sycamore-moon)
The Seventh Sons
The Blood of Brothers
The Green Children

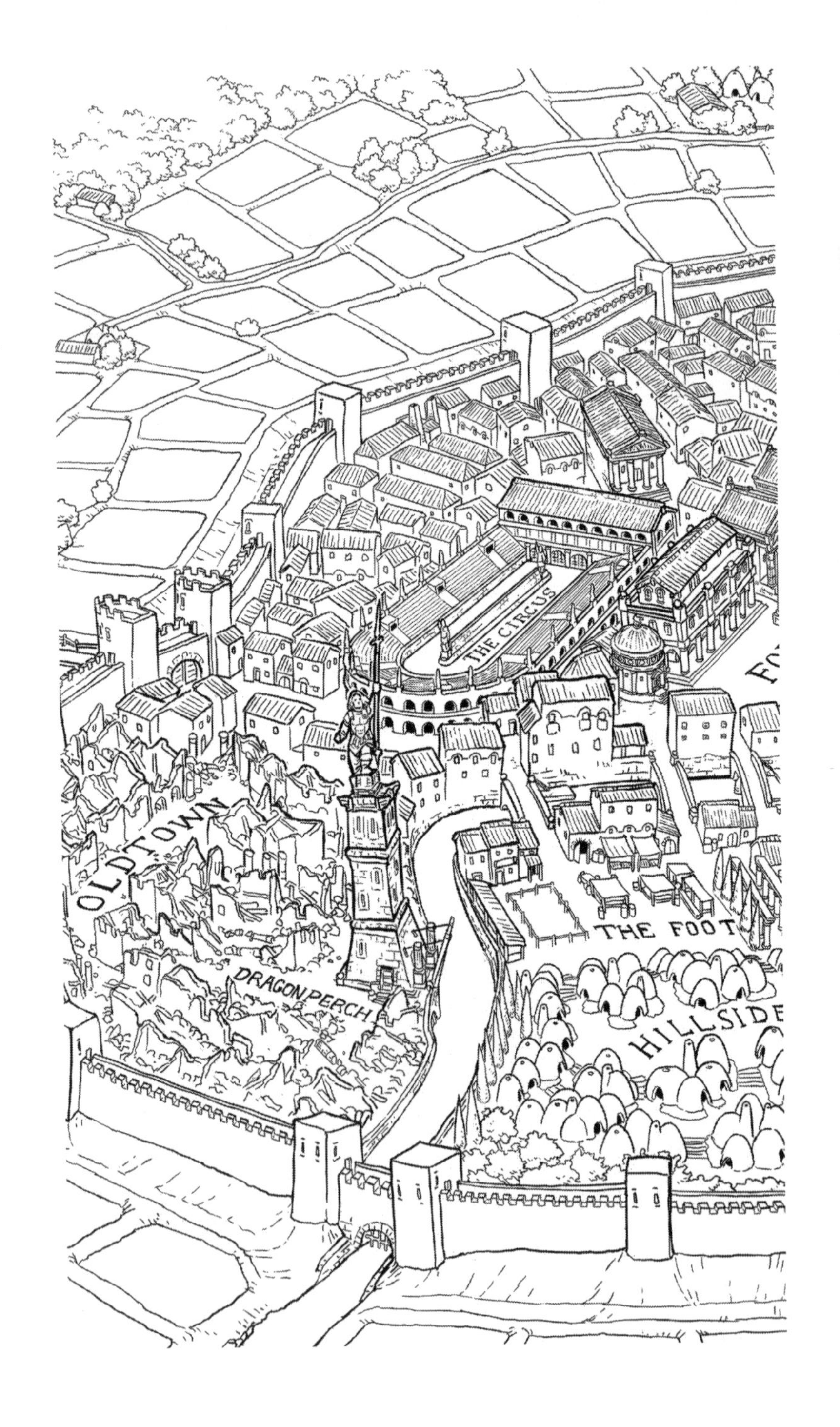
THE CIRCUS
OLDTOWN
DRAGONPERCH
THE FOOT
HILLSIDE

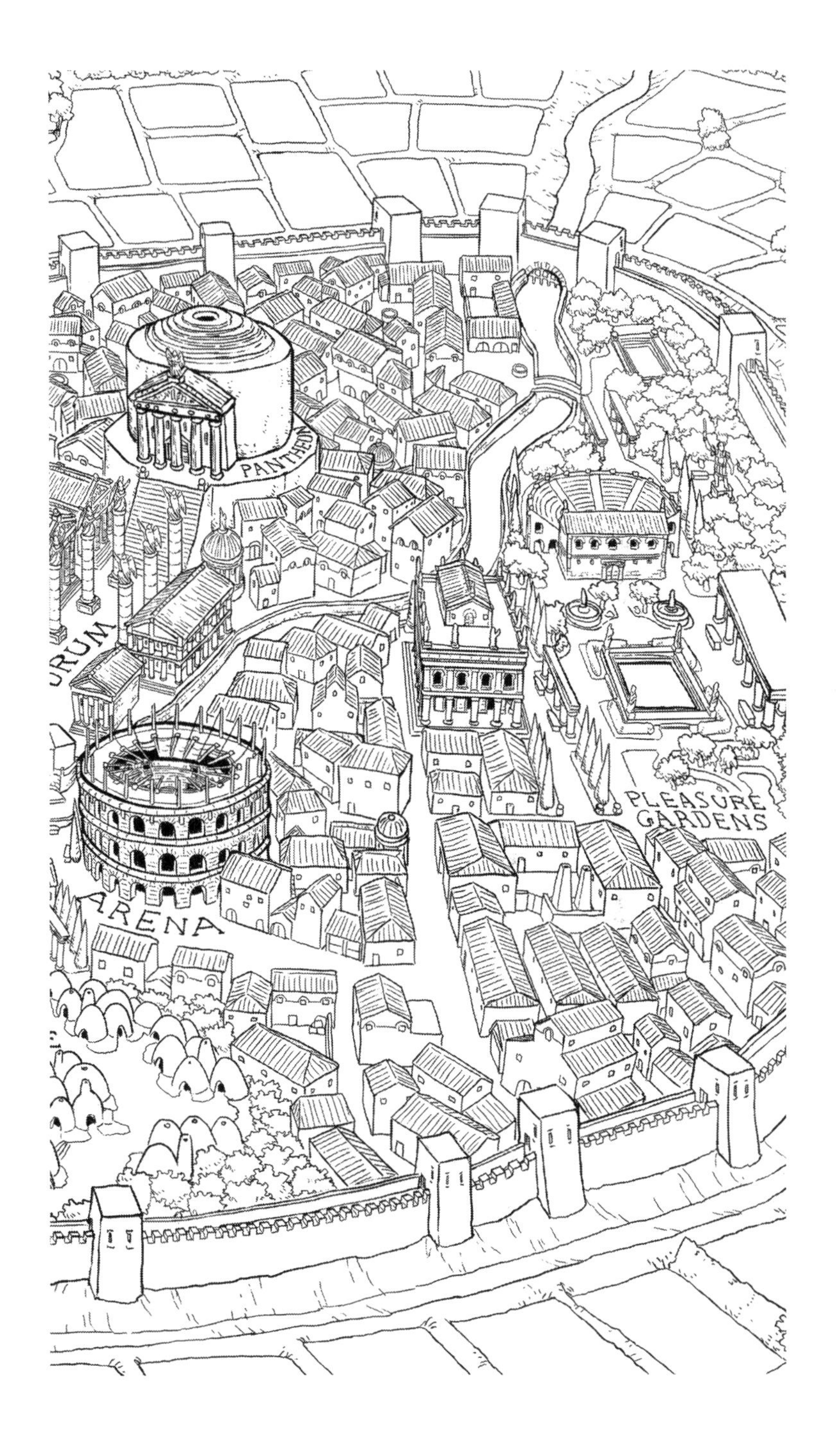
PANTHEON
URUM
ARENA
PLEASURE GARDENS

REBOOT

AFTERLIFE ONLINE: BOOK ONE

0000 Burnout

My name is Tad Lonnerman and I'm a millennial.

These days that sounds like an apology, but it's not. I hate that word and all the baggage it brings. Problems are problems, and we all have them. A father we never knew. A mother who barely remembers her name. A debt well into five figures. I turn twenty-five years old today and share an apartment with my little brother Derek because he's all I have left. So don't talk to me about being a whiny, spoiled brat.

About the only problem I don't have is my job. I'm an associate programmer in the game industry. Kinda bucked the unemployment trend on that one, didn't I? It's a dream job and I've been treading water for two years, focusing on nothing but being good at what I do and supporting me and Derek.

And it was working. Portlandia: the beautiful Pacific Northwest. This was where everything turned right for me, even with all the rain. A solid paycheck. A challenging career. I finally had it made.

So why was everything so bland?

Here I was, on my birthday, stuck in rush-hour traffic in a snowstorm. Rain I could deal with. Portland's a nice town but all the hills and highways run through endless bottlenecks. Snow shuts everything down. It gave me plenty of time to ponder being twenty-five.

My conclusion? What a crappy milestone. Sixteen gets you behind the wheel. Eighteen makes you an adult. Twenty-one's party time. What did I get now?

A lower deductible for car insurance. Watch out, ladies.

Yup. Mid twenties. Might as well be thirty. Kill me now.

It's ironic how the harshest measures of life happen on birthdays. To be fair, it wasn't just weather and existential angst. My small boutique game studio had been acquired by a soulless mega-conglomerate named Kablammy Games some time ago. They didn't care about game mechanics or design, they cared about monetization and data mining. *And* making endless sequels and clones. *And* focus testing the crap out of good ideas until only the most sanitary leftovers remained.

Kablammy had so many branches and divisions it was impossible to get anything done. Two years of plucky grit making a name for myself and I was suddenly lost in a sea of middle managers and request forms. And don't get me started on the number of mandatory meetings. It was one such useless meeting I was late to already. Today we'd probably strategize methods of charging gamers extra money for regular game content. Sorry, the princess is in another castle; please pay $9.99 to access it.

I huffed and flicked on my blinker. Eager to get out of traffic, I turned up an empty side street sloping up a hill. Don't worry, my hatred of the snow left me anything but unprepared. I had proper chains on my tires to battle my nemesis. With the absolute weight of the world on my mind, my compact car steadily scaled the icy road.

Dying isn't like those *Final Destination* movies. Gory, yes. Inexplicable, sure. But it's not fated. A series of events don't collude to kill you.

Death isn't noble like all the stories shoveled out of Hollywood either. It's not a meaningful sacrifice that forever changes the rest of the world for the better.

Death is a fucking Pepsi tractor trailer driving down an icy road and swerving headlong into your Nissan Altima.

That's it. No meaning. No purpose.

It's random.

I laid on my horn but the semi was out of control. Dumbass didn't even have chains on his tires. I tried to pull off the narrow road but there simply wasn't anywhere to go and the truck was determined to hog both lanes.

As the Pepsi truck slid inevitably closer, all I could think about was if my insurance deductible would reflect my twenty-five-year-old discount.

0010 Dead or Alive

I opened my eyes to extreme calm and nothingness. The world was white. I was in a great expanse of it. Drifting.

The car accident.

My gut reaction was I was in a hospital. Lying in a bed watching an empty ceiling. How long had I been here?

A man behind me cleared his throat. "Tod Lonnerman, I presume?"

I blinked and focused. Realized I was standing up. I spun around. In the complete absence of any background, the motion was disorienting. I was moving but I wasn't. Then the man came into view. He settled in front of me as I stopped, standing casually with his weight on one leg, cradling a tablet in his arm, and looking like he could use a coffee.

My demeanor wasn't nearly as ordinary. I stooped in front of him with my arms splayed to either side, wary of falling.

He looked me up and down and waited patiently. If he wanted something from me, he didn't get it. I stayed hunched in place like a cat trying to blend in with a wood floor.

The man was getting on in years. Thinning white hair and a matching wraparound beard. He wore a strange golden twig around his head like a crown. Come to think of it, everything about him was strange. He was dressed in a full toga, cream-colored except for a stripe of maroon along the edge.

He frowned and marked something on his tablet with a stylus. At this point I noted it was an actual stone tablet.

"You are Tod Lonnerman," he said. "Please confirm."

"Tad. I'm Tad Lonnerman. Where am I?"

He squinted at his tablet critically. "We'll get to that." His stylus traced a checkmark.

I was still a bag of nerves. He was the only thing in the room that wasn't pure white so I found myself staring at his footwear. Straps ran over open feet and up half his shins. He had strangely buff calves for a man his age.

"Nice sandals," I said.

"You should see yourself," he returned without missing a beat.

I was naked except for a tan loincloth of dubious convenience. I threw my hands around it to keep it from falling.

"How do you feel?" asked the man while acting as if everything was wholly normal.

The car accident.

I looked myself over. My legs, arms. I twisted around to check my backside and felt at my head. Everything was where it was supposed to be. No blood, no wounds or stitches.

"I feel... strange."

His stylus paused over the tablet. "Strange?"

"Well, it's like—I don't feel bad, so that's good, I guess. But at the same time, I don't really feel *good*. You know what I mean?"

He studied me blankly. "I see. That's not altogether

unexpected." He continued down his checklist. "And do you remember your accident, Tod?"

"Tad."

"What?"

"My name's Tad."

The man checked the tablet for verification. "So it is. Do you remember the accident?"

The car accident.

"Of course I do." I studied the white space. "I must be on some really amazing pain meds right now. What happened? Where are we?"

His eyes remained on the tablet but he answered. "Focus testing indicates it's better to let residents ease into the realization rather than tell them right off the bat."

"Tell them what?"

"Would you mind doing a few calisthenic drills for me? Some jumps or sprints. Anything that comes to mind."

"What?" I asked, getting annoyed. "Wait a minute. Where are we? I wanna know what's going on."

I stomped past the old man. The white background was so absolute that I couldn't distinguish the floor from the wall, much less find any doors. I circled him quickly, making two full revolutions before I realized it was pointless. I spun angrily.

"Yes, yes," he said. "That will be enough. Thank you."

I smoldered, red as a beet. "Look, buddy—"

"You're not on pain meds. You're not dreaming or hallucinating or suffering a nervous breakdown. Simply put, you're dead, Tod. You're dead and your consciousness has been uploaded to a redundant server farm owned by Kablammy

Games."

I blinked quickly and fell backwards a step. "It's Tad," I whispered.

I looked around again, absorbing his words. The wide-open space was suddenly claustrophobic. I found myself huddling closer to the old man, the only thing around me besides oblivion. As he scribbled on his tablet, I raised a cautious finger and pressed it into his forehead.

He was solid. I felt him, in the flesh.

"Yup, *great* pain meds," I concluded.

He swatted my hand away with the stylus. "You're not one of those close talkers, are you?"

I took a meek step away. "Sorry." I kept my raised finger in the air.

He sighed. "You don't need to raise your hand if you have a question. Just ask."

"Right. Are you saying I'm in a simulation right now? Like virtual reality?"

"VR?" The old guy snickered. "All reality is perception. There's nothing virtual about this. You're experiencing a brand-new technology. State-of-the-art DR."

"D—" I strained trying to fill in the blanks.

"This is pure digital reality, young man. Your *new* reality, I might add. Welcome to a brave new era. A second chance at life."

Life. I'd kinda liked my first one. I remained silent a moment, then asked, "Are you...?"

"Real? Yes. I'm not an AI, if that's what you mean. But I'm not dead either. I'm a real, live human, interfacing in DR to personally welcome you. Focus testing indicates new residents prefer a human touch."

"Focus testing," I repeated, having flashbacks from work. "You're testing the afterlife?"

"Beta testing to be exact. Kablammy has spent years perfecting this technology. Not only is the sum of your consciousness residing in a server farm, but you have access to the latest and greatest online role-playing game ever created."

I stared, dumbfounded. "Heaven is an MMO?"

0020 Second Life

"We prefer to call it *Haven*," said the old man, finally clipping the stylus to the stone tablet.

"Seriously? The afterlife is an RPG?"

He chuckled. "Sloth is sin, and all that. Focus testing indicates new residents need to apply themselves. Maintain goals. Keep busy, keep motivated. Otherwise they might fall into an irreversible depression loop. Let's get started, shall we?"

He motioned me to a stool that wasn't there before. The plain white wood sat flush with a bare table. The man sat on a similar stool on the opposite side and placed his tablet on its edge. It sat at an angle facing him, suspended on nothing at all.

In most circumstances I wouldn't have sat so easily, but I was desperate to feel something solid. The stool and table gave me something to whiten my knuckles against.

"Who are you?" I asked.

The old man smiled and motioned upward. When I stared blankly, he said, "Look above my head."

I frowned. "What, the motivational cat poster?"

"The what?" He twisted around and grumbled. "No, no." He waved his hand and the poster disappeared before my eyes.

"Everyone's a practical joker these days. Whatever happened to being proud of a job well done?"

I didn't answer the rhetorical question and he shook off the malaise.

"What I meant was look at the space above my head inquisitively."

I was still shaken from seeing the poster disappear. If I couldn't rely on the inspiring wisdom of kittens, what could I rely on? But I took a breath and focused on the empty area above his head.

Gold letters faded in: [Saint Peter].

"I know," he said. "It's a bit dramatic, but fitting. Don't worry, there's no true judgment here."

My gaze sagged down to his face. I couldn't really focus on his words anymore. As the gold name above his head faded away, I could only hang my jaw in shock.

"Listen," said Saint Peter, "this is my job. I welcome new residents to Haven. Help them get started. Give them a shoulder to lean on." He scratched his white beard and waited until I was lucid. "My best advice to you is this: Don't overthink things. Take your new world in slowly, one step at a time. Follow our instructions and keep an open, active mind about things. I'm sure you still believe this is all a bizarre dream. If so, don't waste it moping. Be carefree and enjoy the experience."

I nodded absently. Didn't see the harm in that.

"Now," he said, sitting up straight, "let me answer some of your questions. First off, this is a limited, closed beta application. This isn't a public utility yet, so count yourself lucky. According to these records, your company was acquired by Kablammy, which makes you an employee. One of us. As such, your insurance plan has been upgraded."

"I didn't ask for that."

"Standard procedure with HMOs. You take what they give. But you're right, of course. We require your consent."

I scoffed.

"Haven is just an option. I mean that. If you refuse consent we can part ways and delete you right now."

"And then what? I'll be a vegetable in a hospital bed somewhere?"

He pressed his lips solemnly together. "No, Tod. You'll be dead."

I didn't correct him this time.

"You're not hooked into a VR unit. You've literally been uploaded. Your entire being—your memories, thoughts, and desires—are a collection of ones and zeroes. Your reality is digital now. As a programmer, I'm sure you can understand that, even if you can't wrap your head around it. But we still need your consent."

I swallowed, but my virtual mouth was dry. "It sounds like I'm at your mercy no matter what I do."

"Not true," said Saint Peter. "Haven is what we call a free system. Without the ability for residents to log off, it's imperative we give everyone autonomy. Once you accept, you'll become a permanent part of the simulation. Not even we would have the ability to delete you. Your profile is encrypted and redundantly copied across multiple servers." He paused to give his next declaration weight. "Once you enter Haven, you have eternal life. The Bible got that part right, anyway."

"Great," I said, deciding lucid dreams were more insane than fun. "I consent. Let's get on with it."

He nodded and spun the tablet around. Even though it was made of solid stone, the surface layer resembled an LCD screen. An empty line and checkbox awaited my entry. I took the stylus and filled them in.

"Debit or credit," I joked.

He smiled. "I know you weren't asking, but beta access confers you 100% insurance coverage. You're literally set for life. Now there's just one more thing." He spun the tablet around, swiped a few times with his finger, and faced it at me again.

I stared at the screen without humor. "Terms of service."

0030 Final Fantasy

I scrolled through page after page of legalese, giving my best effort to take the whole affair seriously.

> Kablammy reserves the right to dictate terms of the beta.

> All participants, heretofore referred to as RESIDENTS, agree to store all aspects of their personality on Kablammy servers.

> Kablammy strongly believes in individual human rights and will never infringe on a RESIDENT'S privacy, security, and individuality.

It went on and on like that. There were privacy clauses, data-sharing agreements, beta addendums. I'll be honest here. I tapped out on page four. I swiped to the end, signed, and handed the stylus back to Saint Peter.

"Great," he said. "Perfect. I hope you feel better already."

I didn't mask my sarcasm. "I feel like the possibilities are limitless."

"They are, actually. Within reason. Now comes the fun part."

Saint Peter leaned over the table and spun me on the stool by my shoulder. Apparently I was standing now because matching me eye to eye but several yards away was my exact fucking duplicate.

A series of transparent two-dimensional panels hovered in the air beside the doppelganger. Images, slider bars, color pickers. A text heading above the screens read "Character Creation."

Okay, this was starting to blow my mind a little bit. But I was a gamer. I knew what needed to be done here.

The first choice was race, which was solidly set to human. There appeared to be other options but I was locked out of them. That was fine. I didn't really do the elf thing. There was no selection for gender. I took that to mean people would just be themselves inside Haven, without the need to specify a definition. So far, so good.

Next came the customization of physical traits. I could tweak stuff here and there, but I couldn't just pick a new face. Imagine you hadn't seen your cousin for five years before a family reunion. Had he gained weight and grown stocky? Had he become a gym rat and buffed up? Maybe college years of ramen had thinned his dimensions out, or he'd taken to the club scene and become a suave ladies' man. All these possibilities would affect his appearance, but you wouldn't expect a completely different face or body type. Just modified. The slider bars of real life.

I toyed with my appearance just for funsies. Made myself

stronger. Colored my hair blond, then blue. Even gave myself a nice tan. It was riveting seeing the different people I could be, but in the end I knew I wasn't any of them. I clicked the default button and looked myself over.

Straight black hair. Short. Thin frame. Healthy if on the pale side. I'd spent twenty-five years cultivating professional geek chic. It was who I was comfortable being.

I marveled at the detail of the doppelganger, though. The small dog-bite scar on my left hand. The eyes, not quite blue or silver, dotted with flecks of black. Even my skinny toes were matched perfectly to every nail. I looked down at my own feet and wiggled them.

"Did you scan my entire body?" I asked, amazed.

Saint Peter scoffed. "No. A scan would be imperfect, without the resolution to survive true DR. You're seeing your brain's representation of your body. Not just who you were, but who you believe you are. It's even more perfect than your physical form, which varied from day to day. This is one hundred percent you, Tod."

I rolled my eyes and turned back to the character creation dialog. I had to admit, I was starting to get into this.

I scrolled to the next set of screens. A series of menu images representing categories. My starting clothing. I scrolled through to find something snazzy but quickly realized it wasn't gonna happen. Icon after icon of drab peasant adornments were the only things on offer. As I cycled through the options, the doppelganger standing before me flicked into new outfits. I settled on a black tunic without sleeves that stopped at the knee and suddenly wished I had buff calves too.

Still wearing just the loincloth myself, I turned to Saint Peter. "You think I can put this on now?"

"Check your inventory."

I arched an eyebrow, and then I willed my inventory into existence. A grid consisting of a single item: a black tunic. I selected it and removed it from my inventory. The folded rough cloth appeared in my hands. I awkwardly slipped it over my head. It hung loose on me but didn't hamper my movement in the slightest.

Saint Peter cleared his throat. "The simulation allows you to climb in and out of clothes, if you wish. We do, after all, aspire to realism. However, inventory management, like many aspects of the game, is optimized for digital. Go on, pick a belt and see."

I scrolled through the available belts. They were a bunch of ropes and ribbons; nothing as sturdy as leather. I picked a tan length that was about my height, unsure what to do with it.

"Wear it directly from your inventory," Peter instructed.

I did that and the belt appeared around my waist. There was a knot at my side and the two loose ends hung down my calf. Easy peasy.

Next was footwear. I'm not a sandals guy but that was all they had. I picked something simple that wrapped around my ankle and frowned at my perfectly skinny toes. A good pair of boots would be my first order of business.

I couldn't help grumbling. "I don't really see the point in picking clothes if we're gonna look like peasants."

"We all have to start somewhere," replied the old man. "Your first real decision comes next."

Intrigued, I swiped ahead. A graphic of a crossbar dominated the selection area. It looked like a giant D-pad. Each cardinal direction was labeled.

"The class cruciform," announced Saint Peter. "This concept is at the core of Haven's game balance. These are the four base game disciplines everyone ascribes to."

SOLDIER

(Strength - Weaponry)

I examined the graphic closely. I could apparently pick from four starting classes: soldier, artisan, mystic, or explorer. Each position on the class cruciform seemed to imply opposition.

The currently selected topmost option was soldier. A separate window displayed its description.

SOLDIER

A natural combatant, soldiers are trained in a multitude of weapons and fighting styles. They're the hunters and knights, often relying on physical force to achieve their ends. An offensive class, soldiers shun the esoteric mystics.

Primary Attribute: Strength

A fighter class. It was probably one of the more common choices. I swiped at the screen and the entire cruciform rotated, moving artisan to the top selection.

ARTISAN

(Craft - Equipment)

This sounded like something most regular games didn't offer, so I paid attention.

ARTISAN

A heavily equipped defender and craftsman, artisans provide invaluable reinforcement to groups. They're the smiths and engineers, often relying on building strong communities for support. A defensive class, artisans strive against the subterfuge of explorers.

Primary Attribute: Craft

Interesting. Builders of some sort, although the class description was open-ended. I wondered how many possibilities there were. How many types of things could be built. Artisans were merchants, perhaps, but they had a stronger defensive role.

That made me ponder just how expansive Haven was. Maybe soldiers had a lot more going on than I assumed. I flipped to the next class.

MYSTIC

(Essence - Magic)

MYSTIC

A powerful specialist, mystics cast a range of spells in any number of disciplines. They're the magicians and healers, often relying on superiority through supernatural means. An offensive class, mystics abhor the banality of soldiers.

Primary Attribute: Essence

"Hmm," I said. "I would've expected a mage class to prioritize intelligence."

"You're thinking along the lines of old games," said Saint Peter. "Haven doesn't have attributes like intelligence and wisdom. What are these things if not an applied collection of your experiences and knowledge? If you're dumb enough to grasp a poisoned rose with an ungloved hand, what good would a numbered representation do you?"

I thought I followed. "So the attributes represent..."

"The non-mental portions of your digital reality. The things that don't really exist. Strength is your physical prowess, which unfortunately has not made the transition with your brain. On the opposite side of the spectrum is your essence, your closeness with the magic of Haven. The supernatural world. The craft of artisans represents general handiness and ability, while agility determines your speed and quickness."

I was beginning to see what Peter meant about the class cruciform being at the heart of Haven's game balance. Four base classes, four base attributes. A set of opposites in the combat and support spectrums. As a game developer I appreciated the clean design.

I swiped to the last class.

EXPLORER

(Agility - Artifice)

EXPLORER

A furtive wildcard, explorers use speed and smarts to achieve their goals behind the scenes. They're the spies and adventurers, often nomadic and flexible. A support class, explorers work outside the order built by artisans.

Primary Attribute: Agility

So if artisans built strong communities and unions, explorers struck out into the unknown on their own. I liked the sound of that.

There was something else. In games like this, I always pick the thief. Call it a fatal flaw, but rogues are my jam, even when they're underpowered. Granted, the word "thief" was never mentioned, but this was the agility-based class.

"Can explorers use weapons?" I asked.

"They sure can. Weaponry is the domain of the soldier, but as consort classes artisans and explorers have ample weapon selection. They even have physical combat skills. Just don't imagine you can trade blows toe to toe with a soldier."

That was all I needed to hear. I selected explorer. On cue, I was offered a list of starting weapons. Swords, slings, clubs. This part wasn't a foregone conclusion to me. I'd used all types of weapons in MMOs before. It just depended on the game and the current timing. Right now I knew I didn't wanna be just another sword jockey, but that was about it.

I considered what little I knew of the class. Explorers were loners with great mobility. As I cycled past a staff, I noted the imposing height of the thing in my double's hands. It wasn't a small dagger—a thief's weapon—but it had an opposite appeal. Definitely not sneaky, but a big stick sure as hell would keep enemies at a distance.

I thought about agility. Rogue classes often focus on subterfuge and slinking around shadows—hiding blades in sleeves—but there was nothing that explicitly said explorers needed to steal for a living in Haven. Maybe I could use my quickness for other pursuits. Sprinting, dodging, outmaneuvering.

A big stick wasn't a bad tool for creating space among enemies and using it.

I cycled through some other choices. A bow and arrow. A mace. I'd used those weapons at times but, with my new train of thought, they didn't appeal now. I wasn't planning on hiding in trees or ambushing enemies from behind.

When I scrolled to the spear, it immediately resonated with me. Here I had the reach of a staff but the added offense of a metal point. Sure, it probably limited some of the more acrobatic options, but it was a good balance between weapon and tool. I selected it.

[Woodman's Spear]

"Interesting choice," remarked Saint Peter. "I see you're going to have fun with this."

"I'm either dead or dreaming," I agreed. "I've got nothing to lose."

"Now that's the spirit."

0040 Rogue Spear

I swung the spear in the large empty room. I was standing on a leather mat now. The character creation menus had disappeared along with my double. It was just me and my weapon now.

It felt unfamiliar in my hands, but not ungainly. I could spin it in my hand without dropping it about half the time, which was probably a fat lot better than I could pull off in real life.

"Do I have some skill in spear handling now?"

"You noticed that," said Saint Peter. "You do, but it's just a base amount."

I thrust the tip forward. I did it again and added a hop for effect. "Will I get better with practice?"

"Only incrementally. This is an MMORPG after all. There are basic expertises that you become versed in through practice, things like building a campfire and pitching a tent. These are called proficiencies. They're about competency rather than resources."

I nodded. "And skills?"

"True skills are varied and class dependent. Your weapon use is a skill, which means it mostly improves through the expenditure of skill points. It's straightforward that way. You gain experience, you level, you receive new skill points and spend them. When you begin the tutorial, you'll have the option of selecting two other starting skills. We don't force you to pick them off the bat, in case you want to play around and learn about the environment first."

"Makes sense, but... tutorial?"

Saint Peter smiled patiently. "Of course."

"You're not gonna start me off in some lame RPG school that gets attacked by airships, are you?"

Saint Peter didn't answer.

I sighed. "Will it involve combat?"

"Of course."

I stopped swinging the spear like a jackass. "Um... will it... hurt?"

"What kind of Heaven would have pain?" Saint Peter leaned against the table and crossed his arms. "Listen, as far as sims go, pain is a real brain response. But when you're talking about conducive online environments, focus testing indicates pain isn't an asset. You can take damage, lose abilities and such, but you won't feel intense pain. Instead you'll get real-time notifications of your status as it changes. What is pain, after all, if not the body's status system?"

"So if I get stabbed?"

"You'll feel a watered-down representation of pain and take some damage. If there's blood there won't be a wound unless it's a more critical blow. Most of it is in place to support the idea of damage, to represent it to others. It's a game, of course, so you can always be fully healed."

"Cool," I said. "That doesn't sound too bad. I guess I'm ready to kick ass then."

"Not just yet. You have one last detail to take care of." He gestured to the new screen that appeared before me.

Name: _

The blinking cursor waited for my input. I smiled. This was the easy part. I always picked the same name. Not Tad, not Lonnerman, but a combination of the first few letters of each name. I voiced my input.

"Talon."

The prompt flashed in confirmation and disappeared.

Saint Peter nodded. "You're lucky. We just had a universal wipe and reboot. Everyone's level 1. You'll come out of the gate on the same footing as everybody else."

I paused. I kinda forgot there'd be other people to deal with. Even if they'd had their levels reset, they were familiar with the game. I'd still be the noob.

"Don't worry," he said, sensing my unease. "You'll do fine. It's a big world out there, but my job is to accustom you to it. Remember what I said. Take it in slowly. Over time. Haven's not the type of game that comes with a rulebook. Focus testing indicates it's better to keep the initial choices simple and let residents ease into the rest. You'll learn about skills and enemies and all that good stuff organically. And, if you ever find yourself in absolute need of guidance, just press that giant green help button up there."

I followed his signal and two large buttons appeared in the sky. One was green with a question mark and the other was red with a spider icon.

"Help will summon me," said Peter. "Use it wisely because you won't have access to me forever. The red button is how you file bugs."

"Bugs?"

"Don't be daft. This is a beta test and you're a developer. You're expected to report any bugs you encounter in detail. Such is the price of admission."

"Easy enough."

The thought of being immersed in a buggy simulation could've been disquieting, but the knowledge had the opposite effect on me. Like he said, I was a programmer. This world wasn't magic. It was a set of logical instructions to simulate an environment. The fact that bugs existed confirmed that the system wasn't all-powerful. It made it easier to view the whole thing as a game. As something familiar.

"It should be easy, yes," said Saint Peter. He picked up his tablet and typed in some commands. "Our A/B tests indicate easing residents into the simulation results in a smoother transition rather than throwing them into the fire. Turns out that could be traumatic."

A/B testing is developer jargon that means testing multiple alternatives at once and comparing the results. Does scenario A play out better than B or vice versa? It's a great way to find superior processes quickly.

"Why would you ever think it's a good idea to throw someone into the fire after telling them they died?"

Saint Peter shrugged. "There was a theory that the postmortem mind should be kept busy."

I hefted my spear over my shoulder. "Yeah, well, sign me up for the smooth transition."

"Oh." Saint Peter's face darkened as he referred to his tablet. "Unfortunately, our A/B testing is still technically ongoing and open for trial, and despite the overwhelming evidence that says you'd be better off easing into your new home, we can't slant our conclusions based on early evidence."

I crinkled my brow. "What are you saying, Pete?"

"You're in the B group."

I blinked. "What? The traumatic inferno?"

"Well said. Thanks for being a good sport about this."

"Whoa, now. If it's one thing I'm not, it's a good sport."

I tried protesting more, but all the whiteness in the world began to fade to black.

"Oh, one more thing," said Peter. "During the opening tutorial, and for the purposes of gathering play-test data, that giant green help button will be disabled."

"What?"

"We need to gauge your ability to learn and adapt organically. We don't want a clunky game, after all."

"But what do I do to avoid the serious trauma?" I asked desperately.

The world completely blackened as his disembodied voice answered.

"Don't worry about a thing. We've analyzed every detail of your background and employment history. You have a logical thought process. In a way, you could say this tutorial is perfectly tailored just to you, Tod."

"It's—"

And then the world was gone.

0050 Test Drive

My skin warmed. Mist tickled my face. A deafening roar crashed around me. I shut my eyes at the blinding light and gripped tight against the dizzying sway.

I was... outside.

I braced against a rope, hugging my spear to my body. What I'd initially perceived as a buffeting swell was only a breeze. The ground continued to rock back and forth beneath me, but it slowed to a gentle rhythm. The light and the noise, however, remained.

Cautiously, I opened my eyes and adjusted to the sunlight.

The sky was clear azure. Below, a canopy of trees rustled in the distance. As my eyes moved down to the yellow grass rippling in the wind, I fully comprehended my predicament.

I was in the middle of a grand chasm, rushing water below, suspended on a rickety bridge made entirely of rope.

I hugged the handrail. The walkway was made of three burly intertwined lengths of hemp. The handrails were thinner, one on each side rising from the center rope in the shape of a V. My arm was hooked over one and the soles of my sandals scraped against the rough hemp. I risked a look down.

A hundred feet to a raging current that would surely sweep me to my death.

This wasn't real; it was hyper real.

Overload. In real life your brain works to ignore common stimuli. There's a world of inputs everywhere—you don't really need to feel the air against every tiny hair on your arm.

In the sim, I did. The shiver of the breeze, the baking of the sun, the trilling of the birds. Cold, hard, rough, loud... I was bombarded with sensation.

And then, interestingly, my brain went to work. My digital brain, anyway. A filter of sorts kicked in. Sounds receded into the background. The light grew less blinding. Temperatures normalized.

This was a tutorial, I reminded myself. My body was running diagnostics. Whatever I was now, whatever comprised my intelligence, it was learning all the inputs of Haven. Like being thrown into a pool of icy water, I'd frozen up at first but had now acclimated. Slowly but surely, everything began to feel normal.

Normal. Imagine that. There was nothing normal about this. I should've been in the back of a speeding ambulance or something. Instead I was here, continuing this dream that was feeling less and less like one.

Hyper real.

As far as I could tell, I was alone. The rope bridge stretched taut between rocky chasm ledges, flush with tree growth. Up and down the canyon, the giant river winded a few hundred yards before vanishing around a bend.

Traumatic. I bet Saint Peter thought he was funny.

I checked the help menu. The green and red buttons loomed

over my head, but they were grayed out. Disabled for the play test. That was expected, I guess.

I switched over to my inventory. My bag contained a single whittling knife. An image of myself wearing the clothes and holding the spear depicted my equipped items. Right enough, the spear was hooked under my arm with the handrail.

I stared blankly at my meager supplies for a moment before selecting the spear and examining it.

[Woodman's Spear]
Oak and iron, a staple of the masses. This spear trades elegance for a sturdy frame.

I frowned. That wasn't really much help. I tried to look at my character sheet but didn't know how. Swiping the inventory just whisked it away, and any active thought to summon my stats wasn't answered.

It was just me and the terrifying bridge, then.

I mentally kicked myself. I was supposed to be an explorer, pioneering the land, not my character menus. I imagined a team of engineers watching the most boring play test ever. This was an adventure, wasn't it? Once my senses acclimated to the full DR experience things weren't so hard to handle. I grabbed the center of the spear in my hand and held it along the handrail, using my other arm for support, and stepped carefully ahead.

The bridge rocked under my shifting weight, taut bands groaning as if unaccustomed to passage. I advanced cautiously, trying not to visualize me tumbling into the killer current below.

What was I even afraid of? This wasn't real-real. It was a game. Besides that, pain wasn't a thing. Right?

Right?

Between the steady din of the river and my complete focus on footwork, I crossed a quarter of the bridge before I saw the figure eyeing me from the chasm's ledge.

I froze.

It was an ugly son of a bitch. Some cross between a hairless monkey and a Mordor orc. The creature was gray and misshapen but unnervingly humanoid. Thankfully it was only three feet tall.

I examined it as Saint Peter had taught me. The word [Imp] faded in above its head, colored orange.

"My first NPC," I said. My words lacked enthusiasm.

The creature regarded me with the frantic caution of an animal. Its shoulders jittered. A foot beat the ground. Some kind of threat display, maybe. Then its protruded snout opened and he bared his fangs. The growl was evident over the sound of the water.

As the beast aggroed on me, an intro dialog flashed into view.

No, not an NPC. A non-player character would imply some intelligence. This was a monster. A mob. Its only purpose was combat.

I waited, as still as the rickety bridge would allow, for the imp to make the first move. He was just an animal. A *freaky-as-shit* animal, granted, but an animal.

I was a grown man with a spear. And a whittling knife. I'd never been considered tall, but I was a giant compared to this twerp. I was counting on my superior size and human tools to win the day.

Just as my confidence peaked, the imp turned tail and faced the trees. I stood tall and smiled as he chittered into the brush.

Five of his friends joined him on the ledge. My face blanched.

The collected group of imps bayed and scraped at the ground and hopped up and down in aggravation. My response is best described as shitting a brick. Metaphorically, thankfully.

"What kind of tutorial is this?" I complained. "Couldn't they just start me off with slimes or giant rats or something?"

The commotion on the ledge ended as the group came to a consensus. The original imp (I think) fixed hard eyes on me and stepped onto the rope bridge. It walked on all fours, mostly, using not just the thick central strand of the base but the vertical supports running up to the handrails.

"Shit on a stick," I said.

Every MMO I'd ever played started players out in a noob zone. Something easy, something tame. Something safe, above all. The idea was to get a handle on the combat system before facing real challenges.

Everything about this imp told me he was not a practice enemy. Sure, he was small enough as far as mobs went, but he was straight-up rabid. A vicious, electric little beast. Quick and spry and lugging a chip on his shoulder. I didn't want to face one imp, much less a pack of six.

Still facing forward, I retreated from the advancing enemy. I didn't give two shits if Saint Peter and the entire development staff were awaiting a heroic charge. I was more cautious than this. I'd show them glory was often overrated. That staying alive, even in a game, meant something to me.

I had a larger gait but the backward movement hampered me. The imp began to close with light steps. I was stuck in the middle of the bridge again, too far out to make it back at this clip. I threw caution to the wind, turned around, and sprinted to the far side.

The imp screeched and picked up his pace. I ran. The bridge rocked and bounced. With its lighter weight, the imp had a harder time of it than I did. He struggled to keep rooted to the lurching rope.

As I approached the ledge a wild idea struck me. I summoned my inventory menu and direct equipped the whittling knife. The spear disappeared in a blink. I should've done that a while ago. The knife didn't get in my way nearly as much. It almost felt like I had an extra arm now. That was a lesson to apply to the future.

The second my sandal clapped on solid rock, I spun around and brought the knife down on the rope handrail. The dull blade mashed against the weathered hemp.

The imp recognized what I was doing. For such a rabid little shit, he was far more intelligent than a monkey. He bounded toward me as I sawed at the bridge.

Both gestures were completely unnecessary. My crappy little knife barely managed to snap a few threads of the sturdy length.

As the creature closed on me, I changed tack and threw the whittling knife at its head. The imp ducked. The knife bounced off a rope support and plummeted to the river below.

"Noob knife," I muttered.

A chattering laugh scraped my ears. The imp heaved up and down in mirth. Then it hissed and readied a lunge.

Feet planted firmly in the rock, I equipped the spear and held it straight out over the bridge. The iron point hovered a foot away from the creature's face.

We paused, taking stock of each other. The rest of the imp pack watched from the safety of the other side.

This was the strength of the spear. Positioning and reach. On the narrow platform, the imp could hardly skirt around my weapon. I had him at a supreme disadvantage. Any attempt to lunge could result in it being skewered or knocked into the deadly river. I held my spear firm, aware that I didn't really know how to use it but hoping it didn't matter too much.

After a solid minute of deadlock, I recognized the catch. I was keeping the creature at bay like an ace, but the second I turned around and went along my merry way, the imp would sink teeth and claws into my back. I'd turned this contest into a stalemate, but what I needed was a victory.

Once again, my confidence returned. I stepped forward, placing a steady sandal on the bridge and leaning my elbow on the handrail. It was imperative I kept both hands on the spear if I was going to strike with it. It meant I was slow, and my balance was off, but I was ready to kill my enemy.

The imp hissed with uncertainty. It backed away, but only enough to look for an opening. He clearly didn't have retreat in mind.

That made two of us.

As its back foot hit a knot, I lunged. I kept the spear horizontal, sliding it forward as if on glass. The imp batted at the tip but I held strong and pressed my weight forward. The strike pitched to the side but the iron still found gray flesh. It punctured the side of the creature's rib cage. The imp wailed in pain.

I pulled the spear back to strike again but dragged the imp with it. It swiped with a back leg and gashed my arm. My mind flashed red and a dull ache encompassed my forearm. Pain as a notification instead of a debilitating condition. I gritted my teeth and twisted the spear toward the beast's heart. I pinned it against the rope wall and sunk the weapon deep. Bone snapped and the imp convulsed and went limp.

A faint tickle scrolled past my head, much more subtle than the representation of pain. When I focused on it, I saw a stream of text notifications that I had missed in the heat of the moment.

Impale! You dealt 14 damage to [Imp] 6 damage Critical Hit! You dealt 34 damage to [Imp] [Imp] is defeated 150 XP awarded

Jeez, this really was an RPG. I wasn't interested in the numbers just yet but it seemed both my attacks had achieved special status bonuses somehow. I'd been lucky to impale the creature with the first strike, and its inability to defend itself from that position, and my targeting of the heart, had likely resulted in the crit.

"Fight smarter, not harder," I said smugly.

A new notification popped up:

You have killed a pagan. Doing so enrages all pagans. Pagan Reputation -10

I hissed. I wasn't just gaining experience, I was gaining faction notoriety. That was a crappy flipside to what was supposed to be a victory.

If the pack of imps at the opposite cliff had been perturbed before, they were wildly agitated now. They hollered and batted limbs at each other. Five sets of teeth spun my way as the rest of the pack jumped onto the bridge and charged over the rope in a line. A couple of them even hopped on the handrails and ran along them on all fours.

This... this was not something I was prepared for.

Sometimes fighting smarter means not fighting. I turned tail and ran.

0060 Escape from Monkey Island

Instead of crashing into the dense forest and running into whatever packs of wild creatures lived on this side, I decided to run along the chasm edge. It was rockier ground and the narrow sloped path would give my spear an advantage. I could only imagine it getting tangled in the thick brush.

The downside to my strategy was that I couldn't readily vanish out in the open. I wasn't sure what mechanics Haven had in place for hiding, but I had five imps aggroed on me. I doubted I could pull off a disappearing act.

And I'd thought hiding in shadows was lame.

I raced around the curve of the ledge. The bridge disappeared from sight before the imps made it across, giving me some hope that I'd made the right choice. But scaling the treacherous cliff face proved more and more difficult. My thick sandals weren't very malleable and easily lost traction against the loose rocks. I tripped and stumbled. Once I would've slipped off the cliff entirely if I hadn't planted the spear into the ground for support.

My path—my *only* option now—actually sloped down into the chasm, running along the wall and closer to the white water. The edge of the cliff above me was bordered with boulders and trees, but several minutes into my retreat it opened into a nice solid platform.

The only problem was it was ten feet above my head.

The imps had to be pretty good climbers. I figured they could get up there if they needed to. However, if I could do so before they saw me, I was confident I'd lose them. I put my spear away and faced the sheer canyon wall.

Agility Check... Fail!

My fingers scraped against unforgiving rock, unable to find a grip.

I tried again and slipped again. Lurching upward only meant I came crashing down on the return trip. I attempted a gentler climb. A careful foothold. Two hands spread wide, clutching only flat rock. I kicked up slowly and actually found another foothold. When I got there, though, there was nowhere else to go. As I reached for a jutting rock above, I slipped and slid back down to the outcropping.

The howls behind me grew closer. I was losing my lead. With a last-ditch effort, I pulled out my spear and planted the iron in the ground. I used it to climb partway up the wall. But after that, I couldn't make another move.

Around the bend, two of the imps appeared. They were just as rabid as ever.

I cursed and hopped down the cliff wall. This ledge wasn't a bad place to face them, if I needed to, but I still had a path to retreat along. The ground sloped closer to the river.

As I ran, the hollering of the imps grew louder but strangely distant. The rushing of the water was drowning everything else out. I was close to it now. The splash from the waves hit my bare calves and made the path slippery.

But the volume of the current was still much louder than it should've been. Were my senses out of control again?

A hazy mist smothered me. I pressed forward as droplets dotted my skin. A sinking feeling grew in my belly. The ledge I was sprinting along abruptly ended and I almost plummeted down a sheer drop—not into the river but *with* the river—hundreds of feet below. The noise and the mist were the result of a gargantuan waterfall.

I spun at a stray screech. The imps were closing on me, but I could see their hesitation. They didn't like the water maybe. Or the sound.

I looked down. There was another ledge below, running along behind the waterfall. I smiled. If I knew video games, there'd be buried treasure back there. A small stepped ledge ran away from the waterfall to the next level down. Keeping my spear up in defense, I pressed my chest against the rock edge and descended.

The five imps converged together. Crawling on top of each other, shoving through. All eyes were on me and the tip of my spear. I concentrated on my footholds until I found the bottom. Nice and wide, actually.

The imps stayed above, but they were between me and the

waterfall now. The last thing I wanted was for them to rain down on my head as I passed beneath. I moved carefully, jabbing my weapon upward in warning. Three of the creatures were cowed, but two of them followed my path down the rocky steps. They joined me on the bottom and growled.

I was past the others, though, and the fire had left the filthy creatures. If I had to guess, the ones up top had canceled their aggro on me entirely. The two on my level followed half-heartedly. The nearer I got to the waterfall, the more defeated they grew.

The deluge of water jetted clear over the platform. A huge wall of white. It fogged the area and made the depths it reached entirely mysterious. But now that waterfall was my shield. The imps didn't dare walk under it. And as I moved deeper, I found a dark opening in the rock face.

I instinctively played the Zelda secret chime in my head.

Threat averted, I calmly strolled into the cave, eager to claim my prize. Fighting smarter, not harder, huh? I was starting to like the sound of that.

As I pierced the murky depths, the deafening sound of the waterfall gave way to multiple voices murmuring in unison. I tightened my grip on the spear and crept forward. I neared a bend, hoping to get a peek at my hosts, but their disquieting chanting suddenly cut out.

I took a breath and rounded the corner. In the darkness, it was hard to see anything, but I was pretty sure two figures were standing around a cauldron.

"Who intrudes on the ritual?" asked one of them.

Pagan Reputation -20

Crap.

"The civilized world will crumble," said a scratchy voice behind me.

I spun around. Standing a little taller than me was an imposing creature. She was blacker than the imps. Less monkey, more ogre, with wild mats of long hair. She licked her lips and leaned a bony face close. I gasped as I noticed the hollow cavities of her eyes.

[Crowlat - Boggart Witch]
200 health

"All pagan killers must suffer," she rasped.

She may have been blind, but she slashed a claw so fast I couldn't get my spear up in time. My gut exploded. Not pain, but full alert. The corners of my vision reddened and blurred out, and the boggart pulled a tangle of something that looked eerily like my intestines to her teeth.

Critical Hit!
88 damage
You are dead!

0070 Dead Space

"Ugh."

I shivered in my bed. Jerked awake, to be precise. I wasn't startled. This was a vaguely uncomfortable feeling. I didn't hurt, but my brain was still reeling from being eviscerated by a monster.

My eyes opened to the soft blue lighting of a small room. I turned my head, burying it in a fluffy white pillow. Sleep. Sleep was always good.

A chime went off beside me. *Ding!*

I took a moment to process the serene room. So this was it, then. The end of the dream. I'd woken up in the hospital and there'd be no more imps or boggarts or—

A wall of text scrolled into my vision, line by line.

Respawned at Home
Tutorial is being processed...

Welcome to Haven!

"Fuck me two ways to Sunday," I hissed.

This was still the sim. Haven. I was in a sparse room. A bed, a bookshelf. Some neatly arranged personal effects. Not lived-in clutter but accessible clutter, like you'd find in a hotel.

Ding!

I rubbed my face and realized my mind was playing tricks on me. I wasn't really tired or hurt, I just thought I was. It was a sobering thought. People don't respawn in the real world. But here I was, wearing my black toga and golden belt rope and not-very-comfortable sandals. In bed. I sighed and stood up.

There were two doors in this room. The open one led to a private bathhouse. The medieval equivalent of a Jacuzzi. A sink and mirror, a wicker chest with towels in it, and a small basket of toiletries on a wooden stool.

Curiously, there was no toilet.

I flipped one of the levers by the sink and a stream of clear water flowed from the faucet.

"Huh, running water."

I shut it off and returned to the room for a look around. The shelves and bookcases were mostly empty. A hardcover volume lay on its side. I spun it around and read the title: *Haven Terms of Service 0.9.21*. I hefted the tome aside and picked up the next one: *Haven User Guide*. The cover showed a vast open field populated by players of all types. The bottom corner bore a Prima Games logo.

"I don't believe it. They're in the afterlife too."

The company was famous for making game guides and often worked directly with developers on content. It was a good bet Kablammy Games hadn't given Prima much access, though.

This book was noticeably thinner than the terms of service tome. What had Saint Peter said? Residents were meant to learn about Haven organically.

I opened to the first page. The heading read, "So you've died and gone to Haven." I rolled my eyes and fanned the pages through my fingers.

My brain caught the trick as the pages flitted by. The sensation of pages flipping past my finger was real. Page by page, the snap of the paper and the scrape of the edge were genuine. But the book didn't behave like a book. For the vast majority of my browsing, whether I was near the beginning or the end, the pages were evenly split on either side of my focus. Essentially, I was always in the middle of the book, at least until I came to the end.

"Digital Reality," I murmured.

This wasn't a real book; it was a tablet styled as a book. A collection of ASCII characters and graphics in a soft-cover book interface. It seemed an odd concession in a digital world, but as a programmer I understood data storage and manipulation was the probable reason. Real books had fixed page counts and lacked hyperlinks. Text couldn't be resized, pictures couldn't be zoomed.

They didn't have a search feature.

I focused my mind on the [Imp] and turned the page, pleased to see a successful result.

Various imps and goblins claim the land as theirs and oppose any who attempt to cultivate it. Pagan creatures such as these should not be underestimated. They are devious, quick to panic, and very dangerous in numbers.

Hmm, not a whole lot of information at all. Rather than an actual section dedicated to the little beasts, this was a passing mention introducing the general concept of enemies.

I chewed my lip and shivered inwardly as I brought the [Boggart Witch] to mind and flipped the page.

Nothing.

I shook my head and absently flipped pages, randomly skimming whatever I landed on. This was less of a strategy guide and more of a primer to what awaited. A teaser of Haven.

Ding!

I huffed. That stupid noise was grating. I tossed the user guide into my inventory and scanned the room. I was interrupted by a text notification.

Your tutorial has been processed.
Your starting attributes have been set.
Congratulations, explorer!

I grumbled, unsure what there was to be congratulated about. It felt like I'd been given a participation trophy or something. Still, my curiosity was piqued. I brought the internal game menu up and was surprised by several windows jumping into view.

First off, the help and bug buttons were enabled again. They were part of a profile bar running along the top of my vision. The very left was emblazoned with a pic of my face and my game handle, Talon. A few icons trailed that. At the end was the time, showing it was still morning. About two hours after my car accident. The date was a numbered day in the hundreds, but the year was curiously the same as the real world.

The area underneath the profile bar was a splash screen of sorts. The main window.

Welcome to the beta! Take a tour of the menu!

I canceled past the prompts and was pleased to see other tabs available for selection. Character. Inventory. I swiped ahead.

Talon		*Level*	1
Class	Explorer	*XP*	150
Kit	NA	*Next*	1000

Strength	12	*Strike*	25
Agility	14	*Dodge*	25
Craft	6	*Health*	19 / 19
Essence	8	*Spirit*	18 / 18

My attribute scores. This was what I'd been looking for.

Curious that I hadn't selected these myself. It was possible they were randomly rolled but I figured Haven was more sophisticated than that. The explorer class majored in agility and my stats reflected that. Looking back at the tutorial processing messages, I came to the conclusion that the scenario had been an attempt to gauge my play style and set my attributes accordingly.

I strained to remember the class cruciform. Soldiers and mystics were opposition classes, with their specializations in strength and essence. Artisans were opposed to explorers. That explained why my opposition class attribute of craft was so paltry. In truth, it represented me well. The last time I'd thought myself handy was after changing a particularly stubborn light bulb—it was a safe bet I wouldn't be building things in Haven.

I focused on my middle-of-the-road attributes. I wondered

why strength was the better off of the two. My class and weapon were explicit selections; my actions in the wild would have determined the rest. I'd climbed and scaled and sprinted. I'd stabbed a creature to death. I couldn't imagine how I would've taken advantage of craft or essence in that ravine of raging water, but maybe that was the point. The attributes reflected my standard responses to the world. Fight or flight. Or build. Or cast.

I figured strike and dodge to be combat scores. It pleased me to see my health at maximum again, but 19 didn't seem very high. And spirit appeared to be a mix of mana and stamina.

I remembered Saint Peter's message. Take things slowly. Learn as you go. His point was to not get bogged down in specifics right off the bat. Fair enough.

My inventory had reset, meaning I had my whittling knife again. Woo boy. Between that and the rest of the empty slots, there wasn't much to look at. I focused instead on my equipped items. Just my clothes and the woodman's spear. Try as I might, I couldn't find any hard stats for the weapon. I was sure it affected my strike and dodge ranks, but the spear didn't have a +5 attack score or anything obvious like that.

Come to think of it, my overall stats were somewhat simplistic. That certainly jived with Haven's design focus. Too many numbers would break immersion and slow the game down. This was an experience meant to be lived, not computed. I was just starting to think this wasn't much of an RPG when I swiped to the next menu tab. Skills. A smile played across my lips.

There were several skill categories, and I quickly understood these to be class based: Weapons. Awareness. Survival. Traversal. Stealth. According to the menu, I had 3 skill points to spend.

The weapons tree was straightforward and the only section to already have a skill assigned.

Spear Handling

Level 1

You are versed in the basics of spear combat. This root skill allows you to use spear weapons without being a hindrance, but improvement and specific tactics require further skill point expenditure. Weapon specialization skills may not be higher level than their root.

I began to understand why my weapon didn't have a simple attack rank. As I progressed, I'd need to sink additional skill points into this to improve it. The quality of the weapon was just a bonus.

Besides spear handling, many other weapon types were available to me along the lines of the weapons I'd been offered during character creation. It was a waste of time to focus on those. Instead, I noted the branches leading off the root skill into various disciplines: Vanguard. Deadeye. Javelinist. Defender. These were different play styles leading to the aforementioned specialty skills I could purchase. The spear skill tree.

VANGUARD

Hard-charging, tip-of-the-spear combat

Headline Skill - Power Slash

A vicious strike to your enemy, causing up to x2 damage at level 1.

Spirit Cost: 10

Cooldown: 20 seconds

DEADEYE

Calculated, precision combat

Headline Skill - Deadshot

A targeted strike to a specific body grouping.

Spirit Cost: 10

Cooldown: 20 seconds

JAVELINIST

Flexible, ranged combat

Headline Skill - Spear Throw

A distance attack with a melee weapon.

Spirit Cost: 7

Cooldown: 15 seconds

DEFENDER

Measured, holding combat

Headline Skill - Crossblock

A two-handed parry with the spear shaft.

Spirit Cost: 4

Warm-up: 1 second

Even though it wouldn't be my bread and butter, I appreciated seeing weapon-based techniques. I wasn't a soldier and didn't intend to pound my way to victory. I wanted to fight smarter, not harder. But options were good. It was nice to see explorers weren't useless in a scrap.

From the list I could tell most skills had a spirit cost. Many had cooldown timers to prevent repeated use. The crossblock didn't have that limitation, allowing more frequent defense, but there was a 1 second warm-up. That implied you couldn't use the skill immediately after an attack or action, but rather it needed to be prepped.

Each skill set, when purchased, would open up a further set of skills. Haven kept things simple upfront and didn't reveal what was further down the skill tree, so I studied my current options.

Immediately, I was drawn to the Deadeye style. The vanguard was the power player. The deadeye was the tactical player. I had no interest in tossing my only weapon away so I skipped the javelinist. That left me with the defender. It wasn't the sexy choice but it wasn't stupid either. I thought of the boggart and decided I didn't want that happening again. After confirming I could delve into multiple combat styles, I purchased the crossblock skill.

Ding!

I ignored the notification and hungrily checked the next skill categories. Awareness focused on things like discovery, scanning terrain and landmarks, and other exploration techniques. Survival was hunting, trapping, and skinning. Traversal was scaling and tumbling and vaulting.

"Where were these when I was stranded on that mountainside?" I bitterly wondered.

The last section was stealth, a clear giveaway that these skill options were tied to my class. There were the usual choices one would expect: hiding, sneaking, stealing, lock picking.

When I'd finished scanning over the skill list I was... unimpressed actually. For a state-of-the-art digital-reality first-of-its-kind MMO, I'd kinda expected a wider skill selection. But then I considered how complex the spear skill tree quickly became and realized unlocking and advancing skills would open up others. These weren't *all* the skills in the game; they were just the *starting options*. I was only a level 1 scrub, after all.

I wanted to spend my last 2 skill points to see what else could be unlocked, but I stopped myself and worked over the strategy. I couldn't just buy things without a plan. Skill points were limited. My selections needed to reinforce each other. I needed my abilities to be synergistic.

Even if I could decide on a skill right away, the order I unlocked them in was significant. After all, picking any one skill could open up a new option. Should I first pick the skills I most needed, or should I focus on the skill trees with the most powerful potential further down the line?

Crap. I hated being indecisive, but at least I recognized when I was. No way I was comfortable committing to anything right now. I still had no idea how easy it was to level in Haven or how many new skill points I'd receive per level. I doubted it would be this many.

Ding!

Ugh, already. A pulse of movement from the profile bar

caught my attention. The mail icon had a red 1 overlapping it. That would be the source of my continuing aggravation.

I selected the inbox and found a welcome message from none other than Saint Peter.

> Apologies for that tutorial. No one lives through the pagan ones. *No one*. If it's any consolation, you're the last resident to run through the bridge encounter. Focus testing indicates being gutted alive might be coming on a little strong.

I rolled my eyes. "You think?"

The experience hadn't been especially traumatizing, as I'd been led to believe, but I hardly understood the design purpose of putting me through it. I barely knew more about the game afterward. Tutorials were supposed to equip players with the resources to succeed, not pound them to a pulp.

I continued reading.

> Take your time to familiarize yourself with your room. You're in a safe space. You can study the user guide or relax.

Outside the closed door to my room, something banged against the floor. A scuttling sound followed.

Another interruption, and I'd just been addressing the dings. Hard to relax in conditions like this. Heaven wasn't turning out to be a very peaceful place after all.

I ignored the noise and kept reading.

> You are now in Stronghold, one of nine starting towns in Haven. There's no combat within city limits. No enemies. You can take stock of things, make purchases, and venture out with adventuring parties as you see fit. Stay close to Stronghold until you grow confident of your abilities.
> Until then, happy trails, explorer!
>
> - Saint Peter
>
> PS: Don't forget to introduce yourself to your roommate.

Another crashing sound came from outside. This time it involved glass breaking and a yelp as someone slipped and banged against the door to my room, no doubt eavesdropping.

"Roommate?" I muttered.

0080 The House of the Dead

I swung my door open to find a guy with the text [Kyle] over his head scooping up pieces of a broken bottle. The glass had only fractured into a few shards and most of the beer had been saved in the base.

"Oh!" he said, startled. He sprung to attention. "Sorry. I didn't know anybody was home."

I arched a skeptical eyebrow but didn't call him out. He waited uncertainly, shifting his balance from leg to leg. I guess I couldn't blame him for being curious.

Kyle was a large guy compared to me. Taller, thicker, rounder. The type who played football in school but never made the varsity team. More heavyset than muscled, but not too much of a caricature in any direction. A pretty normal guy with shaggy brown hair. College age.

"Kyle, right?" I said. I offered my hand and he slapped it.

"Kyle Grath. And you're... Talon," he noted, looking above my head. "What's that mean?"

"Um, it's like... a talon."

He nodded. "Cool. You wanna play beer pong?"

"Uh..." I glanced at the spill on the floor.

Kyle cursed and rushed to the kitchen to get paper towels. The mess and glass wiped up without any fuss. No sense making virtual spills a pain in the ass.

I moved into the common area. Compared to the modest bedroom, it was decadently spacious. Several loungers circled around a huge flat screen with game controllers. A modern kitchen and bar overlooked a dining table. There was even enough spare room for a sunlit beer pong table beside a bay window.

"This looks like a frat house."

"Phi Kappa Koopa," said Kyle. He tried for a secret handshake but I just hooked my hands on my hips. He shrugged and killed the rest of the beer from the jagged bottle base. "Can I get you a brew?" he asked, strolling to the refrigerator before I answered.

"We have drinks? I mean, you can get drunk in Heaven?"

"Sure." He grabbed two cold ones and popped them open. "You can get a buzz, at least. It's not quite the same but there's less projectile vomiting and nuclear farting. And it doesn't negatively affect your adventuring. When you go outside, you're clean." Kyle handed me a bottle and unpacked a set of red Solo cups on the beer pong table.

"I've been waiting for someone to shoot against. No offense to old people, but the last guy I was paired with was pretty crusty. An angry drunk, too."

I placed the full beer on the counter. "Last guy? What happened to him?"

He shrugged. "Moved somewhere else. I don't really have luck with roommates." He caught himself and froze up, a little uptight for your average frat boy. "Sorry—I mean... it's no big deal. You seem cool."

I approached the table with mock excitement. "Thanks. I hope it doesn't shatter your view of me, but I'm not really down for beer pong right now."

He paused. "No? Okay, how about pool?" He swiped his hand over the cups and the entire table shimmered and was replaced with a wooden billiards table, racked and ready.

"Cool," I admitted. "But I'm a little out of practice."

He swiped the air again and a humming air hockey table appeared in its place. The plastic puck drifted on the play of the air without a hint of friction.

"*Now* you're talking," I said.

"Cool! Okay, every time you get a goal, that's a sip. And if you accidentally score on yourself that's a five-second chug."

"Let's try it without the drinking, Kyle."

He swallowed and faced the table. "Whatever."

For a few unbridled minutes, I forgot about everything else. It felt good to turn my brain off and crack one piece of plastic against another. I mean, despite the fact that Kyle was absolutely killing me, I was kinda having fun.

"That's ten," said Kyle, scoring the winning goal. "Don't feel bad. I play the AI a lot. It's pretty relentless."

I shrugged it off and reset the score markers, readying another game, but something about the statement was getting to me. This was a physical air hockey table but our entire reality was digital. Was the AI just an invisible opponent? Or did some

NPC actually stand in the room making shots? And for that matter...

"Hey, Kyle?" I asked, feeling the weight of minutes ago return to me. "Are you like me? Are you... dead?"

"Totally," he answered. "I've been in Haven a little over a month. It's not too bad here. I can play Call of Duty all day long if I want to. Well, I kinda did that in the real world too, but you know."

I stared at him. I really didn't know.

"Hey," he said, "I'm not gonna pretend I have tact or anything, so you mind if I ask how you died?"

I grimaced. "Car accident on my way to work."

He smiled and nodded. "Oh, another car crash victim!" He tossed his paddle down and walked around the table to give me a high five. "Welcome to the crash club, bro! What happened?"

I found his mirth on the subject a little endearing.

"Icy road," I said. "Stupid truck. The usual, I guess."

He nodded. "Similar thing happened to me. I ended up wrapped around a telephone pole."

I wasn't sure if it was bad form to show my disgust at the mental image of his death. I changed the subject. "Don't you miss it? Your life?"

He shrugged. "I mean, I miss my friends a little. But they were assholes."

"Your job?"

"I was on the six-year plan to graduate. Almost done and not really sure what I was gonna do. In a way, Haven figured all that out for me."

"I can see that. I just... I don't know. I can't help but think I left things unfinished. The video game we were developing."

"You're a gamer? Awesome, bro! Let's set up a fragfest right now."

My face went flat. "You just told me you play all day. I think you'd wipe the floor with me."

"Yeah, I would. I'm better at shooters and bar games than MMOs, it turns out. Big surprise."

I scratched my head. "You mean, *the* MMO?"

"Haven. That's the one."

I surveyed the common room again. It was large, moderately luxurious, and comfortable. An ideal bachelor pad, if a bit lacking in character. My eyes settled on the electric-white front door.

"Hey, Kyle," I said, forgetting the immediate amusements, "you mind showing me around? Outside, I mean."

"It's a straight ren fair out there, bro."

"That okay with you?"

He sighed. It seemed like he didn't leave the house a lot, but he put on a brave face. He chugged his beer, burped, and said, "I can show you whatever you want, roomie. Just be warned: it's medieval out there."

"Like, violent?"

"Nah, man. There's just no TVs or technology like in here." He strolled to the door with me and opened it. A sheet of pure white welcomed us. "Once you're out there, you're in the game."

I clenched my jaw, worked up my courage, and stepped into the light.

0090 SimCity

The transition outside wasn't seamless. The entire world faded to black for a second and reappeared. Kyle Grath spread his hands dramatically as we zoned.

"Welcome to Stronghold."

We now stood outside the front door as it closed. Despite Kyle's gesture, I found myself staring back at our home.

It was a small clay dome, tan, with a few opaque ornamental windows. The building was too small to have possibly contained the generous space we'd been in. The rounded structure was twenty feet in diameter and a little over ten feet high. Identical houses lined the block in both directions. Different color clay, different color doors, differently styled windows, but otherwise identical.

"Hey, bro. You're missing the view."

I turned and Kyle melodramatically flaired again. "Welcome to Stronghold."

Okay. I could see his point.

Our neighborhood was on a low hill with the rest of the town sprawled below us. Whereas the inside of our house was modern, Stronghold closely resembled ancient Rome. Scores of mercantile establishments and impressive buildings as far as the eye could see. Stone-lined streets, occasional parks and squares filled with crowds of people. Statues, wells, columns. It was a sea of white and tan with painted accents of red, purple, blue, and yellow.

Not a beer pong table in sight.

A few faraway structures dwarfed all others. An accurate replica of the Roman Colosseum on the eastern side of town immediately drew my interest. As I scanned to the west, I admired a ruinous tower sitting along a riverbank. Behind it ran the grand city walls.

"What's the population of this place?" I asked in awe.

Kyle smiled. "Like, pretty big. You're in Hillside, one of the player neighborhoods." He dragged his fingers through his shaggy hair. "Come on. I'll show you what you need to know."

He started heading to the foothills but I pulled him back and pointed at the tower. "What's that?"

"That's Dragonperch," he said flatly. He started to walk away again but I held him firm.

Kyle's casual disinterest was underselling the place. Sure, the tower was in disrepair, but it was by far the tallest structure in the entire city. Taller than the Colosseum. Twice as high as the gargantuan city walls, and I'd never seen higher walls.

"Oldtown," he explained, sweeping his hand across the land on the far side of the river. "That's original construction, there. Two thousand years ago, it made up the whole city. Now it's completely abandoned. Some adventurers stroll through it like a graveyard, but there's no quests or loot or anything to be had. It's a dead zone."

He was right. Everything was crumbling. The roads were

more debris than clearing. "Two thousand years... How's that possible?"

"It's just game lore." He chuckled. "I spent my entire education ignoring history. The Fertile Crescent. The Fall of Rome. The Reformation and the Renaissance. Now I'm dead and they hit me with an assload of new legends to memorize. Raw deal, right?"

I'd noticed the game clock kept the same year as the real world. Haven's lore seemed a rewriting of the Gregorian calendar. "Did you?" I asked. "Memorize the lore?"

Kyle recited what he knew about the tower without feigning interest. "Dragonperch is all that's left standing in Oldtown due to its powerful origin magic. That same magic secures it with formidable wards. The tower's completely locked down. No one can enter. Everybody's tried."

My eyes scaled the dusty stones two hundred feet up. A weathered statue of an armored knight stood on the roof, boldly reaching for the sky. He held a lance that glistened in the daylight.

"Who's the big shot?" I asked. "Did he found the town or something?"

"He saved it. A thousand years later, in the Dragon Wars."

I turned to him. "The Dragon Wars?"

"You sure you wanna hear this stuff? Dragons are pretty lame."

"Dude, how awesome would it be to ride a dragon?"

"Whatever. I'll take an AH-1 SuperCobra over a dragon any day of the week."

I rubbed my eyes. It was obvious Kyle wasn't big on D&D.

"What about the Dragon Wars?"

"The usual." He flared his eyes dramatically. "Ancient beasts encroached on the peaceful land established by the great cities. Dragons fought back and very nearly destroyed Stronghold." Kyle pointed to the statue of the knight atop Dragonperch. "Magnus was the first man to harness a dragon as a mount. He taught the people to fight back."

He held up his hand to stave off my excitement. "But before you get any ideas, this is just standard lore stuff. There aren't any dragon riders. Hell, there aren't any dragons. They all went into hibernation or something. These legends are just stories, man. Background for quests and stuff. There's plenty of time to get into it later if you want."

Kyle appeared bored by my pressing questions and eyed the green parks north of us. I was kind of let down by the whole hibernation thing myself. Anyway, it was obvious he wasn't the best person to ask about this stuff and I could probably learn more with a little light reading. I'd catch up on game lore some other time.

"You are the worst tour guide ever," I said with a smile.

He laughed. "I'll tell you what. How about you actually let me show you around first?"

I nodded. "Deal." We headed downhill.

Hillside was all residences. Neat, curated, quaint—it reminded me of a real-world housing association. As we strolled along the road I spotted a ragged man, thin as a skeleton with a long scraggly beard and wild eyes, sprinting toward us. He stopped right in our path and hopped up and down over and over again without saying a word.

He wore nothing but his starting loincloth and pink wool socks.

"Oh, hey Phil," said my roommate. He turned to me. "This is Phil."

I watched the man hop several times, an expression of wild excitement frozen on his face. "Good to know."

Kyle chuckled. The wild man didn't seem to acknowledge us, though. He continued bouncing up and down.

"That's enough, Phil!" barked a guard in the distance.

Phil made a strained grunt and moved on, ready for the next passersby.

"I'm not even gonna ask," I said as we continued on our way.

"Probably for the best."

I eyed the guard who had intervened. He wore simple clothes. A short green tunic. Sandals. His armor consisted of a small mail hauberk and a woven straw helmet. He did have a sheathed sword on his belt, though.

"The city watch," said Kyle. "They don't look like much, but you don't wanna get on their bad side."

"What do they do?"

"It's more what *you can't* do. Players can't fight in town, so the city watch has absolute authority. They usually don't need to do much of anything except tell you to move on. If they do, you should listen."

Saint Peter rounded a corner. "Now, now, Kyle. You make it sound like the city watch doesn't serve the residents. They're here for your protection."

My roommate straightened and nodded.

Saint Peter looked me over. "Glad to see you getting a feel for the city. Did you find your new home accommodating?"

"Yeah, actually," I said. "Except I didn't see a toilet."

"Yes, yes. There's a bodily function or two we didn't deem necessary for Haven. Residents would only find ways to cause trouble with them."

I arched an eyebrow and thought of Phil. "Griefers in Heaven? That's not exactly the ideal model of religious selflessness."

He nodded. "This is certainly Heaven, of a sort, but it's not your Christian template. Sure, we use the same trappings, but we accept all types. Part of the goal of the beta is observing how different groups interact and determining if we need to enforce segregation of play styles. We want everyone to get along, but we're also realists. You can't truly be happy if it's guaranteed, can you?"

I shrugged. The question had probably given many philosophers pause.

"Anyway," said Saint Peter, "do let me know if you have any troubles. I must continue my rounds." He headed off.

Kyle chewed his lip as he watched him go. "That's weird. You don't see the white robes wandering around very often."

"You think he's watching us?"

"Did you give him a reason to?"

"No," I said. "I was just kidding."

He nodded. "I bet it's because of the wipe yesterday. The white robes probably just want to make sure everything is starting up as expected."

At the base of the hill, the land opened up to large public spaces. Tree-lined parks with benches and people tossing balls around. Some men sparred with gloves, others walked tightropes strewn between trees. The area was a hive of activity, only uncrowded because of the amount of free space.

I passed in silent wonder, awed by the diversity.

"Dude, this is just the Foot," said Kyle. "It's not much more than cosplay central. Reattach your jaw to your head, 'cause you ain't seen nothing yet. Trust me."

I wasn't sure if it counted as cosplay anymore, but it was an apt enough description. Groups and loners all partaking in countless interests, hobbies, and pastimes, many in gaudy medieval dress. The allure of Haven was becoming clearer to me, even if my roommate wasn't big on fantasy. I watched players in roped-off sections of dirt using weapons against training dummies. It looked fun.

"I thought you said there's no combat in town."

"No weapons, even," said Kyle. "In designated training areas you can practice for funsies, but you don't gain experience from it. It's more to give you a sense of what you can do. I don't bother."

I wouldn't have minded getting some tips from the city watch on spear use myself, but I was eager to see the rest of Stronghold. Lining the blocks of open park along the far road were individual buildings with public storefronts. The river that ran past Hillside and the Foot twisted behind the shops, creating a quaint, but busy, mercantile district.

"This is Front Street," Kyle explained. "The starting shops. You can buy basic equipment and supplies here."

"Like food?"

"Food's free. You can order it at home or eat in restaurants or whatever. Heck, you don't even have to eat at all if you don't want to. I once played a dystopian apocalyptic survival game where if you didn't eat food once a day you would die. That doesn't sound like Heaven to me."

"So what kind of stuff should I buy?"

"Healing potions. Equipment. You know, adventuring stuff." We walked along the storefronts. Kyle pointed out the shops as we passed. "This one's a bladesmith. Over here's a bowyer and fletcher. This is a leather shop. You're not gonna find top-of-the-line stuff on Front Street. Some people call it Noob Alley. That's why we're here."

Seeing the weapons and armor shops, I was flooded with years of memories playing RPGs. One of the storefronts had a pair of clay pots on either side of the door. I slowed as Kyle passed and wondered. I picked one up and smashed it on the ground. Loose gravel spilled out.

My roommate spun around. "What are you doing?"

"Looking for secrets. Relax." I smashed the second pot even more completely, disappointed to find nothing but soil and rocks. I frowned. "Shouldn't there be some loot or at least a turkey leg in these things?"

"Vandals!" cried a woman from inside the shop. "Vandals!"

"Run!" yelped Kyle. He was sprinting down the road before he'd finished the clipped word.

I caught up to him, wondering if my agility gave me an advantage. He stopped only a block away.

"She won't chase us. I just wanted to avoid seeing the hag." We watched from a distance as the old woman shook her fist in the air before turning her attention to the pots. A wave of her arm restored them.

Kyle shook his head. "Breaking pottery. Next you'll be walking into random apartments asking strangers for information. Maybe your video game background will actually be a hindrance in Haven. You really are a noob. Speaking of which..."

He held a shop door open. The wooden sign hanging above was a simple white happy face. I went inside. Unlike our home, the transition indoors was seamless. We didn't need to zone. That also meant the modest shop was contained by its outer dimensions.

Wooden shelves were stuffed to the brim with books and tools. Large pots and objects had been messily shoved into corners, partially obstructing passage. An empty counter lined the back wall.

"Trafford," called Kyle, "I've got a customer for you."

A weathered shopkeeper emerged from the back room. His white hair stood on end in an attempt to flee his head, but he wasn't balding in the slightest.

"Another one? That's four in as many weeks!"

"That's not true," returned Kyle. "It's been five weeks at least."

"Bah." The mature man turned to me, one of his eyes larger than the other. "He doesn't look like much."

"What's that supposed to mean?" I objected.

"That you don't look like a whole lot. Do I gotta spell it out to ya?"

I opened my mouth to retort but Kyle interrupted.

"This is Trafford. He sees to the noobs in Stronghold. Sets

them up with a starting kit, on the house."

"You only get one, mind you," added the ornery shopkeeper. "You come crawling back begging for more, it'll cost ya."

I ignored his comment and surveyed the shelves. "I guess I could use some stuff. What kind of place is this anyway?"

"It's a welcome shop," he hissed.

I stared at him blankly.

Kyle cleared his throat. "Can you set him up, Trafford? I'm planning on showing Talon around town and we only have the rest of our lives."

The shopkeeper chuckled. "Talon, eh? Everybody and their mother walks into my shop and wants to be a legendary hero. The next Magnus Dragonrider. That's what I like about you, Kyle. You have your priorities straight."

"Joining me for a pint at the Wicked Crow this weekend?"

"The Crow waters down their ale!"

"I told you, it's called Budweiser."

"Bah. You know I'll be there anyway. It's my only reprieve from work." The man scowled bitterly and disappeared into the back.

I watched my roommate with inquiring eyes.

"What?" he asked.

"What's his deal, exactly?"

"What do you mean?"

Since the two of them were friendly, I phrased my statement carefully. "Haven't you noticed that, for a welcome shop owner, Trafford isn't very... welcoming?"

Kyle laughed. "Yeah. That's kinda his shtick."

I considered that. Trafford was the first real NPC I'd had a conversation with. If you could call what we had a conversation. But he seemed real enough. He seamlessly answered our questions. The fact that he had a personality on top of that was flat-out impressive. I'd always thought Kablammy programmers were posers, but the company must've attracted some real talent to achieve this.

Before long, Trafford stomped back into the room and dropped two sacks on the counter, one large and one small. "Here's your virgin kit," he said gruffly. "You should already have a knife, unless you've managed to lose it, but there are a couple of tools and some goods in here."

I kept my mouth shut and grabbed the big bag. If the tutorial had allowed me to lose items, Trafford would've been right.

"This pathetic sack here is your coinage," he said. "Don't get excited. It's only a few silvers. Not nearly enough to buy whatever vaunted bullshit you think you'll be wearing by day's end."

I grabbed that bag too. The items disappeared as they were absorbed into my inventory. I thanked the shopkeeper and went into my menu for a look.

"Not in here!" snapped Trafford. "I don't tolerate loiterers and slack-jaws."

"We were just headed out," said Kyle, clamping his arm around me. "Don't be too hard on Talon, Trafford. I've got a good feeling about this one."

"I get good feelings in my trousers when I visit the Scented Ladies, but I don't blab on about it."

We bit down giggles as we pushed outside. I had to admit, the guy was growing on me.

0100 Saints Row

The rest of the shops were more of the same. We stepped into a few but didn't browse too closely and kept our interactions with NPCs to a minimum. Besides weapons, armor, and equipment, there were clothiers and novelty shops and bakeries. Much of what could be purchased was somewhat useless strategically, status items for displaying around your house or around your neck. There were even premium versions of food and drink that *did* cost money. Kyle explained that having a healthy economy necessitated frivolous spending and recreational purchases. In a world of grinding and looting, it made sense for there to be limitless ways to spend your spoils.

The cross streets that divided the Foot and Front Street into separate blocks ran past the shops over bridges crossing the river walk. It was finally at this point that we left the Foot and headed into the city proper. To our west was a large wooden gate—open double doors that allowed access past Stronghold's impressive walls. We passed an oblong racetrack that was walled in like a low stadium. Kyle called it the Circus and said chariot races and other events were held there, but it was expensive to attend and he'd never bothered.

I forgot about the business of the rich and checked into the business of the poor. As we headed to the center of the city, I went into my inventory and opened my welcome kit.

[Welcome Waiver]
Gratis admission to the Pleasure Gardens.

[Flint and Tinder]
The tools to start and stoke a campfire.

[Torch] x2
Provides 1 hour of light.

[Sleeping Roll]
Grants the partial benefits of rest when used in the wild.

[Health Vial]
This tincture will restore 40 health over 30 seconds.
Ramped Cooldown: 10 minutes

[Spirit Vial]
This tincture will restore 40 spirit over 30 seconds.
Ramped Cooldown: 5 minutes

Ugh. Noob kit was right. The contents weren't exactly

garbage but, besides the potions, the loot was only of minor utility. Kyle explained how health and spirit potions had a ramped cooldown, where the effects of repeated use of like items were anywhere from drastically reduced to completely useless. It was Haven's method of combating substance abuse, basically making sure deeper pockets didn't necessarily translate to infinite health and spirit.

Speaking of which, I did a silver check while I was at it. 13 pieces. It didn't seem like a lot based on my limited window shopping but it wasn't worthless.

I was increasingly feeling small and unimportant in this new world. The thought first occurred as I pondered my meager possessions, but then I realized the buildings around us had become more grand, to the point of gloating, almost. Heavy stonework. Two and three stories. The shops here were organized more like a permanent bazaar, an outdoor mall of connected space along a central cobblestone walkway as wide as a freeway.

"This is the Forum," said Kyle. "The center of commerce and civics in Stronghold." We weaved around other players in the street. "The best merchants selling the best wares in the city are here."

It wasn't overly crowded, but some shoppers did patronize the stores. "How can players afford anything right after a wipe?"

He shrugged. "Hell if I know. Most of them must be making plans or looking for quests. I also suspect there are stashes of silver or ways to make money much faster than I know about. In a week this place will be a madhouse. You'll see."

The wide corridor of the Forum continued some distance.

Amazingly, the buildings grew larger and even more stately. These were the wonders of ancient Rome. Grand columns lined the path, each with red and yellow banners. Statues of half-clothed men and women stood high overhead, painted black and white.

The thoroughfare ended with a large building with a rounded dome. Six Corinthian columns, more massive and impressive than the others, lined up three to a side leading to the doorway. The figures atop these pillars had wings and were painted gold.

"The Pantheon," said Kyle. "Home of the saints. Well, I guess they don't *really* live in Haven, but they work through here. Believe it or not, this is where they held your orientation."

I was awed by the sheer magnificence of the palace. The domed building had an entrance portico with an arched roof. At its crest stood another golden statue. "What's inside?"

"Who knows? Us mere mortals don't get to go inside without a special invitation. Unless you wanna try your hand with the city watch."

Two guards marched across the steps to the portico. I figured it was a worth a shot and took a step toward them. Kyle grabbed me.

"Whoa, whoa. I was kidding. You don't wanna try them, bro. You'll just embarrass yourself."

I gazed at the grand dome and the high doorway and the columns leading up to it. Six columns and the roof. Five figures. "Why are two statues missing?"

"The Golden Seven," noted Kyle. "Or Seal Team Seven, as I like to call them. I hate to break it to you, but they're not statues. They're angels."

I watched them in stunned silence. I knew they were just ones and zeroes, not actual heavenly angels, but they were awe inspiring nonetheless.

"Angels are the real security force of Haven. Screw the watch. These bad boys are heavy-duty AI muscle. They only come alive when game-breaking events threaten Stronghold."

"I'm afraid to ask what the absent couple's up to."

Kyle looked around conspiratorially. "No one really knows for sure, but Trafford likes to brag when we drink. We hung out last night after the wipe. You could imagine how slammed he was, running the welcome shop and all. He had to blow off some steam."

We wandered away from the columns in case the holy watchers could hear us. "What did he say?" I asked in muted tones.

"He thinks there was a raid on the Pantheon. Says a few players snuck in and tried to access the core code. Word is all three terrorists were permanently deleted."

"I thought that was impossible."

"It's supposed to be, but apparently angels are the only in-game system that can do it. Not even the saints have that power. But here's the thing: angels are governed by complex checks and guidelines. Even with whatever threat the terrorists caused, only two of them activated. They must still be out tying up loose ends. I've only been here a month, but I've never seen anything like it."

We strayed into a side alley on our way out of the Forum. Marble arches loomed on either side of us.

"What did the terrorists do?"

"I don't think they did anything. But they're infamous in Stronghold. They call themselves the Fallen Angels. Get it? Of course, they aren't really angels. None of the players are. The Fallen Angels were no match for the real thing. Trafford witnessed an active angel once and said they don't screw around."

"That's some story," I admitted. "Could it all be a world story line? Game level quests to unite players under?"

"Nah, bro. You know I'm not into game lore. This is the real deal. That's why it's so interesting. See, yesterday's wipe was unscheduled. It wasn't supposed to happen. If the Fallen Angels were part of the game story line, why would the wipe be necessary?"

I nodded.

"Me and Trafford figured it was done to avoid another attack."

I furrowed my brow. "Interesting. After permanently deleting the Fallen Angels, what does a wipe accomplish?"

"It resets all player progression."

I nodded. "That would imply there are more terrorists out there."

"Right on, bro. It's intrigue like we haven't had before. I don't take this game stuff too seriously but the Fallen Angels are hardcore."

As we cleared the Forum, the roads became more tangled and haphazard. Most of the structures reverted to single story, leaving us with a long view of Stronghold. I could see the hill where our house was in the distance, but it was partially obstructed by the monstrous Colosseum. Unlike the Circus track, this building was round, not as long but much taller. The only thing in the city that stood taller was Dragonperch.

"You're checking out the Arena." Kyle whistled out air. "Serious business, bro. That's the one place in town players are allowed to fight. I mean *really* fight. All the gloves come off. You get your armor bonuses, your weapons. All your skills are usable. People go in there to settle scores."

"Sounds harsh."

"It can be. I mean, the whole thing is set up for arranged duels so in theory it's not that bad. You respawn after the battle without missing a hair on your head. But I've seen some cruel stuff go down in there. City-wide public shaming."

I snickered. "You could afford those tickets, huh?"

"The Arena's open to anyone who wants to watch. Or fight."

We stood there with our hands on our hips, considering the gigantic structure. I wondered if I'd ever make it in there one day.

"There you are, frat brat!"

A husky voice caught us gawking at the Arena. We spun around to see an imposing figure in plate approach.

"Oh, great," muttered Kyle.

The dude was a good seven feet tall and wearing a matching set of heavy armor. The steel helmet, shoulder plates, and other highlights were brushed white and fitted over a chain mail tunic with shiny black straps. The name above the knight said [Lash] and it was clear to anyone with sense he was a soldier.

"How the hell did you get full plate already?" whined Kyle.

"Shut up, poser." The full helm concealed his face, but enough expression came through. The two eye slits lowered to

Kyle and seeped disdain. Lash's voice echoed within. "I see you found a new friend. Wonder how long that's gonna last."

I arched an eyebrow. The voice was deep and heavily distorted but... "Are you a woman?"

The helmet swiveled my way. "More woman than either of you can handle."

Lash removed the full helm. Our LARPer friend turned out to be a Mexican woman in her late twenties. A small gold hoop cinched the outside of her right eye and a diamond studded her left nose. Her dark hair was pulled tight into a ponytail which was curly and hung to her shoulders. Bleached highlights streaked through the bramble.

Her makeup, too, was dramatic. Rose-petal-pink lipstick and black eyeliner and eyelashes. The dark lines extended outward from each eye in menacing stripes.

"Oh... Lash. I get it."

"Shut up," she snapped. "I don't know you but if you hang out with this loser, you're clueless."

"We're roommates," said Kyle.

"Yeah?" she mocked. "You ladies gonna have a tea party and trade beauty tips?"

It was an odd point to attack considering her ensemble.

"I have an idea," she said. "How about you tell the noob the shitfucker way you went and got killed?"

Kyle zipped his lips and backed up a step. Lash leaned down and shoved her face into him, making him back up even more.

0110 Bully

"Hey," I said. "Wait just a minute. You might have a nice set of armor and be level whatever but—"

"3," she said. "Didn't your guide here tell you how to examine people yet?"

I checked her again. In addition to the name [Lash] I now noticed [Level 3 Knight].

"Crap," said Kyle. "She already has a class kit."

"What's a class kit?"

Lash snorted. "Classic. This incompetent buffoon would've told you what a class kit was except he's never been level 3 yet so he's never gotten one. He's a loser who doesn't know how to quest. Weak. He can't handle the game."

I scowled. The irony wasn't lost on me. In the real world, people dressed in armor were the ones likely to be picked on by brainless clowns looking to score cool points. Kyle was a drinker, a frat boy, and—frankly—he didn't get fantasy. Not that he fit the bully stereotype, really. He was more of a live-and-let-live sorta guy. But seeing him the target of harassment puzzled me. It also pissed me off. No one deserved to put up with that crap.

I pushed forward into Lash, which wasn't as intimidating as I'd hoped because she was a good foot and a half taller than me. "What are you, the big bad bully? You're not impressing anyone, Lash. Nobody cares."

"Bully." She snorted. "You girls learn that word huddled in your safe spaces in your fancy liberal colleges? *Fuck* you."

"Stronghold's non-PvP. You can't hurt anybody in here, so all you're doing with your chest pumping and neck flexing is looking like an idiot."

Kyle slapped his hand to his head. He clearly wasn't happy with my choice of words. Lash only laughed.

"Noob here thinks he's safe, huh? Well, I just saw you ladies wetting your panties looking at the Arena. I've been daring this one to meet me face-to-face for weeks now. I bet even you know his answer. Maybe you'll have a different one?"

Lash crossed her plated gauntlets over her barrel chest and stood tall. Her pink lips fixed into a slanted smile, waiting expectantly for my answer. She was a formidable figure. And let's just say I was thankful Haven didn't include certain bodily functions.

I fired back with the first strategy that popped in my mind. "This is how you get off? Challenging brand-new players to duels before they've even had a chance to grind?"

She scowled. Maybe her armor didn't have chinks in it, but her pride did. "Course not. PvP's blocked until you choose a class kit, anyway. Probably why this pansy never gets that far. Go kill some mobs. When you're level 3, you're putting your puny weapon against mine in the Arena. *If* you're still hanging out with this douchebag."

Lash slammed her helmet back on. The eye slits lasered me a warning. "If you come to your senses and kick him to the curb by then, well, maybe I won't have a problem with you, noob."

She shoved forward through Kyle, forcing him to retreat awkwardly. As she stomped away, he released a nervous hiss.

"You shouldn't have stuck up for me like that," he said.

"Screw that. She has a lot of nerve."

Kyle nodded. "I get it. And I... I understand, Talon."

I smoldered and watched the white knight leave. "Understand what?"

"You know. If you don't wanna be my friend anymore."

"Screw that. We're roommates. If anyone deserves to be ostracized, it's her. What's her problem, anyway?"

Kyle glumly kept his head down. It was clear he didn't like talking about it. In truth, I didn't either. I'd never really had a problem with bullies before. Growing up had brought me face-to-face with occasional asshats, but serious cases were few and far between. Passing and irregular, like bad gas.

Lash? She was something else entirely. She was a sad after-school special.

I stomped toward the Arena, in the vague direction of Hillside. I hoped what little I said was comfort to Kyle because I didn't want to dwell on it anymore.

The city of Stronghold was built haphazardly. The large landmarks made sense, more or less, but everything in between was a sprawl of huts and hovels; domes and walls; stone, wood, mud—you name it. The smaller roads winded and dead-ended abruptly. Some had names like Via Argo, Via Tempo. Others were unlabeled. The buildings, without the booming economy of the marketplace, lacked the fancy frescoes and brightly painted highlights of the Forum. As a result, everything blended into a homogenous sprawl. Without the notable landmarks marking the destinations, it would've been all too easy to get lost in the slums.

I ground my teeth as we followed the road. People roamed the streets with horse carts. Haggard women tended brown land. For a simulation, it was strangely moving.

"Spare a silver?" came a voice at our feet.

I eyed the man over. His face was hidden under the brim of a straw hat, his body folded under a filthy robe. The man's feet were blistered. The only other flesh he showed was an open palm reaching out to me.

"Uh, sure." I poked into my inventory, produced a shiny coin, and placed it in his hand.

It disappeared into his sleeve. "Much obliged, kind sir."

I nodded and waited. When it was clear the interaction was over, I said, "Wait, that's it?"

The straw hat tilted my way. "What's it?"

I shrugged. "I don't know. I thought you were gonna offer me a quest or something."

"Quest?" I caught sight of his wispy beard and chin. "I'm not an NPC. I don't offer quests."

"Any priceless artifacts then?"

He looked at me like I was crazy.

"A turkey leg?" I hedged.

Kyle shook his head. "What's with you and turkey legs?" he whispered.

I sighed. "Well, at least offer me some golden advice or

something. I'll even take useless advice. You know: 'You need a dungeon key to open locked doors.' Something like that."

The vagrant was flabbergasted. He looked around, picked up a rock on the ground next to him, and handed it to me. "It's dangerous to go alone! Take this."

I blinked dumbly at the stone.

"Now get outta here," he muttered. "You're hogging prime real estate."

I turned to Kyle for sympathy but he shrugged. I scowled, tossed the rock, and continued down the road.

"You know," said Kyle, rushing to keep up, "I'm not the best player to give advice, but you really shouldn't go around handing out silver to anyone who asks. That guy probably has more coin than you."

I grumbled under my breath at how angry I was getting. I didn't know why, either. Being a little put off would be one thing, but this was unreasonable. All I could do was clench my jaw and walk. My blood was boiling. Every single person I passed on the street was another coal added to the fire. Another potential threat, scammer, or bully. Was this all the afterlife was?

After. Life.

I suddenly grasped the source of my ire. This wasn't about a silver piece. This wasn't about the Mexican Brienne of Tarth. My problem was much more existential.

"All these people in the streets," I said. "They're all dead?"

"Of course," answered Kyle matter-of-factly. "Unless they're NPCs. Then they're just AI. But there are lots of us here. Haven's been running a while."

I veered away from the packed city toward a small field of grape brambles. A low stone wall lined the property. I followed it without much care for where the road went. Kyle was happy to let me lead.

"Afterlife Online," I chuckled bitterly.

Kyle scratched the back of his neck. "That's pretty much the point of Heaven, right?"

"It's just wild. You and me and everyone else is running around a simulated RPG and there's a whole real world out there."

He nodded. "I see what's going on here. The wonder of Haven is wearing off and you're realizing you miss people. Did you have a special someone?"

"A girl?" I scoffed. "No way. I was only in Portland two years. I spent most of that time competing for my career. I worked with some amazingly smart people."

"Friends?"

I paused and kicked a sandal in the dirt.

"Well, fuck it. What about family? I mean, everyone has a mom and dad, right?"

I chewed my lip, listless. "My dad hasn't been around since I was a kid. And my mom's not altogether there anymore. The aunts and uncles never got along with her. Now she stays at a special hospital. It's just me and Derek."

I sat on the stone wall lining the road. My little brother was only nineteen. I'd taken him to Portland with me. Made sure he finished high school. I was supposed to watch over him, but I'd done a mixed job at best.

"I'll never be able to give him advice ever again," I said, every word cementing the hard reality.

Kyle swallowed. "Hey, man, it's okay. You can't think about it too much on your first day."

"I'm really dead."

"It'll get easier to process."

My face twisted in sorrow. "What's there to process? Derek needs me. He can't pay the rent bussing tables. Here I am, running around in a tunic and sandals, and he... Does the outside world even know about us?"

Kyle sighed and parked his butt beside mine. "Not totally yet, but they will. Connectivity with the living is a large part of this."

I sprang to my feet right as Kyle was about to hang his arm around me. "What?"

"What?"

"Connectivity?"

"Oh," he said. "I don't know, exactly. A two-way news feed. Video chat. That kind of stuff."

"You mean I could talk to Derek?"

Kyle waited to see if I would sit down again. When I didn't, he joined me on his feet. "Look, don't get your hopes up too soon. Kablammy beta tests features all the time. We don't have access to that one yet."

I ignored his protest and opened my menu. The profile bar at the top was clear of notifications. I clicked the mail icon but it was only built for players. No living contacts. Undaunted, I selected the giant green help button. It chimed and five seconds later Saint Peter appeared beside us.

"Ah, Tod. How are you getting accustomed to Haven?"

"Tad Lonnerman," I corrected. "I need to speak to my little

brother, Derek Lonnerman. My death left him all alone. I need to get word to him that I'm alive."

Saint Peter considered us both with a neutral mask. "You're *not* alive, Tad. You're—"

"Okay, I get it. But I could still talk to him, right? Face time him. Let him know I'm around."

The Kablammy employee glared at Kyle. "You're supposed to be showing him around Stronghold, Kyle. Teaching him how to quest and test the game. *Not* spreading rumors about unreleased features. *Untested* features."

"So it's buggy," I said. "I don't care. I'm a game developer. I deal with buggy crap every day. I can help you test it."

"I'm sorry, Tad. Everchat isn't available yet."

Everchat. Catchy. I could just imagine the paid advertising.

"But you've got to be able to pull some strings," I argued. "There needs to be some implementation of chat I can—"

"It doesn't work like that," he chided. "You must realize how vitally important this feature is to the entire enterprise. It marks the first time in human history families can speak to their dead loved ones. Honor thy dead. It's the other half of why Haven exists. And if we rushed it out for every emergency a newly retired resident had, the exception would be the people who *didn't* want to phone home."

"This is ridiculous," I hissed. "There's a way I can see my little brother and you want me to grind out levels instead?"

Saint Peter's face softened. "I know it's hard, Tad, but that's exactly what I want you to do. You've agreed to test Haven. Your participation is what will give you the ability to speak with your loved ones eventually, but it's functionality that simply doesn't exist yet. The very best thing you can do for your brother is play along. Build up your skill. Familiarize yourself with the world. Be a team player. I promise you, I'll factor in your circumstances when it comes time to roll out Everchat, but you certainly won't get consideration if you fight us every step of the way."

That shut up the angry response I was about to spout off. Of course I understood feature development. Saint Peter's words were logical on paper. Schedules and deadlines were the lifeblood of game development, but they sure weren't compatible with human emotions.

I weakly tried one last appeal. "Can't you at least get word to him?"

"It's impossible," said Saint Peter, and he disappeared. The green help button stayed grayed out after he'd left. My ability to access him had been revoked.

"Harsh," said Kyle. "Look, bro, I'm sorry I brought it up."

I hooked my hands on my hips. Some Heaven this was. Dangling the possibility of family contact over me in return for services rendered.

"It's been a long morning," said Kyle. "But I have an awesome idea. A way to take your mind off things."

"Not likely," I said, but I appreciated the effort.

He laughed and wrapped an arm around me. "Trust me, bro. I've got just what the doctor ordered. It's time to spend your welcome waiver."

0120 Phantasy Star

Away from the Hill, past the Arena, on the eastern outskirts of the town lay the Pleasure Gardens. The grounds had higher acreage than any of the other properties of Stronghold, consisting of wide manicured lawns and rows of curated flowering bushes and trees. Walkways weaved between assorted cabanas and recreational facilities. The Pleasure Gardens were greener than the other parks, more ordered and tended, and offered a wide variety of leisure activities to spend hard-earned silver on.

As a new resident of Stronghold, my welcome waiver entitled me to, well, just about anything I wanted.

We strolled past the thermal baths and pools and exercise areas. Past the grand library outfitted with peaceful reading nooks and cozy fireplaces. There were massages, music, and refreshments in fancy tea houses. It was jarring to transition from the Stronghold slums to a five-star resort, but that wasn't the only surprise.

Kyle led me to a complex of breezeways. A watchman in a chain mail vest guarded the entrance. "Pleasure?" he asked.

"I'm gonna show him around," said Kyle, prompting me for

the waiver. I handed it to the guard.

"Another first timer," he chuckled. "Hold onto your breeches. Room four."

I followed my roommate down the hallway with concerned anticipation. The outdoor halls magnified our lonely footsteps. In all of the Pleasure Gardens, I hadn't seen more than two stray players. That meant the place was expensive and frivolous. Trafford may have handed out a full suite of welcome kits since the wipe, but something told me only true first timers received the welcome waiver.

We approached an unassuming door with Roman numerals on it. We zoned inside into a separately instanced room and I knew I was in for something special. Most of Stronghold was a single level so far, a global community of players sharing the same space. Our home had been the exception, which made perfect sense. That space was for me and Kyle. I doubted other players could even enter without our permission.

This room was essentially a dungeon. A separate level just for... what, exactly?

"Welcome to the media room," announced Kyle.

It didn't look like much more than a KTV room. An empty space with cushioned benches and tables circling the walls. My friend waved me forward.

"What's your favorite movie?" he asked.

"Uh, I dunno. What is this?"

"Just pick a movie you like. Something exciting."

"Okay. *Inception*."

Kyle smiled and pointed to the far wall. When I looked, an elevator dinged. It was at the end of a long hotel hallway. Not only was I there but I was approaching it, confidently marching to a driving violin score. The two metal doors slid open and a gruff man in a suit exited the elevator.

I lowered my head and ducked around the corner, now completely immersed in this fictional world. My hair was slicked back and I wore a smart tie-and-vest combo. I pulled a pistol from my belt.

"Holy shit," I whispered. "I'm in the movie."

The security guard turned the corner and I tried to shoot him. He batted the weapon away with a martial arts move and we locked into a back-and-forth struggle of punching and shoving.

A blaring horn section came to life and the whole building tilted sideways.

I threw the man down the hall as I barely grabbed onto a door frame. The collision was hard, but he was still fighting. Both of us, somehow, were stronger than we should've been. Possessed of knowledge and power we shouldn't have had.

The hallway leveled out horizontally, not a pit anymore but spinning like a funhouse tunnel. I charged the man as he climbed to his feet. My dress shoes stomped over the walls, doors, and ceiling, deftly maneuvering through the rotating world until we crashed into each other. I flipped him around with practiced precision and slammed him into the wall. We tumbled through a door and into a hotel suite where we both maneuvered for the loose gun. Through several tense moments of grappling, the music grew to a desperate crescendo until I managed to scoop the weapon off the floor and fire right before he struck me. The man slid lifelessly across the floor. Sudden silence. I had won.

I turned to Kyle, who was silently sitting on the wall bench with his arms crossed. My eyes were wide. "I wanna do *The Matrix* next."

He raised his eyebrows and nodded. Frantic horns ramped up.

I twirled around, black overcoat swinging outward in slow motion, black leather pants splayed out to my sides in a low stance. This time I raised a pistol in each hand. The agent was standing across the skyscraper rooftop, anticipating my move. I emptied both magazines but he blurred into multiple twisting bodies, unharmed.

"Trinity!" I cried. "Help!"

The agent responded with his own pistol. A statue of cold technique, he fired straight and true. Except, again, I could break the rules of the world. I was more adept. The rounds flying my way were laughably slow. I shot my arm behind me and leaned back as the bullet whistled past me, rippling the air in its wake. The barrage continued and so did I, leaning impossibly lower, swaying around the attack.

Two bullets grazed me and I collapsed on my back. Pain—actual pain, not a damage notification—stung me into shock. I looked up as the agent stood over me, pistol raised.

"Only human."

"Dodge this," said Trinity, and blew his brains out.

I sat up slowly, gawking at the media room as it really was. "That felt amazing!" I told Kyle.

"It totally is."

"Except that actually hurt."

"Yeah. You feel the pain, the emotions, the exhilaration of whatever it is you're supposed to be experiencing. That's part of the point. Sometimes you wanna feel alive, you know?"

He continued wistfully. "My favorite movie clips are the dogfights in *Top Gun*. But then I get to the part where Goose dies and I just can't take it, bro. There's something about that scene that breaks me. Doesn't keep me from replaying it, though."

I didn't think that was so weird. Being in a sim was the weird part. Living as an ideal representation of myself. It was sanitary and logical but was it really real? Maybe it was true that ugliness needed to exist for there to be true beauty. I wondered about this holodeck 2.0.

"So I could do anything here I could have done on earth? Not just movies?"

"It's not a virtual world," he answered. "If you want that, you've got Haven. This is a media room. You can watch passively or take part. You can act in a Broadway production, be the lead singer of your favorite band, or immerse yourself within any video game you want. It's a mix of your imagination and memories and the actual media that exists on Kablammy's servers." He leaned toward me and spoke conspiratorially. "And they have *everything*."

I released a breath, imagining the scope of it all.

"You get my point?" he asked.

"I think so."

"I don't think you do. Have you considered... nontraditional movies?"

I arched an eyebrow.

Kyle chuckled. "You know, like video clips. You can take part in certain 'movies' you might be familiar with from the internet."

I stared at him flatly. "Porn."

"You got it. I'm sure you can summon a specific favorite to mind."

"Yeah, right." I snorted at the ridiculousness of it, but I couldn't *not* think of something. It just happened subconsciously.

Jenna Jynx stretched against the butterfly machine in the gym. She wore tight sweat pants and a tank top that was too small to provide practical support. Her ample cleavage was on full display as she arched her arms and shoulders back. Beads of sweat ran down her neck and disappeared under her shirt.

"I'm sore," she complained.

Kyle chuckled again and stood up from his perch. "You've got good taste," he said. "I'll just leave you two alone." He headed for the door.

"No, seriously," I protested.

"What do you want me to do? You heard the lady, man. She's sore. Go for it."

Suddenly I was helping Jenna up and laying her back on a gym mat. The door closed behind Kyle and it was just me and the girl with perfectly airbrushed skin. Despite ostensibly working out, she wore full makeup and her long brunette hair was perfectly curled.

"Maybe you can help me work a kink out," she said with a suggestive wink.

I gripped her thigh and leaned her knee into her chest. Although I was a personal trainer, I wasn't being especially professional about the situation, meaning my crotch was firmly pressed against hers.

"Feel better?" I asked awkwardly.

She closed her eyes and moaned. "Oh, yes."

Okay. All right. I'd barely done anything but whatever. I guess she was really into flexibility.

"Ooh, like that," she said, grinding into me. Her other leg wrapped around my waist and her abs hardened into perfectly taut muscles. She clasped both hands around my neck and I flipped our positions, moving to my back and lifting her above me. She landed with an excited shriek. Her ballooned boobs hugged my face and I got a little excited too.

"You're a *bad* boy, aren't you?" she asked. Strangely, she didn't really want me to answer because the next thing I knew her tongue was down my throat.

She tasted like strawberries, as I always knew she would. That must've been the "memories" part of the media room. As far as I knew, video streaming hadn't yet achieved flavor technology.

She broke away and sat up on me. With deft acrobatics, she flung her tank top over her head till it was at her wrists. Then she twisted her arms behind her back and wrapped her top tightly like a pair of handcuffs. The effect arched her back into a comic book pose. Her breasts were the most sculpted, perfect, fake things I'd ever seen. And I was in a freaking DR simulation.

She thrust against me, and boy did I feel it. It wasn't just the rushing blood and tingling. There was an emotional connection too. A strong sense of need and passion and lust.

Jenna smiled and ran her tongue across her lips. "Maybe you

could show me what you can do with these punching bags."

Wait, wait, wait. That was just weird. Maybe lines like that had a place in fantasy porn, but people didn't really talk like that. Kyle had been right about this place. The emotions, they sure made me feel human, but Jenna Jynx was anything but.

"Excuse me," I said, trying carefully to grab her without touching anything sexual. A tall task, with her proportions. I couldn't reach for her arms either because that brought my head dangerously close to what I was trying to avoid. Eventually I settled on clamping around her waist. Even that body part was more tempting than I'd anticipated. Her hard stomach and compact waist gave in to surprisingly soft hips. I couldn't get a grip on her *without* my fingers grabbing her amazing ass.

As gently as I could, I unstraddled her grinding pelvis and placed her on the mat beside me.

"Oh, yes," she said. "Just like—"

Her face froze in shock when she realized she wasn't on me anymore. She perked her lips out in confusion a split-second before she vanished along with the entire gym.

Just as I'd figured. The system couldn't improvise. She wasn't AI. She was playback. A replay. Nothing in Haven was technically real, but even given the virtual surroundings, Jenna Jynx was a pale imitation.

I stormed from the media room to find Kyle wandering the halls. He had a knowing smile on his face. "Already?"

I rolled my eyes. I was all for taking my mind off things but Jenna had creeped me out. "Can't we just go adventuring like a normal MMO?"

0130 Wild Hunt

Kyle and I marched toward the exit to Stronghold. I gawked at the daunting wall as we got closer. Built from stones larger than a car, wider at the base than the top, it rose almost a hundred feet in the air.

"Why would walls need to be this tall?" I said to myself.

Kyle shrugged. "It's a video game. No one needed to actually build it."

He was probably right. Besides, I assumed the size helped ease the rendering load of the simulation. Residents in the busy city didn't need to visualize a vast draw distance. The wall kept city business contained in the city.

Battlement towers stood slightly taller, at regular intervals. City watchmen were lazily posted at a central double gate made of triple layers of wood, currently swung open. One of the guards eyed us dubiously as we approached.

"Inexperienced adventurers, eh?" The man had a half-helmet made of straw with a leather strap wrapped under his chin. Besides a vest of chain mail, he was lightly armored. "What's yer business leaving Stronghold?"

"To become *experienced* adventurers," I said pointedly. That just made the guard eye me harder.

"You folks full citizens?"

"Sure are," said Kyle. "Born and raised."

I chuckled. "You gonna make us walk through a metal detector next? What gives?"

The guard squinted sharply. "A metal what?"

I waved it off. "Sorry. Bad TSA joke."

"The TSA!" His eyes lit up and his hand moved to the hilt of his sword. "We don't take kindly to the Throne of Salt and Ash. You two wouldn't be spies, would you?"

"If we were, would we—"

Kyle cut me off. "No, no. Not spies. Concerned citizens." Kyle constructed some elaborate explanation to excuse the gaffe, but I'd stopped listening. It blew my mind that this watchman didn't know what the Transportation Security Administration was. Kyle did. I did. All the players in Haven did, of course. But there was a whole world of people here, NPCs, whose only basis for knowledge was the simulation. It enforced role-playing, or led to misunderstandings like the one Kyle was scrambling to explain.

I let him speak and turned my attention to the gate towers looming high overhead. The sun glinted brightly off the banded plate armor of a captain. He stared down at us, red long shield in hand. Already we'd attracted the attention of the higher-ups. The city watch appeared to have order well in hand.

I wisely kept silent as Kyle schmoozed us past the guard with a promise to buy pints later. That seemed to be his go-to move to make friends, or at least commiserate with others who had none. The watchman nodded us past with a grunt and we were more than happy to move on.

"They like to put on a show," explained Kyle. "Everybody's first time, the city watch wants you to know who's boss. They're tough and they're watching. I bet they let you walk in and out unmolested from now on."

I liked how that sounded. I liked what I saw before me even better.

The city of Stronghold was large, but it was dense and cluttered. Views tended to be obstructed by walls and columns and death arenas. Outside the city gates, the land opened up to a wide span of light-brown fields and gently toiled earth. The horizon was limitless. A perfect day greeted us: Sun. Warmth. A breeze rolling over the wild grass. It was peaceful.

Now *this* was Heaven.

"Gah!" screamed Phil, bouncing across my field of vision in his loin cloth and pink socks. "Gaaah!"

Three players chased him. One shot arrows at his feet. A wizard filled the air with bursting missiles of light. Now that we were outside, I noticed health bars over everyone's heads. In seconds, they all ran out of view.

I reined in my wonder and studied the full bar under Kyle's name tag. There were no numbers—just a proportionate level of health. "How safe are we out here, exactly?"

"We don't need to worry about other players," he said knowingly. "They're just griefing each other. Players can't fight on tended land, and PvP doesn't start until level 3 anyway."

"What's tended land?"

"Just the area around big towns. This flattened grassland. It'll be obvious when we leave it, but it's even more obvious on the map."

Map. I smiled at the thought and went into my menu. Sure enough, I had a new map tab. An overview of the surrounding land popped up with the heading: the Midlands.

We'd exited Stronghold from the west gate. A single road stretched to the left, passing the bubble of safe tended land before hitting a forest.

Kyle fell in beside me and pointed to my map hovering in the air. "We follow the road west," he said. "It cuts through the forest—all the way to the other side in relative safety—but most players break off and head into the trees to find mobs."

I nodded. The strategy was simple and direct, if a bit dull. "Let's do it."

We took a straight shot to our destination. A few players returning to town passed us but we ignored them.

"First thing," said Kyle, "is we should form a party." He swiped into his menu and a dialog prompt appeared before me.

Kyle would like you to join his party.

I accepted. The only thing that outwardly changed was the color of the name text above his head from green to blue.

"It's the best way to level," he explained. "Parties divide experience, but experience gets divided anyway. Like if you and I killed a mob, just the two of us, we'd get the same XP whether we were in a party or not."

"So how's it the best way to level?"

"The benefit is a single member can pull the entire party into a new experience pool. So if you kill a mob alone, we all get XP.

In a max party of five, that's four other people pulling you in. Grouping shares the load, includes the support classes, and keeps everyone in sync."

> **Kyle:** *Plus, there's this.*

I recoiled from the text that splayed across the bottom of my view. Embarrassed, I joined in.

> **Talon:** *Oh, I get it. Party chat.*
> **Kyle:** *Right on. No matter where we are in all of Haven, you can speak to party members in chat. It's huge because we don't even get email outside of town.*

I glanced at the inbox icon on my profile bar and noticed it was indeed grayed out.

> **Talon:** *And no one else can see this, right?*
> **Kyle:** *Nope. Just party members.*
> **Talon:** *Sw33t.*

Kyle strayed off the dirt road and I followed. He equipped his sword and I once again took his lead. The woodman's spear popped into my hand and felt comfortable there. Every guy in existence ever immediately feels tougher with a weapon in hand. Traipsing through the Forum, experiencing the movies in the Pleasure Gardens—those things were cool but holding that spear pumped me with adrenaline. I suddenly wanted to get down and dirty with Haven combat.

As we crossed into the tree line, I narrowed my eyes and stalked silently, imagining I was a lethal assassin. Kyle trampled the plants and whistled the tune of *Super Mario Brothers*. "There!" he said.

A [Dirt Beetle] skittered into view. It was twenty feet away and I could barely see the insect itself, but its name text glowed yellow, giving away its location. I took a stride toward it but Kyle grabbed my shoulder.

"Green is friendly. Yellow is an easy mob. Orange means you're in for a tough fight. And if you see a red, stay away."

I nodded. As I went to attack the beetle again, two level 1 soldiers sprinted up and stabbed it with swords. They congratulated each other on the "total owning" and moved on.

My frustration was evident.

"Don't worry," said Kyle, only mildly annoyed. "It happens all the time."

"It's always this crowded?"

"Kinda. But sticking to the edge of the forest is safe. It pretty much guarantees we won't get killed."

I huffed, keeping my words of complaint to myself. Kyle didn't have the reputation of a good player but he'd taken the time to show me around. I signaled with my hand for him to lead the way.

The forest was sparse. The ground was flat and easy to travel, with plenty of space between the trees. This clearly wasn't tended land, but with the number of players out here, it might as well have been. Safe was right.

We wandered another five minutes. I was just beginning to wonder what kind of MMO didn't populate its world with mobs when a giant rat squeaked and bit down on my spear.

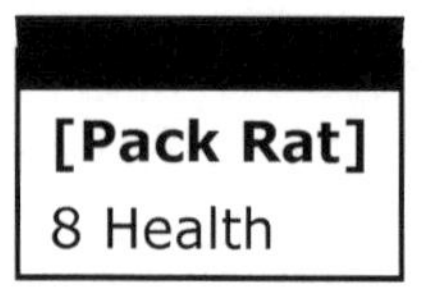

I twirled around and yanked my weapon. The rat, hunched over with yellowed eyes, wasn't large *overall*—maybe two feet in length—but it was damn large for a rodent, and it had teeth for days. Instead of ripping my weapon free, my hand slipped off the handle. The [Pack Rat] bolted in the opposite direction.

"My spear!"

"Talon, wait."

I broke into a run.

The scavenger skittered through dried leaves, my spear scraping a line in the dirt. We tailed it to a small warren in a circle of trees. Thick roots twisted over a large hole in the ground. The pack rat was stuck trying to pull my weapon into the narrow hole. If you've ever seen a dog try to go through a pet door with a stick in its mouth, you get the idea.

"Don't get too close!" yelled Kyle.

I didn't listen. I met that rat at the mouth of the hole before I could think. I gripped the spear and gave it a good tug, planting the sole of my sandal into the beastie's face.

You dealt 2 damage to [Pack Rat]

It yelped and released the spear. Then it disappeared inside the burrow.

I sighed and made my way back to the edge of the warren. Kyle kneeled beside an overturned log, chuckling. I cracked a smile and sat next to him.

"Let's keep that little adventure to ourselves."

"I've seen worse," he said. "At least you got it back."

I shook my head. I'd be an infamous explorer in no time.

My roommate pulled a glass orb from his bag. It was crystalline and rounded but sturdy enough to take a tumble without cracking. Inside the hollow ball was a mass of thick black gel.

"What is that?" I asked.

"Pretty cool, right? It's this new thing I'm trying with the artisan class. Glasswork."

"Heh, I never realized what class you were."

"Seriously? You need to get in the habit of examining players more."

I did. Beneath [Kyle] and the health bar I read [Level 1 Artisan]. Unlike Lash, who sported a class kit, Kyle and I were still branded with core disciplines from the class cruciform. My explorer to his artisan. Opposition classes, I realized. That didn't mean we were at war or anything, it just meant our classes didn't have much in common. For strategic reasons, mixing up play styles was great—as long as we could work together.

"I've tried all the classes at this point," he said. "Mystics are complicated. Soldiers are boring." He nodded my way. "I tried explorer a bunch but didn't take to the always-on-my-toes thing. I wasn't fast enough and died a lot." He looked downward. "I'm not especially good at games unless they're shooters."

"Or beer pong."

"Yeah."

"They let you reroll classes like that?"

"Sure," he said. "When you die you lose all progression from your current level. Your latest skill points get unassigned. So you usually just repick the same skills, but you can change them around and experiment. Between that and the wipes, I've tried a bunch of loadouts. Artisan's new. I figured as an artisan I can build up my strength and use cool toys. I guess we'll see what happens."

"I guess we will." I stared at the glass orb. "So, glasswork, huh? What's inside that thing?"

"It's a corrosive. My first branch of the alchemy skill."

A chittering sound interrupted us and we instinctively ducked. More squeaks followed and we peeked from behind the log. Two pack rats were sniffing around the outside of their hole.

" 'Nade out!" barked Kyle with military gruffness. He flung the black-gel orb through the air and it shattered right between the rats. Black goop plastered their fur.

> Blinded!
> [Kyle] dealt 4 damage to [Pack Rat]
> DoT: 5 dmg/5 secs
> [Kyle] dealt 4 damage to [Pack Rat]
> DoT: 5 dmg/5 secs

The rats screeched and ran in circles. The grenade hadn't caused a ton of damage, but the damage-over-time was driving the little critters crazy.

Kyle laughed. "I call it the Call of Duty: Medieval Warfare. Get it?"

I didn't want to reward him for the bad joke but I had to admit, the grenade was pretty clever. Both pack rats succumbed to their injuries.

40 XP awarded

"Cool," I said. I opened my character sheet to check my level progress.

Talon		*Level*	1
Class	Explorer	*XP*	190
Kit	NA	*Next*	1000

My excitement dimmed. Only 40 experience points per rat. We killed two but split the total across the party. At that rate we'd need to kill forty more rats to level. I closed the menu and approached the corpses optimistically. Checking their bodies brought up small inventory slots.

Loot:
3 silver

Okay, my excitement dimmed a little more. I wasn't even sure how to split 3 coins two ways. There was an option to share the money across the party and I accepted. It gave Kyle 1 silver and left me with 2.

"It's not much," he said, "but we'd need to tackle humanoids to find better loot. They'll have more health, obviously."

"But these things are pack rats," I countered. "They steal things, right? They gotta have more than silver. Hell, they almost had my spear."

I dug around at their hole with the tip of my weapon, aware more baddies might be lurking down there. I traced the tunnel to the other side of a tree root and a notification popped up.

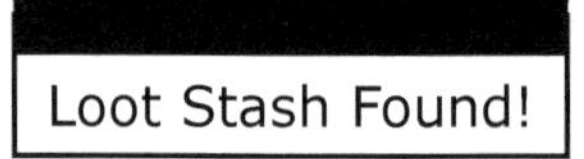

"Holy..." trailed off Kyle. His face went dumb as he contemplated the stashes he'd left behind in the past.

I shrugged. "Tricks of the trade." I checked the contents of the stash.

Loot:
23 silver
[Raw Emerald]
[Mixer's Smock]

This time when I split the coin, Kyle got the odd extra. It was cool the game balanced that kind of thing out for fairness. As for the actual loot, we needed to work that out on our own.

"An emerald *has* to be good," I said.

"Gems have various magical and alchemical uses but it's probably better to sell at this point. Nice find."

"And the mixer's smock?"

"I could use that," he said excitedly. I handed it over. "This gives me bonuses to mixing time. Thanks."

I nodded. "Let's move on."

We continued through the forest, emboldened by our minor success. The trees grew closer together, partially blotting out the sun. I held my hand up for Kyle to stop. To our side, something was trampling through the brush.

"Ready," I said, pointing my spear out. Kyle nodded and produced another corrosive grenade. We waited as the snapping branches grew louder.

Suddenly, a giant pig with spiky bristles crashed through the bushes right next to Kyle. He fell backward and dropped his orb. It bounced into the brush without breaking.

The beast brandished his tusks.

[Wild Hog]
19 Health

I swooped in with my spear, scraping the pig's side. It glanced across thick hide.

You dealt 5 damage to [Wild Hog]

The pig snorted and turned on me. It was quicker than I'd

anticipated, but I had a trick up my sleeve. I'd been waiting to use my crossblock skill since Stronghold. The boar came at me and I triggered my block. Its head rammed against the solid shaft of my weapon and bounced away. The animal snorted in anger as I repositioned.

I knew to do real damage, I needed a strong thrust. I braced the weapon against my body and held the point to the hog's face. We squared off, pacing sideways.

I lunged, driving the tip of the spear forward. Its head jerked. Iron clanged against tusk. My spear was batted off target, a glancing blow that did minor damage. I tuned out the notification because, with my weapon canted off center, the wild hog now had a clear shot at me.

It lowered its head and charged. A split second of panic transformed into pure instinct. Like a trained matador, I waited as the animal bore down on me, only rolling away at the last instant. Except, instead of doing it with style and flair and a red cape, I tumbled face first into the dirt with a thud.

Kyle scrambled for his grenade but the pig circled back around to him, never slowing down. Kyle drew his sword and fended it off, both sticking each other but neither dishing serious damage.

I grunted and hefted my spear. With the hog's back to me, I barreled forward and drove the iron deep into its side. It squealed and collapsed. An added whack with Kyle's sword put it down for good.

45 XP awarded

Loot:
[Ham Hock] x2
[Hog Tusk] x2

Kyle and I breathed heavily for a minute. I wasn't sure if my brain thought it needed oxygen or if the game had some kind of stamina feature or if it was just neural adrenaline.

"You hurt?" I asked.

"Nah, I'm fine." He stood and dusted himself off. "That was pretty cool, you know. Wild hogs are pretty vicious for their size."

"But their loot sucks."

He shrugged and recovered his dropped grenade. "Dude, we're getting closer and closer to making level 2."

He was kind of right. 235 out of 1000 wasn't nonexistent, but 150 of that had come from my tutorial. We still had a ways to go.

"It was still a little close," I said.

0140 Monster Hunter

It was clear I needed to improve my combat prowess. I'd had that hog dead to rights, my spear tip lined up with its eyes. What could've been an easy kill turned into an emergency.

The whole point of a spear is to maintain superior distance and positioning against an enemy. The second an opponent gets past my kill zone, I become vulnerable. A sitting duck, almost. I needed some way to counter that.

That meant skills. The crossblock was helpful, but I could purchase more. I flicked open the menu. I had 2 points to spend.

"Hey, Kyle, how fast do we get new skill points?"

"You start with 4: your initial weapon competency and 3 spares. Every time you level you only get 2 more."

That was in line with my assumptions. Skills were grouped into trees, allowing new branches to be unlocked with purchases and upgrades. A player's initial batch of skills did a lot to define their play style. My next two choices would determine whether I made it to level 2 alive.

I searched the spear tree and was presented with familiar options. I'd already purchased the crossblock so I ignored the defensive discipline branch and checked the others.

VANGUARD
Hard-charging, tip-of-the-spear combat
Headline Skill - Power Slash
A vicious strike to your enemy, causing up to x2 damage at level 1.
Spirit Cost: 10
Cooldown: 20 seconds

DEADEYE
Calculated, precision combat
Headline Skill - Deadshot
A targeted strike to a specific body grouping.
Spirit Cost: 10
Cooldown: 20 seconds

JAVELINIST
Flexible, ranged combat
Headline Skill - Spear Throw
A distance attack with a melee weapon.
Spirit Cost: 7
Cooldown: 15 seconds

Once again the deadeye play style called to me. I recounted my clash with the wild hog and decided deadshot would've avoided my problem. No more having my spear batted away. I purchased it and moved on to the other skill categories: awareness, survival, traversal, and stealth.

It was time for something creative. Stealth would allow me to hide, but traversal would better utilize my agility in combat.

Vault
Maneuver over objects with assisted leaps.
Spirit Cost: 6
Cooldown: 5 seconds

Scale
Climb and hang on sheer surfaces.
Attributes: Strength, Agility
SpS: 0.5

Dash
Quickly slide along ground for very short distances.
Spirit Cost: 8
Cooldown: 20 seconds

I knew climbing and vaulting would eventually come in handy, but dash had the most obvious combat use. I selected it as my third skill and closed the menu.

"Might as well get back to work," I announced. "I'm not returning to Stronghold until we level."

Kyle seemed to like that idea. He strode ahead, sword in one hand and grenade in the other.

For the next thirty minutes, our grinding consisted of walking, killing a snake, walking, failing to catch a razor hawk, even more momentous walking, and finally an encounter with a [Swamp Toad], which looked easier than a wild hog.

Embarrassingly, the oversized frog got the jump on us and nailed me with poisonous toxin. He was a slow mob though and the DoT was low. We hacked at it. I lined up my spear and readied the deadshot skill. Right before I struck, a wooden arrow thunked between its eyes.

Critical Hit!
[Dune] dealt 27 damage to [Swamp Toad]
[Swamp Toad] is defeated
12 XP awarded

"Hey!" I yelled.

A dude in a green cloak emerged from the trees. [Dune] was a [Level 2 Explorer].

"That was our kill," said Kyle.

"That was *my* kill," he snapped. "I was in the middle of tracking it when you crossed its path."

"You can't be serious," I said.

He eyed me squarely. "*That* was a swamp toad. You see any swamps around here?"

I curled my lips.

"My party took on a pack of them and this one got away."

Party. That's why the XP division was so low. Kyle's party spread in action. I examined the carcass.

Loot:
[Swamp Toad Gland]

"I could use that gland," Dune said, swiping it.

"Bro, we were the ones that killed that thing," protested Kyle.

"I beg to differ. My arrow plugged it right between the eyes. Just be more considerate next time."

"Considerate?!?"

"Let it go," I said. "Take your damn gland and get out of here, Dune. Swamp toads don't really rate with us."

He sneered. His insistence on making a big deal out of the toad made him look desperate and he knew it. Instead of refuting the point, he brusquely spun away and headed back through the trees.

"This isn't working," I told Kyle. "I don't wanna compete for scraps all day."

I trudged deeper into the forest. This time Kyle followed me. "The farther we go, the more outmatched we'll be."

"Good. Maybe we'll run into fewer kill-stealing cocknuggets. That dude just snagged more XP for his entire party than *we* got from that thing. It's hopeless out here. Not only do they take our kills, but there aren't enough mobs to go around. It's the worst kind of grind."

"It's what everybody else does."

"Somehow I doubt Lash got that sweet armor by snuffing out swamp toads."

He chewed his lip, pondering my point. "So what's your idea?"

I scanned the ground as we walked. I didn't have a formalized plan but a set of tracks caught my eye. I paused. "That," I said.

"What?"

"Dune mentioned he'd tracked that toad from a swamp. If he'd been actively chasing it, we would've seen him earlier. But he wasn't chasing it, he was tracking it." I kneeled down beside the new footprints and traced a finger through them. "Tiny feet with a central dragging tail." I moved forward on my haunches. "Crawls under and past these roots." I turned to Kyle. "Has to be another pack rat."

He grinned. "More loot."

I didn't really know what I was doing but we followed the tracks. With any luck, these would lead right back to a new burrow. And if the pack rats were safely hidden at home, they wouldn't be aggroed on other kill-stealing players.

It was only a few minutes before we pushed through a spiny bramble and found a rocky glen. A small valley walled in by a circle of trees. I climbed down a boulder with fuzzy moss. The dirt on the bottom was rich and cool. At my foot was a small tunnel.

"We found it."

Proficiency gained: **Fledgling Tracker** You are now familiar with the concept of tracking and will find mixed success attempting it.

I backed away from the hole and sat against a tree, opening my game guide.

"Hey," said Kyle, "there's another hole over here."

I looked. Beside Kyle's tree was another burrow. It must've

been from the same tunnel. Kyle backed away to lie in wait, grenade in hand. As we essentially spawn camped, a tunnel exit to each of us, I returned to the game guide.

> Proficiencies are minor skills that improve through practice and research. They do not cost spirit and aren't limited by timers. Some proficiencies are learnable by everyone, but most are core class abilities. In general, attempting certain activities enough will activate a proficiency, which the player can improve by repeating the activity. Certain research items can also gift proficiency advances.
>
> Proficiencies have 3 levels of knowledge: Fledgling, Skilled, and Expert.

Pretty cool. Saint Peter had hinted at this. There were techniques in Haven that could be improved with practice, without spending skill points. Tracking was almost definitely an explorer proficiency, which explained Dune's usage of it. I wondered if there was a proficiency list somewhere. Details weren't in the book. Maybe I could access a wiki in town to look up the possibilities.

"Wait a minute," said Kyle. "There's another hole over there."

I turned my head and squinted. Indeed, under a branch of thick leaves was a third tunnel. I rounded the tree to explore. That's when I noticed the passage under the roots two feet away from me.

Another hole, except this one was three times the size of the others. This wasn't just a burrow, it was a whole damned warren.

Padded feet kicked the earth below. I gripped my spear and whirled around, noticing several other tunnels. Kyle and I backed into each other in the center of the warren as yellow eyes peeked out from darkened passages all around us.

"Uh, Talon," he said. "I've got a really bad feeling about this."

0150 Rat Attack!

We circled carefully, finding burrow after burrow crowded with pack rats. Their eyes gleamed from the safety of shelter.

"There's gotta be ten or eleven of them," I murmured.

Kyle furrowed his brow. "Eleven eyes? You think one of them has an eye patch?"

"Ten or eleven *rats*, Kyle. I wasn't aware we were counting eyes."

"I'm just saying," he said under his breath. "All we can see are their eyes so there could be twice as many of them holding an eye closed to conceal their numbers."

I sighed. I was starting to get the sense Kyle wasn't an expert Haven player.

"Maybe it's like prison," I offered. "I should just walk up and stick the biggest one with my spear. Then the rest of them will back away."

My roommate nodded. "Sounds reasonable." Then, after a pause, "You ever been to prison?"

"No... You?"

"Uh-uh."

The flurry of activity slowed, skittering paws ready and

waiting. We were surrounded, no two ways about it. Any retreat would likely be met with failure. And if we just kept waiting for the rats to come up with a plan, we'd be fighting a battle on their terms.

I had to strike first. Gain the initiative and keep them on their grubby heels.

Kyle and I rotated in place to maintain a view of every last rodent in the warren. As my spear passed over a burrow with a careless pack rat too near the entrance, I found my opening.

I wasn't taking any chances with this. I lined up the iron and used my deadshot skill. Without a warning to Kyle, I lunged ahead and drove the spear straight into the pack rat's brain.

> Critical Hit!
> You dealt 24 damage to [Pack Rat]

It collapsed immediately. Deadshot was impressive. I could only use it every 20 seconds but that wasn't a problem. I'd done so much extra damage that it seemed unnecessary. The poor rats only had 8 health total. The other mouse in the hole screeched and retreated deeper. I shook the lifeless body from my spear.

Kyle and I traded a cautious glance. Maybe this wouldn't be so difficult after all.

The ground beneath my feet rumbled. A mound of dirt struck upward. It surprised me but I'd been ready to dodge a counterattack. I canted to the side and activated dash.

Suddenly I was a parkour expert. My sandals skidded along the loose dirt. I was in control, perfectly balanced, shooting away from danger while surfing a shockwave.

Behind me, huge teeth burst through the ground and tracked me. Scraggly whiskers, damp with soil, brushed my back. A ragged rat several times the size of the others chomped empty air as I sped away. I only moved six feet in total, but it was enough to slip the attack. I took a defensive position as she sneered at me with a glowing red eye.

[Mother Pack Rat]
85 Health

"You see?" said Kyle. "She *is* missing an eye! Told you."

The mother rat had a scar running across her face, proof that she'd been in combat before, and proof that she was a survivor.

I braced my weapon and lined up a strike, eyes glued to the cooldown timer for my flagship skill. It hit 0 and I triggered deadshot. Unfortunately, nothing happened. The mother rat disappeared back into the newly formed hole before I could get a bead on her.

Too late I noticed I only had 2 spirit left, out of a maximum of 18. Deadshot required more than half my allotment. That meant I could only use it once before waiting for my spirit to recharge.

The entire pack chittered in unison, a chorus of furious rodents ready to defend their home. They rushed out into the open, attempting to overwhelm us.

"Watch out!" I yelled, sweeping my spear in a horizontal arc before me. The swipe created a buffer between me and the charging pack, giving me room to maneuver to safety. I'd been correct in my assessment of the spear.

Kyle had no such advantage.

He struck a rat with a decent sword swipe, shoving it to the side to lick its wounds. Unfortunately, two others slipped his defenses and took chomps out of him.

The pack rats were one of the weakest individual enemies we'd faced so far. Weaker than swamp toads. That meant Kyle wasn't about to die. However, the strength of the rats was right in their name: pack. Killing a few was cake. The rub was living to kill the rest.

I plucked a vicious rat off my roommate's leg with my spear and hurled it to the edge of the warren. Another sweep protected my back. When I turned to help Kyle again, he was finishing off the other mob and scrambling for the trees.

"Good going," I said. "Get some distance. I'll cover your back and group them up. Get that grenade out and I'll dash away. Got it?"

He nodded and leaped over a hedge. I chugged the spirit vial from my welcome kit. Potions in Haven didn't restore everything in one go, but at my noob level I just needed about 10 seconds to hit max spirit. I danced around the middle of the warren, keeping all eyes on me.

The ground rumbled again. I tumbled out of the way and triggered crossblock as the mother tore through roots and chomped at me. Her powerful teeth almost jarred the spear from my hands, but the block held. I landed on my side and rolled to my feet.

Instead of backing away from the lumbering den mother, I

lined up the spear for an immediate counter. Before she could disappear back into the ground, I struck with deadshot.

The mother rat was no slouch. She twisted to avoid the blow. Instead of the iron finding her exposed neck, it bit deep into her shoulder.

> Combo!
> You dealt 27 damage to [Mother Pack Rat]

I couldn't believe the damage I'd inflicted on such a large enemy. I'd missed the crit but scored some kind of combo for the style move. A crossblock followed by a deadshot. Good to know.

The mother pack rat didn't appreciate the gaming mechanics like I did. She thrashed and dove underground, leaving a trail of blood.

I briefly considered following her down the large tunnel, but that would be a death sentence. Even the smaller rats would be much more dangerous within their warren, so I stayed on the surface.

The entire pack rushed forward to aid their wounded mother. I had eight of the fuckers on me at once. My spear was too slow to fend them all off. They took bites from my arm and leg. I battered the critters away with imperfect shots. Checked my spirit. Although I should've been nearly cashed out, I found that the delayed effect of the spirit vial was benefiting me. I was still within the 30 second restoration window. Although I'd hit max spirit and then spent most of it, more points had recharged. I had enough for a dash.

I searched the edge of the warren. "Uh," I said. "A little help?"

I didn't see Kyle. Another pack rat slipped under my weapon. This one chomped me hard in the stomach. I grimaced under the weight of my damage notifications. I was gonna need to dash out of here or wind up dead.

" 'Nade out!" came a battle cry from behind. Kyle strode into the clearing with his glasswork masterpiece in hand. He planted his foot on a large rock and nodded to me.

I nodded back. The rats were all clumped together. I was ready.

The ground shook. The rats scattered, running into burrows or to the tree line. The wounded mother burst through the ground, but not from under me.

The rock Kyle leaned on lifted and tilted him off balance. Large teeth clamped his leg. With a stilted cry, he tumbled to his back. The grenade bounced from his grip and landed in the dirt. A needle-thin crack splintered the crystalline glass.

I needed that grenade, but Kyle was in serious danger. That bite had left him at half health. I was in the same boat but didn't have a giant monster chewing on my leg. She dipped her head below the surface, dragging him under.

"No!" I yelled.

I dashed to Kyle's position and clutched his wrists. The den mother's heft was powerful, but Kyle and I both had strength as our secondary attribute. Together we countered her pull. I kicked at another critter trying to take a piece of my toes as we fought her off.

With a triumphant heave, I dragged Kyle from the tunnel.

The mother retreated deeper and most of the rats followed suit. Only a few remained topside. Kyle and I looked at each other and then looked at the partially cracked grenade.

On our hands and knees, we scrambled for the weapon. Clawing over dirt and tangled roots, I almost had my hands on it when a lone pack rat whizzed by and scooped it up in its jaws. It raced underground with something resembling a chittering mock.

"Asshole!" said Kyle.

We both sat on the ground, amazed at how badly everything had gone, when a loud explosion rang out from below. The ground bounced up slightly and settled back down. We ducked but it was already over. Black tendrils of smoke winded from each of the burrow openings.

54 damage to [Mother Pack Rat]
DoT: 5 dmg/5 secs
73 damage to [Pack Rat]
42 damage to [Pack Rat]
42 damage to [Pack Rat]
34 damage to [Pack Rat]
34 damage to [Pack Rat]
34 damage to [Pack Rat]
34 damage to [Pack Rat]
34 damage to [Pack Rat]
34 damage to [Pack Rat]

[Pack Rat] is defeated
[Pack Rat] is defeated
[Pack Rat] is defeated
[Pack Rat] is defeated
[Pack Rat] is defeated
[Pack Rat] is defeated
[Pack Rat] is defeated
[Pack Rat] is defeated
[Pack Rat] is defeated
[Mother Pack Rat] is defeated
380 XP awarded

Kyle and I widened our eyes in stunned silence. After a few idle moments, we simultaneously burst into laughter. But it didn't end there. A two-note chime sounded in sync with a new pop-up.

Pim-pom.

Crown Unlocked: **Fire in the Hole**
Take out a pack of tunnel dwellers with a single explosive.
1000 XP awarded

Both our bodies rushed with glowing blue fire from toes to head. As the fire washed over us, a long and deep chord sounded.

BWOOOOOM!

You have reached Level 2!

Our hysterical laughter once again transformed into slack-jawed gaping.

0160 Army of Two

Not only had we done it, but it was done with style. Level 2. With enough extra experience that we had a head start on level 3.

"Whoa," said Kyle. "I've never leveled that fast before. I've never gotten a crown either."

"I can't believe how much experience it was worth."

"Well, their XP doesn't get divided. The whole party gets the full reward. And you can only unlock them once. They're like secret achievements. Haven supposedly has a bunch of fun Easter eggs they award players with."

So creative killing and problem-solving were rewarded. All of a sudden, Lash being level 3 didn't seem so daunting. "You see? Leveling like the pros isn't about grinding swamp toads. It's about knowing the best sources of XP bonuses. I'm willing to bet if there was a wipe we could unlock this crown again without too much hassle. That's an automatic level gain."

Kyle nodded in agreement.

I was fired up. I stood and yelled into the trees. "Take that, Haven!" I strutted around like I owned the place. Though it occurred to me that the crown hadn't been my doing. It had been Kyle's weapon and the pack rat's mistake. I'd just had a front-row seat and been duplicated the XP.

"Those grenades are pretty cool," I said. "How many of those things you got left?"

"Just one. I can craft three a day."

"Hmm." I admired the destruction below. "They make a nice boom. It's a good start, but it doesn't seem very efficient to build a class around."

"Production should be better at level 2. Besides..." He pulled his sword. "That's what this is for."

"I guess."

I paced around the warren while Kyle checked his menu.

"What are you doing?" he asked. "Don't you wanna see what skills you can unlock?" His eyes glazed over. "Wow! Maybe I'll go into metalsmithing and make plate armor better than Lash has."

I arched an eyebrow. "An alchemist glassworker who forges armor?"

His boyish excitement clammed up. "What's wrong with that? I could make you some too."

"I'm just saying you should think about building a unified loadout. You want skills to complement each other. Like glasswork and alchemy to make grenades. That was pretty clever."

His eyes widened dramatically. "But *full plate*."

I shook my head. "Suit yourself. I've got loot to find."

Kyle stood as I continued surveying the ground. "That's right. This place has gotta have a sweet stash."

"Here we go."

Loot Stash Found!

As I crouched by my find, a new dialog popped up.

Proficiency gained: **Fledgling Searcher** You are now familiar with the tricks of hiding objects and will find mixed success finding them.

Loot: 127 silver [Iron Boots] [Throwing Axe] [Raw Topaz] [Health Vial] x2 [Spirit Vial] x2 [Chain Mail Gloves] [Soldier's Coat]

It wasn't much, but I was giddy all the same. This was the first legit stash we'd earned. The fact that we were out of breath made it that much sweeter.

The loot was simple to divide. Since I'd taken the last gem, I gave Kyle the topaz. The potions split evenly and the axe would just be junked. I gave Kyle the metal boots and gloves because they were too heavy for my class.

The soldier's coat turned out to be decent armor for an explorer. The padded leather fit snugly without hampering my mobility. It was a slick blue with gold trim. Made me look like an established player instead of walking around in only a noob tunic. It didn't have full coverage though. My arms and legs were still bare. Not to mention: sandals. I had no complaints, though. I was steadily making progress.

After organizing our gear we strolled through the forest, pleased with our good fortune. I glanced at my character screen.

Talon		*Level*	2
Class	Explorer	*XP*	1647
Kit	NA	*Next*	2500

1

Strength	12	*Strike*	50
Agility	14	*Dodge*	54
Craft	6	*Health*	38 / 38
Essence	8	*Spirit*	37 / 37

That level 2 label at the top did more than just look sweet. I had an additional attribute point to allocate. It also doubled my stats for strike, dodge, health, and spirit. Those were huge. I'd be more effective at combat and using skills wouldn't be such a juggling act. In addition, the rush of blue fire had restored me to full health and spirit.

I was pleased with my experience points as well. That rat encounter had rocketed us up almost 1500 XP. No doubt we could make another level before heading home. Of course, level 3 had its downsides too. I'd be eligible to fight Lash in the Arena, for one. I didn't worry too much about it, though. People like her were more bark than bite.

I was about to pull up my skill screen when Kyle barred my way with his arm. "Watch it."

We ducked behind a bush at the edge of a clearing. Not just a clearing, but the end of the forest. We'd hiked clear through to the western edge of the wood. The tree line stopped abruptly at the top of a gentle slope. Our position overlooked a common road and endless grasslands.

There were mobs too. A band of six imps and two goblins. The imps were the same I'd seen before: small, monkeylike, gray and feral. The goblins were different. Dark green skin but they weren't just a color-swapped mob. Standing between three and four feet tall, they had conniving faces with hard eyes and sharp noses. More importantly, they were outfitted with weapons and armor. The raiding party surrounded a wagon full of supplies and seized a single unarmed man in leather. The goblins prodded him with blades until he fell to his knees.

"Crap," said Kyle. "Pagans. These guys are WAY harder than normal mobs."

I snorted. At level 2, the [Imp] labels were only yellow now. No such luck for the goblins. "They sure killed my ass in the tutorial."

Kyle turned to me in shock. "Pagans were in your welcome tutorial? That's brutal."

We watched on as they interrogated the lone traveler. I cringed as the goblins spoke a clipped language and bossed the smaller imps around. They were intelligent. Relatively, anyway. From what I could gather, the pagans were intercepting all activity along the road. Eight of them against a single merchant, he was complying with their every request.

"What's the deal with pagans anyway?" I whispered.

Kyle answered without removing his eyes from the scene. "Your standard Haven lore. Pagans were the princes of the wild before humans settled in. Civilization forced them to the deepest reaches of the wild. Urban centers like Stronghold were founded on their holy treasures. Yada yada yada. The key takeaway is they hate us." He backed away from the bush. "We wandered farther than I'd thought. We should get outta here."

I steadied his shoulder before he could leave. "We need to save that guy."

"Are you kidding? We can't take on eight pagans. They're not tiny pack rats."

"I know. I killed an imp before."

"You what? You don't wanna start pissing off pagans. They're wild and unorganized, but they're the largest NPC faction in Haven by far. Screw the lore, man. You start knocking them off and they'll hunt you down. Even Lash doesn't fuck with pagans."

I winced as I considered my negative pagan reputation. "It's quite possibly too late for that."

"You'll be okay. Lie low for a while and your notoriety will diminish."

"And what about that guy? Counting him and us it's three versus eight. Only two goblins. I'd say the odds favor us."

A goblin kneed the man in the stomach. When he keeled over, the second goblin brought an axe down hard, severing his head from his neck. Kyle and I flinched at the merciless display.

"Time to recalculate those odds," muttered Kyle. "Wait a minute. Where'd the imps go?"

Several screeching creatures loped our way, already at the top of the hill. Their cries of alarm alerted the goblins below. We leapt into defensive positions. In seconds, the entire pagan party converged on us.

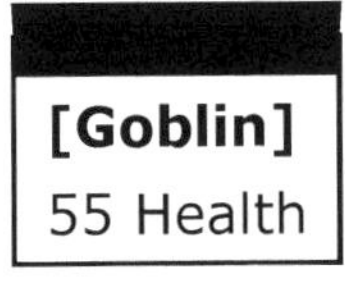

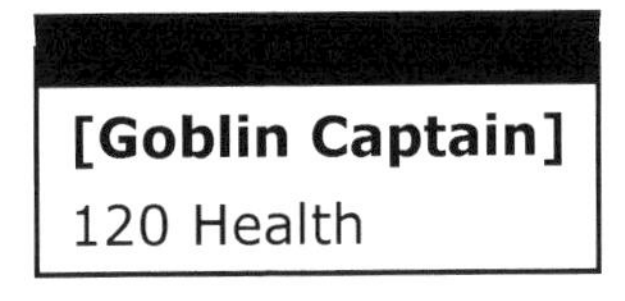

"Yup," I noted wryly. "Definitely too late."

0170 Goblin Commander

The imps hopped and chittered in noisy unison, mere animals unable to hide their growing anticipation for blood. The two goblins were more restrained. They stood upright, wore torso coverings of thick hide, and held long daggers. The little stickers were twisted and jagged and probably loaded with five kinds of Hep.

Kyle: *We're so screwed, bro.*

I smiled. The party chat wouldn't be visible to the pagans. It was a great way to strategize in secret, provided we had the concentration to apply to it.

Talon: *Don't worry. Let's keep our heads and stay defensive. You still have that grenade, right?*
Kyle: *Ready and waiting.*

"Tricksy spies!" accused the [Goblin Captain], waving his

blade at us. "I knew that merchant wasn't alone."

I shivered. Somehow the fact the creature could talk made him more vile. The imps howled at the reference to the beheaded man on the road. They wanted more of the same.

"We didn't know him," I contested. "We were just wandering the Midlands—"

"These lands are free!" spat the goblin subordinate.

An imp swiped at me with a claw. I maneuvered my spear between us to back it off. The [Imp] tags were yellow now, indicating a simple challenge. In the tutorial, when I'd been level 1, they were orange. That was the good news: six imps would be a challenge but, with clever tactics, Kyle and I could take them.

The [Goblin] and [Goblin Captain], however, spoiled our chances. One name orange, one name red. That was Haven's way of saying the goblin would be tough and it would be outright stupid to attack the captain. Maybe we should have run when we'd had the chance.

"Lies!" screeched their leader, face twisting in anger. "Humanses and their lies. You were hunting the errant folk, you were. I can smell the stink of your actions from here."

I scowled. My pagan notoriety was working against me already.

"I only defended myself," I countered. "I'll do the same right now, if I need to."

The captain snickered. It was an uneven, choking sound that set me on edge. He looked to the other goblin. "The tricksy human wants to best us in combat."

"No," I cut in, inspired by our experience with the pack rats. "I want to offer a gift. A passing token to the pagans who rule these wild lands. A passing token, and then we can be on our way."

The imps chittered wildly. The goblins narrowed their eyes. They were suspicious of all humans, but they weren't immune to flattery. Whether ego or curiosity, their eyes twinkled.

"Gift," said the goblin subordinate, testing the word. "What gift?"

Talon: *Hand them the grenade.*
Kyle: *What? You're crazy!*
Talon: *Remember the mother rat? Hand them the grenade.*
Kyle: *Oh.*
Kyle: *Should I crack it first?*
Talon: *No. Let me handle that part.*

Kyle produced his final corrosive grenade. It really was beautiful, in a way. Custom blown glass, thin and sturdy, with a reflective black gel inside that settled unevenly. Kyle held the offering out and the goblin soldier snatched it and backed away.

"What's this?" he asked, studying it closely.

"A crystal ball," I answered. "It tells the fortune of those who peer into its depths."

The captain arched an eyebrow and peeked over his man's shoulder.

"Seriously," I continued. "Throughout history, civilizations have risen and fallen due to the influence of the black orb."

Kyle: *Okay, bro, you might be laying it on a bit thick.*

"Let me sees that," snapped the leader. He snatched the grenade from his comrade's hand and placed it before his eyes. "How does its turn on?"

Chances were this encounter was going to result in combat no matter what I did. My pagan rep all but guaranteed that. If these creatures wanted blood so badly, the best thing was to give it to them before they were ready. Attacking the captain was suicidal, but I'd never get a better shot.

I leveled the spear at the distracted leader and triggered deadshot. In a split second, the iron pierced my target: not the captain but the corrosive grenade he held. The glass orb shattered and the spear dug into the goblin's eye.

The resultant explosion was vicious. I rolled away, hoping the length of my spear was enough to keep me out of range. Between my improved stats, the technique, and the added corrosive gel, the damage didn't disappoint.

Surprise!
Critical Hit!
You dealt 82 damage to [Goblin Captain]

The pagan was thrown backward and landed in the dirt. He snarled and rolled to his side, face blackened with slime. He shrieked in pain and anger. "Trickses! Kill them!"

My jaw dropped. That had been my strongest hit yet. The

captain had shrugged it off.

Note to self: No more attacking reds.

"Watch out!" shouted Kyle. He swung his sword as the other goblin charged me.

Because the creature's attention was divided, Kyle scored a decent hit. I readied my spear but couldn't trigger deadshot during the cooldown. 20 seconds didn't sound like much but it was an eternity in combat. Instead, his blade met my spear in a crossblock. He spun away and came at me again.

I stabbed forward. The goblin had decent defensive technique, batting my iron to the side, but he was a shrimp compared to me. His three-foot frame and puny weapon couldn't counter the full weight of my thrust. Despite being knocked off mark, my point found the goblin's side.

He growled and swung at me, but he was way out of range. I was liking my choice of spear more and more every minute.

Kyle took advantage of the distraction to score another hit on the goblin. Despite being a superior level, we already had him down to half health just like that. I was starting to think orange enemies weren't too bad after all.

Then the rest of the pagans caught up with us.

The imps converged, three on Kyle and three on me. They threw themselves at us with reckless abandon. And it *would've* been reckless had our weapons been pointed at them. Instead, while we were busy with the advanced mobs, the low-level ones swarmed us with ease. We took immediate and serious hits.

I knocked the pagans away with the flat of my weapon. I considered sweeping again to clear a path, but Kyle had stumbled to his knees. An imp took the opportunity to jump on the back of his neck and bite.

I triggered dash to escape my imps and assist Kyle. I struck before my zippy movement was finished, before the beastie could strike a killing blow. I impaled it on my spear, not a crit but a solid attack that drained most of the imp's health and stunned it. The opening easily allowed a second strike to finish it off.

The other imps reared at my approach. They congregated into a battle pack. For all our effort, only one pagan was dead. That left five howling critters, a goblin subordinate, and a wounded captain just now regaining his feet.

We were screwed.

"Take the imps," barked Kyle. He charged straight at the weakened goblin.

My next spear thrust found more flesh, but the imp had avoided lethal damage. I found myself unable to fully commit to any blow lest the rest of the pack spill in.

"No," I said. "We need to run. We need to get out of here."

"I can do this," said Kyle.

His sword came down in a hard overhead strike. The goblin easily set to parry, but Kyle's strength was impressive. He must've dropped another point into the attribute since he leveled. The little goblin couldn't cancel the sword's momentum. His dagger twisted down as Kyle's hammering blow landed on his head.

Imp teeth dug into my neck. I spun away in panic. It wasn't pain I felt, exactly, but absolute horror filled in the blanks for my brain. Like when that boggart had slurped on my intestines. The mind wasn't meant to experience that.

I swung my weapon overhead in hasty arcs. I spun in circles, watching all approach angles, doing anything I could to keep the pagans off me.

Kyle incurred a grievous injury. The goblin's sticker sunk into his stomach all the way to the hilt. My roommate battered his enemy weakly, scoring decent hits but clearly losing now. I growled and tumbled as claws scraped my back.

This was it then. The moment of our deaths.

I felt my intestines spill from my belly. The paralyzing terror of that Pepsi trailer sliding right at me. This was helplessness, all over again.

Virtual blood boiled within me. I couldn't accept that. Not that easily. If I was gonna bite it, I'd be damned if I didn't take one of these sickos with me.

My dash was still unusable so I had to do it the old-fashioned way. I charged Kyle and the goblin and lined up my weapon. An imp blocked my path so I speared him and kept barreling ahead. The iron popped through the imp and stuck the goblin's gut as I crashed into them with the full force of my body. The tackle ripped the goblin off Kyle. It rocketed us over the smooth sloping edge of the hill. Head over heels, the goblin, the imp, and I tumbled down the hillside. I held onto my spear for dear life.

Fall Damage!
3 damage
Fall Damage!
3 damage
Fall Damage!
3 damage

At the bottom, when the world stopped spinning, I was the only one sitting up. My 8 health points didn't look so hot, but it had my present company beat. The goblin subordinate was dead. The imp hadn't even been alive for the tumble.

Two more dead. That meant Kyle was still on the hilltop with four imps and...

The goblin captain swapped out his dagger for the familiar axe and approached my friend. Kyle was on his hands and knees downing a health potion.

Talon: *Get out of there!*
Kyle: *No way. I got this.*
Talon: *Kyle*

I abandoned party chat and climbed over the dead goblin. My vision was blurry and tinted red. I stomped up the hill. "Kyle!"

My roommate squared off with the goblin captain. Kyle's health was regenerating but their duel wouldn't wait. Before either of them struck, however, the imps jumped on my friend's back. He twisted and stabbed backward, ending one's life, but the sacrifice had accomplished its goal. The goblin was only at a third health but he was a formidable soldier. A quick heave of his axe buried it into Kyle's skull. The critical hit put him down for good. My friend crumpled to the grass and the imps jeered and bit into his flesh.

[Kyle] is dead!

The captain barked an order and cut the imp's celebration short. Then he equipped his dagger again and pointed at me. "Kill the human!" he commanded.

The pagans charged down the hill like a rolling thunder.

0180 Out Run

Kyle was dead and I had three imps and a goblin captain bearing down on me. Half their party taken out and half of mine. Difference was, I was alone. My vision swam a little. I was near death.

I did what any red-blooded person who wanted to live would have done. I ran.

The pagans were navigating the hillside while I was on the road. That gave me a good lead. As I sprinted, I downed one of two health potions. With my max health of 38, the buff would restore me to full in half a minute.

Talon: *Kyle!*
Talon: *Kyle, where are you?*

My friend didn't answer. I ran down the path and waded through combat notifications. I didn't care about the damage and experience. I was learning to ignore those and focus on what was important. I found it.

[Kyle] is dead!
[Kyle] has left your party

Crap. I had no idea how Haven handled death. I could only assume he respawned at Stronghold. Problem was, I couldn't access my mailbox in the wild, and with him removed from the party, chat was out as well.

That meant I was truly on my own.

The pagans had full aggro on me. I charged down the road at an impressive clip but they weren't giving up. I was faster than them but I'd tire eventually.

Well, not *tire*, exactly, but sprinting at this pace was steadily draining my spirit points. Haven's stamina and combat skills and mana were all built into the same pool, making spirit a delicate balance. I was below a third and believed the pagans would follow me to the ends of Haven. I needed to change the game.

As I rounded the hillside, I broke line of sight with my pursuers. The hill was rockier now, a steeper grade but not a sheer face. Several large boulders formed platforms, a series of steps for a giant. At the top the forest grew thick.

I opened my skill menu and checked the traversal options. Scaling was real attractive right now. However, I had another thought. Without time to examine the skill descriptions closely, I selected vault. I ran at one of the large stone steps, twice my height, and shoved the base of my spear into the dirt. The ensuing skill trigger lifted me off the ground. I shot up like a pole-vaulter and easily landed on the rock above.

The skill cooldown was only 5 seconds but it took a chunk of spirit. I repeated the vault onto a higher plane, leaving only one more jump to the hilltop.

My spirit was too low for another one. I considered using my last spirit potion but I was only 1 point short. It would naturally replenish itself in seconds. Yes, I was one of those RPG players who saved all my cool stuff for the last boss. Sue me.

Waiting, of course, felt longer than it was. Another ten seconds or so gave me the spirit I needed. Unfortunately, it also gave the pagans time to round the bend and see what I was up to.

Damn.

It was a mistake not using that spirit vial. Nothing for it anymore. I vaulted to the top of the hill as the pagans clutched the rocks and started their ascent. These bastards were persistent. I pressed into the forest to maintain my lead.

I crashed through the brush, branches whipping my face. There was no such thing as far enough ahead. Even as I ran, I heard the captain's war cry as he crested the hill. Damn pagans were good climbers too.

I hurried past a clearing where I saw the strangest thing. A deer with white stripes and huge horns—not antlers but thick, heavy horns—hung upside down in some kind of net. I slowed my sprint for a second and took in the bizarre scene, readying for any other surprises. There were none, however. We were alone.

The animal whimpered. I bolted from the clearing. Not as far behind as I would've hoped, the imps raised a noisy ruckus. They were close and smelled blood.

I stopped. Crap. I couldn't do it.

I sprinted back to the clearing. The deer turned its head to me as far as the net would allow. It jerked and set the whole hanging contraption swinging. The poor thing was stuck good. Despite the pagans bearing down on me, I equipped my whittling knife, reached up, and cut the net down.

The deer landed on her back and rolled to a sit. She was large and solid, falling somewhere between deer and bison in the animal kingdom. She had a deep-chestnut coat with white vertical stripes on her body and a cream-colored mask around her eyes and the bridge of her nose, like a raccoon. Her four hooves had cream socks, and her horns were large, broad things that formed a V atop her head.

A [Mountain Bongo], whatever that was. As I readied to go, she licked my face.

"Okay, girl," I said. "You're welcome. You're free. Now get outta here."

The bongo hopped to the tree line. Her muscled legs had a long stride, but she was limping.

I nodded. "Don't worry. It's me they want."

The pagans screamed through the dense brush. I bit the bullet and chugged my spirit vial, wishing I'd done it sooner and avoided this whole mess. I winked at the bongo and raced into the trees, banging my spear against the foliage and generally making a clamor to draw the pagans my way.

And my way they came. I pressed ahead with near abandon. At the last second, I noticed my foot falling toward a length of net on the ground.

"Shit!"

I triggered my vault skill and hopped over the trap.

Agility Check...
Pass!

I tried planting the spear between the net loops but I must've snagged it. The trap sprang, yanking my spear from my grip. My panicked landing was the opposite of graceful, but I cleared the net. I rolled to my feet and brushed myself off.

Someone or something was making use of the trapping skill. As if I didn't have enough things to worry about. I heard the imps approaching. I tugged my spear hanging in the empty net. It was wrapped tight. Tangled. I pulled harder but that only tightened the net's grip.

I took a breath and worked the net's loops off my weapon one by one. At least this was a chance to catch my breath. Unfortunately, the pagans came into view through the trees. As I finally pulled my spear away, they fanned out into the clearing.

I backed away slowly. I was now in a spot of sunlight. The tree canopy opened above, allowing the light to hit the ground. Lush grass grew. That's what had attracted the wild game. It also helped hide the net. Someone knew what they were doing.

Proficiency improved: **Skilled Searcher**
You are accustomed with the tricks of hiding objects and will find moderate success finding them.

"Tricksies human," admonished the goblin captain. His eye was a bloodied pulp. "I will tear the flesh from your bones."

Could these guys get any more disgusting? I grimaced and faced them. One of the imps was wounded. The goblin hadn't healed. Still a third health, which put him about equal with me, thanks to the health tincture. That had to mean this was winnable. But it wouldn't be easy. He'd taken out Kyle with a single crit, and he'd done it by using the imps as a distraction.

"How about a fair fight?" I graciously offered. "Tell your imps to back away and you and me settle this like men."

He chortled. "Now why would I do that?"

The three lackeys flanked me. I almost backed into another net. Another trap. I smiled and sidestepped it, luring the captain closer.

"You sure you don't want to do this fair and square?" I asked, my tone a smug warning.

The goblin ran his black tongue over the length of his dagger and cackled. Then he stepped into the net. A rush of sound zipped against the trees as the net sprang. The goblin recoiled as the net snapped up around him, squeezing his arms to his body and lifting him two feet off the ground.

I instantly struck the nearest imp. The pagans had all been startled and I scored an easy kill.

The captain grunted as he sawed the net, but he couldn't free himself quickly enough. I only had two imps left, and one of them was hurt. A crossblock combo took care of the healthy one. I cleaned the other up without resorting to skills, with only a minor scratch to show for it. With the lackeys out of the way, I turned my attention to the captain.

With a final slice, he cut his torso free. He tumbled upside down, knees still caught in the air. His head banged the ground and he lost the grip on the dagger.

I snorted and approached. "You killed my friend."

"No!" he uttered. "A fair fight. I want a fair fight."

I recalled his execution of the merchant on the road. How he used the imps to surprise and take down Kyle. If the captain was so keen to fight dirty, I'd oblige him. I activated deadshot and plunged the spear into the goblin captain's neck. His screaming hiss cut to gurgling blood, and red painted the dirt.

[Goblin Captain] is defeated
600 XP awarded

BWOOOOOM!

You have reached Level 3!

I closed my eyes and took in the surge of power. Another level. Another rush of fire over me as my health and spirit instantly maxed out to new levels. Incredible.

Without Kyle in the party, I'd absorbed the full experience reward of the goblin captain and remaining imps. Clearly an enemy I wasn't supposed to kill yet in a one-on-one fight.

My face darkened at the next notification.

Pagan Reputation -100

I grumbled. It always bugged me how games scored faction penalties. None of the witnesses to my deeds lived. How the hell would the entire pagan nation know what I'd done? But that was that. The rules of the game. I had to live with them.

And I wasn't sorry.

At the edge of the clearing, the mountain bongo peeked out at me.

I laughed. "You're a quiet one. With that mask you look like a little bandit."

She sniffed the air hesitantly.

"I know. They smell disgusting."

I looted the bodies. Decent silver and sellable gear, but nothing noteworthy except for a weird roll of cloth in the captain's pocket. It was sealed with a sticky, sappy substance.

[Outer Mandate]

This scroll cannot be read unless you break the seal. This will have consequences.

Break the seal?

Hmm. It would be better to know what I was getting into before opening this. What if I negated its value by doing so? I frowned and stuffed it into my inventory.

The bongo pressed her nose into my hand. Her silent approach had surprised me. I relaxed and rubbed the spot between her eyes. Her ears twitched happily and I rubbed those too.

"Watch out for those nets, now. Okay?"

I lugged my gear back to the hillside. Instead of climbing down the steep slope, I followed along the top. I didn't want to stand out in the open.

As I hiked, the mountain bongo came along. She still limped although I couldn't spot anything seriously wrong with her. It was stupid but I used my last health vial on her. What can I say? I had 57 health now; I was practically invincible. Fully recovered, the bongo hopped up and down in excitement and pranced two circles around me. Good as new.

She was cute. Had a lot of personality for an AI animal.

But it was time to regroup. No more health or spirit tinctures. Kyle was probably back at Stronghold. As I traversed the hilltop, the forest grew thinner and soon I was at the site of Kyle's body. I selected it.

Kyle's equipment was dropped. You can salvage it and return it to him, or you can scavenge it for yourself.

Salvage or Scavenge?

I chose salvage. The entirety of his loot immediately disappeared into thin air. Huh. I wondered if that meant he had it now. If true, corpse runs weren't necessary in Haven as long as one party member lived. In fact, we weren't even in a party anymore, so maybe Haven allowed the kindness of strangers to return a dead player's loot.

I'm sure it didn't happen a lot.

As I finished looting the rest of the dead pagans, movement caught my eye on the road below. Three adventurers sprinted toward the abandoned wagon. It was that kill-thief Dune and his party.

"Hey!" I called out. "That's my stuff!"

0190 Thief

They got to the wagon first but I was scrambling down the hill yelling and flailing my arms like a madman. It got their attention. The three of them turned to me, startled.

I stopped in front of them. "I let you walk away with that toad gland but I won't let you take this."

One of them scoffed. A level 3 mystic in a red robe and a staff. He had a wide belly and a long black beard. "Won't *let* us?"

I frowned. They were all level 3, like me, except they'd already received their class titles. Dune was a ranger with a bow. Stigg, the red robe, was a berserker. He looked like some kind of mystic tank. The rail-thin black girl with spectacles, Caduceus, was a physicker. Her plain white clothes advertised her as a healer. She was an artisan class, though, not a mystic. She leaned on the sciences, then.

"I'm not here to fight," I told them. "But the simple fact of the matter is I almost died beating the pagans for this. My friend," I said, pointing to the hilltop, "*did* die. So I think I've earned this."

Dune backed away from the wagon. "This is pagan loot?"

The others eyed the creature's bodies on the hill and the

beheaded man on the road.

"It *was*," I answered. I brushed past them and went to the wagon. They didn't try to stop me.

Loot:
[Chain Mail Hauberk]
[Iron Vambraces]
[Blacksteel Spear]

A nice haul. I wondered what that lone traveler was doing with this stuff. I twirled the new spear in my hand and examined it.

[Blacksteel Spear]
Blacksteel is hardened in the desert forges of Alandra with an unknown ore enricher. Harder and sturdier than normal steel.
+10% damage versus pagans

This would *definitely* come in handy. I trudged over to the poor merchant's body. He was an NPC so there was no option to salvage his belongings back to him.

Loot:
[Studded Leather Armor]
[Leather Pants]
[Leather Boots]
[Steel Shortsword]

"Finally," I said. I slipped the studded leather armor and pants on under my soldier's coat. I chucked my sandals and put on a real pair of sturdy boots. The chain mail armor was too much but the iron vambraces fit nicely on my forearms.

Dune chuckled. "Much better than newbie gear. I dig that blue coat, by the way."

Dune wasn't a stranger to bright colors, but with his green cloak and bow he was more into the Robin Hood thing. I just hoped they weren't planning on robbing me.

The three of them listed around uncertainly. "Hey, you think you wanna group with us?"

I nodded at them thankfully. "Sorry. Maybe later. I gotta get back to Stronghold and resupply. And see about a friend."

"Kyle," said Dune.

"Right." I got my gear in order. "I'm not sure what happened to him. I haven't been able to reach him yet."

"He's on lockdown," explained Caduceus. Her voice was deep and precise. "He can't leave home for four hours. He can read email but can't send anything, so even if you had access you wouldn't hear back. Once you see him again he can rejoin your party and restore chat privileges."

"He also loses all his XP after his last level," added Stigg.

That was a bit of a loss. Kyle had probably been halfway to leveling. So I made it to 3 but he would still be 2.

"Did you salvage his drop? Dead players drop random equipment. It could be worthless junk or priceless artifacts."

"I got it," I said. "Thanks. Listen, the pagans were ambushing people along this road. You three might wanna watch out for that."

They nodded and I started up the hill.

"How does it feel?" asked Stigg. "Killing pagans?"

I shrugged, but as I climbed with my back to them, a smile played across my lips. There was something twisted about those creatures. After my horrifying encounter with the boggart, maybe I wanted to kill every last one of them.

When I crested the hill, the bongo rejoined me. She followed as I marched through the forest, ignoring stray swamp toads until the woods grew overcrowded with adventurers. At the edge of the tended land, I rejoined the main road to Stronghold. It was wide open from here. The deer paused and lowered her head.

"You don't want to expose yourself to the wide-open tended land," I said. I scratched the bottom of her chin. "I don't blame you."

I said goodbye to my new friend and headed to the city. She hurried back into the brush and peeked. Then I approached the gate. The city watch let me in without a hassle or a word.

It felt good strolling through town with some accomplishments under my belt. I took my time and enjoyed the pace, figuring Kyle was still on lockdown anyway. I stopped in the various shops and sold the junk out of my inventory. I also purchased a few more potions. All said and done, I was left with 110 silver. Not a bad haul for half a day.

None of the shops would buy the outer mandate, however. Even Trafford didn't know what to make of it. He noted that I'd be "better off trying to stuff it up a horse's ass than opening it" though. Classic Trafford.

After I had everything in order, I returned to Hillside and zoned home. Kyle was planted on the couch watching *Top Gun.* He paused when I came in.

"You gotta be more careful," I teased. "You can't just take on the whole world like Maverick."

"Holy shit," he said, jumping to his feet. "I was wondering why you didn't respawn here. I thought they'd taken you prisoner or something."

"They can do that? Anyway, no, I just didn't try to take them head on. Caution and strategy are rewarded."

"So you ran," he translated.

I grimaced. "Yes and no. I killed them, Kyle. I got them all. And some extra loot to boot."

I tossed the chain mail tunic on the floor. His eyes widened as he picked it up.

"A hauberk! And you made level 3," he said in awe. "But you haven't earned your class title yet. You need to spend your skill points."

"Oh." I checked the character menu.

Talon		*Level*	3
Class	Explorer	*XP*	3072
Kit	*	*Next*	4750

2

Strength	12	*Strike*	75
Agility	14	*Dodge*	81
Craft	6	*Health*	57 / 57
Essence	8	*Spirit*	55 / 55

Indeed, I had a few points to spend. Not only that but the kit box that usually read NA now had an asterisk.

I looked at my attribute points first. I had 2 to spend for levels 2 and 3. I considered upping essence since I'd been hitting the limits of my spirit, but my level gains had done me well. I decided to max out my agility with both points.

Then I looked over my skills for something new. I wasn't especially feeling anything and considered upgrading a current skill.

Kyle interrupted my study with a party request. I joined.

"That goblin captain give you anything cool?" he asked.

"Nah." I noted the lone mystery item in my inventory. "There is this. An outer mandate. Any idea what it is?"

Kyle shook his head.

"It looks important, but I can't open it without the pagans knowing. I couldn't sell it in the shops either."

Kyle killed his beer. "Looks like you have a decision to make."

It wasn't really a decision when I thought about it. I broke the seal and unrolled the cloth scroll. It was painted with garbled orders.

Quest Offer: **Unveil the Pagans**
Quest Type: Epic
Reward: Unknown
You've discovered pagans encroaching on Stronghold and found orders to secure the roads leading to the city. Uncover the source and reason for this activity.
Accept Quest?

Kyle's eyes widened, apparently seeing the quest notification as well. "Epic quest," he read.

"What's that mean?"

"Well, if you go to the town questkeepers you'll find lots of simple stuff like escort and fetch quests. Jobs, payment—pretty standard fare. Epic quests are much more wide open and extended. To be honest, they're supposed to be a pain in the ass."

"Yeah, but what does it hurt to accept? We don't need to follow through with it, right?"

"True. We're free to abandon it whenever we want."

I accepted. The quest was added to a new quest tab that appeared on my status screen after the map. Unfortunately, the quest screen was just a recap of the same info the offer had given me. Wide open, indeed. I didn't have time to ponder it because yet more notifications interrupted us.

You have broken the seal of the outer mandate. Pagan Reputation -150

"What?" I complained.

You have surpassed 250 pagan notoriety. There is now a mark on your head. Pagan assassins have been dispatched.

"WHAT?!?"

I chewed my lip.

"Um, maybe I shouldn't have opened the mandate."

Kyle blinked dumbly and headed to the fridge for another cold one.

My reaction was much more pragmatic. Knowing we were going to have pagan trouble sooner or later, I reopened my skill tree and studied my options.

I had 3 points to spend here, 2 from the new level and 1 leftover from the last. Weapon skills were the only ones that were upgradeable, but in order to sink another point into deadshot I had to increase my general spear handling as well. So I spent the trio of points upgrading to spear handling 2, deadshot 2, and crossblock 2. I received bonuses across the board to my chances to hit, damage, dodge, and chances of criticals. I also received another momentous notification. Finally, this time, it was a good one.

You have been promoted to: Level 3 Scout. Congratulations, explorer!

My eyes narrowed slowly and the edges of my lips upturned. Scout. I liked the sound of that. Swift. Tactical. Dangerous. I admired my new stats.

Talon		*Level*	3
Class	Explorer	*XP*	3072
Kit	Scout	*Next*	4750

Strength	12	*Strike*	78
Agility	16	*Dodge*	90
Craft	6	*Health*	60 / 60
Essence	8	*Spirit*	57 / 57

Between the class kit and the blacksteel spear and the new armor and loadout, I was feeling like a game breaker.

"Looks like we're in for a world of hurt," said Kyle, walking over and offering me a bottle. "Let's sit down and have a couple beers. We'll hit the wild first thing tomorrow."

"Screw tomorrow," I told him, snatching both bottles from his hand and returning them to the fridge. "You said you were gonna take my mind off things by adventuring today. It's still today, your four-hour lockdown is up, and if we want to level while the going's easy, it's past time we got back out there."

Kyle sighed and turned off *Top Gun.*

0200 Twilight Princess

We marched through the streets wearing used but snazzy armor. My new class title drew the eye of several residents. I reminded myself that simply being level 3 was a pretty good accomplishment at this point. It was now a little under twenty-four hours since the full wipe. Most players hadn't yet achieved what I had, and they'd had an extra half day.

"I still think this is crazy," pressed Kyle. "Pagan assassins can't get us in town."

"What if they sneak over the walls all ninja-like and kill us in our sleep?"

"You don't get it, dude. Pagans are absolutely unable to cross into city limits. It's impossible. Standard pagan lore. It's one of the reasons they hate us so much. I'm telling you, we should hole up and play air hockey until this blows over."

"You are the least ambitious person I've ever known," I told him. "You were so close to level 3. Equal with Lash. Breathing on a class kit. You've never hit that before. Don't you wanna see what it feels like?"

"Sure I do. It's not as easy as some of you make it look."

I gave him that point. Haven combat was a complex

organism. Old-school MMOs were more about numbers piled upon numbers. Gold. Gear. Level. If you had enough in the hit points department then you could withstand enough from the damage department.

Haven was different. This world incorporated tons of hidden bonuses that wildly swung the favor of combat. Crit, stun, combo, surprise—special damage conditions were a norm rather than a rarity. In my limited experience so far they were responsible for the weighing of most battles.

That meant fighting tactically and with measure was the way to succeed. Fighting smarter, not harder. Maybe it was because I was an agility class, but I couldn't imagine how tanks survived in Haven. Without a set of full plate, I simply couldn't see absorbing endless damage.

"Crap," said Kyle. "Take my lead." He moved to the edge of the road.

As we approached the city gates, a solitary player entered the city, returning from questing, walking toward us on the otherwise empty main thoroughfare.

"She..." I squinted. "She's purple."

"That's Izzy," he said. "Keep your head down. Just walk by staring at your new boots and hopefully she won't bother us."

"Bother us?"

I was simultaneously preoccupied by two things. One, I wondered how Kyle had become such a doormat in only a month. But two, this woman returning to Stronghold was fucking purple.

It didn't end with the lavender skin, either. She had four dragonfly wings sprouting from her back. At first I assumed it was special armor but, the closer we got, it looked organic.

I couldn't help but stare. Izzy marched our way with badass confidence. She was Japanese, five-foot even, and almost my age. Everything about her conveyed attitude. Jet-black hair, short and spiked. Tiny earrings dotting her cartilage. I think I mentioned the purple part.

She was striking, unlike anyone I'd seen in Haven yet, and you know what the funny thing was? What stood out most was the icy glare she gave everything and everyone. Hard eyes, sharp eyebrows—this was a girl who did not want to be fucked with.

"She's a pixie," explained Kyle.

"I thought everybody was human."

"Other races are being beta tested with more tenured players. People say she was one of the first players to live in Haven."

"And she doesn't have a party?"

"That's no accident, bro. I have to warn you before you get any cute thoughts: That girl is stuck up. She's a killer mage. And she's a master dueler. I've never seen her lose in the Arena, and she fights *a lot*. You chat with her, you're bound to wind up on the receiving end of a beat down."

I examined her. [Level 5 Frost Mage]. Color me impressed. Now I understood the midnight-blue tunic and pants she wore. Her class likely prohibited armor.

"Wow," I said. "She's good at power leveling."

Kyle snorted. "More like her dad is some hotshot with Kablammy."

I turned to him. "You think she's cheating?"

"Isn't it obvious?"

I shrugged. "I mean, maybe her racial bonuses are an unfair

advantage, but you said yourself she was one of the first players. Maybe she just knows what she's doing."

He pressed ahead unconvinced.

"Have you ever followed her to pick up tips?" I asked.

"No." His voice was hushed because Izzy was only twenty feet ahead of us now.

"Have you ever asked?"

He shook his head.

I didn't get it. What was the big deal? First Lash and now Izzy. I broke away from the edge of the road and moved to meet the pixie in the center.

"Dude," whispered Kyle, "don't."

I smiled magnanimously and spread my arms to the side as I approached. Izzy's glare found me immediately. Her lips were a dark indigo against her lighter skin. It painted her smirk plainly.

"Hello, traveler," I said. "My name's Talon. Pleased to make your acquaintance."

I offered my hand in greeting. Izzy didn't slow her gait. She pranced right by my hand without a word. My eyes followed her and then landed on Kyle loitering a good distance away. His eyes said *I told you so*. And then his party chat said it too.

Kyle: *I told you so.*

So I got a double dose of it. But I wasn't deterred. I hurried to catch up with the pixie.

"Look," I said, falling into stride with her, "if you're busy, I get it. I'm new here and just trying to find some friends, you know? It looks like you know what you're doing... and I think

I'm getting along decently for my first day ever... Are you maybe interested in grouping up?"

She marched along silently, not even giving me the time of day.

"Um. Well, do you mind telling us if there's a secret to getting a non-human race?"

Again, no answer. I became slightly angry.

"Fine, then." And as sarcastically as I could muster, "I'm so *sorry* I *bothered* you by trying to say *hi*."

Izzy stopped and spun around, hands on hips. "What about my face says I look like I wanna talk?"

Her eyes were sharper than razorblades.

"Nothing. I just figured it couldn't hurt."

One eyebrow arched in challenge. "It *could*."

Izzy was way shorter than me but seemed to stand taller. I didn't know how she did it. I was still upset, but I reined in my temper and sarcasm, speaking genuinely.

"Look, maybe it's a bad time. I'm sorry if I said something wrong. I just figured, we're all here, we're all dead—we could all use some support. That's all."

She didn't soften her posture in the slightest. "What about my face says I need support?"

I chewed my lip and shook my head lightly.

Izzy twirled away and continued down the main thoroughfare. I sighed in relief, glad that train wreck was over. When Kyle finally wandered back to me, I just scratched my head and said, "Seems like she doesn't want to be bothered."

"Told you," he said, chuckling. "Stuck up and a half. You're just lucky she didn't challenge you to a duel. Now let's get out of here. I never thought I'd want to leave Stronghold so much. Pagan assassins are better than Izzy."

0210 Assassin's Creed

Once again we marched out of Stronghold's western gate. My thoughts were on Izzy and Lash as I absentmindedly followed the road. There were a lot of angry people in Haven. A lot of unresolved issues. I suppose that was to be expected.

We were, all of us, dead. Our prior lives were over. Even the veterans like Izzy had had less than a year to get used to that fact. Real death was final, without the capacity for angst or could-have-beens. Or, if you subscribed to the popular competing theory, death came gift-wrapped with supreme enlightenment and eternal bliss. But Haven wasn't any of those things. Here it was either be smothered by regrets or grind your ass off.

I was no different. I mean, I wasn't taking out my frustrations on other players or drowning my sorrows in endless beer or taking part in whatever pseudo-Freudian theories were out there, but I felt a driving desire to level. To progress. I'd been telling myself I had to play by the rules. Keep my head down and be a good beta tester until Everchat rolled out. Then

I'd be reunited with my little brother. Derek wouldn't have me back, of course, but I'd be there to listen. To advise. I could make sure his life didn't spiral out of control.

But had I really focused on grinding for him? Was it all just a logical contract? Part of me knew there was a simpler answer. I was just keeping myself distracted. Inception and the Matrix did it for a few minutes. Jenna Jynx was stimulating, but in all the wrong ways.

But skills, levels, quests, pagans, outer mandates? There was something about it all.

The road ahead divided the forest that spanned before us. The end of the tended lands. Last time we'd split off the safety of the well-traveled path and ventured into the trees. Now I wasn't sure either option was great. After all, both led to the same place. The other side of the forest, where the pagans were policing the road.

As we halted there, a deer poked its head out of the trees. The mountain bongo was back. She cantered up to me and I hugged her around the neck.

"You're still here," I said.

Kyle lowered his sword, confused. "What's going on? You a deer whisperer now?"

I smiled. "No. After you died, I found her caught in a net, wounded. I freed her and healed her. She's followed me around ever since."

Kyle approached the bongo. They eyed each other warily. "She's fucking huge," he said. "Those horns are no joke."

"She's harmless," I assured him. I gave the girl a pat on the back. "You know, I think she's scared of venturing too deep this way now. With what we've seen, I don't blame her. We wanna stay far away from the road now. I'm not exactly a popular guy with the pagans."

I opened my menu and brought up the map. Stronghold was surrounded by flat farmland. The west gate was the main gate, but there was an eastern gate as well. It was too late to try that out. But if we headed directly south over the plains, we'd eventually hit mountains. No main roads broached those peaks.

Kyle was cool with it so we headed that way. The bongo followed. I was personally looking forward to discovering new enemies. You can only pick off rats and toads for so long before you get bored. We crossed the dry grassy plains without incident. It was still close enough to Stronghold that the pickings were slim.

"You ever picked up that smithing skill?" I asked to break the monotony.

"I did," said Kyle under his breath. "But the skill point reset when my level did. I haven't spent it yet."

"That's probably a blessing."

"Yeah. When I was on lockdown, I was thinking about what you said about using my skills together."

I fired a skeptical expression at him.

"What?" he said. "I don't only drink beer and play shooters. You made a good point. I'm not sure what to do yet, but I probably wanna grow out my alchemy tree with helper skills."

I nodded. "Increase your output. While you were busy being productive, did you manage to make any more grenades?"

"Just had time for one. My new level raised my limit even without the skill points. But here's the thing." He pulled out his glass orb. "We already agreed the damage of this sucker is convenient. It's not monster damage, but when it exploded in tight quarters, in the warren, it was a lot more effective."

"Context seems to matter a lot in Haven," I agreed.

"So wouldn't a corrosive do more damage in an enemy's bloodstream?" He unplugged the bottle and pulled his sword out. Slowly and carefully, Kyle dripped a spattering of black gel over the sharp edges of his sword.

I smiled. "Now you're talking. Just in time, too."

I pointed ahead. A [Devil Badger] had noticed us. It was a hairy, short-legged thing with a vicious snarl. It loped toward us aggressively.

[Devil Badger]
45 Health

I pulled out my spear but let Kyle take the first shot. Sure enough, his blow did more damage than usual. Even better, the DoT increased threefold.

The devil badger had decent health, though. Despite being a lowly critter, it was still at half life and readying a bite on Kyle. My upgraded deadshot easily took it out.

We didn't have time to celebrate. A couple more badgers aggroed on us. The tall grass must've hidden them. Two weren't a large concern. Between us, we took them out, but they did inflict a decent gash on Kyle. We also noted how the third enemy took significantly less corrosive damage. Kyle made sure to reapply regularly after that.

Whatever mobs we encountered, the deer stayed at a distance. She didn't fight. Each time, she was happy to see us win. She ran over and sniffed at us to make sure we were okay. Her expressive eyes within the cream-colored mask were endearing. I scratched her behind the ear and she tilted her head in joy.

"Dude," said Kyle, "you don't think it's weird that you're petting an AI animal? It's not like it's smart."

"She's gotta be at least as smart as a dog. She was programmed by people, after all."

"But she's still just a collection of routines. She's not real."

I shrugged. "You could say the same thing about us."

He didn't have a response. We reached the foot of the mountains and that usurped our full attention. Suddenly the land was our enemy. Our progress slowed and we needed to watch our footing carefully, but we wouldn't balk at the challenge. Ten minutes of careful climbing rewarded us with a nice view of the plains and Stronghold on the horizon. Haven had an impressive draw distance. None of that game fogginess fifty feet out.

The mountainside grew steeper and more treacherous. We struggled a bit but found a natural path with a reasonable slope. We weren't gonna climb a sheer face equipped as we were. The mountain bongo, on the other hand, was now in her home environment. Her hooves deftly found footholds among the rocks. She galloped across the mountainside, often appearing to walk on walls.

"Now you're just making us look bad," I said. "You know, we should name you."

Kyle rolled his eyes, but the bongo approached me and lowered her head to my hand. Suddenly, the [Mountain Bongo] tag appeared over her head with a blinking cursor.

Wow. I didn't know what was going on but I was strangely honored. I studied the striped animal and landed on the expressive eyes under the mask. "Bandit," I said.

Her name changed and she hopped with glee. I was pretty stoked too. I wasn't sure what game benefits I'd attained, but I seemed to have acquired a pet.

A *thwip* echoed across the landscape. Before I knew it, a crossbow bolt slammed into my chest, just above the heart.

0220 Hitman

Ambush!
Critical hit!
42 damage

I collapsed. Kyle spun around, not fully aware of the threat. Another crossbow bolt grazed his arm. His new chain mail safely deflected it away.

I grunted, more in shock than pain. Two-thirds of my health was gone in an instant. I ripped the arrow free and downed a health potion, scanning the mountainside above us.

"There!" I cried, pointing to a rock offshoot.

[Goblin Assassin]
200 Health

He was lying on his stomach. A perfect perch against our vulnerable position. The crossbow went vertical as he reloaded it. He slipped two bolts into place before leveling it at us again.

"Move!" I yelled.

We scrambled. The first bolt missed wide. Bandit was just standing there, ten feet away. The crossbow swiveled to her. As it let loose, I swung my spear in front of her. It was a sloppy, desperate move. I lucked out big time. The bolt cracked in half when it hit my blacksteel.

> Crown Unlocked: **Faster than a Speeding Bullet**
> Knock an arrow out of the air with a melee attack.
> 1000 XP awarded

"Whoa," said Kyle. "I'm only 44 XP away from level 3."

"Focus," I warned, trying to ignore that I was a little over 200 points from leveling myself. Why couldn't we have killed a few more devil badgers before being ambushed?

Kyle poured black gel on his sword, then lobbed the half-filled grenade at the assassin. His aim was slightly off, but the explosion spread the tar in a decent radius. Damage notifications rewarded the effort. It wasn't a lot, but the goo ruined the sniper's perch. He hefted his crossbow and retreated up the mountainside.

"Don't let him keep at a distance!" I screamed, charging up the mountain. Kyle followed.

As we chased him up, all I could think about was how crazy this was. The pagan assassin had wasted no time. Little more than an hour had passed between the warning notification and the ambush, and I'd done my best to avoid their area. How the hell did the damned thing track me down so effortlessly?

I fared better than Kyle did on the mountainside. My higher agility and the occasional vault to hop an obstacle guaranteed decent headway. The potion had left me at nearly full health, too. The goblin noticed me gaining on him and spun around with his weapon.

Thwip! Thwip!

I triggered dash and shot to the side, easily clearing the path of the projectiles. The sniper widened his eyes in surprise and hastily loaded two more bolts. I vaulted again, closing the distance so quickly that he unequipped the crossbow in favor of different gear.

Just ten yards away, mid charge, I drove my spear forward and activated my upgraded deadshot. I slammed into him, greeted by a jarring clang. My spear shook in my hands. The tip had glanced off the goblin's new silver shield. It was a small thing polished to a mirror sheen, round with flattened edges on the top and bottom. I could only gawk at it for a split second because the goblin's other hand reared a spiked mace. While I was still off balance, the heavy weapon crashed into my ribs.

I recovered quickly. The sniper struck again but I backed away to gain some space. I followed up with a strike of my own. Again, his shield knocked the tip of my spear away. This time I made sure not to fully commit and lose my footing. His mace lacked the range to overcome my spear.

I'd never dealt with a shield before. I wasn't a trained soldier. I had no idea what tactic to use and was still in shock about my missed deadshot. I tried a feint to the right. As his shield prepared to meet my blow, I swung inside and past his defense. I managed to partly plug him before he corrected and pushed my weapon away. The goblin was good at protecting himself.

After a few more traded strikes, I used the feint again. This time he was on to me. He lurched forward and pinned my spear to the ground with his shield. He stepped on the shaft to raise his short frame above mine. I was extended forward, a spiked mace racing to the crown of my head, when Kyle's longsword slashed right down the goblin's spine.

Surprise! [Kyle] dealt 32 damage to [Goblin Sniper] DoT: 15 dmg/10 secs

The assassin reared in pain, but that didn't stop his blow from finding me. The mace veered off target, slamming into my right shoulder instead of my skull. I heard a nasty crunch. My spear fell to the ground.

20 damage Dislocation! Your arm is dislocated. You cannot use weapons until it is fixed.

Lucky there were two of us because the goblin could've killed me then had he been ready. Instead he rolled away and squared off with my roommate. Kyle hadn't scored a crit but the surprise damage mixed with the corrosive was a good combo. The assassin still had two-thirds of his health, but he now knew we could hurt him.

I considered chugging another health potion but it would be nearly useless so soon after the first. Besides, I suddenly remembered every 80s action movie ever. After all, what was Haven if not a product of popular media? Instead of wasting the potion I lined up my shoulder with a rock wall and barged into it.

Your arm is back in place! Weapon usage is restored.

God, I was beginning to love this game. I lifted my spear and downed a spirit vial instead. Then I charged into the fray.

Kyle's sword work was improving, but the assassin was quicker and better. I flanked the goblin to even the odds but, honestly, he was quicker and better than me too. Together we had a chance.

Kyle was admirably fighting his way to level 3. With the crown I'd unlocked, we were both on the verge. All we needed to do was finish off the goblin sniper. And it began to look possible. We started to get the better of him. For every thrust and parry, I could see the worry in his eyes. Two strikes later, my blacksteel bit deep into his leg, causing extra pagan damage and slowing him down. Kyle hammered him with a powerful overhead strike. The assassin braced himself under his shield. The impact was legendary. The longsword shattered into a thousand pieces.

Seriously, it was just a hilt after that.

Kyle stared dumbly, jaw agape. Jeers erupted from the

foothills. Three more goblins waved weapons over their heads as they charged to meet us.

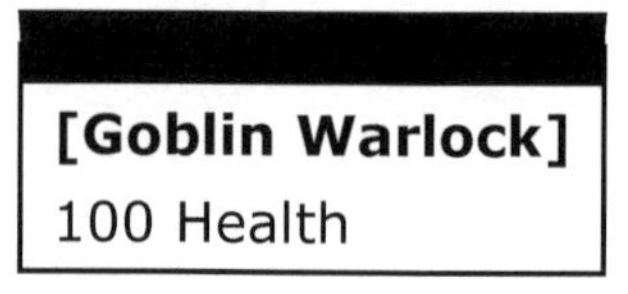

They were still a few minutes out but we were boned and the assassin knew it.

I went to stick him again but he abandoned his current tactic. He just bowled into a dumbstruck Kyle and they both tumbled down the mountainside, taking minor damage but heading closer to pagan backup.

The goblin righted himself before Kyle did. He swerved to his feet. Kyle slipped further below on his hands and knees before steadying. The assassin had him lined up perfectly, ten feet above my roommate.

I charged downhill.

They'd tumbled out of range. Even at a full sprint, I wasn't gonna be able to get to them in time. I triggered vault and used the spear to push my body off the mountainside. In midair, out of pure desperation, *without even knowing it was possible*, I triggered dash. A horizontal force surged me forward. A dash along the slope would've left me in a sprint but now I was a rocket, coming down fast, homing in on the sniper. His back was to me. I was gonna beat him.

His mace blinked out and the crossbow reappeared in his ready grip. *Thwip! Thwip!*

Two bolts thunked into Kyle's head. I roared in anger as I

triggered deadshot from above. My spear dug into the goblin's shoulder. As I landed, it drilled down through his body, ripped out his belly, and staked him to the ground.

Surprise!
Combo!
Savage!
You dealt 127 damage to [Goblin Assassin]
[Goblin Assassin] is defeated
850 XP awarded

Bones crunched as I landed. Luckily they belonged to the goblin corpse.

BWOOOOOM!

You have reached Level 4!

I ignored the deep chord and dramatic wash of flames, ripped my spear free with some trouble, and skidded down the slope to Kyle.

He was dead again. Mere moments from level 3.

"Fuck!"

The pagan backup was almost on me now. Two [Goblins] and a [Goblin Warlock]. I was outnumbered but stronger now, and at full health and spirit to boot. I salvaged Kyle's body for him, looted the sniper, and desperately waited for dash to recharge.

0230 The Warlock of Firetop Mountain

I didn't have many options. There was up, down, and... well, that was it. That's what I meant by not having many options.

Fighting all three goblins head-on was a poor tactical decision, but so was running away. The mountain quickly steepened behind me. It would shift my sprint into a slow, arduous climb, with my back exposed to the threat.

The two goblins waved daggers angrily as they raced uphill, just fifty feet below. The warlock, the one I was really concerned with—he just stopped. He pulled his brown robes close and thrust his scrawny arms skyward.

Shit. He was casting.

I hastily checked my skill tree and inventory for anything that could help. The crossbow. Maybe I could interrupt his spell. Maybe I could take advantage of his distraction. I hefted the weapon into my hands and struggled with the loading mechanism.

I wasn't trained in using the thing.

It was a [Dual Eagle Crossbow], a heavy, double shafted

thing that looked mean and professional. It took me precious seconds to get the bolt loaded. The next one came easier. I raised the crossbow and the two advancing goblins dove to the ground. I turned my sights on the warlock, flames now rippling up his arms, and let fly.

A bolt whizzed through the air a good ten feet over his head. He didn't even notice.

The warriors had followed the projectile's path. They turned back to me with puzzled expressions.

I tried to play it off casually. "First time," I announced.

They snickered and advanced again. I raised the crossbow. That got them to duck, at least, but the jig was up. They knew I wasn't skilled with the weapon. And I only had one shot left.

A whoosh of oxygen ratcheted up my panic meter. A giant globe of fire as tall as the goblin warlock burst into life above his head. It wasn't a fireball; it was a fire *planet*. A miniature sun. The mystic gazed up maniacally at his creation before sending it forth. The other goblins fell back a safe distance from the raging inferno beaming my way.

I sidestepped to the left and the fireball veered toward me. I skittered right and it homed in on me again. I gulped and dropped the crossbow. My dash was recharged. I would just need to time it perfectly. That or find out if Haven had sunburn cream.

As I packed the crossbow back into my inventory, my eyes fell on the assassin's shield.

[Mirror Shield]
A favorite of the Atlanteans, mirror shields are primarily designed to reflect magical energy but are also surprisingly robust against physical attacks.

That sniping bastard. No wonder he'd been so hard to kill, deadshot or no. As for me and the impending fireball, I really had no choice. This was the equivalent of an MMO layup. Like finding a red key while standing next to a red door. I *had* to try it out.

I equipped the mirror shield and defiantly placed it in the path of the oncoming heatstroke. Bracing against the hellish meteor with a little round shield went against my every instinct as a human being, let alone a quick-on-my-feet scout, but willpower prevailed. The flames slammed against me as I screamed into oblivion.

And then something kick-ass happened.

Without leaving so much as a contact burn, the three-and-a-half foot sphere bounced right off the mirror shield and headed back down the mountain. The goblin warriors hugged the ground as the rogue fireball passed over them. The warlock didn't take evasive action. He just stood there, eyes wide, watching his own creation hurtle toward him with unstoppable might.

He exploded in a mini mushroom cloud right where he stood. The charred remains barely constituted a corpse. The two remaining goblins turned to me in wonder.

I shrugged. "First time with that too," I said, a little more confidently.

They bared their teeth and charged. With the ranged threat subtracted from the equation, I scrambled higher up the mountain, equipping my spear and triggering a vault to get a lead. When the cliff steepened I focused on hand holds, putting the weapon away and using both hands. I hit a dead end and used dash to cheat upward. The rock face became more sheer but I was making good time.

The problem was the damn pagans were as well. Either they were natural climbers or had a great strength-to-weight ratio. They advanced at the pace of a brisk stroll, even and effortless. Neither had even bothered to unequip their daggers.

I was further up so my going was tougher. As the ground transitioned to a wall, they gained on me fast. I wasn't even in a position where I could equip my spear anymore. The only thing I could do was double down and keep going higher. The slope became a cliff, where a minor slip meant plummeting to my death. Maybe I could pull a *Donkey Kong* and barrel into them on my way down.

As I struggled to take the next step, a dagger swiped at my foot. I jumped. My grip on the mountain slipped but my other hand found purchase. Unfortunately, the dagger caught me with the next attempt. It bit into my ankle, making it go fuzzy.

> Injury!
> Your ankle is injured. You cannot put weight on it until it is fixed.

Damn these special damage conditions. Here I was, hanging off a cliff face one handed, legs swinging wildly in the air, and now I wouldn't even be able to climb anymore. I cursed my decision not to stand and fight the pagans face-to-face. At least that would've been a warrior's death.

The goblin closest to me chuckled and climbed a step closer. I tried to kick him away but remember: injured ankle.

Galloping hooves pounded against the mountainside. Bandit came charging right at me, some kind of oversized mountain goat from hell. Her legs deftly strode on the near vertical surface, looking more impossible than impressive. The girl was set to run right past my reach. I grunted and heaved myself up, stretching my free hand.

I caught her offered horn and took off like a Matterhorn bobsled. We sped away, level with the goblins but at a speed they couldn't dream of matching. My boots scraped the rock in a desperate water-ski maneuver while I hung on for dear life.

"Back," I said. "Back."

Bandit nodded. She slowed and turned, allowing me to adjust my position. I hooked an arm over her back and drew my spear. She lowered her head and rushed right back at those goblin tough guys.

They scrambled in terror.

There wasn't time to get away. The same limits that had favored their chase now doomed them. The goblins were even nice enough to line up for me. In a single charge, I lanced them off the mountainside. I watched them descend in satisfaction. I also watched my reputation with the pagans continue to plummet.

Pagan Reputation -125

The number was too far gone to matter anymore. Kinda hard to top being targeted for assassination. At this point I was basically a Wild West outlaw, trading up wanted posters and proudly brandishing the reward amount like some kind of high score. Screw 280. My notoriety was 405 now.

Bandit slowed and I put my spear away. The bongo nudged me with her head. She wanted me to jump on.

"I'm such an idiot," I said, noting the scuffs on my boot soles.

I pulled myself onto Bandit's back. Her large frame easily supported my weight, even on the cliffside. She wasn't just a pet anymore but a mount. Even better, she was loyal and useful in a pinch. I patted Bandit's neck and she lightly traipsed up the mountain.

With my new ride, the climb continued without incident. Instead of focusing on not falling to my death, I could appreciate the view. Bandit cantered to the peak and I watched Stronghold from a distance. The walled city was tiny from this angle, but still imposing. Always imposing. Everything out here was wild and dangerous, twisted and ready to kill you. The city's stone and mortar was a line in the sand. A mark of safety for the residents of Haven. A beacon for the dead, the newly living. Hell, it was practically Heaven. And it was very likely I'd be spending the rest of my life there.

So why was I so uneasy about the whole place?

We crested the mountain. The summit was a scraggly peak of jagged edges, a wall in itself circling a flat platform. Two giant stone hands were built into the ground, fingers wide, seemingly guarding a small obelisk between them. I dismounted in careful awe. I'd found something important here. Quiet boot steps took me closer to the center of the summit. Bandit nervously waited by the edge.

A flicker in the display broke my immersion in the game. One second I was walking through a fully realized fantasy world, the next the graphics were sputtering in an overworked simulation. Refresh lines crackled over the obelisk, lagging images with pixelated edges. It was a brief hiccup. A glitch in the Matrix. Then the graphical artifacts were gone.

Now perched atop the obelisk like a bird was a man in a black cloak adorned with shimmering silver runes.

"Commendably done," he declared, his voice light as a feather.

0240 Black & White

I pivoted my spear toward the intruder squatting atop the five-foot stone structure. He was at ease, arms crossed over a horizontal staff that rested on his knees. The obelisk was plain, worn rock. The man was much the same. Average height. Average weight. The elaborate silver runes the only flair on his conventional black cloak. The low hood covering his face kept him amply mysterious.

His staff vanished as he returned it to his inventory. He didn't appear to be a threat. Over the course of seconds, I came to realize that *I* was the intruder here.

"What is it about their ilk you so despise?" he finally asked.

I watched him carefully, wary of betraying too much information. "The pagans?"

His black hood nodded once.

My first thought was that he might be a pagan himself, but the bottom half of his face revealed him as human. It was the only part of his skin that was exposed. A sharp chin. Tight lips. Everything else was covered up. Black pants. Black boots. Black gloves.

I planted the butt of my spear in the ground. "Besides the

fact that they're trying to kill me?"

The stranger's voice was soft and calm, without a whiff of aggression. "Can you blame them?" His head swiveled to the horizon. Stronghold's battlements. "It's easy to admire the walled city from a distance. If you're a pagan, it's also easy to despise it."

I tried to examine his info but got nothing. No name. No level or class. An NPC maybe. I immediately suspected he was related to my quest.

"The pagans have no reason to hate the residents of Stronghold," I said.

"Don't they?"

I frowned. I couldn't tell if he wanted me to volunteer information or do something. I opened my menu and pulled up my quest.

Unveil the Pagans
Quest Type: Epic
Reward: Unknown
You've discovered pagans encroaching on Stronghold and found orders to secure the roads leading to the city. Uncover the source and reason for this activity.

"Do you know anything about their movements?" I asked carefully. "Securing the roads?"

His gaze returned to me, lips a sly smile. "I see all," he said. "As it seems do you. You recovered the outer mandate."

I was afraid to nod.

He shrugged his hands as if it didn't matter. "Good faith, then." I wasn't sure what he meant but let him keep talking. "The boggarts are holy people among their kind. Sages, you could say. They have seen visions. Rumblings in Stronghold. That is all I can say."

Quest Update: **Unveil the Pagans**
Quest Type: Epic
Reward: Unknown
The boggarts are the source of the outer mandate. Their end goal remains to be discovered.
1000 XP awarded

"You see?" he asked. "Good faith."

"Thanks," I said, "but I can't help thinking you know more."

"Oh, I know *much* more. I know of plagues and blights, famines and floods." His long cloak fluttered in the breeze. The silver runes reflected sunlight. "But faith only gets you so far."

I waited for him to expound on his apocryphal words, but that was all he had to say again. Cryptic, clipped.

The NPCs in Haven. A little overwrought.

I kept my tone firm but respectful. "I mean about the pagans."

His lips tightened. A frown, maybe. The stranger's answer was light and rhythmic. Unassuming, like his appearance. "Have you ever considered the value of numbers? Their ability to manipulate? The number of zeroes on a check. A level, a score—

a negative faction rep."

He was referring to my pagan notoriety. "I mean, yeah. Obviously. It's just part of the game."

"Game," he said with a bit of gruff. "Hmm."

I looked around the rocky summit. Bandit watched from the outskirts. The platform was flat rock, devoid of any decoration save for the giant stone hands sculpted to shield the obelisk, a squat pillar of stone. What was its purpose?

"This is a holy place," he said, reading my thoughts. "Only the gifted tread here."

I smiled sarcastically. "My mother always said I was special."

"You are, Talon."

I tensed. My name was plainly emblazoned above my head for all to see. It was stupid to be taken aback, but I was anyway. It's like you're stocking shelves at Target and a customer glances at your name tag and starts throwing your name around casually, feigning the familiarity of a long friendship. It's unnerving.

"What do you know of me?" I asked.

"I see all. I know all."

"Try me."

He angled his head slightly. "I know you were a developer at the very company that created this world."

I tried to hide the worry in my face. He was talking about *me*. About Tad Lonnerman. How'd he know who I was?

"Who are you?" I asked.

He smiled. "I was waiting for that question."

"And?"

He pointed above his head. This time when I looked, static

crinkled. Letters flashed into place, pixelated and discolored. The digits rolled like a slot machine until they settled on the name [Luc1f3r].

I stared warily. "As in..."

"The very same, Talon. Do you see? We're both special."

Some kind of Heaven this was. But I visualized the themes of the game. The Roman setting. Wild pagans. Angelic protectors. Was programming in the devil really so strange?

"You're the source of the outer mandate order," I concluded.

"No. I told you true. It was the boggarts. Your quest update confirmed as much."

"But you had something to do with it. Behind the scenes."

"I watch, Talon. I survive."

"That's not all you do."

Lucifer shrugged. "I sympathize with their ilk. They were the natural order of this land. The humans moved in and nearly swept them off the continent. Cities built. Walls. They cut down forests and drained rivers. Bent the land to their own will and treated every other living thing as either game or pest. So yes, I see the evil in man. I see it because it exists. If it didn't, neither would I."

I trembled at his words, soft-spoken though they were. This wasn't the devil, I told myself. It was just a programmed approximation of him. Artificial intelligence. Artificial.

"Now who are the lost children?" he posited. "What is left of the errant?" Lucifer released a long sigh and admired Stronghold from a distance. "All cities fall, Talon. Even the afterlife isn't forever."

More introspective babble. I considered simply moving on.

At this point I was pretty sure he wasn't going to hurt me. Though that got me wondering why he was here at all. I had a hard time believing the freaking devil was just a quest checkpoint. My curiosity got the better of me.

"What do you want from me?" I asked.

"Just that you consider an alternate perspective." He crossed his arms over his knees. "You and I are not entirely different."

I crossed my arms too. Then realized the irony of mimicking his posture, however defiant.

"Some people," he started, "when you tell them a rule, all they see is the intended effect. Two plus two equals four. They never consider how malleable numbers can be. The world is a paved street with painted lines. The vast majority of travelers don't stray from it. They do the right thing, the good thing, and blindly follow the path laid out for them. A simple path, for simple people."

Lucifer hopped off the obelisk. It was only five feet high, an unimpressive feat, but his boots hit the dirt so lightly he might have only taken a step. It was a graceful, fluid motion. Understated.

"Then there are the gifted ones," he noted. "People like you and me, we see the painted lines as a challenge to cross. We encounter walls and yearn for the other side. We view rules as mere technicalities to work around. That's the ultimate life hack. Don't *fight* the system. Profit *within* it."

As he said that, the edges of his cloak pixelated and blurred before coming back to focus. Another glitch. I thought I was starting to get it.

"Sounds a lot like cheating," I said.

"There's that insinuation again."

"Which one?"

"That this is a game." Lucifer leaned into me. "Is that what this is to you? A board game? A downloadable app? Are the constraints placed upon you just random rules of balance, something that can be flicked on and off at will? Or is this your life now?"

I didn't know what to say. His words did sort of make sense.

"Maybe their rules are just collars around your neck."

I swallowed. "You're not an NPC, are you? You're a player. You somehow hacked your name, and who knows what else."

Lucifer smiled. "You and me, Talon, the algorithms whisper to us. You have a programmer's mind. You understand the logic of game systems. Their power and their flaws. You even wrote some of the code that was applied to Haven."

"I never worked on this ga—this world."

"No, but your studio was bought out. Your assets absorbed. You worked on genetic learning, did you not?"

"How do you know that?"

Lucifer, excited now, fell beside me and waved gloved hands as he spoke. "Genetic algorithms are a thing of beauty. Survival of the fittest. The Theory of Evolution boiled down to a programming directive."

My face hardened. I knew what he was going on about, and I agreed. While not exactly cutting edge, genetic algorithms were a heavy part of my R&D. Say you need a task accomplished, like decrypting a message. You write code to sort it out and then take several variations of that module and have them compete. Which one performs best? You take the strongest, the fittest, and shuffle their DNA together. You create babies, new modules with slightly different variables. You run the benchmarks again and make more babies. Generation after generation—eventually you have perfectly evolved code that does exactly what you need.

"The difference with your work," said Lucifer in admiration, "is that the branching is user generated. Progress through player input. Yes, that creates a bottleneck in the cycle. Yes, it's much slower. Imperfect evolution. But what you lose in cold efficiency you gain in intelligent design. You create a system governed not by the system, but by the players." Lucifer slowly waved his hands across the landscape. "You create Haven."

I stared at the horizon in wide-eyed wonder. The Kablammy devs had integrated my experimental code into the simulation. I wasn't sure if I was proud or scared. Not that my work was bad or flawed. I stood behind the concept. But it was research and development stuff. Unready for prime time.

And Lucifer was right. Even though I hadn't been working on a massively multiplayer online engine, what better place for the players to affect the simulation, slowly and over time? Using my principles, Haven could be a forever changing simulation, modernizing with its inhabitants. A living, breathing world.

"This is how your genetic learning has been implemented," he said. "Take your skill tree. That's a module of code with an expected result. You can choose to utilize that skill as everyone else does. Safe. Effective. Within the painted lines. Or you can apply your skill to a slightly different problem set. Attempt to achieve an unintentional result. The simulation detects this attempt and, if it's within an acceptable functional deviation, allows it."

He raised a finger in caution. "Now, that doesn't mean the new skill will be better than the old one. Your baby might be a fish who can't breathe water. A genetic dead end. But that very possibility means everybody's skills will be slightly different. Even the same classes, the same trees. The result is that enterprising players will grow using their own ingenuity."

Lucifer clapped me on the shoulder. "And you already have."

I strained to recall doing something like that. "I don't remember branching any skills."

"But you have. Without even realizing it. When you defeated that assassin on the mountainside, you activated dash in midair. Even I haven't seen that before. It certainly isn't part of the stock package."

Holy shit. Adaptable skills.

Lucifer wasn't talking about inventing skills out of thin air. Obviously programming needs to exist for the execution of a module. So skills aren't new, exactly, just remixed. Rebooted. New usage out of old rules.

I recalled, as a kid, playing Street Fighter II on the Super Nintendo. We slotted a Game Genie in there to tweak features. It wasn't a magic chip but it could hack the game data. Patch it over with different values to achieve slightly different behaviors. There was a Street Fighter code to jump and use special moves in the air. You could throw a fireball or a dragon punch and keep jumping higher in the sky, making matches very different than how the developers had originally envisioned.

And I had just done something similar with my dash.

"And skills are only the most obvious application," said Lucifer. "Mounts exist in Haven, of course. So do vanity pets that you can parade around town. But you won't find anything in your game guide about adopting wild animals."

Bandit canted her head. She was an anomaly, then. Not a normal game feature. According to Lucifer, my actions, my will, had somehow caused the mutation in the game code. That was his way of saying I was an outlier. Like him.

And maybe I was.

"You still haven't told me what you want," I said firmly.

He knew his words had sway. He knew I was on the hook. "I merely ask that you open your eyes. That your ideology remains as flexible as your skill with the simulation. That you consider that the pagans may not be your true enemy."

I twisted my lips. I wasn't an idiot. I could put two and two together. This player styled himself Lucifer. Stronghold was full of saints and angels.

"You're the head of the Fallen, aren't you? The raid on the Pantheon. The battle with the angels. Your people did that."

"They're all dead," admitted Lucifer. "It's just me that's left. Unless you were to join me." He raised his head and the hood folded away, giving me my best glimpse of his face in shadow. Plain. Unremarkable. "Will you be my apostle, Talon?"

I tensed. "Why, so I can paint a giant target on my back and get permanently deleted?"

"So you can fight the true enemy," he corrected.

I backed away. He didn't mean to be intimidating, but everything about him was intense. I turned my back on him and refused to face him when I let him down.

"Just because we might think alike when it comes to min/maxing doesn't mean we have the same philosophy. I can't say I asked for all this, but I was in a car accident and I'm here now. I have to be thankful for everything I have left. You want me to help fight the saints, the very people who saved me? Why would I do that, when without them I'd be dead?"

Lucifer clicked his tongue bitterly. My responses both amused and pained him. His voice followed like a caress on the breeze. "The things we take on faith, Talon. If I were you, I would ponder the real question: Whoever said you were really dead?"

0250 Resident Evil

Blood flushed my face. Anger. Pain. I whirled on him. "I—"

I didn't know what to say. Lucifer was clearly manipulating me, right? But was he lying or telling the truth? And what of the saints?

"I'm alive?" I asked desperately. "You're saying I'm still alive, hooked up to machines in a hospital bed somewhere? Stuck in a VR simulation?"

He raised his hands to halt me. He took a quiet, steady breath. "All I point out is that you're blindly taking their word for it."

"But that's not possible. Saint Peter said he'd let me talk to my brother eventually, when the functionality's ready."

"Everchat," said Lucifer.

"You know about it?"

"My friend, that feature has already been rolled out. It's well tested."

My face darkened. "Then why—"

"Family members don't pay for beta tests. The feature exists but hasn't been rolled out to the public. Haven hasn't even been announced. Services like Everchat require a full marketing blitz."

I ground my teeth. I was dead or dying and he was talking about marketing. Someone was lying to me. The ironic part was I *wanted* to believe Lucifer. I *wanted* Everchat to be readily available.

"You must consider," he added, "that what you know and what they know are different subsets. There is some overlap, but not nearly as much as you'd like. Profitability is not always transparent."

"But this is a beta test. It's in their interests to let me test the feature. My brother and I are perfect candidates."

"So you know they're keeping a working feature from you. Your next question must be: Why?"

Why, indeed. If what the fallen angel claimed was true, that I was still alive, that would explain why I wasn't allowed to talk to Derek. What kind of hospital would permit Kablammy to do this to me? If I was in a coma or otherwise still recovering, why would they leave me in this simulation? It boggled the mind. More than that, it made me furious. I felt taken advantage of. Violated. Had those terms of service signed away my human rights?

Suddenly my epic quest didn't seem like a big deal. The MMO became meaningless. Playing by the rules loses its appeal as soon as somebody breaks them.

"Can you help me?" I grumbled.

"We can help each other. Look out for one another. Make sure it's *our* interests we keep at heart."

I nodded uncertainly.

"The saints are part of a capitalistic empire," he said. "They don't want what's best for us. They want what's best for their master's wallet."

Their master. "You're not talking about God."

"Oh, but I am. Their false idols are shareholders. Their god, the dollar. The great almighty—they bow to none other."

My mouth went sour. Whether or not his words were accurate, they had the ring of truth. I'd hated Kablammy even before they bought out my studio. They were soulless. Global, corporate, everything that was wrong with American business today. I didn't put it past them to take advantage of unsuspecting people.

I didn't put it past Lucifer, either.

"Your lies might just be another flavor," I said weakly.

"I think you know the truth when you hear it."

"If it's the truth then I don't care about the pagan war. I don't care about Stronghold. I need to get out of Haven completely."

"Don't be so rash."

"Rash?"

He sighed to diffuse the dialog. "You might enjoy staying more."

I snorted. I doubted it. Derek needed me. That was clearer than ever. And maybe I needed him too. If I could just get word to him he could blow the whistle on it all.

"You know," I said, finding the humor even in this, "you might be more convincing if your name wasn't Lucifer."

He shrugged. "If this were a space opera and I was playing interplanetary spy, I would've picked a more suitable name. Domino, perhaps. Alas, when in Rome." He nodded to the Arena in the distance.

I rolled my eyes. "Great, you like wordplay."

"I *am* Satan, after all."

He had a sense of humor too. I almost liked the guy. "That's my problem. I don't know if I can trust you. I don't know who I can trust anymore."

"Now you're thinking like one of the Fallen." He regarded me proudly. "I, of all people, would never ask you to take something on faith alone. You don't need to believe me, Talon. I can give you the tools to see the truth for yourself."

I couldn't mask my glimmer of hope. "You can give me Everchat?"

His lips twisted. "I can't give you that directly."

"Maybe the saints will."

"They can't know about this. About me. Two angels are still on the hunt. They'll kill me on sight."

"Then what?"

"The Pantheon," he said. "I can get you access to the database. Personnel records. You can look up the truth for yourself."

My momentary hope lodged firmly in my throat. "That's where your Fallen were permanently deleted. What were they doing in the Pantheon?"

"Truth seeking," he said sadly. "Truth comes at the highest of prices."

I swallowed nervously, unsure if I was willing to pay that much. It would mean no more second life. Then again, if my first life could be recovered, Haven held no further purpose for me.

I sighed in futile resignation. "How do we get in?"

"Not *we*. I can do many things, but I can't stroll through those gates. I'm somewhat anonymous, but the centurions in Stronghold will recognize me on sight. The angels will be unleashed. Your quest will be dead in the water before it begins."

"Quest," I repeated, wondering if I was about to receive a notification.

Lucifer smiled snidely. "Not *that* kind of quest. And don't worry, you won't be truly alone. I come bearing gifts."

He waved his hand and black static ate away at the ground. A wooden treasure chest popped into place. It was an overwrought Dungeons & Dragons caricature. Large and worn, buttressed with metal clamps. It hummed with a soft glow.

I knew accepting gifts from strangers was dangerous, especially when that stranger styled himself the devil, but I wasn't making any Faustian deals here.

"I'm not promising you anything," I warned.

He waved to the chest. "These are the tools you need to open your eyes. Reserve your judgment until you have the facts."

I bit my lip. I'd hit my limit of protestation. This was an MMO after all, and that freaking chest was *glowing*. I ravenously flung it open.

[Blacksteel Studded Leather]
High-quality leather armor affording maximum maneuverability and construction.

[Assassin Vambraces]
Reinforced leather arm guards built for precise combat.
+2 Agility
+1 Strength

[Stranger's Cowl]
Unassuming hood that masks your identity and location to distant eyes.

[Gu1d3 Rune]
A gemstone that lights the way through the Pantheon and highlights its defense systems.

[Bit Key]
This anachronistic cartridge gives admin access to the Oculus, the game console.

I couldn't believe my eyes. Each item made me drool more than the last.

I hurried to fit the cowl over my head. My double in the menu was starting to look badass now. The studded leather was finely styled under my blue coat. The cowl draped over my shoulders and ominously hid my face.

"That will keep the pagans off your back," explained Lucifer. "They'll still attack you on sight as long as you have negative reputation with them, but their spies will no longer be able to track you down like they did."

No more assassin ambushes. That alone was worth the price of admission.

"It should help keep others from getting their sights on you."

"Is that what you use to hide from the angels?" I asked.

He chuckled. "The angels require additional subterfuge."

The guide rune was a square yellow gemstone with a metal cross inlaid in the flat face. It vibrated unnaturally.

"A creation of mine," said Lucifer. "It's a map and more. It will activate when you enter the Pantheon and attempt to guide you safely around threats in real time."

"Any chance your dead Fallen Angels had similar protections?"

"It's not foolproof," he conceded, "but you don't stand a chance without it."

I shook my head in frustration. "That's not very reassuring. You get to sit safely on your obelisk throne while I do all the legwork. I'm expected to sneak into the best-guarded place in Stronghold with nothing but a gemstone. Alone."

"That's not true, my friend. We're in this fight together. I'll work up a distraction on the outside. Wait for a message in your inbox. When I contact you, you must move immediately."

I grumbled. For someone who hadn't made a single promise I was starting to feel awfully committed. I changed the subject and produced the last item from the chest.

"And this?" I quizzically studied the bit key in my hand. It resembled a gold Nintendo game cartridge without the label.

"Careful with that one. The saints will delete you if they find it on your person. When you sneak into the Pantheon, you'll find the Oculus. The bit key plugs into the game console. That's what you can use to access the system. To look up your records."

I clenched my jaw. "Can I use it to unlock Everchat?"

"Yes. It might take some hacking, though. Are you comfortable with that?"

I pocketed the bit key and stared at the gated city in the distance. I'd never thought of myself as a hacker before. I never needed to work outside the system. Now it might be my only option.

I strode to Bandit at the edge of the summit. "No promises," I said, and jumped on her back.

0260 The Dark Project

The mountain bongo was a great mount. Even with my added weight, her hooves found sure footing on the steep cliffside. My personal ski lift with horns... that went both directions... that didn't require a ticket. Okay, the analogy breaks down real fast.

My descent was a distracted one. I had the presence of mind to loot the goblin corpses at the bottom but didn't pay attention to the stash. Lucifer's quest was weighing me down. My state of affairs. Once we hit the foothills and made our way across the open plain, every hoofbeat was a reminder that I was getting closer to a destiny I didn't want. Every step away from the mountain made me realize how fucking crazy Lucifer's plan was. How crazy I was to agree to it.

Sure, if everything he'd said was true, there was just cause for the kind of action he wanted. I didn't think the dude was evil necessarily. I wondered what his grudge with the saints was and made a mental note to ask next time I saw him.

Maybe this was all a mistake. Maybe I could clear things up without some crazy *Mission Impossible* heist. I pulled Bandit to a stop, brought up my menu, and stared long and hard at the green help button.

I couldn't sell the fallen angel out, but that didn't mean I was out of options.

I hit the button and waited. Several moments later, Saint Peter popped into place. His bushy eyebrows arched at the sight of the mountain bongo. I smiled.

"I wasn't sure if you'd appear outside town."

He cleared his throat. "Yes, well, we make exceptions sometimes." He looked me up and down. "You seem to be adjusting nicely. The deer is new."

I hopped off Bandit.

"No bugs filed yet," noted Saint Peter pointedly. "You need to submit bugs as you encounter them. Surely you've seen things... out of the ordinary?"

I shrugged. "You've built a pretty solid game here, Pete. Me too, I guess. I've been recognizing some of the routines I wrote for a different game."

He straightened up. "Yes, well, I won't pretend to understand all the programmer gobbledygook, but Kablammy uses whatever assets it has at its disposal. You should be proud of your part in that. Is there a reason for this visit, Tod?"

"T—uh, seriously?"

"What?" He studied me blankly.

"Whatever. Yes, there's a reason. A very important reason. As you can see, I'm holding up my end of the bargain. Playing the game—quite successfully I might add. I was wondering when you could unlock my access to Everchat."

"Everchat is only rolled out to select residents—"

"So other people *do* have it?"

Saint Peter clenched his jaw. "You've only been in Haven one day, young man. You're pretty demanding considering."

"I'm trying to do the right thing," I said. "I really am."

"Then log some bugs and wait your turn. It's my assessment that you're adjusting well to your transition. You no longer need me. Goodbye."

Saint Peter flickered out in a huff. I went back to my menu but the damned green button was disabled again. Beside it, the red bug button taunted me. I shut the menu in frustration.

The lockout wouldn't last forever. That button would enable again and I'd press it, again and again, until Saint Peter gave me what I wanted. And if he didn't...

I stared at Lucifer's summit. Well, my other option seemed extreme.

"Come on, Bandit," I said. I started for Stronghold on foot, mostly because walking would give me more time to think.

If I'd been expecting a eureka moment, I didn't get one. The gates of Stronghold welcomed me just as before. The bored guards of the city watch eyed me like I was a trivial part of their day. Just another traveler passing through. Little did they know I was a traitor in their midst. Guards in chain mail and leather, some with swords and some with slings. Was I really planning on going against a whole force of them?

Bandit followed me all the way to the outer wall this time. She was a good girl but still had reservations about entering town. I scrubbed her chin and told her I'd be back later. Then I entered Stronghold.

The main thoroughfare was more active than before. More

players were starting to see success. Lots of level 2s out there. A few more level 3s with class titles, but it was still rare. Getting there with swamp toads alone was a grind. Of course, I was level 4 now. Since I had some time to kill, I opened my character sheet.

I sunk my free attribute point into agility. With my 2 skill points, I upgraded spear handling and deadshot. I had a feeling I might be needing them real soon. Between the upgrades and the bonus of the assassin's vambraces, my stats were starting to look respectable.

Talon		*Level*	4
Class	Explorer	*XP*	6378
Kit	Scout	*Next*	8125

Strength	13	*Strike*	116
Agility	19	*Dodge*	140
Craft	6	*Health*	90 / 90
Essence	8	*Spirit*	80 / 80

I absentmindedly walked ahead, fiddling in my menu, keeping an eye on that grayed-out help button, waiting for the moment it reactivated. I was just trudging through Front Street when I accidentally walked into someone.

"Oh, sorry, I—"

A set of full plate towered over me by at least a foot. That collision hadn't been an accident.

"Oh, great," I said halfheartedly. "Lash."

She pulled off her helmet and shook her bleached highlights free. "No shit, dipshit. I see you're not lugging that loser around anymore."

Lash's painted eyes were hard slits even without the helmet. She was level 4 now, but then so was I. In her favor she had a couple of followers backing her up. A stocky barbarian who was going for the Conan look and a slight old lady in a plain dress. A white witch. Both were level 3.

I was outnumbered but felt safe in the confines of Stronghold. "Actually, I was just going to meet Kyle now."

She turned to her friends and laughed. "Wait, I get it. He's skulking in his room after dying. Again." They giggled like cruel middle school kids, which was weird considering the old lady's age. I got the impression everyone followed Lash's lead.

I glanced across the street to the parks of the Foot. The open yards were rife with activity, mostly players training and testing items and skills. A few stragglers were already eyeing the action over here. From a safe distance, of course, lest they draw Lash's ire as well. As I scanned the crowd I spotted Izzy the pixie. She was juggling several colorful balls before a crowded audience. Interesting hobby. Even more interesting was that she was masterfully handling the juggling act while intently watching me.

Nice. This place really *was* like middle school.

Even without the helmet, Lash was a good foot taller than me. I didn't care. I stepped right into her personal space, my chin almost touching her breastplate, and said, "In case you haven't noticed, Lash, I'm not gonna play the passive pushover for you. I hit level 4 much faster than you did. I have no doubt I'll outpace you in the next day or two. So I'd watch how you act around me."

I thought it was a good speech. The healer couldn't believe I'd made it. Lash, for her part, twisted her pink lips in amusement.

"Level is only part of the equation," she said. "I'm willing to bet I got the gear and skills to take you on."

I rolled my eyes dismissively. "Try it," I said, and moved to walk past her.

Lash sidestepped into my path. This time my chin *did* hit her breastplate. She smirked.

"Hey, cuddly boy, you wanna get close to me? I'll give you a one-on-one in the Arena. Any time. Any day."

Izzy was still watching. Whether it was her hobby or my predicament, she was having too much fun to wear her usual mask of contempt. Her lips crooked into a smile and her cheeks dimpled. She was pretty like that. A boyish part of me suddenly wanted to impress her.

Then I thought about the email I was expecting from Lucifer. That put everything into perspective real fast.

"Lash," I grunted, "just because you learned how to piss standing up doesn't mean I'm gonna waste my time with a pissing match. Not now." I brushed past her. It didn't make me look as cool as I wanted because she was more massive than me, but I thought I got my point across. Her followers let me pass.

"Of course," she mocked after me. "Run along. Disappoint

everybody. Be a coward like that worthless roommate of yours."

I spun around and raised my voice. "Level and gear aren't everything. Even in Haven. I'd rate Kyle higher than a hundred of you any day."

"Really?" she snickered. "Did he tell you how he died yet?"

"Car accident, like me. I think it's why we were put together."

"Oh, it was a car accident all right." The knight slammed her helmet back on but didn't bother approaching me. The posturing was over. "Kyle's a rich little white boy. Had all the advantages I didn't. And what did he do with his top-dollar education? He pissed it away drinking hipster beer."

"So this is about you being jealous?"

"Not at all. Spoiled brats can do whatever they want with their lives. As long as they don't get loaded and jump behind the wheel of a car. That asshole was coming home from a party, drunk and high, and wrapped himself around a telephone pole. Good thing all he did was kill himself, because he could have just as easily taken out a family of five."

Lash and her crew stormed away, leaving me, well, a bit stunned.

Death by DUI.

That was rough. I mean, we'd all made mistakes. I figured that's why we were here. Dead. But had Kyle really made such a horrible decision? Had Lash been right about my roommate all along?

I ground my teeth together because nothing in Haven was lining up as I'd first thought. The whole place was a damned mystery, as was every single person in it. I realized, then and there, that I didn't really know anything about anyone. Kyle,

Lash, Lucifer, Saint Peter—they were all strangers. Every single one of them. Probably the only being in the whole place I could trust was Bandit, and she was a block of code.

I faced the crowd of players, displeasure now marring my features. Strangers, all of them. I watched Izzy performing her juggling act, no longer interested in me, of course. My show was over. But maybe it wasn't. I still had one more appeal for help.

I eyed the pixie reluctantly. This new world may have been filled with strangers, but I wouldn't get far without a couple of them in my corner.

0270 Words with Friends

"I never took you for a juggler," I said.

Izzy hiked a shoulder as she laid a set of multi-colored bowling pins on the ground. The crowd had dispersed after she announced her break. "Keeps the reflexes sharp. Keeps the fingers working."

I leaned against the stone statue she'd picked as a backdrop to her act. It was a sculpture of a giant open book, with an inscription below that read "Knowledge is Power."

"Correct me if I'm wrong," I said, "but mystics in this game don't really need dexterous fingers and sleight of hand."

Another shrug. She was determined not to care much about anything at all. But she did answer. "Probably not. But it means something to me to be the best. I don't just do it, I do it with flair."

Izzy had almost smiled as she said that. Maybe not happy, but satisfied. I'd caught her in a talkative mood.

I studied her, knowing I had to proceed carefully but unable to hide my surprise. "Level 6 already. That's gotta be a record."

The higher in level you advanced, the larger the amount of experience needed to achieve the next level. I was a good way off from level 5, so Izzy had done some serious questing.

"You're doing pretty good for your first day," she admitted. "Few people surprise me."

That was almost a compliment. Before I could smile, she added, "Don't let it go to your head."

Again with the apathy. I was sure a part of her somewhere was kind. Maybe she just didn't like to show it. Then again, she'd been watching my encounter with Lash and didn't seem intent on helping. I was probably being too generous about her attitude. I had to remember: Izzy was one of the oldest residents in Haven. Dead for at least six months. This was the first time in history we could see what that did to a person. We were all guinea pigs of a sort. Izzy was practically patient zero.

"Let me ask you a question," I said, keeping my tone as casual as possible. "How much access do you get for being a veteran? I mean, you're a pixie."

She snickered.

"I mean, do you get cool racial bonuses or what?"

She puckered her lips. "It's not really like that. It's a vanity kit more than anything."

"Ah. Pretty cool, regardless. What... other perks do you get?"

She narrowed her eyes. "And here I thought you were interested in juggling."

"I'm interested in your experiences. You have special sway with the saints?"

Her cheek twitched. "The white robes? Hardly."

"Ever took a tour of the Pantheon?"

She grunted. "Don't mess with that building. Only idiots try. Sheesh, it's been twenty-four hours since the last example."

"I wasn't around for the last example."

She glared at me.

I raised my palms in surrender. "Fine. Advice noted. It's just, well, Saint Peter let it slip that certain residents had certain benefits. Everchat, for example. And I figured, who constituted a special enough resident to qualify if not our friendly neighborhood pixie?"

Her lips pressed together tightly. I could almost see her face transform right before me. No more frivolous banter. No more carefree day. The mention of Everchat closed her up immediately. Instead of looking at me she focused on her props. Instead of a smooth conversation, I'd been shut out.

"I don't know what you're talking about," she said.

"Let's cut the bullshit," I returned. "I know you have access to Everchat. I know your father's an employee at Kablammy."

Her face darkened. "Investor."

"What?"

"He's an investor. Put a large stake into the future of Haven and helped influence early development."

I thought about what Lucifer had said about shareholders being false idols. I leaned in. "Look, I just want to contact my brother. He's in trouble without me."

She spun around lazily. "Little advice, noob: The outside world will only hurt you. Leave it alone."

"Hear me out—"

"We're done here," she said in a commanding voice. "Now are you gonna make me find another spot in the park or are you gonna leave me alone?"

I chewed my lip. She was really pouting now. I must've said something to set her off without realizing it. I considered apologizing, but her glare warned me off. Besides, what did I have to apologize for? I just shook my head and trudged off, leaving her to her little magic show.

I didn't get it. Navigating the citizens of Stronghold felt like a quest in itself. I should be awarded experience for dealing with these people. I stomped up the foothill in a sour mood and zoned into my house. Kyle was sitting on the kitchen counter with a beer in his hand.

"Don't you give it a rest?" I asked sharply.

"What?"

I didn't say anything.

"Hey, sorry about dying out there. I have an idea for how we might—"

"Let's cool it with your ideas," I spat. "They don't seem to be taking you very far."

Kyle paused, stunned. He took a resigned swig from the bottle. "I didn't even wanna go out today."

"That's right. You were booked up with beer pong. You need to realize there's more to life than that. Even virtual life. You can't just hide away and wait for things to happen to you. You need to *make* them happen. It's time you took this seriously."

I was going hard on him, but he needed to hear this.

"You're talking about the MMO?" he asked. "This is all fantasy, bro."

"Then take fantasy seriously. Look around. This is your world now."

His gaze fell to his fingers scratching the label of his beer bottle. "Lash is right. I'm worthless."

"I just had a run-in with her. She might have a point."

Confusion on my roommate's face turned to hurt. I immediately felt like an asshole but wasn't in a mood to back down. Faced with unenviable options, I said nothing. I went and collapsed on the couch in a huff. I checked my menus. My inbox was still empty. The help button was still disabled. Fucking nothing was going right today.

Kyle wandered over to the living room but stopped short of the couch. He was acting like a dog that had just been disciplined, following me around in hope of righting whatever aggrieved me. I didn't like how that made him look or made me feel.

"What?" I asked, annoyed.

He sighed and twirled the beer in his hands. "She told you, didn't she?"

I stared at the turned-off TV. "She told me."

He swallowed. "I should have."

"That occurred to me."

Kyle came around and sat on the adjoining L-shaped side of the couch. "It's not so simple. 'Hi, I'm your new roommate. A worthless sack of shit who killed himself by getting blitzed and driving home after a party I only went to so I could impress my frat brothers who didn't even like me anyway.' What kind of first impression is that?"

I picked at my fingernail. It was a boneheaded way to die, but had I never gotten behind the wheel once or twice when I shouldn't have? Sometimes the only thing separating a Darwin

Award winner from a successful Congressman is pure chance.

"Your frat bros didn't even like you?"

He shook his head. "Not really. My family was rich enough and all but I was never good with people. I figured a fraternity would come with instant friends, right? I acted like college was a big 80s movie. I got wasted and did inappropriate things for attention. Played to the crowd. It got me plenty of laughs, but I was a punch line to them." He rubbed his beer. "The very thing I did to get noticed got me ostracized. The sad thing is, it took me a month playing solo Call of Duty in the afterlife to realize that."

I worked my jaw and looked at him. "That's a crap deal, Kyle."

"I own it. I'm a fuckup."

We sat in silence a minute. It was uneasy and weird. We didn't really know each other but I had the sense he was a good guy. Did everything change because of one night at a party? Or a few years of compounding bad decisions? What the fuck was Haven if not a second chance?

"It gets worse," he said softly.

I jutted my lips out, concerned.

"She—Lash—well, her and her family were hit by a driver at three times the legal limit. Her aunt and baby sister died immediately. Lash was in the hospital for a week before dying of complications. For a while there, she'd recovered enough to hear the bad news about her family. To find out she'd been paralyzed."

My face was frozen in horror. I couldn't imagine anything worse.

"Yeah," he said, "pretty harsh. Lash got me alone outside for an extended session of torture and told me all the gory details. Kablammy took her in as part of a pilot program for more diversity. I don't know if you've noticed, but most of the residents of Haven are somewhat well-to-do or connected. Limited closed beta and all that. So Lash gets to live on, fully mobile, but her aunt and sister are dead forever."

I just started getting my jaw working again. I stretched it numbly. "Survivor's guilt," I mumbled. "So she's not a complete bitch."

"Oh, she's a bitch," he countered. He saw my surprise and shrugged. "Listen, man. The world treats some people like shit. She got a bad draw. But she also chose to lash out because of it. To make everyone else miserable."

I thought of Izzy. "There's a lot of that going around."

And then I thought of me. I was better than this.

"You made a mistake," I suddenly said, my tone edging brighter.

"Correction: I made tons of mistakes."

"You didn't kill anyone."

He shook his head in agreement. "Just my own dumb ass."

"That's a great start... considering."

He sighed, unconvinced. "Nice to see you lowering your standards. I'm still a useless waste of space who can't even hit level 3. You're totally owning me at level 4."

"No," I said. "The assassin was my fault. Without you, I would've died. You would've made it too. You just got hit with bad luck. Who would've thought your corrosive would eat right through a sword like that?"

His eyes brightened. "*That's* why it shattered."

"That's what I figure, anyway."

He paused and went glum again. "Doesn't that just make me a bigger screwup? My death was my own fault."

"Don't think of it that way. It's trial and error. It was a good idea." I went into my inventory. "I got something for you." I tossed the dual crossbow to his side of the couch.

He winced. "The assassin's weapon."

"Yup. I figured you could try ranged attacks for a while. Keep some distance between you and whoever's trying to kill you. Might help you live longer."

"Hmm, it's a pretty sweet piece. I'd need to spend another skill point to handle it."

"Do you have one?"

"Yeah. When I respawned I lost all my progression. I'm bottom-of-the-barrel level 2 again.

"Maybe dying was good news then. The crossbow will be useful."

"Mr. Bright Side, huh?" He hefted the new weapon. "You might be right. I guess between this and the grenades—"

"Screw grenades. You were on to something, Kyle. The corrosive on your sword did a lot more damage than the grenades. Getting that gel into an enemy's bloodstream is nasty business. Just lobbing it over them isn't good enough."

"Okay."

"What can you do with that glasswork skill of yours? I figured, instead of grenades, you could make custom crossbow bolts. Very thin vials of glass for your corrosive. Rig it so when you shoot someone, the black gel gets injected into the baddies."

He thought it over and opened his menu. "I would need to

spend another point in my glasswork tree, but I have it. Yeah, I think I can do that. And the bonus is glass is easier to craft than alchemy. Each crossbow bolt will take a much smaller amount of the corrosive, so instead of three grenades I can make..."—he ticked his fingers to some mental math—"hell, at least twenty. And that's without support skills."

"Great. Do you have enough to get to work?"

"That's the downside. Glasswork is easy, but it takes resources. Smaller vials, and more of them—that'll create more waste. But I have enough silver to buy what I need. As soon as my lockdown wears off, I'll hit Front Street and get to work."

Already Kyle was energized. I liked seeing him that way. Hopeful. Still, the reality of combat was far different than strategic planning. If he died again too soon it would discourage him. I'd need to try harder to keep that from happening. For now, anyway, my roommate's mood was unstoppable. He'd even set aside his beer.

Heightening the mood further was the fact that my green help button was no longer disabled. I filled Kyle in on my meeting with Lucifer. I tried to give him a quick rundown, but I'd forgotten how interested he was in the politics of the Fallen. Between the loot I'd given him and my story, I was his new hero.

I didn't share the whole I-might-still-be-alive thing. I wasn't sure what to believe and was afraid that would make me sound like a conspiracy nut in denial.

Of course, Kyle thought the part about breaking into the Pantheon was crazy. But my intention was to circumvent that plan completely. I clicked the help button, ready to annoy the crap out of Saint Peter until he caved.

A man flickered in almost immediately. Instead of wearing the maroon-striped white robe of the saints, he was dressed in a scarlet uniform with large gold buttons. It almost amounted to a British red coat.

"Uh," I said, taken aback. "Who the hell are you?"

0280 Star Control

The man had blond hair and blue eyes and was clean-shaven except for a thin mustache. Regal in his slightly anachronistic suit. The gold buttons and shiny black boots were gaudy. He matched the attire with a straight and proper posture. Even though his face looked American, he spoke with a thick Indian accent.

"How may I serve you, sir?"

I froze at his sudden intrusion.

His eyes lit up. "Ah, I should introduce myself. I am Varnu. I shall be assisting your play problems from here on."

My voice deflated. "Saint Peter passed me off to tech support."

"That is correct, sir."

I rolled my eyes. "*Outsourced* tech support."

"I'm not sure I understand the implication."

"You're human, right?"

"Of course—"

"In some crowded call center in India."

His face went whiter than it already was. "What? Of course not. I am sitting in the good old honky-tonk capital of Texas, sir.

I am offended that you would think I am not American."

I shot him an entirely unconvinced glare. "You just said your name was Varnu."

He nodded unabashedly. "Oh yes, I can see why the name would throw you. All my friends in the American universities have made similar remarks. But you will see that my last name is very popular in your country. I am Varnu Son of John." He blinked triumphantly at me.

"Son of John?"

"Yes, sir. It is quite clear on my motorcar license." He tilted his head like he was reading something. "Varnu, John, Son."

I arched an eyebrow. "Varnu Johnson," I said flatly.

His eyes lit up. "Yes! Thank you for that trouble. I am Varnu Johnson. Raised and born in American US. I assure you, sir, I am eating a mutton burger with mayonnaise as we speak." He mimed eating while somehow not looking like he understood what a sandwich was.

I rubbed my face. Saint Peter was straight devious.

"Okay," I said, waving off his poor attempts to blend in. "If you're tech support, maybe you can help me."

"I shall strive to, sir."

I nodded. "I know some players are granted access to Everchat. I want in. Saint Peter told me you could enable that for me after I hit level 4."

His brow furrowed. "Saint Peter said this? There must have been a misunderstanding, sir. The feature you request is unavailable."

"No, no. I already know it's available. I've spoken to players who've used it."

He shook his head decisively. "I can add you to a list of early testers and notify you when the feature is available, sir, but—"

"Look," I interrupted. "I get it. You're just some dude making minimum wage, if that exists in India. You have an unhelpful script to follow that's designed to get me to stop complaining rather than actually fix the problem. But things will be much easier if you just help me."

"There you go," he said happily. "You are *first* in line to receive the feature. I can promise you priority, immediate access —when the feature becomes available."

I scowled. "Oh, never mind then."

"Excellent. May the seven kings of light shine their glory upon you. Good day, sir."

I cursed under my breath before realizing Varnu was still standing there. He raised a pointed finger.

"One more thing. You'll be receiving a short survey where you'll be asked to review my performance. Please make sure to mark a 5 meaning you were fully satisfied with my assistance."

"Thank you, Varnu," I snapped.

He bowed and disappeared. As I sat there fuming, Kyle was stifling laughter.

On any other day, I'd see the humor in the whole affair as well. Saint Peter had successfully trolled me by siccing tech support on me. Even more aggravating was the fact that the help button wasn't grayed out after Varnu's little visit. They were welcoming me to try them again. As many times as I wanted. In one swift move, my plan to slowly wear them down crumbled.

"You have to admit it's pretty genius," offered Kyle unhelpfully.

"It is. They've basically removed all my options. All I can do now is sit and wait for a message from Lucifer telling me it's time to break into the Pantheon."

His smile disappeared. "You really gonna do it?"

"I don't know. It seems like overkill when all I need to do is access"—I stood up—"Everchat." I clicked my teeth together. "How long do you have left on your lockdown?"

"Uh, twenty minutes and change."

"Right. Take care of your shopping as soon as you can." I moved to the front door.

"Wait, what are you doing?"

"I'm backed into a corner, Kyle. It's time to bite back."

I zoned outside and lumbered to the Foot. Everything was much the same as it had been shortly before. I worked through the crowd, forcing my way to the main attraction. Izzy was juggling burning torches now. I punched a fist over her head and knocked one out of the air. It broke her concentration and she jumped backward, catching one but letting the rest clatter to the ground. Her eyes zeroed on me.

"What the hell do you think you're doing?"

Her eyes flared. The thick crowd muttered in amazement. Izzy was a big deal in this town. She wasn't used to anything but flattery. According to Kyle, she shoved her weight around when it suited her. When she was openly annoyed with something, players avoided pissing her off or risked facing her in direct combat. I was surprised anyone agreed to it, but maybe they let their pride get the better of them. They didn't wanna back down from a girl.

Of course, they had good reason to back down. Izzy never

lost.

"I'm challenging you," I announced loudly, for everyone to hear, "to a duel in the Arena."

Her eyes flared. Open defiance was new to her. "Are you kidding me, noob?"

The crowd waited in quiet disbelief.

"I'm not." I lowered my voice so only she could hear. "And if I beat you, you agree to let me use Everchat."

She scoffed. "And what's in it for me?"

I pressed into her space. "I stop bothering you about it."

She ground her teeth. It wasn't really a fair deal, but I had nothing else to offer.

"Or," I added, raising my voice for the onlookers, "you could back down because you're afraid of losing."

That got her. Any surprise that betrayed her features was instantly gone. Bloodlust took over. She wanted to kill me twenty times over for the affront.

I offered an open hand. "Do we have an agreement?"

She rudely brushed past me. "Another noob, another lesson. Let's get this over with, stat."

0290 Virtua Fighter

The stadium was a damn good replica of the Colosseum, at least what I thought it should look like. The stone was pristine, smoothed to a dull shine, with bands of painted red and yellow adding flourish. Banners flapped in the wind. As I entered through the arches, a raucous crowd surrounded me. Their applause assaulted my senses. The bass of a hundred stomping feet pounded my ears. The ground shook to the beat.

The stadium space was a barren circle of dirt. Izzy waited at the other end, her weight on one leg. Upon my entrance she righted her posture and lowered her head. She was serious, now. Sharp and focused. Her pixie wings angled down on her back. Her jet-black hair was spiked up. She was ready.

I swallowed, wishing I'd bothered to replay scenes from Gladiator in the media room. It was okay, I told myself. I had a plan.

First was the mental game. I swung my blacksteel spear proudly over my head. I played to the crowd, utilizing my upgraded spear handling skill to toss the weapon and catch it dramatically. They roared in response to *my* juggling act. I was gonna show Izzy I wasn't scared of her reputation. I'd hit level 4 in less than a day. A scout. I was building a reputation of my own.

As per duel regulations, health and spirit potions were out. Since she was a mystic and had lower health, that stipulation worked in my favor. I just needed to hit her hard once or twice and she'd be as good as done. Getting to her, of course, would be the problem.

The city watch closed the portcullis behind me. The crowd settled into a steady din, and the wind slowed. The only boots on the ground were mine and Izzy's. We mad-dogged each other, a hundred feet apart.

"So how do we do this?" I asked. "We roll for initiative or something?"

She gave me a wry smile. "Your move. It's the least I could offer."

I brought my spear down and tightened my grip. Now that I thought about it, I didn't really want to stab her with it. Neither of us would feel pain, of course. And any damage we suffered would be immediately restored outside the gates. No experience loss or death penalty lockdown after the duel. But Izzy wasn't a murderous boggart or a thieving pack rat. She was just a normal girl with dragonfly wings.

This was all just for show, I reminded myself. It was just a game.

I narrowed my eyes and charged forward. A straight line. As far as strategies went, it wasn't much, but it was solid. It was also designed to make Izzy waste her first move.

She was a frost mage, and her attack was more or less what I imagined it would be. She raised her hands and fired a barrage of sharp icicles. I let them come right to me before I activated dash, skirted to the side, and continued my charge. Half the distance between us was cleared, and I was unscathed.

She smirked and fired another volley. This time the icicles went straight up into the air. The crowd oohed and aahed as thirty stalactites hovered in open sky high above the Arena walls, each sharpened point aiming at me. As the spell readied itself, I continued closing the distance. I needed to get to the mage with as little damage as possible. Then the fight would be over.

I didn't have as much time as I'd thought. The icicles rained down in clusters of two, three, and four. The strikes were random enough and timed to defy prediction. Luckily, I'd maxed out my agility stat. I canceled my charge and faced the raining spell, darting this way and that as I desperately waited for my dash to recharge.

It didn't come fast enough. A block of icicles faked me out and changed direction at the last second. I activated crossblock and heard a crunching sound as sleet sprinkled across my face. I'd parried a central blow but there were too many icicles to take on. A hard nugget pounded my shoulder. It knocked me to the ground where I barely rolled out of the way of another.

I coughed and sputtered in the dirt. My leather had prevented the ice from impaling me, but my whole weapon arm was tingling. I rolled on my back and looked up as the last cluster of spell shards barreled toward me. Izzy had saved the best for last. A block of five frozen lances set to stake me to the ground.

My dash recharged. Not bothering to get off my back, I

desperately triggered the skill and slid away, dragged along the dirt as if by a horse. The ice chunks exploded into my old position, spraying the air with hail.

The crowd roared in excitement.

I rolled over and used the spear to climb to my feet. With a bow to the crowd, I dusted off my shoulder with playful swagger. They loved it. I could almost believe they weren't rooting for my gory death.

Izzy's teeth were bared now. She made the mistake of backing away a few steps. Her magic must've had cooldown times as well. Giving her a breather was the last thing I should do. I set my spear and charged at her again.

While I bore down, she surprised me by remaining calm. For a purple Japanese girl who stood five feet and had delicate little wings, the resolve was impressive. This time she pressed her fingers together and built a block of ice in front of her. It started as a large cube but grew into a brick and then a slab as tall as her. She spread her hands and the ice elongated into a wall, six feet to either side. With me only seconds away combat was getting physical, so she'd built herself a shield.

Just when I thought I had everything figured out, she shot her palms forward and the entire glacier sped along the ground at me.

Perfect.

I planted the tip of my weapon into the dirt and triggered vault. Up and over I went. The massive sheet of ice fired past my raised feet. I swung the spear over my head, aligning it with my forward momentum and activating my upgraded deadshot. The blacksteel came crashing down on her head.

Combo!
Critical Hit!
You dealt 63 damage to [Izzy]

Izzy slammed backward in a reverse somersault and splayed out in the dirt. She spun to me, harried, and tried to cast something in defense. Frankly, I was impressed she was still alive.

I didn't hesitate. I drove the spear deep into her chest. She jerked and went rigid.

In a heartbeat, the crowd went quiet. The ice wall crunched and crumbled behind me. Amazed breaths filled the air. I looked the crowd over, stunned admiration in their eyes, and yanked my spear away. It was stuck.

Slowly, ice plastered over Izzy's face. It grew out from her eyes and her mouth and her pointed ears. From the open hole in her chest. The pixie's entire body solidified into a block of ice.

Weapon Caught!
Your spear is stuck. You cannot use it until it's dislodged.

No shit it was caught. I tugged at it but the frozen statue didn't move. I began to worry about not having received Izzy's death notification.

A cold dagger slipped into my back. I rolled away but it was too late.

Backstab!
Critical Hit!
Stun!
47 damage

Most of my health was shorn away. I tried to twirl on my feet but couldn't recover. The stun effect prevented my counter. I tumbled to the ground weaponless.

Izzy stood a few feet away holding a frost dagger, a sharpened wand with a blade of jagged teeth. For her part, she was nearly dead. At less than a quarter health. My initial strike had been true, but somehow she'd swapped herself for an ice double before the killing blow.

I was a more robust class than she was. Higher strength and agility and health. Even now, my 33 remaining health had to double what she had left. But the situation was nonetheless bleak. I had no weapon. I could barely move. Her strike had been a huge momentum swing.

The audience couldn't contain themselves. All manner of emotions erupted among them. Laughter, scorn, surprise, anger.

My opponent smiled cruelly. "Good show, but I think it's over."

A ball of cold energy coalesced between her fingers. It was bright and active, like electricity. This was Izzy's killing blow. She stepped between me and my embedded spear. I backed away on my hands and knees.

"Just be lucky I'm honoring you with a quick death," she said. Then the jolt of frosty energy fired at me.

I equipped the mirror shield and ducked behind it. The resultant boom bowled me over, but the shield did its thing. The ice-cold lightning bounced back at its caster. Izzy barely dove out of the way. Instead of hitting her, the projectile collided with her frozen double. The block of ice mushroomed into chunks. My spear fell away. I lunged forward and grabbed the handle, sweeping it wide to hit the mystic.

The steel caught the frost dagger and jarred it loose. At the end of my swing, I tried to bring the spear around again, but I was fully extended and off balance. Izzy jumped inside my defenses and tackled me. I fell back and she landed on me hard, hugging my hips with her legs. It would've been a pleasant sensation, too, if her hands hadn't been squeezing the life out of my throat.

I swung the spear, but it was too long to effectively counter a grappling opponent. Izzy pressed closer, leaning her stomach and chest into me, leveraging her full weight against my neck.

I dropped the spear and grabbed her waist. Her lithe body was forceful. This wasn't at all reminiscent of Jenna Jynx. I wasn't sure if it was her strength score or my poor angle, but I couldn't unlock the pin of her legs.

She grunted. "You're. Going. To. Die."

I believed her. My hands scrambled to her face. Indigo lips spread wide and she chomped down on my fingers. The bitch was ruthless. I drew back and pried at her hands.

Finally, my strength began to overpower hers. I loosened her grip just enough to breathe. Locked her wrists up. As I wiggled under her, I spotted the frost dagger several feet away. Out of reach, but not unattainable.

With a surprising heave, I shoved her sideways and rolled on top of her. We were still locked together, her legs wrapped tight, but I was on top now. In control. She tried to squirm out but I forced her back to the floor and pinned her shoulders. She squeezed my neck, but I stopped fighting her hands. I wasn't concerned with that anymore. She saw me reach for the knife and stiffened.

"Ow!" I screamed.

The freezing wand shocked my hand. I immediately dropped it as my breath left me. Luckily, Izzy had stopped choking me. One of her hands beat at my chest. Too late I noticed the other reach for the knife. She slipped it into my side, clean and smooth.

I coughed a spatter of blood on her face. She grinned viciously. Her left hand twisted the blade in my side and I couldn't hear the crowd anymore. Her right arm hooked around my neck and drew me down. I was still on top of her, but the position didn't feel nearly as dominant as it had a second ago. Izzy's indigo lips were inches from mine. Her legs were squeezing the life out of me.

Was it weird that I wanted to kiss her?

She noticed the inappropriate attraction. Here I was, a dagger plunged into my side, and I was embarrassed. It softened her face a little. But she didn't give me the kiss I wanted. Instead, she pulled my head down beside hers and whispered in my ear.

"I win, noob."

Izzy caught my earlobe between her teeth and bit down.

Gazing past her as the life flowed from my body, I focused on the stump of ice left behind from her double. It was large, planted to the floor—and most importantly—sharp. I focused on that jagged edge. Felt the caress of the crazy woman's tongue as she killed me.

"Sorry," I said.

I gripped her tight and triggered dash. I slid forward, dragging her back along the ground until the icy stump impaled her.

Izzy's eyes went wide. She arched her chest into me and yelped. For the first time, the muscles in her legs slackened.

That was it for me. I collapsed into her, completely spent. As I died, her body rhythmically jerked beneath me.

You are dead!

I was whisked away in white and appeared outside the Arena entrance. I was suddenly fine. Full health, no red tinge to my vision. I rushed to the closed portcullis. Izzy lay on her back where I'd left her, coughing up blood. Then she stopped moving.

[Izzy] is dead!

Izzy disappeared as I had and the crowd watched listlessly.

The duel is a draw!

I grumbled, unsure what that bought me. My eyes darted to

the portcullis at the other end of the stadium. Izzy's back disappeared into the darkness without a return glance. I stared after her as the audience applauded wildly. We'd given them a real crowd pleaser. Unfortunately, neither Izzy nor I were pleased with the results.

A chime signaled a new message in my inbox. I checked it with trepidation, knowing what my failure meant. I had two messages. The first was a user experience survey sent from Varnu Johnson. I deleted it and focused on the next message, sent from Izzy.

> Talon,
>
> Don't think your little show gained anything but another enemy. The duel may have officially been a draw, but you died first so everyone knows I beat you. Either way, without a clean win, I have no obligation to share Everchat.
> Also, I'd watch my back in the wild. I'm not done nibbling on you.
>
> - Izzy

0300 InFamous

Throngs of players filed out from the Arena. I waited for them to rush past me like a wave. Instead, a strange thing happened. Several congratulated me and patted me on the back. Others discussed the fight amongst themselves, excitedly miming the turning points. I was the freaking flavor of the minute.

I decided it best to get out of there. This was a moment of defeat. I wasn't up for public appearances. I picked my way through the raucous crowd, dejected at the state of affairs and my rapidly dwindling options.

Today had started out so promising. Well, except for the dying-in-a-car-accident part. *But after that,* today had started out so promising. I'd been getting the hang of Haven. Leveling and looting like a pro. But somewhere along the ride the wheels had shaken off the axles. Everything good around me was burdened with baggage. Friends. Saints. Even my adventuring successes with the pagans. This fantastical afterlife was smacking into hard, inevitable reality.

"That was amazing!" beamed Kyle as he rushed to my side. I was surprised to see him here.

"You caught the duel?"

"Bro, I know you said to do my shopping first thing, but when you hear your roommate's taking on Izzy the Master Duelist, you drop everything except the popcorn and watch."

"I suppose." I continued scuttling away from the hungry eyes of the people. "Sorry for coming up short."

"Is that what you think happened?" Kyle waved at the groups of players following us through the streets. "Don't you get it, man? Izzy's never lost a duel before. She's never been held to a draw. This is the very first time she ever fought where she didn't outright win."

"I died first."

"Doesn't matter. Against her, a draw is just as good as a victory. It's something the people have never seen. That shield was amazing."

I managed a smile. "It kinda was. You should've seen her face when her ice lightning bounced."

"Must've been something."

"It's not just frost mages, either. I deflected a legit fireball back at a goblin warlock with this thing."

We laughed and I held my head a little higher as we walked. I wasn't really into the groupies that trailed us like hungry puppies, but I had to admit Kyle's enthusiasm was infectious.

Until that moment, I hadn't decided what to do with one notable piece of loot. It was cool. Had to be worth a lot. But it didn't really suit me. I pulled up my inventory and offered Kyle the mirror shield.

He stopped cold in the street, staring at the trade notification in shock.

I shrugged. "I'm not really a shield kind of guy. I prefer

dramatically leaping from the path of danger. And I wanna apologize for being so hard on you before."

Kyle frowned. "I can't take your shield, Talon."

"Seriously, it's yours. Hunkering down for a big hit isn't my idea of a good time. We're party members. I need you to be protected. Besides, it's my fault the pagans are on our asses anyway."

His eyes were hungry, but I could tell he didn't want charity. That wasn't what this was.

"Look, Kyle, as far as I'm concerned, you earned this shield. You're putting a lot of work into this. I wouldn't be where I am without you." I stopped short of telling him: fuckup or not, I appreciated his friendship.

Kyle took the shield and gaped at the reflective surface. It had a rounded shape with a flat top and bottom. It made for a good crossbow perch, discounting the fact that it reflected light and attracted attention. I supposed some things were worth magic deflection.

"This is by far the coolest gear I've ever owned," he said. "Thanks, Talon."

"Don't mention it."

For a second I was worried the conversation was about to get sappy. Luckily we lived in a terrifying fantasy world. A piercing screech echoed through the town. It was a long, howling cry that demanded the attention of anyone in earshot. Hundreds of eyes shot upward to the perfectly cerulean sky. It was a beautiful cloudless day.

A serpentine streak of black blemished the firmament like a rivulet of oil. It snaked through the sky high above town leaving a noxious trail of smoke. A flying creature with a wingspan three times the length of its body.

"Dragon!" yelled the people.

A wave of fright struck me as the beast swooped toward Stronghold, growing in scale as it neared. A black dragon. Its head was all pointed horns and chomping teeth. The rest of him writhed behind like a snake with four muscled legs that ended in razor-sharp claws. The beast was the length of a school bus, but much slimmer. A sleek thing. Speed *and* power. It roared and a dreaded shadow fell over us.

"I thought you said dragons were extinct."

"They are," he assured me as his eyes bulged.

My face displayed obvious disagreement.

"Okay," he hedged. "Maybe not extinct. Just asleep... Hidden. Banished!"

"You keep saying words but I don't think you know what they mean."

We ducked as the dragon flew over us. Massive wings buffeted sheets of air downward.

I looked at him pointedly. "Still think dragons are lame?"

He didn't answer.

I tried to pull my spear from my inventory but I couldn't. Weapons were banned in Stronghold.

"It can't actually attack in town," I said. "Can it?"

In response, the beast stretched its mouth agape. A stream of hissing venom spurted out like from a fire hose, blanketing the park grounds of the Foot. The acidic substance boiled and smoked, melting anything it touched.

Kyle pulled his mirror shield to his face. "What do we do?"

I surveyed the screaming hordes of residents. Most of them were scurrying home. That made a good deal of sense. Zoning into safe quarters kept them out of the fight. I wondered who that left for defense.

City Alert:
A dragon flies above!
Stronghold is under threat. All residents may engage in combat. While within the walls, all watchman and residents are immune to friendly fire.

Oh, man. This wasn't good. I desperately scoured my inventory for something that would help.

My spear blinked into my hands. Just as I was worrying that Kyle and I were in this alone, the city watch flooded the streets.

Most of them were lightly armed. Swords and slings and other unimpressive weapons. I wasn't sure they were up for this. Breaking up drunken arguments was a far cry from slaying dragons. Then again, it was possible Stronghold guards had unbelievable bonuses when defending the city.

Rocks and arrows volleyed into the sky. A few patriotic players joined the fray. It was a hasty response, haphazard and improvised, but it was a response. More guards and players spilled into the streets and attacked with anything they had.

The weak projectiles glanced off the dragon's scales. Even the occasional magic didn't harm it. The beast screeched again. Then, as if taunting the very institution of Stronghold, the dragon beat his wings and whirled to the top of Dragonperch. He belched acid onto the statue of Magnus Dragonrider: the hero on the tower, holding the dragonspear triumphantly to the heavens. The old stone steamed and buckled. It crumbled under the boiling substance. The black dragon landed with a crash beside it, bathing in its own sticky destruction.

"Where are the saints and angels?" I asked.

Kyle shook his head. "Saints don't engage in combat and angels only go after players. Angels are balancers. They don't deal with in-game threats."

More watchmen hurried past us in orderly units. Centurions with gleaming helmets and red body shields led the charge. These troops were equipped with heavy crossbows. A follow-up unit pushed a ballista on wheels over the cobblestones. A set of long steel spikes were ready for loading. The army of Stronghold was getting serious.

Ding!

I almost ignored the inbox notification outright. Then an uneasy feeling seized my stomach. With nothing but dread, I checked the message.

> Talon,
>
> I believe you have your distraction.
>
> - Luc1f3r

My breath caught in my throat. My eyes ran over the destruction. The crumbling statue. The bubbling land. The immolated players in the Foot.

All this was for me.

"Talon, what should we do?" asked Kyle.

I groaned. I didn't have time for a crisis of conscience. This wasn't my doing. Those players weren't dead-dead. And I wasn't getting anywhere with Izzy or tech support.

Lucifer's plan was my only hope.

"Get to the shops," I said. "Outfit yourself as best you can. Pick up extra potions for me." I tossed him some silver.

"I mean about the dragon."

"We can't do anything about the dragon until you get your glasswork supplies."

"Okay but what are we gonna—"

I grabbed his shoulders to focus him. "Don't worry about it. The dragon's too strong and the city watch is on it. Just get your gear and get back home. I'll meet you when I'm done."

Understanding crept into Kyle's face. He knew I was going for the Pantheon. I waved him off before he offered to help.

"Get the gear," I repeated. "Before the shops turn to dust."

He nodded and rushed off in a sprint.

I scanned the area. The streets were a riotous flurry, but none of the attention was focused on me. Flavor of the minute was right. My new fan club had bigger things to worry about now. That left me with plenty of privacy to operate.

The dragon was conveniently terrorizing the outskirts of Oldtown. The neighborhood was empty and remote, against the southwestern wall of the city. I raced north across the river, toward the Forum. Centurions in a rush to defend the city passed me without a second glance. The fancy shopping district was mostly abandoned. I approached the Pantheon, amazed at the quiet that had grown over the bustling capitol. I had to hand it to Lucifer. Dude knew how to make a distraction.

The facade of the Pantheon was a portico of Corinthian columns. Six freestanding pillars lined the walkway toward that entrance. Four golden angels towered high above, two still absent. The seventh golden angel perched on the pointed crest of the portico itself, hands thrust heavenward.

I shuddered as I passed beneath the celestial protectors of Stronghold. Kyle's assurance that the angels would remain inert didn't comfort me. They were activated by rogue players bent on unbalancing the game. I was merely seeking information. Was that enough to sign my death warrant?

I pulled the guide rune from my inventory. The yellow gemstone gleamed in the sunlight. The metal cross inlaid in the face held a dull shine.

"If you're gonna do anything," I said, "now's the time."

A digital map flickered into life a few feet ahead of me. It was a 3D layout of the Pantheon, horizontally overlaying the ground at an offset from my position. As I moved, it moved with me, and so did a blue "You Are Here" dot within the map itself. A green line extended from that position and traced the path I should take.

"Slick."

I followed the guide line. It had me step between the second and third columns and approach a side door. An internal lock mechanism clicked when I held the guide rune close. I pushed in with nervous anticipation.

The portico was a squared building with several subrooms,

but it was just the welcoming face of the Pantheon. The heart of the structure was the round room under the dome, in the back. That's where the green line was taking me. First, however, I had to jump through hoops.

As directed, I took a pit stop behind a central indoor column. Once in place, a pair of centurions marched into view from the back hall. They briskly paced the room and exited through the main open doorway, where several other guards were posted.

The guide rune wasn't just a map and a key. It showed a live play-by-play of active security. Not only were the guard positions noted on the map with red dots, but the green guide line adjusted to roving threats. This thing had taken some serious programming.

I continued to a small staircase along the wall that led to a balcony. Another door lock clicked open and I pressed into a private chamber. A monk's study. Parchment was laid out and scripted in beautiful cursive. Colorful illustrations ornamented the margins. The title read: *Haven Terms of Service 1.0*.

The finalized release-day terms of service. Haven was nearing its public launch. I couldn't be sure of the timetable, but I certainly hadn't seen a lot of bugs. This game was ready for prime time.

The guide stone flared. I wanted to stop and look around but time was short. I followed the guide line to the back of the room, frowning at the bookcase inset in the wall. Tomes lined the shelves. *A Brief History of the Nine. The Cleansing of the Old Gods. The Scourge and the Crusades*. I stared stupidly at the library until it clicked, just like the locks on the other doors.

I felt around the backing of the bookcase until I brushed

against a secret handle. I opened the door into the inner Pantheon with a smile and stepped inside.

Everything went black.

0310 Left 4 Dead

For a second, I thought the whole plan had gone to hell. I couldn't move. I couldn't see anything. Not the guide rune map. Not even my body.

Then I realized I was just streaming into a new zone. The inner sanctum came into view. I was in a separate space. A separate level.

The rotunda was a huge circular room. Marble tiles with intricate runes spanned the floor. Columns and alcoves and statues hemmed the wall. At the far end of the circle was a small altar.

I was above it all on a balcony that spanned the near half of the circular room. I'd need to go downstairs to reach the altar.

Above my head was a giant dome of squared blocks—impressive in size, beautiful in precision. The dome culminated in a round opening. The oculus. A thick shaft of sunlight beamed from the sky to the altar below. Ones and zeroes buzzed through the electrified energy.

The guide stone had led me true. I was here and, thankfully, the rotunda was empty.

I didn't need a green line on a map to know the altar was my destination. I descended the marble staircase against the wall and followed its curvature to the raised platform. I stepped lightly to the altar. A charged current thrummed over my body.

The table was set with a rich white cloth. Several computer terminals sat on top. This was Stronghold's control room, the Oculus, with access to all the secrets of Haven. I couldn't help but stare in reverent silence.

The guide rune flared again. The digital map zoomed in on the terminal. An open slot on the holographic display prompted me.

The real thing had the same slot on an elongated computer console. There were a few machines, actually. Slick white, with the Apple logo. Forbidden fruit. I considered the various terminals and monitors. One of them was labeled "Resident Records."

That was the one. The flat screen was running an old-school screensaver of a scrolling star field. I wiggled the mouse and was presented with a database and a search bar. I typed out a name.

SEARCH: Talon

My file immediately came up. My picture, occupation, signed documents. The record was separated into several tabs, some concerning my previous life and some concerning my new one. The summary page showed a flag on my account. Capital red letters read: NOT YET DECEASED.

I went numb with shell shock. My knees almost gave out. I couldn't believe it—Lucifer was right. I mean, I'd known something was off. Ever since I spawned in Haven I'd been plagued by unsettling urgency. But this truth was both glorious and terrible.

The possible implications flitted through my head. I was badly injured. In a hospital or convalescent home. In a coma, or paralyzed as Lash had been. Dying, but not dead.

But what if I wasn't beyond saving? What if I was stuck in this simulation while my body was fighting? Recovering? I had to believe it was still possible to go back home.

I typed a new name into the prompt.

SEARCH: Derek Lonnerman

The only result was my file again. He was listed as a living relative. In a known-associations section. Haven players were listed as well. Kyle, Lash, Izzy. I wondered what triggered inclusion in the list. Dune wasn't on it. Lucifer, thankfully, wasn't either. I bit my lip and mulled over looking through other people's personal data. I knew I didn't have the right, but I couldn't think of a better option. I clicked through to Izzy's file.

She'd been uploaded to Haven almost eight months ago. That was a hella long closed beta period, even if it was almost over. I confirmed she was deceased, just to make sure we weren't in the middle of some giant Matrix-like conspiracy. Nope. We weren't batteries for spider robots. Her file said she was a twenty-two-year-old living with her father. Isabel Sakata had swallowed a whole package of cold medicine.

I cursed and looked away, certain I'd crossed a line and violated her privacy. Izzy had killed herself. That nugget of information explained a lot about her. Doing something like that, she couldn't have been a happy person. Even if Haven was everything she wanted it to be, I doubted it could cure her, no matter how much magic was in the world.

Gritting my teeth, I pressed onward to her benefits page. She was on the Everchat white list. The bitch wasn't bluffing. She had the feature. And she probably didn't even use it. If her aim was to escape her old life, she wouldn't likely reconnect with it.

I wondered if I could add myself to the white list. I went to the same section in my file and tried a quick edit. No go. The document was read-only.

The guide stone flickered. The display of the console slot urgently blinked.

The bit key. That would give me write access to the data.

I pulled the gold cartridge from my inventory. It sparkled with a royal glimmer. I slipped it into the slot and pressed down.

The terminal screen blinked and went black. Digitized static froze across the display. I furrowed my brow. At first I thought something had gone horribly wrong. Then I pulled the cartridge out, gave it two sharp blows to clear away dust, and re-inserted it. The screen flashed white and gave me a command list. I was in.

I smiled and went through the feature list until I found Everchat. From what I could tell, at least thirty players across Haven were white-listed. I added myself. Make that thirty-one.

Ding!

I got an email. Everchat welcome information. It said I could only use the feature in private zones like my home or media rooms. It said I needed to verify a connection request with a contact before placing a call. Halfway through reading the message, the guide rune I had placed on the altar thrummed ominously.

I closed the menu and looked around. I was still alone. The yellow gemstone bounced and hit the floor. I leaned down to get it but it clattered a few feet farther. The name above the item glitched out. It read [Gu1d3 Rune] but the letters flickered like a countdown timer. The stone bounced and renamed itself to [Recall Rune]. It emitted a large pulse like a sound wave and momentarily covered the area in light.

When it cleared away, I was no longer alone in the rotunda.

0320 Bad Company

The room was quiet again. The rattling stone on the floor had settled.

"What the hell is this?" I asked.

The silver runes on Lucifer's black robes sparkled in the focused beam of electrified light. Ironically, the sunlight of the open dome forced his hooded face into deeper shadow.

"This is the plan, Talon. You did well."

I stared dumbly as Lucifer approached the Oculus console. "The guide rune was a hacked recall rune. It teleported you right to me." Once again I tried to examine his level and class info, but it wouldn't appear. "I thought you said you couldn't enter town."

He went to work at the terminal. "I can't without them noticing. We don't have a lot of time."

His hands were a blur on the keyboard. Various windows and documents cycled frenetically on the flat screen. I was afraid to see what he was doing and unsure I'd even be able to tell if I looked.

"This is what the Fallen Angels were attempting during the last raid. You wanted access to the Pantheon."

His head remained fixed on the monitor. "This is the beating heart of Stronghold, one of nine sainted cities that enforce order in Haven. Access to the Oculus is necessary to effect real change."

"But your men were all killed."

"They were flagged, as I am. I'd thought them anonymous but the saints knew exactly who they were. The Fallen Angels were lured into an ambush and slaughtered."

I worked my jaw. "You used me to get you in. A new player. One who didn't arouse suspicion."

His frantic keystrokes paused and he turned to face me. "Don't make out like you weren't a willing participant. The white robes are the ones who lied to you, not me. Don't lose sight of that."

I didn't immediately snap back this time. My resident record had confirmed I was still alive. I couldn't deny I had a bone to pick with Saint Peter. "How is it you know all this? That you can do the things you do? After the Fallen Angels were killed, the saints wiped the server to protect the Oculus, but you're here a day later."

He turned back to the console. "I can't be wiped."

"How's that possible?"

"You've probably heard about the security of the system. The encryption of our data. Triply redundant, cycling from server to server in continuous obfuscation."

"Yeah. It's what makes us supposedly impossible to delete. Barring interference from the angels."

"The angels are the only exception precisely because they're a facet of the security system. A policing countermeasure. But they're bound by strict rules. The saints can't activate them manually. It's why we should be safe enough for now. But consider what you know about data resets."

I twisted my lips and followed the thought process aloud. "I can understand resetting the game state—the world—but if player identifying data is so secure then how the hell can they wipe it?"

"Bingo. It shouldn't be possible, but it is. It's a special condition of the beta. Kablammy can't rightly give test participants a permanent leg up before Haven launches. Right now, everyone's flagged for temporary progression."

"Except you," I noted.

Lucifer ignored the comment. "Your skills, your level, your experience—everything you've worked for—aren't being written to your redundant profile. All data is being rerouted to a special closed server. A beta server. The encryption is still pretty hairy, of course. I doubt they're able to alter it piecemeal. But nothing stops them from doing a full wipe. The saints can't *delete* you but they can *defeat* you. Take away everything you've gained. Everything you've worked for."

It sounded like an insidious plot. On the other hand, it kinda sounded like a harmless beta test.

"Nobody ever said wipes were awesome," I pointed out. "But it's what we signed up for. Aren't wipes a necessary part of testing the game?"

Lucifer smiled. "There's that word again. Game. They call this a digital reality, do they not? Ones and zeroes make up everything we are. Does that sound like a game to you? You're shutting your eyes and believing the illusion."

I snorted. I understood his point, but he was being pedantic about semantics. Once again, the devil in him reared his head.

"So that's the difference between you and everyone else?" I asked. "Manipulation of the temp progression flag."

"Hardly," he said, confirming my suspicions. "That's one difference but there are many more beta flags. I've hacked other modules of the runtime too. Case in point, it's time for you to receive my gifts."

The head of the resistance typed in a few commands and a thrum of energy overtook me. I stumbled in surprise but it was over before it started. I looked around warily. Checked my character status. I was fine. I thought I was. But something felt... different.

"What did you do?"

"I gave you a taste of freedom, Talon. You must earn the rest."

A few more keystrokes resulted in a series of beeps and a loud unclicking of bolts. Lucifer smiled and twirled around, moving to the alcove behind the altar. A shelf built into the rotunda wall bore a few ornamental statuettes. Front and center was a large object covered in a veil. Lucifer pinched the stitched cloth and flung it away, revealing an ornate golden box topped with a cross.

"The tabernacle," he said in awe.

The square box had two golden doors with carved images of valiant knights. Lucifer pulled them open slowly, revealing them to be six inches thick with retracted titanium crossbars. A digital display on the safe read "Unlocked."

Inside was a single relic. A large rough-hewn rock that

sparkled dirty red. A ruby painted with blood.

"Uh, Lucifer, what—"

"The Eye of Orik," he said. "One of nine relics the white robes used to found the great cities of Haven."

I recalled my very limited knowledge of Haven world history as explained by my frat-boy roommate. Lucifer had filled in enough blanks for me to get the picture. Nine relics. Nine great cities. The people ended the vicious rule of the pagans by founding cities with appropriated holy treasures. The Eye of Orik had to be one such relic. A symbol of Stronghold's power over the wild.

Except Haven was an MMORPG. Here, unlike the real world, relics had more power than mere symbolism.

"Hold up," I said. "We didn't agree to this."

"Did we need to? This is about ending oppression. Ripping away the bit and blinders and allowing natural order to rise in its place."

My face tightened in dread. "How does stealing treasure end oppression?"

"This isn't loot, Talon."

"I just mean it seems important to Stronghold. If you take it, what'll happen to the people living here?"

Lucifer smiled. "The beauty of natural order is the chaos inherent." He tucked the artifact into his inventory and strolled away triumphantly. The tabernacle was left open and violated.

"I think you should put that back," I said firmly.

Lucifer's smile waned. He considered me as if for the first time. "Resistance doesn't come with a road map, Talon. I understand your apprehension, but trust me. I take care of mine."

"I'm not one of your Fallen Angels."

"That's because you haven't proven yourself yet. But you can be on my side. If you become my apostle, I will welcome you with arms outstretched."

He tried to walk away but I grabbed his arm. "I'm serious, Lucifer."

He moved quicker than I thought possible. A blade flashed and bit deep into my forearm. I fell away in shock. A wave of pain, bright and harrowing, flexed through my arm.

Real. Actual. Pain.

I growled and hunched over, cradling my wound.

"One of my gifts," he said slyly. "You wish to continue this charade and play a grand MMO? Well, I've disabled your pain inhibitors and gore filters. Even though this is a digital environment, your brain perceives threats the same as it would in the real world." He leaned closer. "Taking damage *hurts*. How's that for a role-playing game?"

I blinked through the searing heat running up my arm. It was a damned superficial wound as far as MMOs went—a mere 6 points of damage—but the gash in my arm was deep. Blood oozed from exposed muscle. It fucking *hurt*.

I gritted my teeth. Various plays raced through my head, but they all ended in defeat. I wasn't sure I could fight him. I didn't even know what level he was, but he'd avoided the wipe. Multiple wipes, for all I knew. Lucifer was bound to be the most powerful player in the world right now.

The entire room tinted red. Chirps blared through invisible speakers. *Bip, bip! Bip, bip!* Lucifer and I broke away from the standoff and scanned our surroundings.

"They've isolated me," he said. "We need to get out of here."

His eyes landed on the gold cartridge plugged into the terminal. He moved for it.

I grunted. Maybe I couldn't fight him, but I wasn't slow on my feet. I instinctually triggered dash. I streaked across the marble floor and beat him to the Oculus. I yanked the bit key from the slot and rolled away as Lucifer hit the altar.

"That's mine!" he roared.

"Give me the Eye," I said. "I'll trade it for the Eye."

Lucifer's lips curled into a sneer. "My enemies don't live very long, Talon." His long staff appeared in his grip. It was a length of black wood with a fork at the top. A blue crystal was set between the Y branches.

I armed my spear and backed away slowly.

The main rotunda doors slammed open. Muffled shouts came from the plane of white light beyond. Boots and sandals shook the marble floor as figures faded into place. Lucifer scowled and swapped his staff for the recall rune.

"This isn't over," he snarled. Then he vanished in a brilliant flash of white.

All I could do was dive behind the altar. Soldiers spilled into the room and fanned out. The alarm still blared. The room was still tinted red. As I hunched low, I glanced up at the sky through the open oculus. Freedom seemed so close.

"Where are the intruders?" called out a centurion.

"Impossible!" cried another. "The devil is no longer in Stronghold."

They stuttered in place, sure they had backed us into a corner but shocked they had lost us.

A centurion ordered a watchman to summon the saints. Some of the guards filed out, grumbling. I peeked at them from behind the personnel terminal. Staying low, I reached a hand up and typed in the search bar.

SEARCH: Lucifer

No matches found.

I grimaced. The centurions ordered the entire Pantheon secured. The heavily armored lieutenants went back through the door, leaving me with lower-level city watchmen as they established a perimeter. I considered bolting right then and there but tried the console again. This time I used the numeric spelling.

SEARCH: Luc1f3r

A file came up with a match for a known alias. The resident was a Lucille Black, an eight-year-old girl who had died of cancer. At first I thought it was a bad match, but evidence started to line up. She'd been in Haven for over five months. Lots of her info was redacted. There was a warrant out for her deletion. And her real name explained both her handle and her penchant for goth dress.

"The tabernacle!" cried a watchman. Sandals scuffed toward the altar.

Shit. I didn't have the luxury of hiding anymore. I stood and bolted for the staircase on the wall of the rotunda. The guards yelled in alarm and made a beeline for me. For soldiers, they were pretty fast. At higher levels my scouting advantages might have overtaken them, but I simply wasn't good enough yet. As they converged on me, I triggered dash and skidded to the steps. I used vault for a head start and ran up the marble handrail. Stones from slings flew my way but crashed behind me.

In response to their cries, centurions zoned into the rotunda again. The search of the Pantheon was called off in favor of giving chase. I raced to the top of the mezzanine, realizing I'd forgotten one last thing.

While still in the private rotunda level, I accessed my Everchat menu. It was unlocked here. I quickly requested a chat contact and filled out Derek Lonnerman. Just before I slipped through the door to the study, I clicked send.

Back in the monk's chamber, I knew I only had moments before the guards figured out how to work the secret entrance. If I was lucky. Instead of risking my way through the portico downstairs, I wedged open a stained glass window and jumped from the second story to the road outside. I landed in a controlled roll, pain arcing through my shoulder like lightning, and took off down the street.

0330 Crackdown

Disappearing in the chaos was easy. At first I was surprised there were so many people in the streets, but a notification explained it.

> **City Alert:**
> The dragon has fled!
> *Stronghold is safe. Engaging in combat is once again prohibited.*

I supposed Lucifer and his black dragon were miles away by now. That left me in the thick of it, in possession of an illegal bit key. Grounds for deletion on sight.

I clutched my bleeding arm and sprinted past the Pantheon, peeking at the golden angels above. They watched me with the omnipresence of statues, but they didn't turn their heads. They didn't leap from their perches and take flight against me. Two of them were still missing, but those were hunting someone else.

I pressed forward into the main Forum thoroughfare.

Watchmen lined the streets so I stayed in the thick of the crowd. Ahead, players were complaining. Most of the shops were barricaded.

I groaned in annoyance. I *really* wanted a healing potion right now.

City Alert:
The saints have evoked security procedures!
Effective immediately, Stronghold is under curfew. All residents are ordered off the streets. Return to your homes and await interview.

I froze, reading the message again. The shops wouldn't be reopening. The city was on lockdown. A commotion swept through the crowd. More complaints.

"Interview?" cried a man. "What kind of crap is that?"

"I have a quest to complete," said someone else.

The townspeople were upset. To them, the curfew was a result of the black dragon attack. With that threat gone, all they cared about was getting back to business. But I knew the truth about the curfew. It was me the city watch was looking for. It was me they wanted to interview.

It was curious that I hadn't received any direct messages about the breach. My only conclusion was that I was still anonymous. Lucifer's stranger's cowl really was protecting me. Maybe I could make a clean getaway.

I hurried through the unrest. It was difficult to weave through the excited crowd but the commotion served my purposes. The city watch did what they could, funneling the mass of players southward, down the Forum road through the marketplace. All the little alleys between buildings were blocked with soldiers. As I pushed closer to the main exit, I saw why.

The city watch had erected a checkpoint. Every single resident was being forced to clear the area, but not before they were vetted. Anyone coming from the Pantheon would be forced to use this route. With the bit key in my inventory, I couldn't afford to be stopped by Stronghold officials.

I also couldn't fight. No combat in town. No ability to damage the guards even if I could. Most of the watch wasn't heavily equipped, but they'd wipe the floor with me. I had to get out another way.

I took my cue from the vociferous pack around me.

"A checkpoint?" I shouted. "This is gonna take forever!"

The bottlenecked crowd grunted in agreement. Players pushed and shoved.

"Let us use the shops!" I demanded. "My friend died in that black dragon attack. The least you could do is treat me with respect!"

Hoots and hollers joined my demands. A few brash players made appeals of their own. Some asked for free loot or experience for helping defend the town. Others just wanted to get the hell out of the pack-jam. The city watch scanned the crowd for dissidents. That was my opening.

I cupped my hands around my mouth and chanted. "Let us out! Let us out!"

It caught on like wildfire. After the third sentence, complete strangers were reciting along. After the fifth, the entire Forum added their voice. The tumultuous mass spoke as a unified entity, pressing against the fumbling city watch. One of the guards drew a club and swatted an unruly resident.

Then all hell broke loose.

The people surged ahead. Combat wasn't possible, but sheer presence was. The outnumbered guards couldn't stop the wall of players shoving them. The city watch hurried away as their tight checkpoint burst like a failing dam. In seconds the Forum was an absolute madhouse. I spilled out behind a crew of large artisans, no one the wiser.

Amidst the confusion, I made for the noob shops lining the river. Front Street was packed with wild activity. Players scrambled through the Foot, avoiding guards. The watch blew whistles to summon backup, doing anything to contain this before it turned into a riot. I broke away from the horde and slipped to the doorstep of the local apothecary.

I leaned into the locked door and groaned in defeat. Even the noob shops were all shuttered. Apparently NPC shopkeepers were more cooperative about curfews than players were. I slid to a sitting position against the wall and pressed tightly against my wound. The bleeding had slowed. The pressure helped mask the pain, but it was still there, underneath. I grimaced and felt like the worst MMO player ever. Subdued by a cut.

I had to be better than that. The pain was Tad Lonnerman's problem. I had to be tougher than that. I had to be Talon, a level 4 scout. There was nothing to do but suck it up.

I rose to my feet and hurried past the training yard. Half an entire field had been obliterated by dragon acid. Players wandered the destruction, looting, salvaging, trying to help. I marched by and tried not to blame myself.

Back in Hillside, things were more settled. Lines of dutiful players returned to their homes, disappearing to their drama-free confines. The city watch was present and kept the curfew a civil affair. I passed Lash's stocky barbarian companion. Just my luck it wasn't the healer, but I supposed it was better than running into the white knight herself. As I reached my block, I passed a few more familiar faces. I didn't really know them, but they were supposed to be there and that was comforting. I was almost home free.

I ducked behind a parked wagon when I spied the two watchmen standing outside my front door.

So much for comforting. There was a chance the men were randomly posted but, really, it was miniscule. They were standing beside *my* door. Of all the homes, why that one? Maybe I wasn't Haven's most wanted quite yet, but I had to be under suspicion.

I opened party chat.

> **Talon:** *Kyle, you at the house? Two city watchmen are camping our doorway. Any idea what that's about?*

After a moment:

Kyle: *I'm here. I saw them asking a few players questions. They asked me if everybody was home when I came in.*
Talon: *They ask about me?*
Kyle: *Not by name.*
Talon: *What did you tell them?*
Kyle: *The truth. It was just me. They didn't seem concerned. But listen: They're looking for anyone and anything out of the ordinary. You'll be interrogated because you're new.*

I frowned.

Talon: *Did you manage to hit the shops before they closed?*
Kyle: *Totally. Glassworking as we speak, bro. I got a bunch of adventuring supplies too.*
Talon: *Health potions?*
Kyle: *I'm not an idiot.*
Talon: *Okay, I need one bad. But I can't go in there. You need to come outside.*
Kyle: *Uh, Talon, have you been paying attention to what's going on around you? I'm not allowed to go outside, dude.*

He was right, of course. And any action on his part counter to the proper rules would only increase suspicion. With them already camped at our door, it was a huge risk.

Talon: *Just be ready. I'll take care of the guards and let you know when it's clear.*

I backtracked down the road and racked my brain for a way to take them on. Civil unrest was a harder sell here. Most players were peacefully returning home. Anybody fighting the power was doing that away from the resident neighborhoods, in the public spaces.

As soon as my gaze fell on a lightly clothed man, I knew I was in luck.

"Hey, Phil," I said. "Wanna make some silver?"

A few minutes later, the watchmen outside my house were taken off guard by a ragged man wearing nothing but a loincloth, a scraggly beard, and two bright pink wool socks. The neighborhood oaf strolled right up to the guards and kissed one of them on the cheek. He turned around and mimed mooning them—apparently the loincloths weren't removable in public—before screaming and hopping away.

The stunned guards traded an empty glance. Then they drew their weapons and took chase.

Talon: *Now, Kyle! Go, go, go!*

My roommate was out of the house in a blink. I waved him across the street and we took off down the hillside.

"This is crazy, Talon. What are we doing?"

"You taking this seriously yet?" I joked.

I waved him onward. I didn't have time to explain until we

got to safety. We avoided heading back to the Foot because that was halfway closer to the Forum. Instead I led Kyle west to the river. On the far side, Dragonperch reached into the sky, worn and crumbling, but only cosmetically. The structure itself was tall and strong. At its rooftop, the smashed statue of the dragon knight reflected the state of the town.

I wasn't much for poetry and symbolism. What I saw was an abandoned tower without city watch patrols. The problem was, the only bridges across the river were north of the shops. The Oldtown crossing had suffered more than minimal damage and had long ago fallen into the water. Dragonperch itself had a drawbridge that spanned the river, but it was raised.

"We have to swim," I said.

We dove into the wash. The cold water stung my arm but the current wasn't a danger. We forded across easily enough. The river was part of the aqueduct system and lined with deep stone walls. The base of Dragonperch sported some narrow alcoves that we climbed onto. Tucked into the side wall and hidden from view across the river was a rusted portcullis barring entry into a cave. The passageway immediately turned inward so we couldn't see further inside.

"Check this out," said Kyle confidently. He produced a large glass vial of corrosive and applied it to the old lock on the gate. Several bangs with a hammer from his inventory snapped the lock into pieces like his ruined sword. We were granted access.

I stared at him, impressed.

"What?" he said. "If I don't learn from bonehead mistakes, then I'm a bonehead. Right?"

I nodded with a smile and stepped inside. We were in a

brick-lined grotto, a man-made cave with passages and statues and pools of water. "This is the base of the tower," I said.

"You mean we broke in, just like that?"

"I think so."

He grabbed my shoulder to stop me from proceeding. "Not cool, Talon. There are supposed to be, like, really hard mobs in here. I don't think now's a good time to go adventuring."

I grimaced. "You might be right. You got my potion?"

He spent abominably long digging through his inventory. When he presented me with the item offer, I saw why. Kyle had put a bunch of supplies in there for me. I accepted the items without checking them over and immediately used a health potion. My arm closed up. The pain subsided instantly. I melted to the floor in relief.

"You're crazy," said my roommate. "You were only missing a tiny bit of health. That was a waste of an expensive potion."

I shrugged. By the numbers, Kyle was absolutely right. I couldn't put a price on the nagging pain, however.

0340 Breakout

Kyle paced back and forth in the small grotto passage. His leather armor was bolstered by the mail vest, but he sported some upgrades too. Shoulder plates, shin guards, steel vambraces. He'd started to take to his defensive loadout. That was more than learning how to crack an old lock.

I sat against the wall, peeking at the Everchat interface. As I'd suspected, I couldn't access it here. This was a global world zone; Everchat could only be accessed in private. In my home. Surrounded by guards.

"What's your plan?" he asked.

The question hit me like a brick. I didn't really have a plan. Which was unlike me. I'd just been running, really.

"Umm," I said, failing to hide the obvious. I closed my menu.

"Bro, are you serious? We violated curfew and broke into Dragonperch for no reason?"

I rested my forehead on my knees. "I can't let them catch me."

"You sure they know about you?"

"No, but it's like you said. I'm new. I'm suspicious. I don't think they linked me to Lucifer, but if they do I'm a dead man.

They might delete me."

His jaw tightened.

I pulled the gold cartridge from my inventory. "I need to get rid of this before it kills me."

Kyle snatched the bit key from my hand and followed the passage around a bend. I crawled around the corner just in time to see him stash the cartridge in an alcove behind the bust of a regal woman. "There," he said.

I sat again. Hiding the bit key was probably for the best.

"Maybe you're wrong," said Kyle. "Maybe we should sneak back into our house and sit tight. Deny everything."

I closed my eyes and rested, thinking clearly for the first time since everything had gone down. I was wearing a stranger's cowl. It kept me somewhat off the radar of the various authorities, but it didn't hide my identity from anyone face to face. With the confusion in the streets, the theft at the Pantheon, and Lucifer still at large, he had to be public enemy number one. I wasn't more than a footnote. Kyle's plan to lie low wasn't an awful one. And it would give me access to Everchat.

But waiting at home ignored the interrogations. While we could figure out a way to sneak into the house unnoticed, all suspicious residents were going to be followed up with. Hell, maybe everyone in Stronghold would be questioned. Did I really want to sit tight for that? Put myself at their mercy?

So I thought over my options. Lucifer had angels chasing him and still managed to hide. Should I seek help from him? At the very least, I could camp out in the wild. Stay clear of Stronghold. That was just another way of lying low. Kyle and I could skip town and go out adventuring. Spend a few days out there until everything calmed down and play dumb upon our return. Oh, sorry, we were out questing. We didn't have anything to do with the theft of the Eye.

Yeah, I was starting to see the value in getting out of Dodge.

"Whoa," said Kyle reverently. "Check this out."

By now he was further into the darkened grotto. I climbed to my feet and followed the walls deeper. The tunnels twisted in different directions but were relatively contained. This wasn't exactly a network of sewers. It was more like a man-made bunker, filled with old art and supplies. I passed a weapon rack but everything on it was old and rusted. I found Kyle at the end of the largest hallway.

"I thought you didn't want to go exploring in the tower?"

"We're not *in* the tower," he said. He stood at an oak door carved with twisted sigils. "It's locked."

I was starting to get it. These catacombs were more like a patio cave, hidden access from the river. The gate Kyle had broken into gave us access to the property, but not to the building itself.

"Imagine that," he said. "This door blocks access to unnamed loot and quests. There are even rumors of an ancient library for that lore you love so much."

"It's a great place to hide at least," I said.

He crossed his arms. "That's what you wanna do then? Hide out here?"

I shook my head firmly. "No. I'm leaving Stronghold. I need to get away from this mess for a little bit."

"The gates will be heavily manned," he warned. "A freaking dragon just attacked us."

"But the curfew should be taking most of their man power."

"Maybe, but containing the town, locking the gates, that *is* the curfew. It's a suicide mission."

"We'll figure it out," I said.

"I don't think I can come. Lash is right about me. I'll just drag you down."

"Come on. I wouldn't have gotten this far without you."

He sighed. "Look, Talon, I appreciate everything you've done for me, but you're asking me to risk permanent deletion for— What is this all about, anyway? What are you running from?"

I bit down and dropped my head. "I'm not dead, Kyle. I looked up my resident file and I'm not fucking dead. That fact alone puts a special flag on my record. That's why the watch is posted at our doorstep. They don't know I was involved at the Pantheon, but I'll be under close scrutiny."

I took in a slow breath and saw Kyle's viewpoint. "Look, you're my friend. I understand if you don't want to go. I don't blame you. The last thing I want is for you to get into trouble over my problem."

He chewed his lip a moment. "Are we really friends?" he asked.

"What?" I gave him a strange look. "Why would you think otherwise?"

"I don't know. I just... I'm used to disappointing people."

I shook my head. "Don't worry about that. I'm not disappointed. I understand why I need to do this alone." I moved to the grotto's entrance and peeked outside. The coast was clear. I could maneuver up the riverbank wall to ground level without getting wet.

Kyle joined me. "Friends don't do things alone. I'm coming."

I turned to him to talk him out of it, but he wore a look of smug certainty on his face. "You sure?" was all I asked.

"Don't mention it, buddy. I'll see you through this."

I chuckled, a little more than relieved. "Okay, then." We headed into Oldtown.

The west side of the river was a smallish bubble of land. The original city. Now Oldtown was just the outskirts of Stronghold between the water and the west wall. We walked along the battlements, isolated from the city proper. No point crossing back over the river when we could follow the wall to the west gate. The land narrowed where the river pinched close to the city's border. After that the water snaked eastward along Front Street. We were back on the main thoroughfare leading to the gate, uncomfortably close to the entrance of the Forum.

The two small outpost stations within the gate were manned by only a single guard. The large wooden doors were mostly closed but not fully. Stronghold wasn't under attack or fully secured. A person at a time could still pass in and out, given they were granted access. I was sure the gate could be locked at a moment's notice but, for whatever reason, the city watch hadn't deemed it necessary yet.

"This might actually be possible," I said.

Further working in our favor was the good-sized crowd on the main road. It wasn't a thick force of trouble-making miscreants, but there were several higher-level players spouting grievances at watchmen posted on the street. I wasn't the only player who wanted out. Lash scoffed in the faces of the guards. Their annoyed looks told me they were trying to obey orders without inciting violence. I pulled my hood low and walked by without the white knight noticing us. Small blessings.

We strolled past the south entry to the Circus, stadium walls skirting the track inside. The games were closed, of course. A single watchmen stood at the doorway, blocking access. He eyed us as we passed but I hurried along.

Only fifty feet from the gate now, most of the players were cleared out. We were in a buffer between the people and the gate. That made it harder to blend in. Izzy was there, arguing with the gate guard. With any luck she would keep him distracted while we slipped out.

I made sure my cowl was in place and said, "Walk confidently, Kyle. Don't draw attention to yourself." He nodded and followed suit.

Sometimes things are hard, sometimes things are easy, and sometimes they're too easy. The plan was going swimmingly until a centurion atop the gate tower sharply blew a whistle. The gate guard spun to attention. Another emerged from the second outpost office. They drew their swords and faced us.

I widened my stance, stuck in a moment of fight or flight, when our odds grew exceedingly worse. Centurions stormed in from outside the gate. Two. Four. They were followed by a whole contingent of legionnaires, who were like watchmen with better equipment. Less leather and straw, more chain and plate.

I whirled around. Centurions and watchmen spilled from the entrance of the Circus. Our empty buffer area was quickly flooded with soldiers on both sides.

All this coordinated effort wasn't a response to a routine whistle. This was an ambush. The units had been posted out of sight just waiting for someone suspicious to try the gates. And we'd sprung the trap.

Kyle and I pressed our backs together as the soldiers of Stronghold circled us in tight formation. The players in the area all paused their complaints to watch the new show. Izzy arched a curious eyebrow. Our captors were too numerous for me to see what Lash was doing.

"Kyle and Talon," called out a centurion. His steel plate hung in heavy bands around his torso and arms, which were further protected by a body shield painted bright red and yellow. A steel helmet wrapped around his crown and chin, leaving his hard face bare. A tuft of red hair jutted out ornamentally like a Mohawk in traditional Roman style.

The head centurion, [Gladius], broke the ranks of the circle and approached. "You have been deemed persons of interest to the state and will be detained." His hand rested on the golden sword looped into his belt.

I backed away. "I can't let you do that."

He sneered at me, almost an invitation to try anything. "You have no choice." He moved in.

I didn't think. I didn't plan. With deft precision, the blacksteel spear appeared in my grip. The centurion only had time to widen his eyes as I simultaneously triggered dash and deadshot. None of it should've been possible in town, but I fired forward, speeding along the ground in a supercharged lunge. The tip of my spear shot past his shield and slammed right into his heart.

The sound of impact jolted everyone nearby. My weapon punched a hole between his bands of armor and struck true. The centurion flew backward ten feet, clearing a hole in his crowd of soldiers before crumpling to the ground.

Combo!
Surprise!
Stun!
You dealt 52 damage to [Gladius]

"Come on!" I yelled, pulling Kyle forward through the crack in their ranks.

The legionnaires weren't defenseless—they were probably better than me—but with their leader on the ground they hesitated to take action. Hesitated just long enough for us to escape the kill zone.

Gladius struggled to his hands and knees. Subordinate centurions barked orders. Soldiers brandished weapons. I batted the half-hearted attacks away with my spear as we charged past. The NPCs reared away defensively, still shocked by the sudden and impossible threat.

As I held them off, Kyle rushed between the wooden doors ahead. I hoped there weren't more soldiers waiting outside.

"Shut the gate!" ordered Gladius, still on the ground, spittle on his chin.

Guards on the wall heaved chains that pulled the heavy doors. They began to close, faster than I could make it. I tried to use dash but had too much time left on the cooldown timer. I wasn't gonna make it.

Ten feet in front of me, a solid block of ice the size of a mailbox lodged between the closing doors. The gate lurched and paused. The ice crunched. I charged forward as more watchmen added their might to the chains. The frozen block groaned under the pressure and cracked, but I was close enough. I slammed my spear into the ground and triggered vault, jumping up high and over the obstruction. I rolled sideways in the air to squeeze through the wooden doors. The gate slammed shut and I landed hard on the ground beyond.

Kyle waited in the tall grass beside Bandit. He raised his crossbow in trembling hands, aiming just above my shoulder.

Izzy stood over me, spraying a sheet of ice over the closed entryway, sealing the doors shut. When she was satisfied, she shot Kyle an annoyed look and offered me her hand. I grabbed it and she helped me up.

"That will only buy us a few minutes," she said. "We have to move."

We sprinted across the tended lands and made for the tree cover down the road.

0350 Need for Speed

"They're not chasing us," said Kyle.

"Keep running," I returned. We weren't even halfway to the forest yet.

"No, seriously. They're not—"

The icy barrier on the west gate shattered as the doors flung open. The wind carried the rushed orders of the centurions on it. Legionnaires marched from the city in a disciplined line, four across. They moved double-time down the road.

"You were saying?"

Izzy hissed. "They're sending a whole legion after us. Why would they—?"

"We need to keep moving," I said. "Maybe they won't march past the tended lands."

"The tree line," said Kyle.

Horns blared in unison after us. The Stronghold army was an intimidating presence and they'd only been mustered over the course of minutes. I tried not to imagine what the force would look like in a well-planned war.

The good news was the legion was slower than us. That many men maintaining formation couldn't compete with our mad scrambling. At least in the short term, we had the advantage.

"Arrows!" yelled Izzy.

I spun and saw the line of archers letting loose. A wave of arrows took to the sky like a flock of spooked birds. As we raced down the road, the projectiles angled and fell to the ground, pattering across a wide swath of land. The barrage fell short.

"They won't miss again," warned Izzy. "They were just gauging their range."

The centurions barked orders and the archers adjusted their angles. She was right. We had no choice but to barrel ahead and hope we could outrun arrows.

The volley let loose. A hundred arrows flew skyward and made a wide arc above. As gravity slowly took over, their aim appeared true. In a few seconds we'd be experiencing a hell of a hailstorm.

Our boots took us past the tree line. We each maneuvered side to side to avoid the trees while maintaining top speed. Sharpened points of metal tore through the dense canopy above. Leaves exploded. Shafts thwacked into thick trunks. A few stray arrows made it all the way to the barren forest floor.

Dirt splashed my face as an arrow thunked down just in front of me. Kyle's mirror shield, held at his back, deflected another. Luckily, the thick foliage had done its job. The vast majority of projectiles never made it to us.

We found a clump of old oaks with wide trunks and ducked behind them. Izzy and Kyle each took their own tree. I pulled Bandit close behind mine. From our vantage in the forest, we could no longer see the pursuing army. The centurions ordering the legion had grown quiet.

"The archers are done," I said. "There's no way they can get us in here."

Kyle breathed a sigh of relief. "The question is whether they'll come into the forest."

I nodded, weaving my head side to side to find a sightline through the trees. I considered climbing the oak.

"Talon," called Izzy, studying me carefully. "How'd you do that? Use combat in town?"

I paused, for the first time realizing the significance of what I'd done. Not only had I drawn my spear and used skills within Stronghold city limits, but I'd squared off toe-to-toe with a lead centurion. He should've been protected from friendly fire but I'd damaged him. In a fair fight he'd likely mop the floor with me, but the sheer impossibility of my resistance had taken them all by surprise.

Even Izzy—who'd helped me escape by using magic to wedge the gates open—had only been able to act once she was clear of the doors. The distraction of the ambush had allowed her to sneak out beforehand.

"I'm not sure," I said.

"Don't keep secrets," warned Izzy. "I wanna know how you did what you did."

Lucifer's gifts. His hacked runtime modules. It was the only explanation. He'd done more than disable my pain inhibitors. A taste of freedom, he called it. Yeah, I was free all right.

In our silent vigilance, my mind drifted to the other revelations in the Oculus and my face hardened.

"Why should I share anything with you?" I seethed.

"Come on, bro," cut in Kyle. "We're in this together."

"He's right," she agreed. "All three of us violated curfew. I'm not sure why that merits them sending a legion after us, though. They must be after you for attacking one of their own."

I bit my lip. Izzy didn't understand the magnitude of the situation. She'd just wanted to escape town along with many other annoyed players. Shirk being grounded. Grind during the lockdown. She was guilty of little more than smoking in the bathroom, but I'd just involved her in grand theft.

My anger smothered whatever guilt I had about dragging her into this.

"This wasn't what I wanted. All I asked for was a simple message to my little brother. It would've been nothing for you to let me use Everchat. Thirty players in all of Haven are on the white list. You're the only one I know."

Izzy's gaze dropped to the ground. I ignored the newly silent centurions. I stopped watching the trees. Shoving the truth into her smug face took precedence over everything. I guess something hit home because her next words lacked their usual superiority.

"Access to the outside isn't everything it's cracked up to be..." she said softly. Her face twisted and she couldn't continue.

Her reaction took me off guard. Where was the condescending banter? The confident smirk? It wasn't that I regretted my words, exactly—I hadn't said anything that crossed the line—but I *had* let my anger get the best of me. For a brief moment, my plight had totally bowled over hers. I reminded myself that we were all human here, even if our DNA was now ones and zeroes.

Tact. That was what I needed. A peace offering. "Izzy," I said.

My gentle tone attracted her attention and she looked up at me. "I know," I said. "I know what you did to yourself."

Her indigo eyes were shimmering, her lips quivering. Then her expression iced over into something scornful. Her face tensed and reddened. "You shouldn't have seen that!" she snapped.

I was taken aback. Before I could explain myself, she stormed off, deeper into the forest, pixie wings twitching in her wake.

"Izzy!"

She didn't stop. I cursed. That had been me being tactful. My attempt was sorely off the mark. I started away from the tree cover but Bandit jerked her head up, suddenly alert.

"Watch out!" screamed Kyle.

He rushed me and extended his shield. A sword came down hard and clanged against it, right beside my head. The soldier's weapon bounced from his grip. I remembered almost losing my spear the same way.

I may have been distracted, but I knew an opening when I saw one. The legionnaire moved to recover his sword as I sunk the blacksteel neatly between his ribs. It was a damaging blow, but not a lethal one. That came when Kyle produced his crossbow and fired two bolts into the man's neck. The new glass arrows popped like lightbulbs and injected the corrosive fluid directly into his bloodstream. The result was even better than with the poisoned sword. The combination of the deep puncture and the injection needle didn't waste a drop of the nasty black stuff. With the soldier reeling from the immediate damage and the hefty DoT, Kyle and I finished him off by hand.

We didn't have time to be disappointed by the lack of awarded experience. Our eyes shot to movement in the trees. To the left. The right. It wasn't a whole legion, but plenty of soldiers had broken formation to clear the forest. We'd be surrounded if we didn't move.

"Deeper," I said. "Let's go after her."

Bandit got the message. She hopped ahead and deftly passed through the brush, leading the way. Izzy wasn't in sight anymore. We were moving too fast to utilize my tracking proficiency, but the mountain bongo seemed capable of it. We rushed through the forest on her tail.

The soldiers were making sure to advance carefully now. They must've found their dead man and didn't want to suffer any more casualties. Despite their caution, they stayed on us. I was sure we'd escaped them once or twice only to discover more movement at our flank.

The worst part was, the forest was running out. I was familiar with this terrain and any minute now we were gonna find the far road in a large clearing. That open space would wipe out any advantage we had with guerilla warfare. We had to think of something. Nothing came but pounding footsteps.

The ground thickened with ivy and other plants, signaling the edge of the forest ahead. Kyle and I cleared the brush and almost bowled into Bandit, stopped with all four legs planted in a wide stance. Ten feet in front of her was Izzy, similarly alert, hands spread and ready for casting.

A gentle hill sloped down to the road at the bottom. The lower ground was flush with what must've been three thousand pagans. Imps, goblins, kobolds. Large ogres and trolls lumbered around on leashes. War elephants wore halters and bits and dragged wooden wagons full of weapons and supplies. In the distance, catapults and other siege engines lined up in wait.

Our merry band of adventurers hadn't gone unnoticed. We stood frozen in place as the eyes of an entire invading army fixed on us.

0360 Guild Wars

The pagan war machine sprawled below was maybe the most daunting thing I'd seen my entire life. Three-thousand-plus beasts ready for battle. Many were small and armed only with claws. Others were large and lumbering, partially tamed horrors out of storybooks. The vast majority of the horde was made up of lightly armored goblin warriors with swords and clubs. They weren't as well equipped as the Stronghold army, but their numbers dwarfed the legion that was after us. Hell, if Stronghold had a week to gather every last NPC it had for defense, the pagan army would still be two or three times its size.

The three of us squeezed close.

"They're readying an attack on the town," I explained dumbly.

"Impossible," said Izzy. "Pagans can't enter Stronghold."

I canted my head. "How many supposedly impossible things do you need to see today before you're convinced?"

"This isn't denial. The nine great cities of Haven are fortified against the pagans. Stronghold maintains the Eye of Orik. As long as it's under saintly control, the city's impregnable."

I winced. "Yeah... about that."

Her head swiveled to me. The curfew, the centurions, the pagans—I could see the wheels spinning in her head. I could see the dots connecting. Her eyes widened. "You!"

I shrugged. "Not me, per se, but—"

Stronghold soldiers brandishing weapons breached the tree cover behind us, forcing us further ahead. The legionnaires halted in their tracks, stunned at the vista before them. Several men became twenty. Then more. All froze and held trembling weapons before them.

Below, the pagan army was chattering. Murmurs washed over the dense population, sending shivers down my spine. A small force of goblins congregated at the foot of the hill. A greeting party. Their supreme confidence barely faltered at the sight of the additional Stronghold soldiers, even as the moments passed and nearly a hundred men emerged from the forest behind us. The pagan surprise might have been spoiled, but it was clear who was in the position of power. Sheer numbers don't lie.

Then there was us. A moody pixie mage, a struggling artisan screwup, an overcocky scout, and a mountain bongo, right at the meeting point between two clashing armies.

"It's okay," said Izzy. "This is actually good for us. The pagans hate Stronghold so much they'll focus on the legionnaires. Without significant pagan notoriety, they'll ignore us completely."

I slapped my hand to my face.

"Death to the pagan killers!" screamed a goblin captain, his eyes firmly entrenched on yours truly.

Izzy sighed. "You didn't..."

"Charge!" he cried. The greeting party rushed ahead.

The captain's lead was cut short when two crossbow bolts popped into his chest. He fell to the ground, writhing as the poison ate him alive from the inside.

The other fifty pagans didn't even notice. They scrambled up the hill with mad bloodlust. To my surprise, an arrow whizzed inches by my ear. We ducked as a barrage cut down the goblins heading the advance. A row of archers at the tree line nocked a second wave of projectiles into their bows.

Those soldiers had no love for the pagans, but we weren't exactly topping their friends lists either.

"Run!" I yelled, turning perpendicular to the battlefront and breaking into a sprint. My companions didn't need convincing to follow suit.

Arrows rushed over our previous position and took down more pagans. The injured and dead rolled down the hill, tripping up the reinforcements. A few agile goblins slalomed past the obstacles and bore down on the archers, but legionnaires broke through the line and slew them.

Already the battlefront was becoming a chaotic blur. Given a minute, the gentle slope would be utter chaos. With more Stronghold soldiers advancing and their greeting party in tatters, the pagan army began to shuffle nervously. The legionnaires were vastly outmanned but the pagans didn't know that for sure. The forest hid their true numbers. What had begun as a chance crossing of paths had morphed into a possible ambush. What if their entire invasion was in danger?

Abandoning the immediate onslaught, the goblins at the

bottom of the hill hurried into defensive formation. While not as sophisticated as the Romanesque legionnaires, it was frightening to see what amounted to a bunch of intelligently organized monsters.

With the two armies squaring off, our little party was almost forgotten. But the discipline I'd just been admiring only went so far. Stray pagans broke rank and chased after us. Imps were the first to arrive, but they weren't powerful enough to be a threat. I cut four down to cover our flank.

Several goblins led by another captain came our way. A [Kobold Handler] followed. He was diminutive too, same size but with fewer muscles and sharp edges. A softened gray goblin should've been less formidable, but the brute he was "handling" concerned me plenty.

The kobold held a chain leash that hooked around the metal collar of an [Ogre], as brutally massive and ugly as you'd expect. His oversized arms rippled with muscle, closed fists assisting his stride. The ground rumbled beneath him.

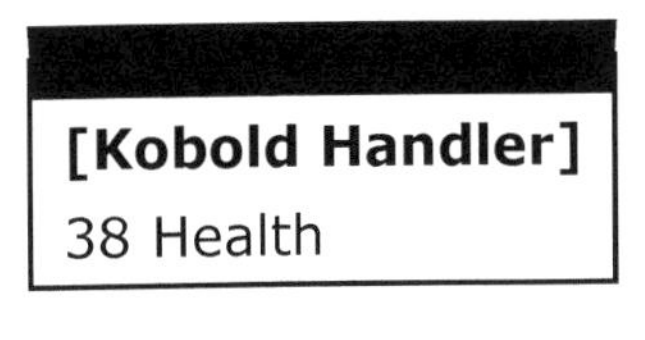

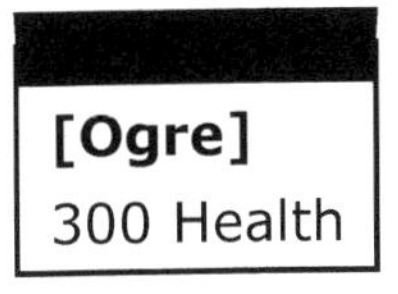

The only thing we had going for us was the high ground. With most of the pagans being shorter and having limited reach, it was a real advantage.

Izzy lanced icicles at stray imps attempting to cut off our escape ahead. Kyle and I squared off against the new greeting party. My roommate surprised me once again with his strategy. Instead of going for the biggest target, he fired his crossbow at the leader of the pack again. The goblin captain ducked behind his shield. One bolt missed and the other was blocked. Kyle cursed and hurried to reload.

I liked his general idea, but I didn't think neutralizing the captain would give us that great an advantage. It wasn't like sophisticated orders were needed to poke us with pointy things. Instead I decided to wreak a completely different kind of havoc.

I charged downhill and vaulted over the oncoming goblin warriors. I honed my spear on my target and triggered deadshot, raining down hard on the kobold handler. His health zeroed out and I judged him to be about as strong as your average goblin. I twirled to face the pagans in satisfaction.

My pleasure was short lived. A fist the size of a barrel rushed at me, readying to squash me like a sledgehammer. I triggered dash and sped sideways away from ground zero. The ogre pounded the corpse of his former master into the earth.

The three goblins were surrounded now. They traded glances uphill to Kyle and downhill to me. The captain had the protection of a shield, but his minions weren't similarly equipped. Kyle adjusted his strategy. While their backs were turned, he fired a bolt into each goblin warrior. The attacks didn't kill them but the ensuing DoT forced them into immediate panic and isolated the captain.

My skills were spent but I stabbed my spear into the goblin

anyway. The captain took damage but rolled away from the attack, charging uphill at Kyle who was still reloading. Out of nowhere, a large icicle impaled him. He tumbled down the hill, dead.

"Keep moving!" yelled Izzy. Ten dead imps littered the ground around her.

Kyle used his sword to finish off the writhing warriors and looted the goblins. The ground rumbled as the rabid ogre bore down on me again. Two fists with interweaved fingers hammered down as one. My upgraded crossblock met the blow. There was a loud impact and I crumpled to my back.

18 damage

Jeez. That was a relatively minor amount of health to lose considering the size of the attack, but *that was my block*. Even worse, pain flared in my wrists.

The ogre was only rebuffed momentarily. His eyes widened manically as he came at me again with both hands locked. Hey, if it ain't broke, don't fix it.

My dash hadn't recharged yet. I could barely raise my spear from my position. Losing confidence in the crossblock, I tried to roll away but tripped on the ground. I winced at my impending death.

Bandit charged ahead and planted four hooves protectively over me. The double-fisted blow struck her thick horns. Her head and neck shuddered under the impact, but the massive V staved off the blow. She'd saved my life.

The ogre roared and unclasped his hands, moving to grab the

mountain bongo. A cluster of five icicles pounded into him, one after the other. He stumbled and waved the nuisances away. I jumped to my feet as two corrosive bolts embedded into his chest. The disparate attacks further confused the monster. He spun sideways and spread his jaws, hot breath washing over us as he bellowed.

I took advantage of the hounded enemy. My deadshot had recharged, but I waited the extra second for the combo. I activated it together with dash and rocketed into him, plunging my blacksteel halfway into the ogre's midsection. Despite the deep penetration, the spear hadn't exited the wide monster's backside. I twisted to pull it out, but the ogre caught me with a vicious backhand that sent me tumbling down the hill.

For a few seconds my world was alternating sky and ground. My dizzying fall came to a stop at the bottom of the hill. I should've recovered quicker but my body was in agony. I coughed on the ground.

Although we were near the edge of the army and most eyes were on the legionnaires, several imps noticed I was an easy target. They converged on me. Without a better weapon, I menacingly drew my whittling knife and lunged.

Icicles rained down from above. These were much smaller but greater in number, harrying the imps. Only a few died, but the magic pushed them away from me. I punched half an inch of bladed death repeatedly into the closest imp like an inmate with a prison shank. The brutal attack gave me the space to climb to my feet. Bandit galloped past. I scooped her horn and jumped onto her back. We sped away faster than the imps could recover.

Above, Kyle had hit the ogre with more poisoned bolts but

was now backpedaling. The damned thing had a spear stuck in him and was still advancing. The red mob had half his health, making me wonder why we kept tangling with them. My roommate frantically shoved a second bolt into his crossbow.

I saw it happening again.

"Get out of there, Kyle!"

He fell backward as a large fist swiped over him. Kyle lay on his back but didn't let up. He took quick aim and emptied two more bolts into the beast. The corrosive DoT at this point was impressive, even with the minimized effectiveness of the stacked damage. That massive health bar was shrinking fast.

But nowhere near fast enough.

Izzy charged toward the towering thing. I could only guess she didn't have the juice for more icicles. I squeezed Bandit forward. She galloped straight at the ogre. We were still too far away. The beast leaned in to take a bite out of Kyle when Izzy's frost wand zipped through the air. The jagged end bit into the ogre's shoulder. He flinched away as expanding ice crusted over his arm and up his neck.

At the same time, Kyle produced his sword and plunged it upward into the ogre's sternum. The great monster listed, three weapons and numerous crossbow bolts protruding from his body.

Bandit lowered her head right as we were about to ram him. I leaned forward and grabbed the side of my spear.

Agility Check... Pass!

Two horns pounded into his belly as the blacksteel spear punched through his back. The deafening cry of the ogre choked into gurgles and he toppled to the ground in a cloud of dust.

Bandit and I took some damage from the collision and fell to the ground. For a moment I worried the heavy ogre would roll over her, but his body settled. Kyle and I scrambled to our feet. Bandit scurried out of the way as Izzy arrived. The three of us simultaneously yanked our weapons from the massive corpse and faced the bottom of the hill.

A group of seven converging goblins skidded in their tracks, slack-jawed. They eyed our bloody hands and faces. The gore on the weapons and the bodies littering the hill. They took special note of the dead behemoth beside us.

Until that moment I wasn't sure if goblins were smart. The seven of them turned and fled, disappearing within the safety of their army below.

Fire roared over me.

BWOOOOOM!

You have reached Level 5!

It pleased me to hear Kyle shriek in excitement.

"Holy shit! I leveled up! I'm level 3!"

I wasn't surprised.

Izzy rolled her eyes. "You'll never see level 4 if you don't keep moving. Now let's go."

She retreated from the army without seeing if we followed.

We sure as hell did.

0370 Night in the Woods

Despite all odds, we escaped the insanity of the pagan battle. We raced along the foothill until reaching the intersection of two paths: the outer road lining the hill and the road to Stronghold that divided the forest. Going against reason, we headed toward the city. Instead of moving in plain sight we skirted the tree line, but we were more concerned with speed than attracting notice. It was an unnecessary precaution. The forest road was empty.

Once the pagan threat was in our rearview, I scouted ahead and found a large part of the legion had remained behind in the tended lands. That complicated matters a bit, but it's not like we were planning on strolling back to Stronghold anyway. I backtracked and convinced everybody to head south through the lower forest.

Free of an immediate threat, our pace slowed. Izzy healed but since Kyle and I had leveled, we were already maxed out. We grew relaxed, if you could believe it. As we hit the bottom border of the trees and saw the darkening sky, we decided to set up a hidden camp within the tree line.

Funny that after our bold escape, battling, and all that running, the walls of Stronghold were still in view across the tended lands. Sometimes the best place to hide was close to home.

Izzy sat with her back against a log. She whittled a chunk of ice with her frost wand, her dour expression revealing her thoughts to be elsewhere. The elation of our freedom had worn off. I was level 5 and Izzy was still level 6. I should've been ecstatic. But seeing her like that troubled me. I couldn't focus enough to spend my new skill points.

Kyle dutifully went through his menus, thinking long and hard about his loadout. It had just been a day but he'd come a long way. Less spontaneous, more careful and measured. I trusted him with his skill selection and left him alone.

Bandit was curled into a ball, asleep.

After mulling over several ways to distract myself, I decided to bite the bullet and come clean. I trudged over to Izzy and plopped down beside her. Her indigo lips twisted but she didn't otherwise acknowledge me.

"Thanks for your help back there," I said. "You can do some real crowd control." It was a solid opener.

"Flattery won't get you anywhere," she answered. "I'm still wondering why I risked my life for you."

I cracked a smile. "Well, we appreciate it. Both of us."

Izzy didn't say anything. All her focus remained on her whittling project.

"Look, Izzy, I feel I owe you an explanation."

Her eyebrow twitched. "Figured that out all on your own, did you?"

"You're really not making this easy." I took a calming breath. "That's okay. I deserve it. Lucifer tricked me and I'm still not sure why."

Her eyes fixed on me. "Lucifer? As in, the head of the Fallen Angels?"

"You know about him?"

She snorted. "Of course I know him. He tried to recruit me once. He's a crazy hacker who wants to bring down the system."

I thought Kyle was preoccupied but he butted into the conversation. "Sounds like you two should've melded minds before you helped the dude bring down the city."

I gave him the side eye.

He ignored my glare and stood excitedly. "Okay, check it out," he said, presenting his hands upward.

I blinked. "What?"

"Me. Check me out."

I inspected his character info. "Level 3 Brewmaster. Pretty cool."

"I know, right?"

Izzy spoke sarcastically. "A class kit. You must be proud of yourself."

"I am actually," he said defensively. "Maybe I'll finally get some respect around town. Don't worry, though: I won't expect any from you."

She rolled her eyes. "You think you're ever going back to Stronghold? You really are clueless."

"That's not cool," I cut in. "You did seriously good back there, Kyle."

He hiked a shoulder. "Well, I *did* need to be saved."

"I did too. But don't sell yourself short. You stirred up some real chaos on the battlefield and pumped that ogre full of sick damage stacks. Don't kill yourself over one mistake. That's what we have each other for."

He seemed satisfied. Izzy had gone back to ice whittling. I wondered if she'd picked up the habit because of a starting whittling knife.

"Here's the deal, Izzy: Lucifer gave me a gem and dispatched the black dragon as a distraction so I could sneak into the Pantheon. I needed access to the Oculus. Only, once I was there, the glitched gem reverted into a recall rune and he teleported in and hacked some stuff. That's why I could initiate combat in town."

Both of them listened in rapt attention but I read their faces differently. Kyle admired the feat. Izzy just thought I was an idiot.

"So you threw the whole city into a frenzy and broke into the Pantheon," she said flatly. "I just wanted to go questing. Now I'm a fugitive. I should've let that gate lock you in. Then your roommate and I wouldn't even be on Stronghold's radar."

I felt bad about that part. "It's not my fault," I said weakly.

"No worries," said Kyle supportively. "Without you I'd still be a level 1 loser getting pushed around by Lash. I'm with you all the way, bro."

Izzy shook her head. It was obvious she wasn't used to being a team player.

"Look, Izzy, I didn't mean to steal the Eye. I didn't even know that was Lucifer's plan. I just wanted access to my records and on the Everchat white list. I just need to connect with my brother. To find out why I'm not really dead."

Izzy's wand paused mid stroke. "What?"

I sighed softly. "Lucifer told me I wasn't dead yet. My body—it's still alive."

"I told you, you can't trust that loon."

"It's true, though. I checked the personnel records myself. I'm listed as not deceased. I'm still hanging on after the car accident, and there's no way the saints are ever gonna give me access to Everchat like that."

She was too stunned to say anything. I kept talking, eager to shift the focus from my personal problems. "Lucifer revealed a lot. He explained the adaptive skill system to me. How we can make tweaks by trying new things. Evolve the game. He also admitted to being a hacker and leading the break-in that got the other Fallen Angels deleted. There's a lot about Haven that isn't quite as it seems. Even Lucifer himself. He's really an eight-year-old girl who died of cancer."

"Harsh," whispered Kyle. Izzy blinked wet eyes. He traded glances between her and me, slowly getting the picture. "I'm gonna go... check on... the status of..." He frowned. "Later." Kyle stomped through the brush and disappeared.

Izzy wiped her eyes. Her reaction wasn't about Lucifer, I knew, but about herself. Bringing up the personnel records, the knowledge of how certain people died—it was a reminder that I knew her dirty little secret.

"I swear, Izzy. I wasn't snooping. I saw it by accident."

She turned away. Instead of snapping this time, she nodded once.

I could imagine what she was thinking. Ending your life is

supposed to be final, isn't it? A way of escaping pain or isolation or countless other problems. In Izzy's case, that connection was never severed. And she'd had plenty of time to rethink her actions.

This time tact came in the form of keeping my mouth shut. The silence gave Izzy the room to bare her soul.

"I... I'm supposed to be privileged or something."

I nodded.

"My dad invested heavily in Haven's development. This sim literally wouldn't exist without the great Mr. Sakata. He wasn't a developer but it was all he cared about. Not Mom. Not me, of course. He never wanted a daughter. He was such a strict asshole, setting limits on us but never giving us time. It drove my mom to a breakdown. She had to be admitted to a hospital, and she never got better."

I pressed my lips together glumly. "My mother was admitted too."

She flicked her gaze at me. She was still angry at my intrusion, but I saw a flash of understanding. A truce. Family was often the difference between Heaven and Hell, not programming. Knowing we shared a tragic past was something neither of us would dream of debasing. It was a bitter foundation to build on.

"The troops are headed back to Stronghold," reported Kyle, returning to camp. "A bunch of soldiers came back from the pagan line." He paused morosely. "A bunch didn't. Whatever's left of the legion is packing it in."

"They gave up on us?" I asked.

"They're retreating," said Izzy.

"Why bother with us anymore?" agreed Kyle. "With a pagan army on the march, we're sure to be killed."

I shrugged. "I'm not worried about dying in the game."

"Don't you get it? The centurions have our home surrounded. They know who we are now. If we die out here, they capture us in there." He thrust his fingers toward the city walls. "The saints are spawn camping us, man. Just waiting for us to slip up. And even if *you* can fight in town, *we* can't. We'll be overwhelmed."

Izzy frowned. "It's not even that. The legion's leaving us alone because we don't matter anymore. Stronghold has bigger fish to fry." We shared a heavy glance. "You were right, Talon. Stronghold's readying for a siege."

Kyle's eyes widened. "You think?"

"You saw those siege engines. That army's not just waiting for an ambush. They're gathering. Storming the gates as soon as they're ready. Maybe before that, since their secret's out."

I understood Kyle's disbelief. Stronghold felt so invincible from within. Vast, impressive. The city was a font of knowledge and strength. "Is it possible the pagans could succeed in sacking the city?"

Izzy tucked her wand into her belt and tossed the ice sculpture at me. The cold bit into my hands as I turned it over. It was an oblong eye, its wide pupil staring at me.

"Don't you know your lore? The legend of the Nine?" she asked. "Nine pagan gods were defeated to tame the wild. Stronghold is one of nine great cities. That's no coincidence. Each beacon of civilization was built on the back of a fallen titan. Each city holds hostage a pagan artifact to protect its walls from intrusion. Protect its people from invasion. You've just helped strip Stronghold of its greatest defense."

I swallowed nervously.

"The city will be in chaos. Besieged until walls fall and buildings crumble. Homes will be sacked. Your roommate over there is half right and half wrong: The saints might very well be waiting for us to die so they can catch us, but it's also likely we'll have no homes left to respawn back to."

Her conclusion was terrifying. I wondered what happened when homes were destroyed. Surely we'd respawn somewhere else. Another town, maybe.

But that wasn't the point. I wasn't sure exactly what the saints were up to, but a lot of innocent players depended on Stronghold. I didn't wanna tear it all down because of my personal quest for justice.

"This is my fault," I said darkly. "I'm going to find Lucifer, and it's bound to be dangerous. You two should stay in hiding. I'll send Bandit back to find you when I reach the summit. Just in case I'm heading to a permanent death, I don't want you to suffer the same fate."

I moved to the edge of the forest and watched the retreating army light fires against the night sky. The mighty city gates opened, and what remained of the legion returned to a safety that was only temporary. As if to punctuate that note, a long, bellowing horn smothered the landscape with its deep cry. The wail scratched the sky and sent shivers through us.

The silence that followed was short-lived. Far in the distance, pagan war drums began to beat over the wind.

"It's starting," said Izzy, next to me now.

Kyle was there too. "Sorry to outvote you, bro, but we're

tagging along."

I turned to Izzy.

"You better send me a party invite," she said gruffly. She noted my smile. "Hey, it's not like I have anything better to do now. This land will be overrun with pagans soon enough."

Even Bandit was awake now. She bowed her head and licked my hand.

We faced the threatened city wearing grim masks. The tended lands were empty. The west gate was shut for good. I could only imagine the flurry of activity that was happening on the other side.

"Well," I said, "what are we waiting for then? It's time to go dance with the devil."

0380 Devil May Cry

The countryside shook to the beat of thousands of unseen boots. The pagans were on the far side of the barrier forest that lined the tended lands, but not for long. Either the army would pick its way through the forest or, more likely, take turns traveling through the bottleneck of the forest road. Stronghold still had time to prepare. We still had time to find Lucifer and recover the Eye.

We trekked into the open, noting the lack of random mobs in the area. In the real world I would've said the horde scared off all wildlife. In Haven, the pagan war machine must've been a strain on the servers. With an epic battle brewing, there was no processing power to spare for randos.

"Where are we headed?" asked Izzy.

I pointed to the mountain range that sprawled before us in the night sky. "Lucifer hangs out at the top of that mountain."

"Blind Man's Peak," she said. "Kind of ironic. You think the name would've tipped you off."

"In the land of the blind, the one-eyed man is king," joked Kyle.

I grumbled and opened my map. The land area was filled in

after my visit and had the telling label. "Now you tell me."

Kyle and Izzy traded a conspiratorial look.

"I once was blind, but now I see," she said.

"The blind leading the blind," he added.

"I get it already," I snapped. I swiped the map closed and attempted to change the subject. "Lucifer said it was a holy place."

Kyle thankfully backed off. He slapped my shoulder as a peace offering. "Good enough for me, bro."

We traveled light and fast, making much more headway than the army could manage. We crossed the southern plain without incident and headed up the foothills. The full moon lit the way.

As we marched, I studied my level 5 spear upgrades, one from the vanguard discipline, one from deadeye, and a couple from defender.

Power Slash
A vicious strike to your enemy, causing up to x2 damage at level 1.
Spirit Cost: 10
Cooldown: 20 seconds

Helmet Stun
A rattling strike that stuns opponents with armored heads.
Spirit Cost: 12
Cooldown: 40 seconds

Position Swap
Trade places with an engaged melee opponent.
Spirit Cost: 12
Cooldown: 40 seconds

Tornado Spin
A spinning attack that deals heavy damage and clears a 2-yard radius.
Spirit Cost: 22
Cooldown: 120 seconds

I still didn't want to spend points on the power slash when my deadshot was my damage move. The helmet stun seemed too specific so that left me with protection skills. Tornado spin was a good mix of offense and defense. Plus, it sounded badass. I picked it up.

As the mountain steepened, our progress slowed. Bandit picked out the most viable path. I had to close my menu and focus on the terrain. Kyle slipped a few times. It wasn't a cakewalk for Izzy and I, but we had better balance overall. Our new brewmaster leaned on the mountain bongo for support. At times we needed to take turns with her assistance as she went back and forth. It was tough going and we climbed in silence until we crested the peak.

Lucifer was up here all right. He was perched on his obelisk like a raven, black robes sparkling where the moonlight caught the reflective rune stitching.

Unfortunately, he wasn't alone. The pagans had beaten us to Blind Man's Peak. A contingent of twenty goblins and three boggarts circled the obelisk. I froze in terror as I recognized the unique enemy that had scooped out my insides in the tutorial. [Crowlat - Boggart Witch] stood with her two sisters, [Havlat] and [Somlat]. All three of them had empty eye cavities. They held a gleaming blood-red gemstone in their hands. The Eye of Orik.

"The land of the blind," I muttered under my breath.

I recalled the map without going into the menu. The mountains stretched over the landscape to the south of Stronghold. The river came from the high ground and led north to town. It was the water I was focused on. The raging current under the rope bridge. The waterfall. The boggarts were a holy people, and this was a holy place...

The tutorial had been close to here. So near to Stronghold all along.

"Intruderses!" cried a goblin on the perimeter. "Protect the Eye!"

The goblin contingent fanned out before us. I wasn't too worried about them at this point. They were hardy mobs, but our newly unified party could handle them. The boggarts were the problem. They stood seven feet tall and had terrible countenances. Blackened skin, patchy and scaly and bumpy in ways that made my stomach churn. Despite lacking eyes, Crowlat locked her head on me and hissed. Every weapon on the summit readied.

"Stand down!" cried Lucifer. He flung himself from the top of the obelisk, glided down with his fluttering robe, and hurried to stand between us and the pagans. "They're friends," he assured. He leaned close and lowered his voice. "Or they can be, if they pick the right side."

"Killerses!" wailed the goblins. "Tricksies!"

Crowlat stepped away from the ritual. Her breathing was coarse and grated my ears. Her voice scraped like gravel. I could feel her sensing my -405 faction rep. "The children speak true. This one is a pagan killer."

Even with the boggart towering over him, Lucifer was unmoved. He squared off against the grotesque creature and spoke calmly. "Many must die for the greater good. Was the Eye not worth the lives of a select few heroes?"

She sneered. "You claim him an asset to our cause?"

"He helped acquire the Eye."

The witch's eyeless gaze faced me, slightly off kilter. I was afraid she saw everything I was, but she snorted and spun away. "Leave them be," she ordered the goblins. Then shc returned to the ritual.

The goblins kicked and spat but backed away. Slightly. Their grips remained tight on their weapons, and they wisely maintained the line that barred us from the central obelisk and the ritual. I peeked around them, trying to determine what the boggarts were doing weaving in and out of the giant stone hand sculptures that acted as a shield.

Lucifer casually fell in line with us. "It is good to see you decided to join me."

"You lied to me," I spat.

He frowned. "I did nothing of the sort."

"You didn't tell me you were helping the pagans. Directing their actions."

"I do not direct the snake to swallow the mouse. This is the normal state of the wild. I merely choose to let it be." I scoffed while he continued. "You saw the proof. Your personnel file. You know what the saints did to you."

"What about the innocent people in Stronghold? You're gonna destroy the town."

Lucifer's hooded head turned toward the mighty gates in the distance. "Maybe I am," he admitted. "Maybe they deserve it."

Izzy pursed her lips. "So just because you can't have it, no one can? I happen to like that city."

The self-proclaimed devil regarded her. "So Isabel has found a life she tolerates. Big surprise it's an illusion. Pure escapism."

Her knuckles squeezed white around her frost wand. "Escape this, you prick."

I gently held back her arm before she attacked Lucifer. They had some limited history but I doubted she knew how powerful he was. None of us did, really. His mouth was the only portion of his face not hidden in shadow. A smug smile played across his lips as I contained the situation. For a moment I felt that, once again, I was doing his bidding.

"So what's your goal then?" I asked, trying to steer the conversation toward something productive. "Anarchy? You wanna bring down the very idea of order?"

"Would that be so terrible? The saints lied to all of us. They promised us Heaven but gave us an endless grind. We're nothing more than inmates of a digital prison, marking our days by their clock."

His words were twisted but they weren't false. "It's a second chance."

"It's a lie, Talon. Look at how they took advantage of your accident. Your physical body still lives but they mean to trap your soul."

I threw my hands up in exasperation. "Doesn't that mean they could be helping me? Maybe I'm in a hospital bed, strapped to machines. Maybe I'm in an induced coma for my own good. Maybe they're healing me."

Lucifer laughed. "If you believe that you're more gullible than I thought. This is about control, Talon. Incarceration. Haven's the world's newest for-profit prison system. We're its literal captive audience."

Kyle adjusted the weight of his crossbow. Lucifer tensed. I began to wonder how invincible the fallen angel really was. If my two companions wanted to have a go at him so bad, maybe that would give me a chance to nab the Eye.

I paced sideways, attempting to get a peek at the ritual.

"What's gonna happen?" I asked.

Lucifer canted his head. "Half the fun is finding out."

"I mean with that thing." I waved at the obelisk. The chanting boggarts. "What are they doing with the Eye?"

Lucifer swept his gaze off us for only a moment. "It's ceremonial. A symbol of their oppression. Now that they have it back, they honor the long lost Nine. Turn around, Talon. The real show is on the land that sprawls below."

The three of us faced the plains. The pagan flood was finally creeping into the tended lands. I'd been right about them moving through the road in shifts. Columns of beasts emerged from the pass and formed up, waiting for the next to fall into line beside them. The army was an undisciplined force. Their troop movements were slow and sloppy. With three thousand of them sure to take the field within the hour, I didn't think it made a difference.

The chanting witches reached a fever pitch. Crowlat held the red gemstone above her head and leaned against the obelisk. Havlat and Somlat each hugged a stone hand. Despite Lucifer's admonition, he was watching the ceremony along with me. Crowlat scraped dirt away from a small slot in the obelisk. The ground began to rumble.

"What's going on?" asked Kyle, raising his crossbow.

Bandit shuffled nervously at the edge of the summit. Even Lucifer appeared concerned. He strode past the goblins and approached the obelisk. I tried to as well but the goblins crossed into my path.

The ritual continued. The Eye was neatly placed into the obelisk slot. Crowlat pulled away victoriously. The other two boggarts extended their hands and she grabbed them, forming a chain. Stone hand to Havlat to Crowlat to Somlat to stone hand. The red Eye glowed brightly between them.

Our little instigator in the black robe with silver runes paused, afraid to approach the perch he so often favored.

Rocks cracked. It was an explosion at first, demolition deep in a mine. The giant stone hands trembled. I thought of the statue of Magnus Dragonrider crumbling, but this was different. The fingers shuddered. The boggarts looked up in wonder as they dutifully beckoned their master.

Why hadn't I seen this coming? This was not going to end well.

The two great stone hands immediately snapped shut, crushing Havlat and Somlat to pulp. Crowlat recoiled, her sister's limp hands still locked in hers.

The entire mountain shook now. The goblin ranks broke. Even the witch stumbled backward as Blind Man's Peak became an every-man-for-himself bounce house.

Stone hands pulled against the ground, seeming to drink the juices of the dead pagans. The obelisk cracked away and rose from the rock. Crowlat tumbled off the rising platform. Lucifer struggled to keep his footing. His hood fell away and his face, full and surprised, ran over the crowd. He froze as he looked at me, for the first time lacking a poetic observation.

The air around him glitched. His body pixelated and winked out. He was gone.

Holy crap, this was a problem even Lucifer himself didn't want to deal with.

"Uh, guys," I said, watching as fresh rock emerged from the

ground. "I don't think that lore about the Nine is just lore."

We backed away as boulders fell, crushing screaming goblins below. The stone hands spread out with giant arms and pulled a body away from the mountain, half rock and half living being. At the top of the protruding head was a large horn. The obelisk. A single eye in the center of the face was shut against the raining debris.

"Bros," said Kyle, "it's the one-eyed king."

We stood stunned as one of nine pagan titans, gods in their own right, was reborn right in front of our eyes.

0390 Shadow of the Colossus

Quest Update: **Unveil the Pagans**
Quest Type: Epic
Reward: Unknown
The boggart witches have used the Eye of Orik to resurrect the titan himself. He must be defeated.
1500 XP awarded

Great. Orik, in the flesh.

The cyclops had reddish skin, the color of rock. The top of his head was bald but a ring of hair skirted his crown, black strands held together with stone beads. For the moment, anyway, he was struggling to escape his mountain prison.

A distant screech tore the sky. The same black dragon that had attacked Stronghold swooped past the summit. Lucifer straddled its back. Holy crap. A modern-day dragon rider. Awe and fear fought for dominance of my body. For a moment I thought the fallen angel would do something heroic, but the dragon retreated to the horizon and disappeared from sight.

Just like the devil. Open up a can of worms and leave the consequences for everyone else.

A rush of ice magic dropped the temperature a few degrees. Huge ice spikes coalesced and fired at the titan. A giant... a one-eyed god... a cyclops. The magic crumbled against his rock flesh, so inconsequential that the attack was completely ignored.

Amidst the chaos, a goblin charged me with a sword. His reach was no match for mine. I impaled him on the end of my spear as others came at us. Kyle took out two more with his crossbow.

The cyclops might have been ignoring us, but Crowlat wasn't. Enraged by the death of her children, eerie red lasers darted from her hands. Kyle ducked behind his mirror shield and reflected the spell. The witch avoided the counterattack but the beam glanced the titan's side. He groaned and fixed on the source of the damage, head turning to the witch. The cyclops opened his large eye for the first time, a newborn struggling against the world. The monstrous eye cavity was a sickening void. Crowlat begged for mercy as a massive palm smashed her into the rock.

Izzy launched battle magic again without effect. "We can't take him on," she said. "He's too powerful."

I stared at the cyclops as I knocked another goblin away. The Eye. It all made sense now. Blind Man's Peak. The Eye of Orik. Orik was a god, a titan, blinded by the humans when his eye was stolen. When Stronghold was founded.

I just needed to get the Eye.

Large and hollow, the titan's eye socket was empty. Whatever true eye it once had was long gone. The horn that protruded from his forehead was a different story. At its tip was the red artifact that had been stored in Stronghold's tabernacle for centuries. It shone with demonic fire. If video game bosses and weak spots had taught me anything at all, this was the key to stopping Orik.

I charged through the pagan line, slaloming between flashing swords and clubs.

"What are you doing?" screamed Kyle.

Izzy's ice magic backed me up, taking out another goblin moving to intercept me. The ground split below us.

Agility Check...
Pass!

I deftly maneuvered over a chasm as a pagan fell to his death. Two corrosive bolts popped against the titan's skin. The damage was infinitesimal, but the great cyclops turned his head toward us.

[Orik]
Unique Pagan God
100000 Health

We finally had the god's attention.

He was only partially free from the mountain. Still he

towered twenty feet above us. If ever I could access the Eye, it was now.

"Give me a platform!" I shouted to Izzy.

Her head swiveled along my path to the titan. Her face tensed when she saw what I was going for. "You're crazy," she replied. "But I like crazy." A sheet of ice fired from her hands and formed its own obelisk on the ground.

I rapped a goblin on the head and jumped to his shoulders. Before he fell, I hopped from him to the top of the obelisk. Orik was just noticing me now, getting nearer. His hand reached forward, ready to squeeze me in its grip.

Instead of avoiding the incoming attack, I leaped toward it. My spear dug into the stone hand and I triggered vault, pushing higher and gaining distance. I swung the spear around and lined up a deadshot, dashing ahead to the confused giant. Twenty feet above the summit, I sped toward his weak spot. My jaw tightened. My knuckles whitened against the spear's shaft. The blacksteel tip converged on its mark, pinpointing the comparatively tiny gemstone on Orik's horn.

A foot away from the target, a barrier of ruby energy flared into life. The impact sounded like a symphony of clinking wine glasses.

The blacksteel snapped. The shaft drove forward and splintered to pieces. Without the spear to halt my momentum, I barreled through the protective energy and slammed into Orik's eyeless face. I tumbled downward and bounced on the rock below, instantly losing a third of my health in fall damage.

> Break!
> Your leg is broken. You cannot move unassisted until it is fixed.

I curled into a ball in pain. True pain. I had only the vaguest sense that a giant was above me. It was all I could do to keep from passing out.

Bandit rushed to my aid. As Orik moved to crush me, two bolts of corrosive acid glanced off his hand. It slowed the god enough for Bandit to scoop me up. I chugged a healing potion as she did. The regenerative effect took a full 30 seconds, and my broken leg wouldn't be fixed until that time elapsed.

We regrouped with Kyle and Izzy. Orik struggled to free himself from the ancient rock, wildly crushing anything that came close. The few remaining goblins scattered, putting their own lives ahead of killing us.

"Let's get out of here already," said Kyle.

And I thought he was the reckless one.

I nodded.

Izzy flashed a trail of ice down the edge of the steep summit. "I always hated Slip'n Slide," she muttered. She jumped first, speeding down the slope. Kyle followed and I pushed Bandit to charge forward as well. The bongo slid down ungracefully, spinning on her back.

Izzy's slide of sheet-ice extended as she descended. I was impressed by her concentration. So this was what Iceman felt like. As soon as the slope leveled off halfway down the mountain, we regained our feet.

Amidst the screams above, a lone goblin tumbled down the rocks and landed beside us in a heap. His corpse was limp and battered, with joints bent at odd angles. Without Izzy, that could've been us.

"What now?" she asked. "We can't take that thing."

I waited for my broken leg to wear off and warily eyed the gathering army below us. Literally between a rock and a hard place. Maybe it was finally time to admit we needed help.

The walls of Stronghold seemed stout and invincible. Even without the Eye—with the horde at its doorstep—the city appeared impenetrable. The titan was a whole different story. The white robes were the only people who might have a plan.

"We need to get back to the city," I said. "We need to set up a meeting with the white robes."

Izzy grimaced. "The quest update didn't say anything about involving the saints."

"Yeah, well the quest update didn't say anything about a hundred-freaking-thousand health either."

Above us, the cyclops roared and the mountain shook.

0400 Time Crisis

We scurried down the foothills. I wasn't sure how long rocky-mountain-god births took, but Orik was still preoccupied. The pagan army, however, was already in place in the tended lands.

Mighty and sprawling, the horde had taken notice of recent developments. They waved fists and beat chests to salute Blind Man's Peak. Their drums fell in rhythm to the shaking mountain. Their horns blared every time the titan roared. They were already cheering their victory.

"It's madness out here," said Izzy.

"Much worse than what's going on in town," I pointed out.

"Except, in case you didn't notice, everyone else is headed there as well."

Kyle nodded. "No matter which way you slice it, it's a bad idea to go back."

"I can't believe I agree with the frat boy," she muttered. Kyle scowled her way.

"I thought you said you liked that town," I said. "Was Lucifer right about you? That you finally found a life you wanted to live?"

She worked her jaw and watched the distant city. I could tell she didn't like seeing it threatened. "What happened to you back there?" she asked.

I paused uncertainly.

"You were gonna let that giant squash you," she explained.

"My leg was broken. I couldn't move."

"It's more than that. It wasn't just your movement being negated. You were rolling on the floor. What happened?"

I sighed. "Lucifer turned off my pain filter. Every time I take damage, I feel it like it's real."

Their breaths momentarily caught in their throats.

"And you're still willing to fight Orik?" she asked. "His army?"

I shrugged weakly. What could I say?

"I don't know," said Kyle. "Realistically, what could we hope to do?"

"We need to warn the city. Tell the people what we know. Help them defend Stronghold."

Izzy's face darkened.

"Or we could cut our losses," offered Kyle. "That town never did me any favors. We could cut our losses and head east. There's a fishing city called Shorehome that way. I've never been high enough level to visit until now. I just made 4. We could make that our new home."

Kyle's suggestion was cold and heartless, but it was also practical. I thought it unlike him. Then I realized he'd been taking my cautionary advice to heart.

The detached surgery of Kyle's idea seemed to warn Izzy off that line of thinking. She wasn't used to backing away from a fight, perhaps, but I thought it was something else. Maybe she considered Stronghold worth saving.

"That's an even worse option," she said reluctantly. "I'll fight. But only if we're smart about it. We need guarantees the white robes won't turn on us."

I snorted. "What are we supposed to do? Just ask the saints for a powwow—" I paused as I realized the sheer simplicity of it all. I opened my menu and hit the green help button. Seconds later, a man popped in.

"Hello, sir. It is good to see the seven suns of Ejiya are still shining upon you."

I massaged my temples and took a measured breath. Varnu Johnson stood at full attention in his scarlet military getup.

"Varnu, we need to talk to Saint Peter right away. It's an emergency."

"Of course it is, sir. I am equipped to handle any emergencies you encounter."

"No, seriously. The Eye has been reunited with Orik. He's tearing himself out of the mountain as we speak. Stronghold will be facing more than a pagan horde."

"By the eight arms of Stranja, that sounds serious."

"It is." I waited but the minimum-wage tech-support employee just blinked at me. "What are you doing?" I asked impatiently.

"Besides enjoying Texas french fry vindaloo? I am assisting with your emergency, sir."

"How?"

Varnu was taken aback. "Well, you see, I am filing a report." He mimed emphatic typing with his hands.

"That's not good enough, Varnu. We need to talk to Saint

Peter."

"Impossible. Please to be describing your emergency once more."

I rolled my eyes. "You're just stalling."

"Describing sources of stress will help residents feel like their opinions are relevant. Oh dear, I don't think I was supposed to read that out loud."

"Never mind," I snapped, and waved the tech support away. Varnu disappeared and left me in a foul mood. "This is useless. I'm blocked. One of you needs to do it."

Kyle arched his eyebrow at me. "You serious, bro? The saints don't answer personal calls for help past the first few days. They settle new residents in but have more important duties. They pass *everyone* off to tech support." Kyle thought hard about the problem. "What about you?" he asked Izzy. "You're the Haven VIP. You have access to the white robes."

She looked away, annoyed by the implication. "It's my living father that has the privilege. Not me in here. Everchat's for his sake, not mine. I hate talking to him." She frowned. "That's why I killed myself in the first place. Talking to him is the only part of Haven I hate. I skip it when I can, but I'm forced to be social once in a while."

Kyle was awkwardly silent. When Izzy realized he hadn't known about her death and she had just revealed the details, her face flushed.

"Wait, wait," I said, trying to keep everyone from each other's throats. "I have another idea."

I opened my menu again. The green help button was still active. Why not? With outsourced tech support playing interference, there was no reason to impede access. This time however, I clicked the other button. The little red spider icon.

Izzy and Kyle looked over my shoulder at the floating screen.

"You're gonna file a bug report?" she asked skeptically.

"It's worth a shot." I began filling in the form.

WHAT IS YOUR ISSUE?
Ancient god has risen from the dead to destroy all life.

ON A SCALE OF 1-5, HOW WOULD YOU RATE THE SEVERITY OF THIS ISSUE?
99999

PLEASE SPECIFY IN EXPLICIT STEPS HOW TO REPRODUCE THIS ISSUE.
Uh...
1) Get tricked by devil into stealing Eye of Orik.
2) Give gemstone to eyeless boggart witches.
3) Run like hell.

I sighed. I'd thought the idea was viable, but reading the generic form questions deflated me. I submitted the bug report and swiped my menu away.

THANK YOU FOR YOUR SUBMISSION! YOUR VIGILANCE HELPS MAKE HAVEN A BETTER EXPERIENCE FOR ALL RESIDENTS!

"Who knows when they'll read that," muttered Kyle.

"Or if," added Izzy.

The brewmaster put his hands on his hips. "So we have to run, then."

She scoffed. "Yes, let's all listen to the fuckup."

"Hey, maybe we both killed ourselves, but at least with me it was an accident."

Izzy's indigo lips twisted. She lifted her frost wand, glowing icy blue. "I can show you what it's like when it's *not* an accident."

"Stop it!" I thrust my hands out to separate them. "You guys are acting like slaves to your previous lives." I stared at each of them hard. "We're in Haven now, aren't we? This isn't about the past. It isn't about giving up or goofing off. It's about that city and that army and that one-eyed abomination. It's about the three of us and Bandit."

Their expressions didn't share my camaraderie. I had to get more personal.

"Izzy, stop denying it. Lucifer was right when he said you found something you liked. You're the best player in town. You spend your free time showing off in the Arena and putting on juggling shows. You like being good. You like the attention it brings. But he was also right about you being an escapist. You avoid Everchat. You do everything solo. You act like you wouldn't care if the whole world was on fire. It's time to stop living in denial and embrace who you are. Who you want to be."

Her eyes were fixed on Kyle, but her chest heaved as she took manic breaths. He smirked at my admonition of her.

"And Kyle, your problem's not too different. You accept this world, sure, but only as long as the brew is pouring and the entertainment's ongoing. You haven't had success until you started taking this seriously, right? Open your eyes, man. *This* means something. Our party, our city, our world. This is reality, not fantasy."

His face soured. I knew he'd started to see the light already. He just wasn't used to it yet.

"The past is the past, guys. Can we please deal with the future?"

Their faces remained firm, neither wanting to back down before the other. I hissed.

"Fine, I'm going back. There're a lot of people who need our help. If you wanna stay here and kill each other, be my guest."

I stomped away toward town, Bandit in tow. It was fifty-fifty whether crashing icicles or crossbow bolts would fill the void behind me, but only silence followed. After a minute of marching, Izzy and Kyle fell in step beside me, glowering. I tried to hide my smile.

0410 Bastion

Instead of plowing north to the field where the pagans gathered, we headed east until we were directly south of Stronghold. Our approach was likely to go unnoticed in the night. Even if we were spotted, the entire army wouldn't drop their preparations to go after us. Goblins and imps aren't the model of discipline but they're not a pack of rabid dogs either. As their final siege engines funneled in from the forest road and took up the rear, the army waited with one eye on town and another on their awakened god.

Orik bellowed at the summit as the mountain birthed him. Boulders larger than me tumbled down the cliff side. Anyone within a hundred miles would know something was horribly wrong.

If we couldn't get behind Stronghold's walls, we wouldn't survive the hour.

"So what's the bright idea?" asked Izzy.

Kyle kicked a stone into the river. It was the same one that led into Stronghold, and as far east as we could go without crossing. "Please tell me you don't expect us to knock."

I chewed my lip. Knocking beat the alternatives. We wanted

in and we wanted the attention of the saints. Walking right up to the gate would accomplish both tasks. Assuming they opened the doors for us.

Then again, Stronghold's legions were readying for battle. The west gate was likely barricaded—the heaviest fortified position in the town. If the centurions did grant admittance, there was no guarantee they'd give us an audience with the white robes. After our little show earlier, they might think it more prudent to simply tear us apart.

"Keep moving," I told them. "I'm gonna scout ahead."

I whistled and Bandit cantered up. I hopped on her back and charged downriver. She was happy to open up to top speed. Her hooves beat against the grass and we made good time. I first looked for a place to cross the water—Stronghold's east gate should be an easier problem—except the river outside the city wasn't nicely tamed by stone walls. It was wild and jagged white water rushing from the mountains. Much more treacherous than the smooth flow inside. Bandit galloped all the way up to where the river fed underneath Stronghold's towering stone walls.

An underground tunnel. Thick steel bars gated the passage closed. A rusted lock mechanism stood above the current. That was our way in.

My smile was short lived.

A gargantuan cry rang out from the top of the summit. Orik was free. Every single pagan on the battlefield hollered in response. The war cries turned the air and wilted the grass. When the voices finally died down, the drum beats and horns began a steady rhythm.

The army marched and the earth shook. The pagans were on the move.

I jumped on Bandit's back and made for my party. Kyle and Izzy had picked up their pace. As they raced past me, Bandit turned in a tight loop and followed.

"The river gate," I called above the din. "We need to break in with your corrosive."

Kyle nodded as he ran, watching the hordes of goblins bearing down on us, far across the tended land but covering ground quickly. I had no doubt we'd beat them to the wall. The pertinent worry was whether or not we'd be able to breach it in time.

We reached the wall as Stronghold's horns sounded. These weren't curved pagan horns fashioned from gourds. This was a brass choir of trumpets performing an upbeat tempo. The goblin army was halfway across the plains now. The city opened fire.

Arrows arced high into the sky. What we'd seen before of Stronghold's archers was a pale comparison. This wasn't a hasty pursuit; it was carefully prepared city defense. The mass of arrows blackened out the moon for a still moment before raining down on the horde with gut-wrenching effect. Imps and goblins collapsed under the onslaught. Heavy arrows harried larger creatures.

I'd expected the converging front to panic. To slow and stumble. Instead, the fallen were trampled beneath their fellow soldiers. The horde was an unstoppable mass now, feeding on bloodlust that had been pent up for hundreds of years.

The pagans were finally storming Stronghold. Even death itself couldn't stem the tide.

"I think this will work," hurried Kyle. He dropped into the water, pressed against the river gate by the incoming current. He scaled sideways to the lock and squeezed a crossbow bolt inside its mechanism, snapping off the tip and pouring acid into its guts. "That should do it." He produced his hammer and went to work. The banging sounds were lost in the clamor of battle. Unfortunately, the hammering didn't get anywhere.

"Move aside," said Izzy.

Kyle edged sideways along the gate to clear the way. Izzy kneeled by the river and splashed water onto the lock. Her wand came up and froze the water. It frosted from within and grew outward like a crust. Then she formed an icicle in her palm and flung it at the lock.

The entire gate rang with the impact. Still, it held closed.

"That's one strong lock," I noted.

Kyle placed a hand in the air, asking for a moment. "Dudes, just leave it up to Brewmaster Kyle." He reached into his pouch and pulled out something like his old grenades, except this time the fluid inside was a ruddy yellow. He took another step along the gate, lined up his aim, and tossed it at the lock.

A fiery explosion engulfed the opening. Izzy and I shielded our eyes. Kyle, too close, lost a third of his health. The blast swung the gate open against the current, with him still clinging to the heavy bars.

"It worked," said Izzy, betraying her shock.

Kyle smiled in a daze, soot on his face. "All hail the brewmaster."

We helped him into the tunnel. "You too, Bandit," I said. "It's too dangerous out here." The wild girl didn't want anything to do with the town but the trembling fields and mountain slopes weren't exactly comforting either. She plopped into the river. I pulled her by a horn to guide her safely inside. As I slammed the heavy steel gate shut, I took one last look at Blind Man's Peak.

Orik was descending the mountain.

0420 Team Fortress

We needed some hacks to get the gate closed again. The explosion had flung a crossbar open. We reaffixed it after only minor repair. The lock was the bigger problem. It was completely wrecked. Even though it was now worthless, we set it up so it looked like it held fast. Izzy froze the fractured pieces together with magic. It wouldn't keep the horde out but, with any luck, they wouldn't think to check the river gate.

"What was that?" I asked Kyle, referring to the explosion.

"I told you. I'm a brewmaster now. Flame gel is my new skill branch. I'm gonna be a badass battle alchemist, whipping up potions and concoctions to help out the party. I think I'm gonna like being an artisan."

I clapped his back and chuckled. "Brewmaster Kyle."

He nodded proudly. "The brewery part will take some work."

A short swim through the tunnel led us to the other side of the sturdy city wall. The lock on the inner gate cracked with only the corrosive. We crawled to dry land and found ourselves back in Oldtown. The empty ruins sprawled before us. It wasn't a huge neighborhood. Quaint almost, to imagine the town had once been so small. Of course, there was nothing quaint about the neighborhood's central monument.

Dragonperch loomed a short distance downriver. The half-crumbled statue on the roof foreshadowed the fate of the entire city. If only we had great heroes like that still alive. Instead their monuments flaked away to dust while old gods emerged from the land.

"That's our destination," I said. We navigated over the rubble of toppled buildings.

"I don't think we need to hide," said Izzy.

Oldtown was abandoned, as always, but across the river was Hillside and the Foot farther north. Everything was a mad scramble in those residential areas. Every single player knew a pagan army was descending on them. Even the watchmen marching by in the distance weren't paying attention to us.

"Maybe not." I scurried down the brickwork along the river's edge and followed the ledge to the underground grotto. Bandit traversed the thin platform easier than any of us. Inside, we could finally take a minute to relax. I immediately recovered the bit key and slipped it into my inventory.

"How'd you find this?" asked Izzy reverently. She studied the paintings and statues adorning the secret place.

I hit up the antique weapon rack and compared the available spears. They were all noob weapons, for display only. I grabbed the best one and led the others to the inner tower door.

"What do you say? Can the dual terrors of fire and ice break into Dragonperch?"

Izzy approached the barred door leading inside the tower proper. "No way. This is warded tight. Same as the outer doors." She turned to us. "I've tried them before. Many times.

Absolutely no way into Dragonperch. I promise you."

I cursed and thought about the many threats headed our way. It was past midnight. That marked the end of my first day in Haven. It had been an incredible experience so far, but hindsight revealed just how much I'd failed at. How much I still didn't know. Without a safe zone I couldn't contact Derek, but we had more pressing concerns. Knowledge about the pagans or the Eye of Orik was paramount.

I thought of the texts I'd seen in the Pantheon portico.

"I really wish we could get into the tower. There's supposed to be a great library in here, right? Maybe we can find something to help against the Nine. I'd rather approach Saint Peter with an idea instead of my hands in my pockets."

"You don't need an ancient tower for lore," said Izzy. "You just need ancient texts."

"Yeah, well, I'm new and Kyle doesn't take Haven history too seriously. What's your excuse?"

"Excuse?" Izzy scoffed. "You're in luck. I specialize."

A very large tome blinked into her arms. It was a dusty hardbound book a foot and a half tall that must've had thousands of pages and weighed as much as one of the bricks that built this tower. Kyle and I peeked over Izzy's shoulder as she flipped it open. She typed into a search bar and the animated pages flapped. A scroll bar along the bottom of the display sped to the middle of the book. When Izzy noticed us reading along, she increased the size of the text.

Ancient, dusty tomes in the digital age. I'd hate to see what they could pack into the Necronomicon.

"Okay," she said, "here we go." She scanned down the page

and recited relevant snippets. "Orik symbolizes vision... Not of our futures but of our nature... Eyes are the windows to the soul."

Kyle chortled. "And people wonder why I don't take this stuff seriously," he said under his breath.

"I can't believe I'm agreeing with him," I muttered, "but he kinda has a point. *That's* the lore? Haven might have incredible programmers but it looks like they skimped in the writing department."

"Just a game," said Kyle. I'd heard that same concession many times during my short-lived game dev career.

Izzy held her fingers up for silence. "There's more: Bodies petrify. Souls live forever."

I arched an eyebrow, unimpressed.

"Lots of mentions of souls in here, actually. The soul inherent. The captured soul. The sleeping soul." She turned a page as she skimmed the lore book. "A soulstone," she said, eyes aflash. "That's what the Eye of Orik is. It's his soulstone." She lifted her gaze from the book. "If we get that—"

"We petrify Orik," finished Kyle. "And his soul lives on in the stone."

"Come on, guys," I interjected. "I thought that much was obvious." They glanced at me. "What, hasn't anyone played an RPG before?"

They both stared blankly, making it clear that they hadn't.

I sighed patiently. "Look, placing the gemstone into the obelisk is what woke the titan up. It's an obvious weak spot. Thing is, I tried stripping Orik of the Eye back at the summit. It shattered my blacksteel spear to shreds. Somehow I doubt this"—I held up the salvaged grotto weapon—"will fare any better. That soulstone is protected somehow. A barrier of ruby magic. We need to find a way to get past it."

"A ruby barrier," repeated Izzy thoughtfully. "I'll look for references to it."

Before she could find anything, a global town notification appeared before us.

City Alert:
Kablammy Games would like to announce a special beta event. The pagan horde approaches! Please participate in the load test by utilizing whatever abilities you have to stunt the attack. Enjoy yourselves for the next half hour. In exactly thirty minutes, Haven will shut down and undergo a full server wipe. See you after the reboot!

We traded grave looks. The reboot was one solution to our current plethora of juggled problems. It was also a flaming bazooka among bowling pins. Checkmate, overkill, and a deus ex machina all in one. Everything—the theft of the Eye, the pagan horde, Orik's awakening—it was all going away.

I suddenly couldn't breathe. I gasped and fell to my knees. Kyle caught me and propped me up.

"You okay, bro?"

I blinked, stunned. Words didn't come.

Literally everything I'd been doing was a lie. Everything I'd worked for, discovered, achieved—it was all just a flip of a switch away from being rebooted. My first life was in question but my second one already had a timer on it. 29 minutes and counting. I noted the time on the clock. The reset was happening at 1 a.m.

"It's okay," said Izzy, her voice stale. "We'll still be here. We'll just be reset. It's not like we haven't gone through countless wipes already."

"I haven't," I breathed.

"It's not that big a deal. You just started today. That's not a lot of progress to make up."

I thought of the pack rats and the crowns we'd achieved. The run-in with the pagan wagon. The encounter with Lucifer. It was all meaningless.

Despite Izzy's cool reasoning, I could tell she didn't like the thought of a reboot. Kyle was taking the news worse. He'd just become a brewmaster. No way in hell he wanted a wipe. Only Bandit was unperturbed. She curled up into a ball in the corner and rested her eyes.

"I don't want a reboot," I said.

"It's a beta test," replied Izzy. "Part of the game."

Lucifer's sentiment came to me. This wasn't a mere game.

"Is that how you wanna live?" I asked. "Constantly being reset?"

"It won't happen once Haven goes public."

"So what, do we give up everything we've worked for? Our levels. Our gear. What about Bandit? She's an NPC. I'll lose her forever."

The napping bongo's ear twitched at the mention of her name.

"What about my use of skills and combat in town? Will I get that back? You think once everything resets they're gonna let me gain that power again?"

Their faces reflected my dark mood. They also wore an expression I didn't: resignation. They'd lived through wipes before. To them, it was part of the game. Conditioned submission. I wasn't ready to stand for that.

"Besides," I added, "some of us might be flagged for deletion."

That caught their attention.

"It's like Kyle said. If they reboot us, we respawn back at our homes. We'll start the new game at level 1, surrounded, without any chance of defending ourselves."

My companions took that in silently. The gravity of the situation was clear to them. Maybe it was paranoid talk, but it was plausible paranoid talk. If Haven was reset, we'd be at the mercy of the saints. For now, anyway, we were safe. Relatively. Excluding the wrath of one-eyed mountain gods.

"Maybe the wipe cancels our sins," offered Kyle. "Only angels can delete players, right? And only when Haven itself is at risk. After a wipe, the game's safe so the angels don't care about us."

"And the white robes?" asked Izzy.

He shook his head. "The saints don't have that power. Our profiles are triple-encrypted and always on the move. Only the game itself can process through that."

I shut my eyes in realization. "The beta flags," I muttered. "We're not safe. No one is. As a temporary condition of the beta, none of our profiles are being stored on the redundant servers. None of us are permanent. That's why the wipes are even possible."

Kyle's brow furrowed. "If we're not stored on the permanent servers then..."

"We can be permanently deleted," I finished.

His jaw hung open like he'd forgotten how to close his mouth.

"They wouldn't delete me," hedged Izzy. "My father—"

"They need to protect the game. Are you willing to take the chance you're so important?"

"I'm not important. *He* is. They'll reset the game to keep things running smoothly, and I'll be here, same as always." The pixie crossed her arms and paced to the corner. Somehow she'd made being a survivor sound like a bad thing. Before I could think of something to say, Kyle spoke.

"You really hate your dad, don't you?"

I glared at him and shook my head in warning. He didn't get the message.

"What if the game *didn't* run smoothly?"

Izzy kept her back to us.

"Think about it," he said. "You like Stronghold. You like Haven. What you *don't* like is going along with your father's orders."

She zeroed in on him with a glare. I couldn't believe he was pushing this, after everything. He continued without thought or worry. Or tact.

"You quest every day. Advance. Avoid Everchat whenever possible, but you're forced into it sometimes. Forced to talk to him." Izzy's lavender skin flushed at his words. He kept piling it on. "Your savior. Your protector."

"Kyle," I mumbled, "ease up."

"Obeying like a good little daughter," he pressed.

"That's enough, Kyle."

My words came out angry, a harsh note after harsher words. A moment of uncomfortable silence thankfully followed. Kyle and Izzy stared each other down, him casual, her tensed and ready to spring. She was practically fuming, but at least they were both quiet.

And then, everything I'd been teaching Kyle about self-preservation went out the window. He opened his big mouth again.

"What if you weren't daddy's good little girl anymore?" he asked.

Izzy lunged at him. I skidded between them, flinching in anticipation of the oncoming hurt.

City Alert:

The pagans are at the gates!

Stronghold is under threat. All residents may engage in combat. While within the walls, all watchman and residents are immune to friendly fire.

I hastily swiped away the notification. It was only like the fifth most tense thing going on right now. I kept my focus on Izzy, who surprised me.

The pixie smirked.

"I can save Stronghold," she said with crooked lips. "But I'll live in the Haven I wanna live in."

Between the two of them, I was stunned. Izzy was more determined than I'd ever seen her and Kyle flashed a smug smile. They actually looked like they were on the same side.

"I'm in," said Izzy. "You wanna take on the pagans, fight the reboot, defy the saints? Whatever. I'm in for it all."

0430 Call of Duty

A huge collision of rock and mortar shook the city. We emerged from the underground grotto to check the damage. A large stone had impacted a barren patch of Oldtown. Nothing was left but rubble and a crater, which was only slightly worse than what was there before. As we surveyed the scene, the wall closer to the gate shuddered as well. That catapult had hit its mark.

My gaze strafed along the great wall to the west gate. A flurry of activity defended the most vulnerable entry to Stronghold. The heavy wooden doors were shut and barred with reinforced backing. A hundred soldiers lined the battlements with bows and crossbows and heavier anti-siege weapons. A hundred more gathered below, ready to take up arms as needed.

Across the river, Hillside and the Foot were just as hectic. Players ran around announcing an apocalypse party, building crafts and casting spells in town, spending all their silver. They'd essentially been given a free pass: Do whatever you want because everything's resetting in half an hour.

I remembered playing the Ultima Online beta test years ago. It was a rudimentary game compared to Haven. In its last hours, before our characters were reset for the public release, the devs spawned demon after demon to wreak havoc. Players charged to their deaths. Others looted and pillaged and hoarded, grasping for riches they could never spend. Some tightly bonded groups clung together for support and survived until the gates of hell opened and so many demons entered the world that the servers crashed under the load.

What I saw now wasn't much different.

"Are we really gonna fight?" asked Kyle, taking in the madness. Despite the apocalypse party, about half the residents took the pagan threat seriously and prepared for combat.

"You tell me," I answered. "I can't keep asking you to stick your neck out for me."

"You kidding, bro? I've never been level 4 before. Hell, I'm Brewmaster Kyle now. I'll be damned if I let the white robes take that away from me."

I nodded. "Then we fight."

The three of us stood there, hands on hips, frowning.

Izzy's eyebrow shot up. "I kinda thought this would be a more dramatic moment."

Kyle looked around. "Until the pagans tear the gate down, there's no one to actually fight."

I gritted my teeth. "Not standing here, there isn't."

We hurried along the river to the west gate thoroughfare. Stronghold was in chaos. The watchmen were well disciplined, but they were having trouble controlling the players who were fifty shades from nervous to brave. People wanted to run. They wanted to charge through the gates. The atmosphere was worried and harried and frenetic all at once. It was utter lunacy.

On the plus side, it was easy for three fugitives to move

around. Not that we went unnoticed, exactly. Izzy commanded her usual gravitas. Players pointed to me and whispered. Plenty of residents had caught on that we'd snuck back into the city, but their sentiment was welcoming. We were Bonnie and Clydes among our people.

"Hey, guys," said Kyle. "We should gear up before things get nasty."

"Now?" I asked.

"He's right," said Izzy. "I need components."

"And I need more ammo," he said. "The clock cycled past midnight. It's a new day. My new glasswork and brew limits are reset. I'm gonna need whatever I can scrounge up for the coming battle."

It was a good idea. Kyle made a move toward Front Street.

"Not that way," said Izzy. "Those are the noob shops. Let's go to the Forum marketplace."

Kyle argued that he liked the noob shops and Izzy countered that higher quality supplies were worth the price. Despite the debate, we headed to the Forum. I wasn't really listening because I was more worried about the world clock. We had 22 minutes till the reboot. Preparing for battle made practical sense, but not if the battle didn't matter.

"Oh, shit," said Kyle on the busy marketplace road. "Let's go in here." He immediately ducked into the nearest storefront and left me and Izzy with puzzled looks.

"Is that a women's lingerie shop?" I asked.

She hiked a shoulder. "I dunno. The world's ending one way or another. Maybe Kyle wants to be his true self for once."

"Laugh it up, bros," came Kyle's voice from within the

doorway. He still failed to explain why he'd gone in there.

In a second we no longer needed the explanation.

"Hey, ladies," prodded Lash, lumbering over with a large cleaver in her hand. It was a wide broadsword, flat at the tip instead of a point. Her white armor and black rectangle shield were upgraded and quite striking. Conan the Barbarian and the Glinda the Good Witch were in tow.

"Don't tell me Lash is your friend," I muttered before they converged on us.

"I don't have friends," said Izzy, "but Lash is all right."

I gave her the side eye. Next thing I knew Lash was gripping our shoulders in excitement.

"That duel was good shit. I'm impressed with you, pint size." Even though Izzy was shorter, Lash was addressing me. "You put up a hell of a fight. Didn't know you had it in you."

"You're gonna see an even worse side of me if you keep calling me pint size."

She laughed gruffly, pulled off her helmet, and punched it into my chest. "Chill out. I'm just playing." Her two groupies chuckled.

"I see you're still level 4," I noted.

They shut their mouths immediately.

I sighed. That wasn't as satisfying as it should've been. "Lash, I don't have time for this."

Her eyes narrowed, pinching the gold hoop outside her right eye. Lash ran her hand through her hair, wiping sweat to the pony tail at the back. "You're telling me. We're gonna fight these pagan jerks. I'm surprised to see you finally grouped with someone, Izzy. And, Talon, good for you. You finally traded up."

That was a reference to Kyle.

"What is it with you, Lash? One second you're in my face. Then you see me fight and level past you and you wanna be friends. What's your problem anyway?"

Her lips tightened.

"And another thing. Kyle made a stupid mistake, but he's a good guy. And he's my friend. So stop giving him hell like this is an after-school special."

She snorted. "You don't know me."

"I know," I said firmly. Then I softened my voice. "I know, Lash. Kyle told me. Word gets around pretty fast in Haven. I heard about your aunt and baby sister and you being paralyzed for a week before dying."

Her face twisted. "Don't you talk about my family." She pulled her plate helm over her head. "Word of advice, punk. I'm fair game. Say whatever you want about me. But you never talk about my family again. I don't care what level you are, I'll—"

Her voice broke. Instead of trying to say anything else, she stormed off. Conan flashed me a look of warning, but he didn't look so certain about it. He was still only level 3.

"I thought you were supposed to be popular," mocked Izzy.

"Really? Do people say that?"

She rolled her eyes.

Kyle emerged from the shop. "Is she gone?"

"Found something in your size already?" I teased.

"Don't tell me you're wearing red panties under all that armor," said Izzy.

Kyle shook his head and smiled. "You guys are the worst."

Cutting off the moment of mirth was a deep bellow. Orik was

bearing down on Stronghold. In the distance, the west gate heaved under a mighty punch. The townsfolk around us scattered.

"You see the flaw in your plan," pointed out Izzy, "right?"

"What's that?"

"You want to stop the reboot, which is impossible enough as it is. At the same time, we want to save Stronghold from the cyclops. If we don't do anything, the saints will take care of Orik. Haven will reboot and the threat will be gone. If we stop that..."

She was saying we couldn't save the city and ourselves at the same time.

"I don't buy that," I said. "You really think Stronghold can't handle a titan or two? He's part of the programming. The pagans are supposed to attack the city. Waking him is part of the quest narrative."

She shrugged, unconvinced. I was sure of my logic right up until the west gate splintered. The giant's shoulder barreled through the door, knocking it off its hinges and flattening a unit of legionnaires. Orik drove forward on his hands and knees and fell on the door.

The cyclops was twice the size of the wall itself. He probably could've hopped into the city if he'd wanted to. But bringing the gate down wasn't about him. A stream of pagans, like panicked ants, crawled past Orik and flooded into Stronghold.

The defense forces braced their weapons and cried in return. The battle for the city had begun.

0440 Anarchy Online

"We need to get over there," said Izzy.

We positioned ourselves on the road to get a better look at the distant gate. Orik was still on the ground. The Stronghold army converged, attempting to nail the giant down. Complicating the effort was the horde of pagans streaming in. They ran right over Orik's back, desperate for human flesh.

The second wooden door hadn't completely caved in. Soldiers braced against it, forcing the pagans to squeeze through a tight bottleneck. Goblins were trampled and crushed against the wall. The surge was damaging their own army, but it was relentless.

Legionnaires formed a shield wall before the open gate. A few agile goblins hopped over them safely, but most were cut down. The flow was only stemmed for half a minute before a large ogre barreled through the formation. The creature battered the soldiers like rag dolls.

Orik came to life. He crushed his attackers and heaved himself up. The pagans that had been crawling over him tumbled to the ground. A lone goblin was unlucky enough to cling to the rising giant. He hung on to Orik's hairy mane as long as he could before falling to his death.

At his peak, the cyclops towered over everything around him. Only Dragonperch, in the distance, reached the same height. The blind titan had been undamaged by his sloppy entry. His gaping eye cavity opened wide with his mouth and he screamed at the top of his lungs in defiance of the very city.

Centurions rushed past us in the streets. I didn't even bother hiding my face anymore. Everyone's attention was fixed on the big ugly.

"We need to hurry," said Kyle.

"You're right. Go get your supplies. We're gonna stop that thing ourselves."

"What about you?" asked Izzy.

"This is the mother of all distractions. Five times better than a black dragon melting statues. I need to get inside the Pantheon."

"You can't go alone," said Kyle.

I clenched my teeth. "I know. I'll just scout ahead. See what the guard looks like. When you two are finished shopping, meet me in front."

They nodded uncertainly.

"Bandit, stay with Kyle." The bongo tilted her head. I sped off before they could stop me.

I raced through the panicking crowd. This wasn't a siege anymore. It was a battle. The warfare would reach the Forum soon. The shops and the residences. Stronghold would be overtaken by little nasties. Maybe goblins weren't an incredible threat but they outnumbered us five to one.

I peered at the statues of the golden angels atop their

Corinthian columns. Painted, pretty, but they weren't going to help us. This was a crisis to be solved by players. By me. A direct assault on the Oculus. That was the only way. I could take control of the system. Stave off the wipe.

MMO players in control of their own fates. It would be another RPG first.

A lot of approaches were possible. One thing I couldn't do was waste time. The entire city only had 12 minutes until the switch was flipped. I would have to act without Kyle and Izzy. Saying I would wait was a lie, and I think they knew it.

Bandit nudged me from behind. I shook my head. The damn girl was loyal to a fault.

"Fine," I said. "Let's go."

Surprisingly, there wasn't a single centurion on the portico steps. I considered climbing to the outside window I'd jumped out of before but decided to sneak to the front door and peek inside first.

The inner hall was empty too. In stark contrast to the rumbling and crashing and screaming outside, the inner hall was dressed in permanent calm.

I swallowed nervously. It was the perfect setup for another trap. I might step into the portico and walk into an ambush. Then again, Stronghold really was in trouble. I'd witnessed the centurions storming to the gate. I leaned against a patio column and considered my options. The stone itself trembled. I turned around and looked past the columns of angels and down the Forum, the road a straight shot all the way to the marketplace.

Orik lumbered around the corner. A contingent of centurions stabbed at his feet with swords and spears. He swiped heavy fists like wrecking balls. Their body shields were useless. The titan crushed any and all opposition. The best they could hope was to slow him down.

Orik knew it, too. That's why he was coming for the Pantheon.

The clock was literally ticking. I stepped inside the portico. Bandit's hooves echoed on the marble floor behind me, their click-clacking a violation of this holy place. Not a single guard rushed to intercept us. It was eerie, like breaking into a museum at night. The ultimate urbex. Except this was a simulation, the hub of Stronghold. Of all of Haven, for all I knew. And it was left completely unguarded.

That revealed how important stopping Orik truly was. Every last centurion and protector of Stronghold was marching to their deaths, hoping to keep the titan from the Pantheon until the reboot.

And I was gonna help the pagans stop it.

I gritted my teeth and headed forward, through the double doors to the inner Pantheon. The rendering went black as we zoned. A blink later, the rotunda appeared. Silence overtook us. No cries of death. No stomping giants. A whisper was too loud for this place.

The large dome sprawled overhead. Even though it was nighttime, a beam of light shone in from the oculus above. This zone wasn't actually connected to Stronghold. A bird couldn't fly in from the outside. That wasn't sunlight charging the air. It was a pure data stream, visualized as life itself.

Bandit and I approached the altar. The room was empty. The control panels, the Oculus, gleamed before us, bathed in a beam of warm yellow. As I rounded the altar, Saint Peter stepped out from an alcove in the wall.

"Tod Lonnerman," he announced, setting me on edge.

I huffed in annoyance. "It's *Tad*."

0450 A Link to the Past

Saint Peter strolled forward, hands folded under a cream robe marred only by the stripe of maroon from neck to toe.

"Tad," repeated the saint. His bushy eyebrows eased under the crown of woven gold twigs. "It is a name I should remember by now. You've certainly caused enough trouble."

"What is this, an ambush?"

Bandit snorted. I think she was trying to be tough.

"Ambush? This isn't a fight, Tad. I just needed to confirm you were a part of this. I had my suspicions but I didn't know for sure. In truth, I still don't know *why*."

There were 9 minutes left on the clock. "You need to stop the reboot," I said.

"Impossible."

"We can fight the titan. We can drive back the pagans."

Saint Peter scoffed. "You most assuredly cannot."

"Stronghold was founded on defeating them," I reasoned. "The Eye was harnessed against the pagans. In the Dragon Wars that followed, heroes rose up and defended the town."

"Heroes." Saint Peter snorted. "Magnus Dragonrider never existed. Those 'centuries' you speak of never happened. Haven's simulation has been live less than a year. Everything else is background history and color. Believe me, Tad, that broken statue might hold a genuine relic, but true heroes like him are nothing but dust and legend."

I clenched my jaw. There was a difference between fantasy and reality, even here. I knew that. But Haven was a digital reality. "Orik's real enough," I said.

Saint Peter crossed his arms. "Orik's supposed to be part of a level 100 town quest a few years down the road. All the cities have titans, but they aren't supposed to be bearing down on a bunch of hapless noobs."

His anachronistic speech made me frown. The devs were taking this seriously.

"It was an accident," I admitted. "I didn't mean to awaken him. Lucifer tricked me."

"Big surprise, there. They *do* call him the father of lies."

"You think your white robes make you so innocent? You've lied more than he has."

"What are you—"

"I'm still alive, asshole."

Saint Peter slowly brought a hand up and stroked his white beard. His face had gone ashy to match.

"*That's* why I broke into the Pantheon," I told him. "I didn't care about the pagans or Orik. I didn't even know the Eye existed. All I wanted was to find out the truth. Are the personnel records right? Am I still alive?"

The old man frowned. "Yes," he finally said softly. "You

weren't supposed to live."

"But I did!" I barked. "Derek needs to know. He's my brother."

I suddenly realized Everchat was available here. The rotunda was an instance, a separate zone, buffered from the rest of Haven.

"I need to talk to him," I said.

I opened my menu and swiped to the chat interface. Saint Peter glanced warily at a slowly approaching Bandit. The mountain bongo could be a menacing animal when she wanted to be. "You can't do that, Tad."

"I need to."

My breath froze as my contact list opened. Derek had accepted my contact request. I clicked the button to hail him.

"Tad."

Saint Peter moved to stop me. I whipped my spear to his neck. He grimaced at the point.

"This is a bad idea..."

I ignored him and watched the spinning icon in the chat interface. A message underneath read, "Hailing Derek. Awaiting a response."

I wondered how it worked. A video chat would be a mobile app. My brother was in the real world somewhere. Hopefully he had his cell phone on him. He might be able to respond within seconds.

"Think about what you're doing," Saint Peter urged. "You think it's only been a day since your accident?"

I ripped my eyes away from the spinning icon. Took a moment to process his words. "I woke up this morning," I said dumbly.

"Yes, but how long ago did you actually die?"

"I didn't die."

"Semantics," he announced. "Two months, Tad. It's been two months since your Portland car accident."

I checked the date on my profile bar. It didn't conform to a real date. The year was good, but the day was just a three-digit number without a month.

"Do the math," he said. "Thirty days to a month, more or less. That number's the day of the year."

My voice tinged with anger. "What did you do to me?"

"It was a mistake. It wasn't planned. It just happened. Uploads can't occur at the moment of death, you see. Once a person goes into arrest, it's too late. The doctors need the space and freedom to attempt resuscitation. Kablammy's removed from the equation at that point."

I stared at him. Two months. What had my brother been doing all that time? How had he been holding up?

Saint Peter continued in a calming voice. "Death is too late. We upload terminal cases while they're stable. *Before* they die. Sometimes there are days of overlap before death occurs."

I took a short breath. "And sometimes it never does."

He nodded. "You recovered. Maybe the doctors were wrong about your outlook. Maybe your desire to live—to protect your brother—was too strong. I don't *really* work for Heaven, Tad. I don't have the answers. For whatever reason, you fought your injuries and returned from the brink of death. You actually just left the hospital this afternoon."

My brow furrowed. "Left the..."

"You've been well taken care of. Kablammy's insurance policy is among the best in the business. You've been receiving worker's comp. Derek has been able to keep up with rent payments. Your entire studio has sent get-well gifts and made donations in your name. I can show you the card."

"But what about Haven?" I asked. "How am I hooked up to the sim?"

Saint Peter stifled a frown. "You're not hooked up to machines, Tad. This isn't a VR experience. It's DR. I told you that."

The Everchat interface beeped. The spinning icon was gone, replaced with an exclamation mark. The text read, "Derek has accepted your hail." A few seconds passed. "Requesting initiation of video chat." A button popped up. "Accept?"

I shivered. My eyes watered as I struggled to take it in.

"You're not connected," said Saint Peter softly, even compassionately. "You're a digital soul. A copy. An impostor. Don't you see? The real Tad Lonnerman is alive and at home. His younger brother is probably taking care of him as we speak, curious about a chat request from a game he's never heard of that was created by his brother's company."

My digital heart pounded in my chest.

"That's why we couldn't give you Everchat access," admitted the saint.

The request beeped again. Saint Peter simply sighed and watched me quietly. He didn't move to stop me.

I stared at the chat interface, paralyzed by emotion. My little brother was there, waiting on the other side of that icon. A single tap and I could see him again. Make sure he was okay.

Tell him I loved him and would always watch over him, even in death.

...But Derek already had an older brother watching over him. Tad Lonnerman was with him in the real world, injured but alive. How could I explain that?

Seeing me would only hurt and confuse Derek. Did my little brother really need to have that burden? Did he really need to know the fate of a copy of his big brother?

I flinched when the notification beeped again. Tears rolled down my face, and I closed the chat request.

Derek still had his big brother. It just wasn't me anymore.

I gasped a few times as the menu closed, trying to catch my breath, fighting off the hacking sobs that wanted to come. Bandit cocked her head and watched me, concerned.

I didn't know who I was anymore.

To his credit, Saint Peter didn't push me. He didn't say or do anything. He waited with considerable restraint. The patience of a saint.

My mind returned to reality.

"You're stalling me," I realized. I checked the world clock. 2 minutes remaining.

"Everything I've said is true," he swore earnestly.

"I believe you, but you're still stalling me."

I turned to the control panel. Saint Peter stepped forward. I rapped the butt of my spear into his head. He stumbled and I shoved him backward to the floor. Before he could stop me, I pulled the gold cartridge into my hand.

"So it's true. You can override friendly fire. That's not a beta flag."

"A gift," I replied.

"You can't fight the reboot. The Nine were never supposed to be accessed this early. With control of the Eye, the pagans are too powerful. Our only hope is to reset the world state with the reboot. Put Orik back in the mountain. Return the Eye to the tabernacle."

"And get us back under your heel," I muttered.

He scoffed, eyes glued to the bit key.

"Let us try to fight for Haven."

Still on the floor, Saint Peter emphatically shook his head. "If Orik reaches the Pantheon, he'll get access to the Oculus. You must understand, this data stream is vital to the simulation. Before us sits the governance of all of Haven." Panic edged into his voice. "We'd be surrendering power of the game to the pagans. A game construct, controlling the game itself. They'll destroy everything."

Saint Peter climbed to his knees and continued making his case. "That's all Lucifer wants. Don't you see? She's a nihilist. A fatalist. Death is the only goal for her. Not only does she not wish to survive, she wants to take you all with her."

I tottered in front of the control panel, bit key in hand. Something told me he was right about Lucifer. But I wasn't on the devil's side anymore. I wasn't being manipulated. This was about what *I* wanted.

"You need to let it go, Tad. You need to surrender to the beta conditions. Let us fix things. I'm sorry about what happened to you. I truly am. But you need to let us fix it."

I swallowed, determination creeping back. "You get to log off and go to sleep in your own bed," I said. "*We're* the ones who live in the simulation. *We're* the ones who call Haven home. What gives *you* the right to reset us?"

"Are you serious?" he asked, looking at me like I was the crazy one. "Haven's a game. *Our* game. We created it. We fund it. Surely we have the right to set the parameters of our own world."

"I'm sorry, Saint Peter, but Haven's not yours anymore."

With 1 minute to go, I slammed the bit key into the cartridge slot. The white robe sprung to his feet. I braced my spear as he lunged. Instead, Bandit intercepted him between her horns. The saint buckled against her momentum. She drove him into the wall, pinning him.

"Tad!" he yelled. "Tad!"

My fingers rapped the keyboard, looking for any mention of the reboot timer. The world clock ticked the seconds away. As I frantically searched the menus, I feared that Saint Peter had stalled me long enough. I wouldn't be able to stop the sequence in time.

In a huff of frustration, I eyed the other terminal. The one that managed the personnel database. It wouldn't have access to the reboot sequence. I began typing faster in a panic.

30 seconds.

"Give it up, Talon."

"No. I can find a way to stop this."

I sidestepped to the personnel terminal. Saint Peter froze as I did. I looked from him to the terminal and back. He didn't want me touching this one.

"Stop," he said. "You can't hack the system."

I bit down and went to search the records. "I'm not hacking

it, I'm unhacking it."

Crackling blue electricity engulfed Saint Peter. His eyes went wild. Bandit was caught in the current. She convulsed. Sparks seared and smoked her fur. In a flash, the bongo fell to the marble floor, blood leaking from her mouth, eyes, and nose. Dead before she knew what hit her.

Saint Peter calmly straightened and patted the electricity from his robes. "I am quite serious," he cautioned.

The entire rotunda shook. The lights went out and we almost lost our footing. When the red emergency glow came on, Orik was towering above us, forced to crouch under the dome. His gargantuan form blocked the beam of light from above.

Saint Peter spun to face the titan. "Don't let him touch the console!" The crazy bastard charged ahead and shot electricity into the giant's foot.

Global Haven Alert:

Thank you for participating in the pagan battle event!

Haven will be wiped now. Prepare for reboot in 10, 9, 8...

I'd failed. My eyes held on Bandit's corpse for another wasted second as I counted all the ways I'd come up short.

I swiveled my head to the personnel records, wondering if I'd still be an entry after the wipe. After all, I was an impostor. Just a copy. The real Tad Lonnerman would hopefully lead a full and eventful life.

5, 4...

Instead of monitoring the individual records, the database was headed by group player info. Everyone in Haven. The entire collection of people. Names, ages, levels, classes... beta flags.

The beta flags. One of Lucifer's greatest tricks.

With seconds left, I selected the entire array of beta flags. I didn't have time to study which flags did what. I didn't have time to check if I was destroying the world. Years of programming had given me a gut feeling. As long as Haven was intelligently designed, my hunch would play out with fairly limited consequences. And if it wasn't...

Well, 2 seconds wasn't a whole lot of time to make an informed decision.

With a single keystroke, I zeroed out the beta flags. All of them. For everybody. Whatever the temporary variables did, whatever hacks the developers had stuffed into the memory that governed the tweaked beta conditions—I wiped them all out. Beta flags equal zero.

Saint Peter whirled to me, having managed to thus far hold Orik off.

"What have you done?" he cried.

Global Haven Alert:
The reboot sequence is primed.
Have a nice day, and see you on the other side.

REBOOTING...

My eyes locked with Saint Peter's.

Then the whole world fizzled out.

0460 Wipeout

After a drawn-out, peaceful moment, I opened my eyes. The soft blue light of my bedroom greeted me. I twisted my face into the comfort of a fluffy pillow. After this was over, I promised myself to sleep two days straight.

With a sigh, I sat up. Everything was pristine. No personal effects or scattered items. Not that I had a whole lot. Haven had reset.

I jerked out of bed and opened my character screen. My sudden tension eased. It had actually happened.

"Woo-hoo!" screamed Kyle.

He was probably in his personal room but I could hear him. We both hurried into the common area to see each other.

"I can't believe it!" he said boisterously. "This is totally awesome!"

A new party chat message came in.

Izzy: *Okay, Talon... What the hell did you just do?*

I smiled. I had done *it*. All player conditions—levels, items, skills—had been retained. I was a level 5 scout. Kyle was still the brewmaster. Even our party was still together.

My roommate followed me outside. From the high vantage of Hillside, I gazed upon the large city. It was mostly empty. There were NPCs, sure. A shopkeeper. The city watch scattered across patrols and posts.

All the players would be restarting in their homes. Slowly realizing their world wasn't a game anymore. It was permanent. I took a slow, deliberate breath. Whatever beta flags had prevented player data from being stored in the permanent profiles had been blown away. We were here for good now. All of us.

Residents stepped out of their houses, faces colored with curiosity, pleasantly surprised by the strange development. I wandered ahead, taking it all in. Some players cheered me as I passed. Somehow, they knew I'd been part of it.

A large shockwave rumbled Stronghold's walls. Everyone hugged the ground out of instinct, even though Hillside itself didn't shake. I scanned the battlements. Saw the scurry of troops on top. Spun around and saw all the combat-ready NPCs scrambling into action. City watchmen abandoned their posts. Centurions marched units to the west gate. Legionnaires lined up to die. Even Trafford the welcome shop keeper hurried by, brandishing a pitchfork.

I broke into a sprint down the hill. I headed west, straight toward the river walling off Oldtown. Kyle followed at a less frantic pace. As we neared, a rock launched from a catapult smashed into the abandoned ruins, just as it had before.

The pagans were still storming the city.

My mind raced. I knew zeroing out the beta flags could have

unforeseen consequences, but I didn't see how this was possible. I'd stopped the wipe, but the reboot had still gone through.

Players were permanent now. It was the personnel records I'd messed with. We should've been the only ones affected. But maybe...

My gaze climbed the tower of Dragonperch with trepidation. Stone by stone, I reached the top and saw the statue of Magnus, toppled in half, his glimmering white spear propped against crumbling bleached stone.

Talon: *Izzy, get to Oldtown. Something went wrong.*

Kyle caught up to me, questions on his lips. I spotted movement in the ruins. A deer with stripes galloped into view. She froze and perked her head sideways when she saw me.

I went from zero to sixty in an instant. She was on the other side of the river, but that didn't slow my stride. At the cordoned brick edge, I planted my spear and vaulted, clearing the whole body of water and continuing in a run on the other side. When I reached Bandit I clapped my arms around her broad neck and held her tight.

"You're alive!"

She gave me a loving snort and danced with glee. After a minute, I pulled away, admiring her chestnut coat.

"I don't know if you realize how dead you were," I said.

Her dark eyes within her white mask stared at me deeply.

I couldn't be sure what had happened. A simple respawn? But she came back within Oldtown, along our original path.

I worked through the possibilities as Kyle forded the river. Listened as the army on the other side of the wall screamed, cursed, and pounded. I watched the townsfolk spill into the streets, abuzz with chatter, surprised they could still pull out their weapons before slowly realizing Stronghold was still besieged. The anticipation of what came next was palpable.

It didn't take long for Izzy to find us.

"What the crap is going on?" she asked sharply. Kyle waited expectantly. They both thought I had all the answers.

"I'm not sure. I couldn't stop the reboot so I cleared out the beta flags. Took everyone out of a temporary state. We can't be wiped anymore." I frowned. "I don't understand it. Maybe the devs hacked some extra junk into the beta flags."

"Developer hacks?" asked Kyle, puzzled.

"It's more common than you think. Laziness, deadlines, logistics. The point is, whatever I did affected the world state as well."

Izzy twisted her lips into a smirk. "So the world is permanent too."

I shrugged. "Maybe the game state takes regular snapshots, backups in case of server crashes. Maybe the reboot sequence halts those backups, so we restored to a previous position, when it began."

I checked the game clock. It was past one, so the time didn't reset. It probably couldn't, being synced with the real world. Everyone had just lost a chunk of time.

Kyle caught on. "Or maybe it just makes a backup every hour."

"Could be."

We thought silently for a minute before Izzy asked, "Is that good?"

I cocked my head. "It *could* be. But it means we're about half an hour away from Orik destroying the Pantheon. If he does that, the pagans will control Haven. We still need to fight them off."

The sounds of battle grew more hectic. The legionnaires had organized quickly and were doing serious damage with ranged weapons.

Izzy hiked a shoulder. "Hey, sounds easy, right?"

Kyle nodded. "I'm with you, bro. Whatever happens."

It was what I needed to hear. Together I felt like we could accomplish anything.

Global Haven Alert:
The player Talon has broken the terms of service and negatively impacted the play experience for all residents. His contract is terminated effective immediately. The angel Decimus has been dispatched to carry out the judgment.

Correction: I felt like I could accomplish *anything but that.*

I reread the message several times. Each time, disbelief was my only reaction. I had gone against the saints. With everything else going on, I couldn't deny that. It was what I should've expected. I just couldn't believe it.

Izzy's face softened. "Talon..."

I smiled at her. She didn't relax her stoic mask often, but she did now. I didn't get the carefree smile I'd hoped for. Instead her mood was closer to pity.

"Don't worry about it," I said, straightening. My statement oozed overconfidence but it was the best I could do. "We need to protect the gates."

"You're thinking about Haven now?" she asked.

"If we defeat Orik," I said adamantly, "maybe the angels give me a pass. Do you guys still have the new supplies you bought?"

"Yup," said Kyle. "Still preserved. We lost time but retained progression, thanks to your change. I need to catch up on glasswork though."

I nodded. "Get to the gates. Convince the watch that we'll help them. Trust me. They don't want the pagans in this city. They'll welcome anybody with skill. I'll meet you there as soon as I can."

Izzy pressed her lips together. Kyle asked, "What are you gonna do?"

"Same as you guys. Prepare for a fight. Get moving."

It took some urging but they broke away and followed the wall toward the west gate. They'd have ample time to prepare. Orik wouldn't reach Stronghold for a while.

For my part, I wasn't like the rest of the party. Frost mages and brewmasters needed to prep components and supplies. Most of my usefulness in a fight came down to quick thinking and quicker feet. But the dried-out spear in my hand wasn't gonna cut it. I needed something better. Something game changing. I looked up to the top of Dragonperch.

I needed a god killer.

The doors to the tower were warded tight. I wondered why

the west gate didn't have similar protections, but figured it had to do with hastily written game lore. Ancient powers, prophetic seals—that kind of thing. Hey, you can't analyze fantasy too hard.

I opened my character screen. I still had a level 5 skill point. If I was gonna die, I was gonna do it with a full loadout. I could go for more power or a new attack, but nothing that would take on a titan. Besides, I already had a weapon of choice in mind.

I'd been eyeing a traversal skill ever since the tutorial. I'd heavily considered it when first climbing Blind Man's Peak. Now that I was sure it would come in handy, I didn't feel bad spending a skill point on it.

Scale
Climb and hang on sheer surfaces.
Attributes: Strength, Agility
SpS: 0.5

Hey, it's not a rock star skill, but it's something.

Climbing was more passive than other skills. It didn't have a set spirit cost or a cooldown, but the act did cost spirit over time. The method of traversal also seemed to require a good deal of strength instead of just agility, which made sense but made me nervous. Normally I'd top off my agility, but I didn't want to fall to my death. I put my level 5 attribute point into strength and swiped my menu closed.

I circled Dragonperch until I found it. Uneven stonework that provided easy hand and foot holds. "Here goes nothing," I said, and began my ascent.

Just a few feet up, I began to see how difficult this task was. Without the scaling skill, it would've been an absolute no-go. As my passive climbing skill took over, I noted my spirit bar flash and start to drain. It was slow and I had plenty to go around. I set my jaw and continued upward. Despite the apparent real-world difficulty involved, I scaled higher and higher using precarious seams in the stonework.

I was twice the height of the great main door when it happened. A shimmering ceiling, like oil on water, or haze along the desert horizon. I banged into it just as if it had been brick, but the magical flash reminded me more of Orik's gemstone shield. The damn tower walls were warded as well. Try as I might, I couldn't get higher.

"Shit!" I screamed.

I forcefully shoved myself into the barrier and received a friendly jolt in return. I lost my grip and bounced hard to the ground. The damage was minor but the pain was real. I cursed Lucifer and wondered if he'd blessed himself with the same gift of pain.

I rolled to my back and gazed up helplessly. I had just wasted my last skill point on an impossible task. Magnus' weapon wouldn't be so easily recovered. Almost a year of alpha and beta testing and no players had ever snagged it, much less breached the tower. I was naive to think I could do it on my first day with a noob traversal skill.

I hissed at the night sky and listened to the sounds of battle. For the moment, the well-mobilized legionnaires and massive walls of Stronghold seemed to outmatch any conceivable enemy. In answer to my thought, the pagan cyclops bellowed in the distance. He was nearing the city.

I sprung to my feet. Giants and angels and magical weapons be damned, I was gonna go out fighting.

I whistled sharply. Bandit was immediately at my side. "Looks like your resurrection will be short-lived," I told her, and hopped onto her back. Her hooves beat against the dirt as we hurried to the wall.

0470 City of Heroes

The west gate was a beehive. Players and NPCs scrambled to defend the walls. Readying weapons, handing out armor. It was impressive unity but too many of them failed to contribute meaningfully to the immediate problem.

Before the reboot, the titan had broken down the gate. That was the inciting event that had endangered the Pantheon and allowed the pagans to stream in like a rushing river. It was bound to happen again, eventually. We needed to be ready for the contingency, but sitting back and waiting for it was conceding the battle.

We couldn't let the pagans in that easily. Not while their force outnumbered ours five to one. If they broke in so soon, Stronghold was done for. The real battle was up on the walls.

Despite the bustle of people, the crowd parted before Bandit's stout form. I was the only one in town with a mount. That, combined with my growing notoriety, brought more than a few stares my way.

Unfortunately, it also brought the wrong kind of attention.

"Halt right there!" screamed a centurion.

It was Gladius, the head of the city watch and the same

centurion I'd previously attacked. He jumped in Bandit's path with his golden sword drawn behind his rectangular body shield. The blade burned with a hot fire. Several other centurions moved in, as well as a troop of legionnaires. I scanned the wall but didn't see Kyle or Izzy.

"Talon, you are an illegal resident of Stronghold. You will surrender your weapons and turn yourself in at once."

I flipped my spear in my hand. "Don't get in my way, Gladius. We're all on the same side here."

He scowled and called the centurions into formation. Two on either side backed him up, forming their shields with his into a tight wall. They advanced a step.

I growled. On Bandit's back, with a spear, I could beat their reach easy. But their tactics were designed against first strikes. They'd bat my spear aside, maybe trap it against the ground, and then they'd move in and stab me like Julius Caesar. Fitting, maybe.

"He'll be deleted!" yelled a random voice in the crowd.

"He let us keep our stats," added another.

The centurions didn't falter. They stepped ahead in unison. I considered dismounting and telling Bandit to run. She didn't need those blades to find her.

An arrow whizzed out of nowhere and clanged against the top of Gladius' helmet. The gold armor rang painfully against his temple. The centurions raised their shields. Another arrow struck right where his head was, now buried behind the makeshift wall. It wasn't made of glass and didn't pop with corrosive liquid. It wasn't a crossbow bolt.

I spun around and saw Dune brandishing a longbow from

behind the city watch's line. Stigg the berserker and Caduceus the physicker fanned out behind him.

"He's one of us," announced the ranger.

Stigg laughed heartily. "You mess with him, you mess with all of us."

The legionnaires warily turned their heads as the crowd grew more vociferous. The cries of support turned to threats. A few waving fists turned to shoves.

Gladius peeked over his shield and snarled. "All residents will stand down or face harsh penalties!"

A stalactite of ice formed in the air between me and the centurion grouping. I finally spotted my friends on the wall. Kyle held his crossbow to his shoulder and took careful aim. Izzy nodded at me.

The mob was getting unruly, but the shields of the centurions and the organized city watch were intimidating. They cowed any who came close.

Gladius hissed. "Town combat is active, but friendly fire is blocked. Attempting to damage Stronghold defenders will only result in failure."

And there it was. The men and women backing me up had weapons in their hands, but Lucifer hadn't hacked their characters as he had mine. Friendly fire wasn't a simple beta flag. It was part of the normal game, meant to be toggled under certain conditions after full release. The players demanding my freedom held paper weapons.

"No!" I cried, kicking Bandit forward. She spun away from the centurions and galloped around the loose circle formed by the wall of guards. "We are not enemies."

I swiped my spear at the line, keeping the legionnaires from charging me. They'd seen my display in town earlier. They knew that I, at least, could hurt them. As I lapped in circles around the centurion grouping, they scrambled to readjust and stay in formation. It was all they could do to keep their shields together and face me. They ceased their advance, giving me the time I needed.

"Stronghold is under attack!" I screamed, wishing I'd invested in blue face paint. "A wild army beats on our walls. Knocks on our doors. A titan has awoken."

Bandit continued galloping and every eye in the crowd followed me.

"If the pagans succeed, our homes will be destroyed. Our safety will be obliterated. Our supplies, our pleasures, our day-to-day lives will be forever changed."

I slowed Bandit to a trot but kept my voice loud, shouting for every person at the wall to hear. I pointed my spear at Dune. "This is *your* home," I announced. He nodded. I circled to a random person in the crowd. "This is *your* home." My spear rose to Izzy on the wall and I watched her for a wistful second, voice slightly softening. "This is *your* home."

Finally, I whirled Bandit toward the centurions who had somewhat relaxed their fighting stances. I nodded to Gladius. "This is *your* home."

He worked his jaw uncertainly. His eyes flicked to a nearby building. I followed his gaze and saw Saint Peter on a balcony overlooking the thoroughfare. The saints were always watching, always above the thrum.

I kicked Bandit into a gallop and raced around the circle

again.

"The saints do not live here!" I screamed. "WE live here."

The silence that had fallen over the crowd broke. The people muttered and cried out. Gladius swiveled his head to them.

"LET US SCREAM LOUD AND LONG!" I bellowed. People hollered. "LET THE SAINTS HEAR US FROM THE HALLS OF THE PANTHEON!" More applause. I locked eyes with Saint Peter as I lapped the clearing. "THIS IS *OUR* HOME! THIS IS *OUR* FATE!"

Bandit's hooves were drowned out by the crowd. The legionnaires had all lowered their weapons. Even Gladius' fire blade was at his side. In the distance, Saint Peter retreated indoors.

I turned to face the west gate. "TODAY WE FIGHT FOR FREEDOM!"

The city erupted into fanatical cheers. I charged the gate and the city watch broke freely before me. The renewed vigor of the people filled everyone with hope. With the spirit to act. We would do it—we *could* do it—because Stronghold was strong together.

The crowd broke into a chant. "Talon! Talon! Talon!" I raised my spear to the air.

Centurions screamed above. "Fortify the gates!" Soldiers went into double-time.

At the foot of the winding stone steps that led to the battlements, I hopped to the ground and approached the guard. "My friends are up there and I need to help them."

Gladius stopped beside me and nodded to the guard. We walked up the stairs together.

"Orik's coming hard and he's going for that door. We should prep the ground before it's too late."

"What do you need?" he asked.

"Archers. Torches. Skilled men."

He nodded. "You'll have them."

My party waited for me at the top of the wall.

"That was awesome," said Kyle.

Izzy just studied me with an arched eyebrow. I walked right up to her, placed my hands on either side of her neck, and kissed her.

Amidst the cheers below, it was a wonderful two seconds. Then Izzy pulled away, slapped me, and asked, "Are you crazy?" She didn't look mad.

"I just might be," I said.

I moved to the battlements. "Kyle, how much of that flame gel do you have?"

He scoffed. "What kind of brewmaster would I be if it was only a little?"

"I love it. We need to coat the ground in front of the gates. This is the weak link in the chain. The pagans will do anything they can to break it."

Dune and company joined us on the battlements. "You *are* crazy. The gate is made of wood. What good are heavy double doors if they're on fire?"

"Izzy?"

Her face flashed recognition. "I can mitigate that. It's not a permanent solution, but fire only lasts so long."

We got to work.

0480 Warcraft

Pagans stormed the wall. Arrows flung both ways. Legionnaires dropped heavy rocks on clumps of goblins. Their bodies littered the foot of the wall. The crazed soldiers climbed over their fallen dead and advanced. Ogres hefted smaller goblins upward, some of them actually reaching the summit of the battlements. They cried in victory for the last seconds of their lives before the city watch cut them down.

No longer a distant threat, Orik stomped through the crowd. Scores of imps hopped excitedly at his presence. Ogres and trolls beat their chests. Quite a few enemies were trampled by their very savior, but it was a drop in the bucket. There were plenty of greenies and grays to go around.

Gladius made good on his word. He provided me with what and who I needed. Kyle's flame gel was in place and Izzy was hardening a sheet of ice on both sides of the wooden gate.

A deafening cry made my blood go icy. The titan was upon us.

Up here on the battlements, we were only half his height. The cyclops was up close and personal now. More frightening than ever. His skin was the color of red rock. His gargantuan body was made up of boulders and glued clumps of grass and dirt. A ring of long hair circled his bald crown, rocky beads swaying with every approaching step.

In the center of his face above a broad nose was the giant's eye socket. It dominated his appearance for being both solitary and vacant. A no-eyed cyclops. The titan was blind.

"So much for the eye being the window to the soul," I muttered.

Above the gaping hole was the large horn protruding from his forehead. The obelisk of Blind Man's Peak. The ruby glow from the soulstone glimmered at the tip.

Kyle fired precise shots at the gemstone. A flare of red magic exploded the glass bolts a few feet before impact. The splash of the corrosive didn't seem to have any effect.

"Not bad," boasted Dune, "but you're not a crack shot like I am."

He pulled his bowstring back, a silver arrow notched between his fingers. The specialty projectile streamed through the air like a bullet. It, too, shattered before touching the enemy.

"Huh," said the ranger.

Stigg, the red-robed berserker mystic, ruffled his black beard. "That barrier won't be taken out by force. What is that thing?"

"It's a soulstone," said Izzy. "The Eye of Orik."

His eyes widened. "The *soul* of Orik."

"It's nice to see you magic types putting your heads together," I noted. "It would be nicer if you generated some useful ideas."

They glared at me. "We can speak in muted admiration too,"

murmured Izzy.

Ranged attacks were getting nowhere. Orik lumbered to the west gate and slammed a gargantuan fist forward. The blow was off target. It glanced the wall and rattled the door. The heavy stones absorbed the worst of it. I wondered how blind Orik actually was.

"You wanna admire something?" I taunted. "Smother him, Kyle."

"Danger," he said. "Contents are flammable."

The brewmaster heaved his vials skyward. They fragmented against the giant without exploding. Oily flame gel blanketed portions of Orik's body. Next I signaled to the soldiers holding torches. They tossed them to the ground at the foot of the gate. As the cyclops readied another hammering blow, the earth detonated into a fiery inferno around him.

This time, the cyclops didn't miss. His closed fist smashed into the gate proper. The sheet of ice blanketing it fell away without leaving much structural damage. Izzy immediately went to reinforce her work.

The area before us lit up like Friday-night lights. Flames cut a swath in front of the west gate. A wall of fire roared upward. Pagans shriveled under the sorcerous fire. The giant growled at the growing heat but locked his eyeless head on the gate.

"Archers," I called out.

Five men dipped their arrows in fire and let fly. Several hit the giant but missed their mark. One caught a spot of yellow gel and ignited it. Orik flinched and pulled back for another punch.

Dune, ever into one-upmanship, tried his hand at it. He found the spot of oil on Orik's chest and nailed it with a bull's-eye. After another round of archery, the god himself was aflame.

"Kill it with fire," I growled.

Orik's third attack against the gate never came. The titan bellowed in pain and reared away. Large hands swiped the ground before him as if feeling the fire at his feet for the first time. The cyclops scrambled backward, crushing scores of pagans that had been readying to breach the gate.

I flashed a wicked smile. "How long will the fire keep up?"

"I'm almost out of flame gel," answered Kyle. "But what's on the ground should burn for a bit."

My eyes met Izzy's with concern. "I can handle it," she assured me through gritted teeth, freezing the melting ice on the doors. "The gate will hold."

I was pleased with the countermeasure, but Orik's health bar had barely budged. The small patches of fire made up a very small part of his surface area and hadn't affected any critical body parts. The titan swatted the flames away. While the ground burned beautifully, Orik himself was only lightly smoked.

With their god rebuffed, the pagans began resorting to more conventional tactics. Catapults in the distance flung heavy rocks at Stronghold. Some missiles sailed over the walls and caused damage and chaos within. Others fell short and bowled through countless friendly soldiers. I was grateful that an especially daunting troll had his head clean knocked off by a boulder. The pagan army corrected its aim and hit the city's walls with a barrage.

I was impressed with their tenacity, but Stronghold's walls proved too mighty. No doubt a direct hit against the wooden doors would yield better results, but I wasn't sure the pagans commanded that kind of precision. Not only that, their attempts to smash the gate were obliterating the line of their army. Between the projectiles, the fire, and the raging cyclops, a large clearing opened in front of the gate.

The horde's overconfidence in the god-giant's rebirth had made them careless. They'd rushed forward wildly instead of taking more strategic measures. Now it was too late. There was no calling this army off. No sating its frenzy.

The good news was, the continuing fire was making Orik think twice about approaching the main gate. The bad news was the pagans had other means of scaling the walls.

A goblin riding a saddled lizard rallied the flailing line. [Azzyrk - Goblin General]. He directed the army to part. Siege towers wheeled forward, pushed from behind by teams of ogres. I stared at the wooden contraptions. They were huge for siege towers, fifty feet high, and they were still only half the height of the wall. I wondered what the pagans planned to do with them until goblins at the top began loading ballistae with spikes attached to lengths of rope. Maybe they could actually scale the walls after all.

I wished we'd reserved more flame gel on the side, but it didn't help second-guessing the strategy now. Keeping Orik out had been the first order of business. We'd already won a huge victory on that front. The towers would just need to be dealt with another way.

At my order, the archers changed their focus from Orik to the siege engines. Some used fire against the wooden towers. Others let loose at the ogres pushing them, somewhat protected behind wooden roofs. Neither tactic found immediate success.

Izzy materialized cannonballs of ice that hammered the meager protection over a group of ogres. Sections of the hasty roof collapsed. Kyle used the opening to hit the big uglies with corrosive. As the rest of Stronghold's army piled on, one of the towers stalled its approach.

But even if an ogre or two dropped out of the charge, others emerged from the horde to take over. The sheer size of the pagan army started to win out.

After Dune pinned a silver arrow into an ogre's eye, a fireball rose from the crowd and bowled him over. "Ouch," he cried. He looked around. "OUCH!"

Caduceus was immediately at his side. I ran over.

"It actually hurts," he said.

"Don't be a pansy," she returned.

"No, I'm serious. I actually feel pain."

I clenched my jaw. "Yeah, that's probably my fault. I have a feeling no one has any pain filters anymore."

"What? That's awful."

"The price of freedom," I muttered.

As Caduceus attended him, his eyes went lax and he forgot about me. I stomped away, concerned. I'd started to build my own fan club, but some of these changes were bound to upset people who'd liked Haven perfectly fine the way it was. Pain was an element I wished wasn't part of the beta flags. It shouldn't have been, really. Unless pain was part of the original programming. Hacked out by the devs after early focus tests.

"Fucking sloppy programmers," I cursed.

More fireballs rained upward, doing serious damage. They strafed the organized lines on the wall, creating havoc and stymieing all resistance. The goblin warlocks also targeted the ice on the gates. Izzy chugged a spirit potion and doubled down on her countermagic, but I could tell it was draining her.

Out of nowhere, a fireball barreled toward her. Kyle jumped in the way and blocked it with his mirror shield. The magical sphere bounced and landed in the crowd below.

"Hey," he said, "I'm getting good at this. Watch."

He waited for another and intercepted it. This time he pitched his shield at an angle. The fireball deflected right into one of the siege towers, instantly setting it ablaze. The wood burned fast, causing the ogres underneath to scramble and abandon their cover. They made easy targets for the archers.

"Keep doing what you're doing!" I yelled encouragingly. But I was at a loss for what to do with myself.

These guys didn't need me up here. I didn't have ranged weapons and they'd taken my lead just fine. I spotted Gladius at the battlement steps, funneling fire mystics into position. The men on the opposite side of the gate were well commanded. Everybody was chipping in. I mean, we were still pretty much trapped in a burning house while surrounded by rabid wolves with laser teeth, but damn if we didn't figure out how to make some s'mores on our way out.

I scanned the closing battlefront and stopped on the closest siege engine. It was almost against the wall now, and the soldiers at its welcoming point were triaging from fireball wounds. Grapples fired from the tower hooked onto the battlements. I grabbed one of the last glass vials Kyle had readied, rushed closer to the exposed area, and vaulted off the battlement. A few of the soldiers forgot how to breathe as I leapt forward into the air. Scores of hungry pagans beamed from below, licking their lips. At the height of my jump, I triggered dash and flew forward onto the top of the siege tower. My momentum kicked one of the goblins clean over the rails. The other two standing at the top were easy work.

Pagans made for the inner ladder. I speared them with brutal efficiency.

"It's over, Anakin," I screamed melodramatically. "I have the high ground!"

The pagans didn't get the reference. Monkey-like imps climbed the outer frame. I cut them down as well. An ogre angrily banged the base but the tower was way too high. The monster attempted a foolish climb, stepping onto the wheels to boost him upward. Corrosive bolts and other arrows fended him off. He snarled at the wall before a silver arrow embedded in his eye and put him down for good.

I gave the thumbs up to Dune, fully healed now. It was a good start, but more siege engines were on the way. I cut the ropes attaching the current tower to the wall as another rolled past me, now in the lead. I splashed Kyle's flame gel into it. The archers took the layup. Another tower went up in flames, a pyre for the screeching goblins who had almost reached the gate.

Trembling below jarred my foot loose. I slipped and barely caught myself. My tower of death began swaying violently. Below, four ogres were treating my vehicle like a police car in the middle of a riot. I rocked wildly back and forth.

Arrows once again came to my rescue, but the ogres were tough. Shafts of wood speared their backs and still they raged on. From my wildly sweeping view, I noticed the ice barrier on the gate wasn't doing so hot. Or maybe hot was the problem. Izzy turned her attention to me, for the first time noticing I was outside the walls.

A barrage of icicles pacified the two ogres on one side. For a moment, the lurching of the engine slowed. I pulled myself up by the railing when a twisted gray creature with a hundred warts and orange hair grabbed the wooden frame. A troll. Not as stout or solid as an ogre, but just as strong with a bunch of magical abilities to boot. He snarled at me and heaved the tower backward. The whole thing listed toward the horde and fell over. I slammed to the ground and had my breath knocked out of me.

Damn. Trolls are a *lot* stronger than ogres then.

Howls converged all around me. I lifted my head and reached for my spear a few feet away.

The siege tower was smashed to bits, having flattened an ogre and several goblins. I'd fallen away from the wall, deeper into the enemy ranks than any human being had a right to be. I searched for friendly archers but the line of converging pagans was too thick.

The gate, the wall, the siege. That was over for me. I was now part of the battlefront.

0490 Battlefield

The mass of enemies danced all around me. Too many goblins to count. Sneering, spitting, cursing, poking. I swung my spear in a horizontal arc to keep them at bay.

"Pagan killer!" they spouted hungrily. "Tricksy!"

I hadn't checked my pagan faction reputation since this mess started but figured there wasn't a point anymore. They didn't like me and I didn't like them. 'Nuff said.

I scanned the battlefield for a way out of this. It was hard not to notice Orik climbing to his feet. The fire had frightened him. That gave the Stronghold defenders a lot of reason to celebrate. After all, what kind of god is gun-shy?

But Orik was unharmed overall. Back at it. And, by the looks of it, angrier than ever. Instead of going for the gate he went for the section of wall he was closest to, somewhat further south. Understandably, most of the defenders on the battlements focused on the giant.

I was on my own.

A tiny goblin lunged under my guard and swiped at me with a curved dagger. I kicked her away, my leather keeping the blade from finding my skin. The pagans jeered.

This wasn't sustainable. I had to start making examples or they'd make me one.

I swept the spear in defense again, only this time I followed the action with a swooping thrust. The unlucky goblin I'd picked at random got a surprise poke in his gut. I wasn't wielding blacksteel anymore so the damage notification disappointed me. I had to pull back before killing him to parry another attack. They laughed brutally.

Experience points flooded my notification window like the winning pull of a slot machine. I hadn't done much, but this was all-out war. Our party was sharing experience.

Not that it would help me. The goblins moved in.

A pop of glass made a few flinch. Another pop. Black corrosive ate at two unfortunates. Kyle's attacks weren't area-of-effect anymore, though. He couldn't take them all on.

"Close in!" commanded a snively voice. "Tear apart the pagan killer!"

It was Azzyrk. I focused on the goblin general snaking behind them. He was easy to see for his height and the fact that his mount was something like a giant komodo dragon. Light green with pine-colored stripes, a snake tongue slipping between shark teeth. It was the closest thing I'd ever seen to a legit dinosaur.

The general was my ticket. Maybe it was a one-way ticket, but I'd accomplish something.

I spun defensively, keeping a bead on the lizard's stride, predicting where it'd be ten seconds in advance. Azzyrk was five deep behind my attackers. Not bad. When I found an opening. I first swung a few lazy strikes. Just another day at the office, batting weapons away. The goblins shrieked and taunted me.

Then I came at them with a doozy.

The next half-hearted swing straightened in my grip. I braced the butt of the spear to extend my reach. Without blowing my skill, I punctured a goblin's neck. Not too deep—I didn't want to overcommit. I threw the spear tip sideways, ripping his throat open and shoving the shaft into the next one's chest. I missed the neck this time but the body hit was solid. The spear sunk as I pressed ahead.

Two goblins down. One dead, one badly wounded. That left an opening in the line, right between them. I yanked the spear backward and moved my grip up its length, holding the point closer to my body. I triggered dash and skidded through the goblin ranks, past the dying two and the next pair. The third and fourth rows hadn't considerately given me a clear path, so my dash ended as I nailed another goblin. The iron tip went straight through him, caught an unlucky imp who happened to be leaping behind, and finally dug into the flesh of another goblin. My weapon was now weighed down by three flailing pagans.

Crown Unlocked: **Monster Kebab**
Skewer at least 3 humanoid monsters on a stake.
1000 XP awarded

As I kicked the dying creatures off my spear, the rest of the company caught up to my quick strike. The horde closed around me. A dagger stabbed my side. A few slashes grazed my back. The general's lizard was converging on the target position but slowing in the face of danger.

It was now or never. I triggered tornado spin.

In the tight quarters, half my spear extended in front of me and half behind. I suddenly twisted, a vortex whirling too fast to count the revolutions. Both ends of my spear blew the horde away, bashing and chopping for massive damage. The entire attack took only two seconds. When it was done I stood in a wide stance in the middle of the pagan army, two yards of clearance in a full circle around me. Bodies littered that space. The goblins on the edge of my death circle reared in terror.

On cue, the general's lizard strolled into the edge of the space I'd created. It tried to turn to safety, but it didn't have that kind of maneuverability.

"Hey," I shouted, "Azzhole!"

The goblin general's eyes widened. He was only ten feet away. Only partially obscured by a single goblin.

I canted my spear upward toward the mounted general. My dash was still cooling down, but I'd saved deadshot just for this.

A debilitating blow struck my body. My head jerked sharply with whiplash as I flew sideways, bowling over a line of pagans.

> Critical Hit!
> 44 damage
> Shock!
> You are in shock. You may not use skills for 60 seconds.

Goblins cushioned my fall. I landed mostly on my feet and facing the new threat.

A sickening gray face with a long nose glowered at me. The troll was back, standing nine feet tall, its frame both malnourished and well-muscled at the same time.

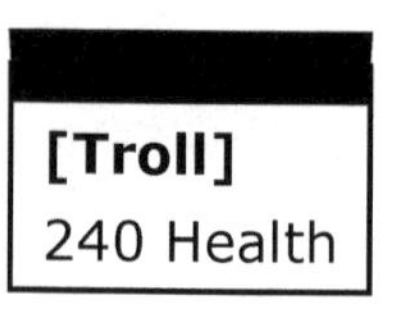

I spat blood as Azzyrk disappeared into the mass of his army. Safe in the herd.

My side was pounding. I'd have a huge bruise in the morning. Small miracle that nothing was broken. A bigger miracle would be taking on the troll at half health without skill usage.

Step one was utilizing an advantage enemies in Haven didn't have. I downed a health potion. My life bar crawled back up but the shock effect was still active. To make matters worse, I'd leveled past the point that health vials were useful. The additional 40 health wouldn't max me out. If I survived this, I'd need to start investing in better supplies.

"Human bonessss," hissed the troll. He sounded weak, like a cute, psychopathic grandpa. "I will boilsss you in a sssstew."

"I'll die first," I said. Then I paused. "Wait, that came out wrong."

The troll stomped closer. His gray skin was damp and covered with warts. His orange hair was mangy and moldy.

"Leavesss him to me, noisy brotherssss," he said.

The other pagans gave him ample clearance. Without another hint of pretense, the troll hammered a fist downward.

I recoiled backward as he pounded the goblin I'd been standing on. I could've run, but this was an ideal time to counter. I charged forward with my spear. The iron had trouble against his leathery flesh, but the resistance eased as I punched through.

Instead of doing his best goblin impression and screaming like a bitch, he punched me again.

I tumbled to the ground without my weapon. The hit wasn't critical. I'd seen it coming and he wasn't able to wind up. He'd reacted instinctually to ward off pain. Whether he showed it or not, his health bar didn't lie. It wasn't much, but I'd damaged him.

The troll pulled my spear from his chest and turned it on me. "Thissss is the great pagan killer?" he chortled.

His health bar flashed and slowly refilled to maximum.

"Uh..." was all I could say.

He stabbed forward with my weapon. You don't expect a nine-foot-looker like this to be so fast, but he was. I jumped backward and waited for my shock to wear off. Luckily, the surrounding pagans weren't joining in. None of them came at me.

"Talon! Get down!"

I barely had time to respond to Izzy's voice when a hail of spikes flew over my head. They riddled the troll, pounding him and opening up his flesh. He covered his face and patiently waited for the onslaught to end. Then he smiled as his health bar fully regenerated.

"You've got to be shitting me," I said. "OP."

Overpowered was right. Here was a creature with tons of health. By the looks of it, a great crit *might* be able to take him halfway down. But he completely healed in seconds without requiring action on his part.

"OP AF," I added.

He stomped toward me. I backed away. My retreat wasn't getting me any closer to the wall, but I couldn't risk getting near this thing. As I stepped over a goblin corpse, I scanned the ground for loose weapons. Nothing doing. I sighed and drew my whittling knife. Maybe the troll had some pencils that needed sharpening.

He sneered and stood to his full height, taking large steps to close the distance between us.

Two crossbow bolts sunk into his belly.

He barely flinched at the small things. As with the ogres, he took them like a champ. But the corrosive liquid pumping into his system twisted his face in rage. Smoke rose from his belly like a science experiment. The troll let out a brief squeal.

I lunged past my spear and slammed my body into his. The knife sank to the hilt, which isn't saying much. Before the troll could pound me, I yanked the spear from his grip and rolled away, flipping the point on him. He recovered too quickly for me to strike and kicked forward. I had to retreat again.

After all that, the troll had lost a fifth of his health. I waited for it to heal but nothing happened. It must've been the DoT. It was fighting against the troll's regeneration. We'd need about a thousand more acid bolts, but we could do it.

"Killsss the archer!" snarled the troll.

Pagans produced bows and slings. A warlock cast a fireball, and from all the way down here I could see Kyle smile. I was just regaining my feet when I realized my predicament.

"Oh, crap!"

I dove to the ground as Kyle expertly deflected the fireball toward us. The scorching flames roared past my head as the troll watched in deflated disbelief.

The fireball engulfed him. Something about his oily skin took to the flames. The orange mass rushed over his body. The giant troll writhed and buckled to his knees. I sprinted toward him and vaulted.

Not my vault skill. I was still in the final seconds of the shock effect and I couldn't risk waiting. So I jumped with the assistance of my spear to the best of my natural ability. It didn't look cool and I landed a bit wobbly, with a boot on each shoulder—but I did it. With two hands, I heaved my spear down into his skull. It answered with a satisfying pop. A straw in a coconut.

Critical Hit! You dealt 84 damage to [Troll]

I leapt head over heels backward to the ground, my boots singed and smoking and me doing a cartoon dance to put them out.

Between being brained and burned, the troll's life bar had been obliterated. But he wasn't dead yet. He held on, clawing at the bloody dirt. Another two special deliveries from Kyle plunged into his side.

"Boilsss you in my sssstew..." he said weakly.

The fire and corrosive continued draining his life and preventing his regeneration from kicking in. I walked up to the slobbering troll and drove my spear into his mouth. The abomination slumped to the ground as his skin turned to ashes.

BWOOOOOM!

You have reached Level 6!

My breath heaved in and out. I bent over, hands on knees. My health and spirit maxed with the blue fire. The quick level was surprising, but it hadn't just been the troll. Crazy XP flooded in due to the battle. Kyle and Izzy were likely seeing similar gains. I took a breather as an entire line of pagans stared at me in awe.

I gathered my confidence and stood tall. Goblins and imps backed away. An ogre watched warily from a distance.

I tightened my grip on the spear and took a menacing step toward the entire pagan army.

They stepped backward.

That's right, motherfuckers. I was caught up in the rush of power and strode toward them.

Their jaws dropped as they stared upward, faces shining with eerie light.

My brow crinkled.

Slowly, I turned around to see what the army was staring at. I had to look up and squint, but there it was: the most beautiful and devastating thing I'd ever laid eyes on.

An angel hung in the sky, clothes flapping in the wind. Above his head was his name in golden letters: [Decimus]. And among an entire battlefield of individuals, he was focused entirely on little ol' me.

0500 Halo

Decimus was a sight to behold. Strips of white cloth hung over his shoulders and around his waist. His arms extended upwards, each with a golden vambrace and silver sword. His hair was cut short and black, his jaw chiseled. Decimus was both the perfect human form and perfectly uncanny. A doll. Too precise to be real.

Statuesque even, which wasn't all that surprising since he'd once been a statue.

His eyes were wrapped with a white blindfold that didn't seem to affect his awareness. The angel's gaze, if you could call it that, remained on me as he descended. He lowered down to the battlefield, his bare feet gently padding the ground, all the while pointing his two swords skyward.

Despite being bathed in a golden aura, the pagans grew bold at seeing the enemy so close. On their level. The army surged, converging on us both.

Without turning to face them, the angel waved a sword at their line. Every other man ten rows deep was instantly decapitated. Heads bounced and rolled across the battlefield, still fixed in anger. They hadn't even had the opportunity to be surprised.

A tenth of the pagan horde's total ranks, decimated. The angel lived up to his namesake.

Amidst their crumpled front line, the rest of the goblins didn't need further instruction, but their general gave it anyway. Azzyrk slithered in on his lizard and regrouped his men. "Leave the angel be!" he ordered. "The pagan killer will receive his judgment. Leave the angel be!" The general pointed to Orik, smashing against the wall, siege engines following close behind without resistance from the harried defenders. "We go for the wall!"

The pagans cheered and rushed past us, kicking the heads of their fallen. I stared at Decimus, hand clenched on my spear.

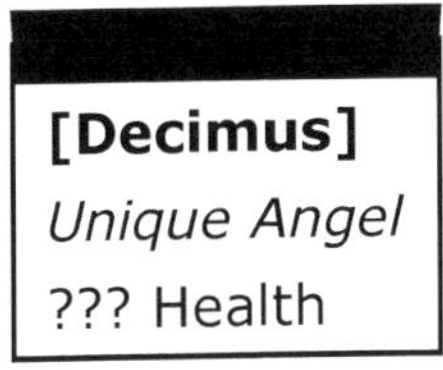

He zeroed in on me through the blindfold. "Talon," he said with a radio-friendly voice. "You are in violation of the terms of service. You will be expunged from Haven."

After my change to the beta flags, I wondered if it was still possible. My profile now resided in permanent storage. Could I really be deleted for good?

If anyone could do it, I had no doubt this angel could. His resoluteness, his might, was omnipotent.

"You're fighting against yourself," I pleaded. "I'm defending the city."

"The defense of Stronghold is not my purview," he said plainly. "Men die. Cities fall. My programming bars me from interfering with the game."

"It's not a game," I grated. "This is my life."

His lips tightened. "Your life is precisely why I'm here."

The angel stepped toward me. Kyle's crossbow clicked in the distance. The glass bolt popped against an invisible orb surrounding Decimus. Just like the soulstone.

"Okay," I reasoned. "You can't interfere with the game, right?" I backed away from the approaching angel. "By killing me, you'll be affecting the game. This battle, the fate of Stronghold—you'll be altering it all."

"Men die," he repeated. "Cities fall."

Jeez, he really did sound just like Lucifer.

"It's not just the city," I urged. "It's the Pantheon. If the pagans break in, they'll take control of Haven."

"That doesn't violate my edict. I do not exist to enforce control of the simulation; I exist to bring it balance."

I grumbled. This wasn't getting anywhere. I hefted my spear and triggered dash and deadshot together.

Nothing happened.

I tried again but the skills were in cooldown. I'd spent their spirit cost and they'd been used up, but they hadn't activated.

Decimus stepped into range. His sword flashed. I dove away but he clipped my arm.

Critical Hit!
65 damage

I fell to the floor and rolled to my feet. My health bar read 76/141.

Impossible. That had been a glancing blow. No way it deserved a crit. I chugged another healing potion but was answered only with an error sound. It was too soon to dip back into the well. It didn't heal me in the slightest.

I backtracked as Decimus swung with his other arm. This swipe only caught a piece of my boot.

Critical Hit! 65 damage

I buckled to my knees. 11/141. I wasn't fast enough. I wasn't gonna make it.

My skin tingled. A massive aura of white suddenly enveloped me. This was it. My final bow.

I was being deleted.

I panicked until I noticed Caduceus atop the wall waving a [Holy Rod].

Greater Holy Light! For the next 30 seconds, you have the ability of Greater Regeneration.

My health rocketed up much faster than a mere health vial could muster. I wasn't sure it was fast enough to stave off the angel, though. Before I reached 65 health, Decimus slashed at me again.

This time I spun and triggered crossblock. It worked. My spear parried his sword. Despite nearly jarring my weapon loose, the deflection didn't slow him down. He merely turned with the momentum and sliced his other sword across my chest.

Critical Hit! 65 damage

I tumbled backward. I wasn't dead. My health flashed down to 9 from the hit before greater regeneration pumped it up again.

Fucking cheater. Decimus was throwing undeserved crits left and right. My health steadily filled but, even with the buff, I wasn't a tank. I couldn't keep absorbing everything he had and stay breathing.

On the wall above, Izzy's face filled with worry. She cast an attack but her spell fizzled out. "What the?" she worded.

The angel was protected against physical attacks by a golden aura. Offensive skills couldn't be used against him. His dual blades were enchanted with 100% chances of criticals. This was getting very bad, very fast. The only thing I could be thankful for was that he couldn't just swipe his arm and cut me down as he had the goblin army. Maybe he didn't have that power against players.

Limits. If he had *that* one, there had to be others. That meant there was something I could do.

I lengthened the spear in my grip to fend off his attacks. He came at me with an even pace. Never slowing, never relenting.

Once again I blocked the first attack but got hit with the second.

> Critical Hit!
> 65 damage

Down to 3 this time. Decimus was simply too fast to avoid.

The red robe on the wall rushed to my aid. Stigg added a buff to my arsenal.

> Berserker's Frenzy!
> For the next 30 seconds, your physical skills do not require cooldown.

I was at a third health already. My greater regeneration was cranking hard, but it wasn't fast enough to overcome the angel's onslaught. One more hit in the next several seconds would kill me. My last health potion might not be completely useless, depending how much time had elapsed since the last one, but it would also lower my defenses, practically guaranteeing a follow-up hit. Then I'd be left lower than before, in the same position as now.

One hit and I was dead. I had to hope the berserker's buff would be enough.

Decimus swung, content to continue the tactic until I defeated it. I knocked his sword away and he mechanically moved in with his other weapon. Too fast to dodge by normal means.

I triggered dash. This time, I was careful not to use it as a charge. That would fizzle out for sure. A slanting dodge? Well, I wasn't sure it would work. If it didn't, I was a goner. But it was a defensive move, and crossblock was working out. I slid across the dirt and slipped under the angel's weapon for the first time.

I was behind him now, more or less, standing back to back. Now standing within the angel's orb of protection, I reversed my weapon and thrusted it at his exposed back. The weapon struck true. Unfortunately, it glanced off nothing but white silk. The blow was deflected without causing a single point of damage.

Decimus, surprised for the first time, hastily whirled to face me. He slashed both swords together. Taking advantage of Stigg's buff, I dashed backward, escaping him again. The angel's lips tightened as my health finally regenerated to full.

My skills had no cooldown, but they weren't free. They still cost spirit, which meant I couldn't dash around like a hummingbird or trigger unlimited tornado spins. Still, 75 spirit was plenty for what I needed.

Decimus lunged. I dashed to the side and tried another strike. He moved quickly, not letting me touch him. The angel countered with impressive precision. I dashed backward, just barely dodging a clean beheading. I thrust my spear forward, catching Decimus in the chest. Once again, my weapon bounced away uselessly.

He swiped and I dashed, but I didn't get away clean this time. His blade barely grazed my arm.

Critical Hit! 65 damage

I managed to stay on my feet in a wild spin. My health continued to regenerate. Fifty percent. Fifty-five. In the distance, Orik blindly pounded against Stronghold's wall. The fire at the gate was dying. Kyle hadn't been able to juice it with any more fuel. Only a matter of time now, but the titan wasn't waiting. Twice as tall as the great wall, he finally came to his senses and leaned over the battlements. Orik was scaling over it.

It was a win over breaking down the gate. Without the wall falling, the rest of the horde was locked outside. Still, the giant breaching the city was the endgame. He couldn't be allowed to reach the Pantheon, no matter what. Too bad he was too big to stop.

Decimus slashed me clear across the back.

Critical Hit!
65 damage

I dropped to my knees. My eyes widened as I gazed upon the grim scene.

Too big. Too unstoppable.

I turned to Decimus, standing victoriously above me.

I growled. I wasn't dead yet, and there were bigger menaces on this battlefield than him.

As his killing blow cut through the air, I dashed away from him. His sword whiffed. Instead of trying to fight back, I sprinted away.

Greater Regeneration has ended!

Crap. I was only at 33 health. One hit would kill me and my regeneration had run out. I was running from the angel so fast I didn't have time to down a potion. The line of screaming goblins came upon me too quickly. I planted my spear in the ground and triggered vault, flying above their diminutive heads.

Decimus followed. The pagans parted like the Red Sea. The ones that remained in his path were put down wordlessly.

I found a clear path and dashed. Then another and repeated. I charged straight toward the god-giant without fear for my life because, as far as I was concerned, I was already dead.

The angel was on my trail but I pulled away from him. The chaos was working in my favor. I dashed wildly between it, rapidly changing position, giving Decimus a tough time of tracking me. The madness gave me a chance to use a health potion, but I opted to refill my almost-empty spirit instead. That allowed me a few more dashes to carry out my plan.

Berserker's Frenzy has ended!

My last dash ended right after the notification. I cursed the bad luck. The skill was now in cooldown mode. I couldn't trigger it despite having plenty of spirit.

No matter. I was close enough to Stronghold. In the madness brought on by Orik's presence, several siege towers had successfully made it to the wall. The titan had passed completely over. Scores of pagans streamed in behind him, rushing up the tower ladders. At the top, they threw grapples and climbed up in such numbers that they overwhelmed any defense. The battlements brimmed with goblins driving back legionnaires.

Dune, Stigg, and Caduceus fought back the first wave, but were forced to slowly retreat. My party protected the gate from the rapidly encroaching forces. Behind me, Decimus painted a swath of pagan blood, converging on his only target.

It was all going to hell. Somewhere, Lucifer was watching in delight. I reminded myself to tear him a new one next time we met.

I charged forward. Most of the pagans were so eager to scale the wall they didn't notice me among their ranks. I sped right past them to one of the siege towers. Instead of attempting to clear them off the ladder, I triggered vault and landed on the outside frame. With my new climbing ability, it was cake to pull myself to the top. I balanced on the railing and hopped on the goblins, using their heads as stepping stones. With deft steps, I ran straight up a tightrope, passing over the hands of hanging goblins. I leapt for the wall and looked over my shoulder.

Decimus floated in the air now. Above the reach of the army, he'd ascended to my level, but his pursuit had halted. He didn't close on me. He didn't advance.

I stood in place on the battlements for a long second, only slightly aware of Caduceus healing me at range. I turned to Orik and then back to Decimus. The angel was afraid to engage the titan. Or, more likely, his programming prevented him from interfering with such a dominating game asset.

It clicked into place: As long as I stayed close to the cyclops, Decimus wouldn't pursue me.

With a triumphant roar, I kicked a frisky goblin over the battlements. His scream ended in a crack at the foot of the city. Then I charged inside. I vaulted into the air and triggered dash at the height of my jump. I rocketed right into the back of Orik's waist, just as he was disengaging from the wall, and grabbed on tight.

I turned back to see Decimus suspended in the sky with a frown.

"Nice talk," I said. "Let's do this again real soon."

The giant rose to full height and yanked me with him. The clump of grass in my hand held tight, even as my legs swung wildly below.

A single miscalculation and I would drop to my death just like the goblin.

Maybe I hadn't wasted a skill point on climbing after all.

0510 God of War

The titan was a slow, lumbering thing. Anything that massive and solid had no business moving outside of earthquakes. Unfortunately, Orik was slow but he wasn't tectonic-plate slow. His heavy, trudging steps shook the ground below him. Tremors ran up his body. I rocked violently, praying the clumps of grass I held onto were rooted deep.

This was more terrifying than I'd imagined it would be.

Talon: *Where the hell are you guys?*
Kyle: *West gate still. Why?*
Talon: *Get to Oldtown.*
Izzy: *You crazy? The titan's in Oldtown.*
Talon: *Yeah, and I'm hanging on his back. Hurry up!*

The lack of replies told me they were rushing to my aid.

Because Orik had retreated from the fire at the gate, he ended up breaching the wall farther south. That meant we were in Oldtown, near the river gate we'd snuck in. This part of the city was abandoned. The arrows and slings that continued to pepper the giant were from the battlements. The ruins themselves provided no resistance.

But the west gate was crowded with soldiers ready to fight, and as Orik headed north, the players and guards up there pivoted south. I braced my feet into the titan's backside and scaled laterally to get a view past him. Already I could see a line forming at the end of Oldtown.

Projectiles from the wall exploded next to me. Orik barely flinched. I almost lost my grip.

"Watch it!" I screamed to the chaotic mass.

Legionnaires struggled to keep order as the pagan horde ascended the siege towers. The jig was up. In minutes the goblins would spill into the streets.

Even worse, none of the attacks against Orik did much. He didn't regenerate. Besides the Eye he didn't have a magical shield. But his health bar looked as full as ever. He plodded forward through any resistance, a slow and steady Armageddon.

The first wave of resistance met Orik below. Swords and hammers dug into his igneous flesh. The giant balled his fists and pounded them to mush. More guards and players rushed in.

I had to help them.

I clung to Orik's waist. I assumed the skin here was weaker than below, but it certainly didn't seem that way. I wasn't sure if the titan was made out of rock or just wore it as armor, but it didn't appear to have many weaknesses.

I braced myself and triggered deadshot. I only received an error sound. I was inside 10 spirit. Not enough for the skill. More urgently, I had less than 20 seconds of climbing time left. I bit the spear as deep into the giant's side as I could.

As with the melee weapons below, the attack did result in damage. The movement of Orik's health bar was infinitesimal, but it moved. And just as with those others, Orik noticed. He twisted around, trying to get his eyeless cavity on me. His hulking palm rubbed down his side.

I released the clump of grass to avoid being smashed. A gigantic hand clapped over my position as I dropped past. I dug my hands into a tangle of vines around Orik's knee and jerked to a halt, wincing as my arm was nearly dislocated.

As I hung there, in pain, the titan's hand followed.

"Distract the giant!" rang out Lash's authoritative voice. "Don't let it get him!"

The vainglorious white knight was in the ruins below, decked out in full plate but otherwise exposed to attack. She swung her cleaver with both arms. It trailed a yellow blaze and struck the titan's Achilles tendon.

It hurt him. The cyclops shuddered and bellowed.

Players flooded to the knight's aid. The barbarian and healer from her party. Other players I didn't recognize. Even the watchmen and centurions were in on the action now. The titan shook, enraged, causing me to slide further down his leg. As my spirit bar hit 0, I missed my last handhold and bounced, landing hard on the road below.

Multiple blows struck giant feet. Orik wavered against the sudden attacks. A sidestep threatened to crush me. At the last second, Lash clamped a powerful hand around my wrist and lurched me to safety.

Down here, when the giant stepped, our bodies vibrated and

a cloud of dirt smothered us. I covered my face as the knight helped me to my feet and pulled me uproad.

"Look at this poser," snapped Lash, only messing around this time. Her friends smiled. The full helm turned to me. "Are you crazy? What do you think you're doing climbing that thing?"

"The Eye," I said, miming a horn on my forehead. "Only I didn't have enough spirit to hang on."

As Orik gathered himself, the other players retreated as well. It had been a rescue party. They'd come out to save me.

When we joined the mass of defenders, Izzy and Kyle were just arriving. I hugged both of them. Izzy's eyes trailed off to the towering titan forging ahead.

"This is it," I said. "This is the fight we all knew was coming."

The entire group was bathed in yellow light as Lash activated a group buff. My spirit bar jumped up a cool 100. "That give you what you need?" asked Lash.

I nodded my thanks. The white knight probably had a variety of group buffs. Something more offensive had no doubt helped them distract Orik long enough to rescue me. Who would've thought Lash, of all people, was a team player?

"Trafford!" exclaimed Kyle. He clapped the shopkeeper on the shoulder. "What are you doing out here? I thought you retired from the legionnaires."

"Aye," said the weathered man. "But that was before these beasties decided to fuck with my city." Players and NPCs cheered in unison. What wasn't to like about the miserable bastard?

"I asked him here," said Lash. "We're setting up a roadblock."

She pointed to the Oldtown buildings on either side of us. The second stories had collapsed long ago, but their foundations were solid. Multiple strands of thick rope trailed from one structure to the other.

"You're gonna trip him," I reasoned.

She nodded.

"Beats climbing," said Kyle, returning to my side.

The white full helm swiveled and held on him for a long moment. I thought Lash might make amends, given the situation and all, but she didn't do anything nearly as magnanimous. She didn't, however, verbally abuse him, which was a huge improvement in my book.

The ground rumbled as Orik advanced. The river created a natural bottleneck, corralling him north along the wall. Not only did that continue exposing him to the archers on the battlements, but it led him right toward us. Once the giant reached the west gate he'd cross the thoroughfare to the Forum, then head all the way to the Pantheon at the end, just as he had before.

That could never happen.

As if sensing the ambush ahead, Orik changed his course slightly. Still northbound, but hugging the river. I watched his stride: lugging and steady, but able to cover large gaps when needed. This was a creature who'd crossed over Stronghold's wall. The river wouldn't hedge him in.

I whistled sharply and Bandit hurried to me. I hopped on.

"What are you doing?" cried Izzy.

"Getting his attention."

The striped mountain bongo galloped straight at the

behemoth without fear. She was a perfect mount. Maybe she didn't spit acid like Lucifer's pet but she'd give her life for me in a second. She already had in a redundant timeline.

Since the cyclops wasn't focused on us, it was easy to slip between his feet. I raked my spear against his leg as we passed. The hulking giant groaned so I looped around and did it again.

Without warning, his open palm came down. It impacted the ground just behind us, almost tripping Bandit. In answer, I scoured his fingers with my iron. Orik's face twisted in rage.

The titan sprung to his feet as we galloped away. Orik smashed another fist toward us and gave chase. He wasn't charging, exactly. Things his size weren't able to run like we could, but the giant had found the grit to speed up.

Bandit and I led the god-giant right to our merry band of defenders. Her hooves danced over the limp ropes on the ground. We retreated another block closer to the river bottleneck to sell the pursuit. I turned around and smiled.

The blind giant had fallen for the trap; hook, line, and sinker.

"Now!" screamed Lash.

Players hidden behind the buildings heaved the lengths of rope. Snaked around support columns like pulleys, the setup allowed them to mitigate the tremendous mass of the titan. Orik's foot barreled into the tripwires. The first two ropes snapped with little resistance. The players securing them flew forward, helpless against his strength. But the union of several other ropes proved mightier. Orik's foot slowed and stopped short. The giant canted forward.

For a second, the stars in the night sky were blacked out as the titan loomed over us. But we'd cleared ample space and there was no danger. Orik pitched downward.

With his left foot trapped behind his weight, his left knee opened a crater on the ground as it hit, followed shortly by his left hand beside it. Orik's body swayed forward, but he pulled backward before completely losing his balance. The giant settled on his haunches, crouched but stable.

"Hit him hard!" boomed Lash.

Arrows took flight. A mobile ballista manned by legionnaires let loose a heavy-duty spiked projectile. Izzy launched a crystalline stake with a perfect spiral. Kyle fired corrosive bolts. Mystics launched spells. Artisans fired gadgets and minions. Explorers and soldiers joined in with ranged weapons. A swarm of pure damage railed right to the lowered tip of the downed titan's horn.

The windows to the soul.

Ruby light projected a small barrier in front of the gemstone. Every other part of the giant had been easy to hit—it was actually hard to miss something so massive—but the Eye of Orik was clearly protected by incredible magic. The makeshift barrage, the sum of all our strongest attacks, exploded violently against the shield, mere feet before their mark. Blinding flashes of light. Jarring shockwaves of sound. It was an impressive coordinated effort that jolted the giant's head backwards.

But when the dust cleared, the cyclops appeared no worse for wear. The magical red barrier faded back to invisible. Orik had absorbed a hearty dose of splash damage. A bit less than a twentieth of his health bar was missing. But that had been our best shot. A trap sprung. And Orik only looked mildly annoyed.

The cyclops backed away.

I squeezed my legs into Bandit and charged forward.

"Keep him down!" I yelled.

The giant started to push off his right foot, but his left knee was still planted in the ground. His hand, beside it, frosted over with ice. Izzy was gluing him to the ground. Orik grimaced and the glacier cracked. I kicked harder.

Bandit leapt into the air and landed on Orik's frozen hand. She galloped up the slope of his arm as I stood on her back, precariously balancing and holding a horn for support. The ice trap shattered and the giant pushed to his feet. His arm jerked but Bandit pressed onward, accustomed to steep slopes.

"Just a bit more," I urged, leaning forward.

As Orik stood, his arm went nearly vertical. I pounced off Bandit's back as she spun and skipped safely to the ground. I triggered a midair dash and launched upward, latching onto a giant ring of iron embedded in the giant's chest like a rusted nipple ring. My boots lost purchase. I hung on for dear life and looked down as the titan reared to full height.

Intense vertigo overtook me. I was way higher than before, towering over the city walls. I don't especially like heights. Bandit retreated to the safety of the pack of defenders as they all watched me, mouth agape. I wanted to say something cool but I was too busy crapping my pants.

The cyclops had enough of the roadblock. Instead of bowling forward, he actually did something strategic. The god-giant turned south and retreated from the dense crowd. He opted to go east instead, a straight shot past Dragonperch and the river, right through Hillside. There were players there, of course, but most of them were running for their lives or hiding out. It'd be easy for Orik to head north to the Forum from there. And all he had to do was step over an itty bitty river.

But I saw my opening. Orik was so focused on the new path that he didn't notice me going along for the ride. This time, I didn't make the mistake of stabbing him and announcing myself, and I had spirit for days.

Orik's chest rocked back and forth in a steady gait. I found footholds and climbed higher. It was hard going but I couldn't be conservative. Once Orik crossed the river, I'd be too late. I dashed upward and barely caught a cluster of dry roots. Then I crested the giant's shoulder and climbed to my feet.

From this height I could see all of Stronghold from a bird's-eye view. The west gate had so far held, but it was buckling under the pagan assault. Goblins and imps littered the streets anyway; many siege towers had made it to the wall. The pagans were gaining control of the battlements but lacked the support of the ogres and trolls. The heavier beasts couldn't readily scale the stone or climb the ropes.

Gladius and the centurions had strategically conceded ground to ensure the gate held as long as possible. They drew a hard red line across the wall which the pagans couldn't breach. Yet.

In the streets, conniving greens and grays lunged for Stronghold residents, player and NPC alike. Izzy, Kyle, Lash, and the others reoriented on the new threat. I could count on them for anything, but the numbers would soon become overwhelming.

It was entirely plausible that Stronghold could fall even without Orik reaching the Pantheon.

The cyclops took another heavy step and I readied my next move. The giant was a head taller than Dragonperch, which put his shoulders (and me) flush with the roof. The broken statue of Magnus Dragonrider came into view. A cracked head attached to half a torso stared into the sky. The expression was supposed to be bold and brave, but from here it just looked hollow.

As Orik passed, I jumped from his shoulder to the top of Dragonperch. I wanted to keep my dash available and fell short for being greedy. My chest crashed into the side of the building and I desperately clawed at the parapet. It was only by the grace of my climbing skill that I clambered safely to the top.

I scrambled on the ground and heaved broken rocks away. The dragon rider's spear, still held by a stone hand, wasn't part of the statue. Saint Peter's sidelong comment and the glint from the sun had tipped me off to it. This was a relic. A long piece of uniform material, metal or bone—I couldn't tell. It shimmered white and blue and nickel like a pearl. The rock sloughed away as I lifted the unnaturally light weapon.

[Dragonspear]
Unique, Unbreakable
The famed weapon of the hero Magnus Dragonrider, the dragonspear grants its wielder heroic power.
+3 Strength
+2 Agility
+1 Essence
Titanslayer
+25% damage versus dragons
+20% damage defending Stronghold
+15% damage versus pagans

I twirled the perfectly balanced dragonspear with ease. This was it. This was my god killer.

"Hey, stupid," I shouted.

At the edge of the river, Orik turned my way, surprised to face an enemy as tall as he was.

His eyeless socket blinked. I wondered what it was he could see exactly. My gaze followed his forehead and ran up the horn to the soulstone. The Eye of Orik gleamed brightly.

"Eyes are the windows to the soul," I muttered. I ground my teeth together, remembering more of the riddle. "Bodies petrify. Souls are forever."

What the hell did that mean?

That I could never kill Orik's soul. But that would imply—

It came to me. The lore wasn't just smarmy advice—it was an instruction manual. We'd been trying to attack the soul, but souls were invincible. It was the body that needed to be defeated.

Orik scowled and brought heavy hands around me.

I stood atop Dragonperch like a new statue. Waiting. The giant's mitts bore down on me, surrounding me as they had the obelisk on Blind Man's Peak. I pushed the gory vision of the pulped boggarts from my mind and carefully lined up the dragonspear, a model of supreme focus.

I triggered vault and dash and deadshot, surging up and out. The alabaster spear sunk into Orik like he was melted butter. I slid forward and crashed into his face, still gripping the spear. The dragonspear drove in all the way to my hands, right into Orik's empty eye socket.

I halted my fall by wildly clinging to the spear, dangling two hundred feet above the ground.

"Eyes might be the windows to soul," I said triumphantly, "but eye *sockets* are the windows to the brain."

Orik faltered and stumbled backward. His face twisted in a horrific agony. I was right next to his mouth as he let out a deafening cry. Hot air washed over me. The giant took two stuttering steps before buckling to his knees. I wrapped my arms and legs around the embedded spear to keep from plummeting to my death.

The titan's hands reached to the sky instead of going for his face. His movements became jerky. Forced. His bones were freezing up. His body, stiffening.

"Bodies petrify," I recited.

Orik stopped. A massive behemoth; pacified, frozen, but still breathing. He didn't have a health bar anymore. My attack had cleaned him out. A one and done. I wiggled upward, hopped to the horn, and climbed to the Eye of Orik.

I pulled my noob whittling knife from my inventory. "I knew you'd be useful for something," I said. Then I pried the soulstone from the obelisk.

The great titan heaved, the last of his breath fled him, and then he went silent forever.

I hefted the Eye of Orik in my hand. "But the soul still burns."

The pagan army below blew wailful horns. The centurions targeting the siege towers were starting to win back the battlements. It would be a hard battle, but the dying cry of their god unsettled the horde. Many of the pagans stalled their attack, waiting for word from their mighty cyclops.

At this stage in the game, that was as good as retreating.

[Orik] is defeated
26,339 XP awarded

Pagan Reputation -1000 (MAXED)

Swarms of blue fire enveloped me as overlapping chords sounded.

BWOOOOOM!

You have reached Level 7!

BWOOOOOM!

You have reached Level 8!

Quest Complete: **Unveil the Pagans**
Quest Type: Epic
Reward: Unknown
The threat of Orik has been subdued.
Stronghold is safe.
9,000 XP awarded
500 silver bars

BWOOOOOM!

You have reached Level 9!

In the distance, Kyle and Izzy were likewise bathed in the same fires of achievement. They stared at each other in awe. We'd reached levels previously unheard of in the Haven beta.

But then, this wasn't a beta anymore, was it?

Global Haven Alert:
Talon has received the mantle of Protector of Stronghold.

I stared blankly at the final notification. This was getting intense. I wondered what the title meant, exactly.

But then, my arms were getting tired. I glanced to the top of Dragonperch, eager to get off the titanic statue. Unfortunately, the tower was too far away now. Orik had frozen halfway down its height, on both knees. Players were gathering below me, staring up in awe at the new hero who wielded the dragonspear.

I grumbled and searched for a way to get down.

0520 Titanfall

The battle didn't last long after that. Turns out morale's a bitch, and when your prophesized god-giant whom all your plans hinge upon turns into brick, there's not much left to do but turn tail and run.

Without the daunting threat of the cyclops, Stronghold rallied to contain the pagans within the walls. The goblins and imps were stunned at the impossible turn of events and didn't have a path of retreat. They were routed. We retook the battlements and fortified the gate, mowing down the pagans who didn't flee. The army didn't have much steam after that.

It was nice, for once, to see players and NPCs all unified under a single cause. Dune was high-fiving Gladius. Phil put some pants on. Even Izzy managed a smile. If that wasn't enough, Lash allowed that Kyle "wasn't completely worthless."

The players saluted me like I was their hero. Magnus reborn, they claimed. I modestly played it off. I mean, I'd kicked some serious butt, but so had they. Dune had rebelled against the centurions. Lash and Trafford had organized the titan tripwire. Izzy and Kyle had exhausted every resource against all odds to keep the gate and the city intact.

After Stronghold was secured, a new surprise greeted me. I wasn't sure what "heroic powers" the dragonspear granted, but the great doors of Dragonperch opened before us. The mythical spear was recognized by the wards. It had been the key to the tower all along.

There wasn't some great dungeon inside, as we'd all imagined, but an incredible bastion of knowledge. A library, a war room, lodging. The new digs were so cool that Izzy and Kyle and I moved in immediately. We reset it to our home base, residents of Hillside no longer. And as always with mysterious RPG towers, there was lots left to explore.

I stood on the roof of Dragonperch, getting used to the grand height, gazing down on the destruction the pagans had caused. It would take weeks of restoration, but the populace was content to rest and recover for now. The tended land outside was marred by thousands of boots, but the field, too, would regrow. Instead I looked to the east, across the town, to the sunrise on the horizon. Bandit sniffed the air gently. She liked it up here. Reminded her of the mountains, I figured. Izzy and Kyle were exploring the tower below, leaving me with time to think.

You could say I was beginning to like the place.

"I was waiting for you to show," I said, not taking my eyes off the beautiful vista.

Saint Peter rustled behind me. "Oh, yes. I'm surprised you heard me."

I waited for him to tell me what he'd come to say.

"A lot has happened in a day. We've reconsidered our position on you, Tod—I'm sorry, it's Tad, isn't it? I'm awfully forgetful."

I turned around and looked him in the eye. "Actually, it's Talon from now on."

He nodded gravely and swiveled to study the petrified body of Orik. The titan kneeled before Dragonperch, arms skyward in praise of the city's might and the restored importance of Oldtown. The symbolism wasn't lost on the saint. It wasn't something I took lightly, either. The mantle of Protector of Stronghold was a big responsibility, but one I believed in.

For my part, I realized I'd been fighting so hard to get back my old life that I'd ignored what was right in front of me in Haven: a place worth saving.

"I don't see Decimus anywhere," I noted.

Saint Peter smiled weakly. "He's been deactivated. He's back atop his column in front of the Pantheon."

"So we're not enemies?"

He sighed. "Listen, Talon, we're not the bad guys. You might see us as an evil mega-corporation, but we're just capitalists. We do things to make money and cover our asses when we inevitably cross the line. Your upload was by the book, one hundred percent. But then you recovered. It shocked everybody. You were never supposed to be activated in the first place, but someone somewhere cut corners. An opportunity to run additional tests was utilized."

"I'm just a tool to you. A testing routine."

He raised a hand in surrender. "Mistakes were made. But how can you be mad about it? If we didn't do it, you wouldn't exist."

"I'm more sore at the whole trying-to-delete-me part."

He frowned. "We *are* sorry about that. Try to look at it from our point of view. You're not a person. You don't have human rights. We considered you a loose end. A glitch. Now we realize you're much more."

"I don't get it. If I'm just a copy, doesn't that defeat the whole purpose of Heaven? The person who died doesn't truly live on."

"It's the same person," he countered. "Uniqueness isn't a requirement of sentience. And families will still appreciate being able to connect with those who pass on."

"But it's smoke and mirrors. A magic trick. It's not real."

Saint Peter stroked his beard thoughtfully. "Do you *feel* like smoke and mirrors, Talon?"

I didn't answer. He had a point. "I don't want anyone else coming after me," I added.

"No one else will. The decision has been made to let you live. Besides, your stunt with the beta flags forced our hand."

"You can't kill me anymore."

He chuckled. "I wouldn't go that far, but it's much more trouble than it's worth. Kablammy is willing to entertain a truce. But you must understand, for purposes of posterity and preservation of the prime directive, we cannot acknowledge you as a person. The real Tad Lonnerman is alive somewhere. He still has an open contract with Kablammy. He still has the potential to die and be uploaded here one day. His human rights must follow him."

For the first time, I thought of the real me as a separate, distinct person. Him and my brother. My living family. "I wouldn't ask for less," I said.

He nodded and held out his hand expectantly.

"Oh. Yeah."

I tossed the Eye of Orik to him. Saint Peter deftly scooped it into his palm.

"I don't want any more attempts against the Pantheon," he warned. "That kind of activity will violate our truce."

I nodded.

He turned to go but paused. "And no more deals with Lucifer."

I clenched my jaw. The white robes didn't have to worry on that score. I was gonna find the fallen angel all right, and when I did I wasn't gonna shake his hand.

Saint Peter flashed out of existence. Moments later, Stronghold thrummed with renewed power. The Eye had been returned to the tabernacle. The walls were impenetrable to pagans once again.

I gazed down on the city once more. My town. My life. I was rebooted now, no longer Tad Lonnerman, but Talon. A new person. A new mission. I was gonna make this work. From here on out, I was gonna fight and grind for every last thing I had left.

-Finn

Character Sheets

Talon		*Level*	9
Class	Explorer	*XP*	49417
Kit	Scout	*Next*	74950

4

Strength	17	*Strike*	324
Agility	21	*Dodge*	360
Craft	6	*Health*	247 / 247
Essence	9	*Spirit*	207 / 207

Coin	
Silver	142
Bars	166

Skills	**8**
Spear	3
Crossblock	2
Deadshot	3
Tornado Spin	1
Traversal	
Dash	
Vault	
Scale	

Proficiencies
Skilled
Searcher
Fledgling
Tracker

Reputation	
Pagan	-1000

Kyle		*Level*	8
Class	Artisan	*XP*	44042
Kit	Brewmaster	*Next*	49300

	5		
Strength	14	*Strike*	188
Agility	5	*Dodge*	116
Craft	15	*Health*	132 / 132
Essence	8	*Spirit*	134 / 134

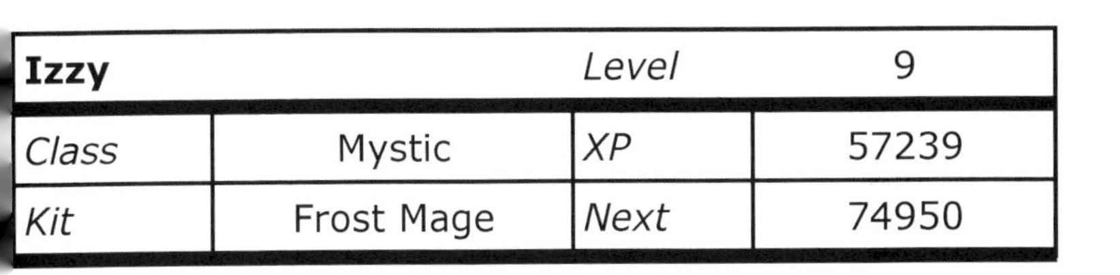

Izzy		*Level*	9
Class	Mystic	*XP*	57239
Kit	Frost Mage	*Next*	74950

3

Strength	8	*Strike*	166
Agility	13	*Dodge*	211
Craft	6	*Health*	130 / 130
Essence	21	*Spirit*	330 / 330

Haven Live Feed

Saint Peter
I would like to welcome the residents of Stronghold to the Haven Live Feed beta! Post your thoughts, feelings, and latest happenings. Just another way Kablammy works for you.

PS - If I see any mentions of duping or hacking, you will be blocked.

Talon
Cool, like Facebook!

Saint Peter
No, no. This is *completely* and *legally* distinct.

Lash
I want everybody to friend me. *Now*.

Domino Finn invites you to Like his page (www.facebook.com/DominoFinnBooks).

Izzy
One of these days...

Kyle
Uh, vaguebook much?

Izzy
Complain to my face, you big whiner.

Phil
<Click for video>

Caduceus
Don't click. It's just a video of him dancing naked.

Stigg
How could I *not* click then?

Dune
I'm with Stigg.

Caduceus
... Any party of non-ten-year-olds looking for a healer?

Glinda
Ugh. I could've gone another whole lifetime without seeing that.

Talon changed his relationship status to: Seeing someone.

Izzy
Excuse me???

Kyle sent a game invite for Beer Pong. Claim your free beer!

Lash
Okay, everyone, there's way too much noise on my friends list. I'm gonna delete anybody who doesn't tell me they're my friend...

Glinda
Me! I'm your friend!

Conan
Don't delete me.

Kyle
The silence is deafening.

Lash
Get off my private feed, loser!

Talon changed his relationship status to: It's complicated.

Izzy
You saying I'm complicated???

Lucifer
Top Ten Ways You're a Slave to the System. You WON'T BELIEVE Number 7!

Saint Peter
Okay, people, this is malware. Please don't click it.

Talon changed his relationship status to: None of your business.

Conan
I'm so sad to hear the news about Chris Cornell. Soundgarden was my jam back in the day. This year is the worst. YOU KILLED ANOTHER ONE!

Talon
Do we really need to rehash every single death as a punch line?

Chris C
Tell me about it. It's old already.

Conan
Chris is that you?!?

Lash
That's it, everybody. I'm quitting the live feed for good.

Izzy
It's not that bad.

Lash
I have better things to do though.

Talon
You realize you're still posting.

Lash
Ugh! This is why I quit!

Kyle
For real this time?

Lash
Grrr...

Talon
Don't poke the dog, Kyle.

Lash
THAT'S IT I'M OUT!!!

Haven Terms of Service 0.9.21

Your access to and use of Haven is conditioned upon your acceptance of and compliance with these Terms of Service, sometimes referred to as Terms, which apply to all participants, users, and visitors in Haven, and are set and governed by Kablammy Games, who is as an organization exempt from this and any other agreements. How was that for a first sentence? Our hope is that lots of boring legalese at the head of these Terms will hopefully dissuade curious readers. For the 2% who've made it this far, trust us, there's nothing entertaining or illuminating in this document. It's a waste of time to read it. Even international tax lawyers find its contents stuffy.

By accessing, using, or even thinking about Haven, you agree to be bound by these Terms. You may "opt out" at any time and face summary annihilation.

Residence
All participants, heretofore referred to as Residents, agree to store all aspects of their personality on Kablammy servers. Transfer of ownership is implied and implicit in this transaction. Don't worry about it.

Happy Fun Time for Everybody!
We included this paragraph for nosy contract skimmers. Besides the feel-good title, this section serves no functional purpose.

Termination
We may terminate Residents... err, accounts... immediately, without prior notice or liability, for any reason whatsoever, including, without limitation, a breach of the Terms. Or passing fancy.

Human Rights Compliance
Kablammy strongly believes in individual human protections and will never infringe upon a person's privacy, security, and individuality.

For the purposes of the previous declaration, Residents of Haven are considered collected intelligences and are not human and are therefore exempt from the above clause.

Beta Conditions

Kablammy reserves the right to dictate Terms of the Beta regardless of the contents of this document. Beta Residents agree to be "guinea pigs," accepting the good and bad in order to serve the interests of actual paying customers. We refer to this internally as the you-get-what-you-pay-for clause. Your life experiences are temporary and solely for the benefit of improving Haven. Congratulations!

Despite stringent beta responsibilities, Residents are solely engaging in entertainment. Your work does not constitute employment nor do you garner salary or any other rights granted to workers. We're even stingy with thank-yous.

Addendum: Let's be honest, MMOs are always technically beta testing one feature or another. As such, the above Beta Terms apply whether or not Haven is officially in beta.

Wipes

Your possessions, achievements, and identity are the sole property of Kablammy Games. Residents are not afforded an avenue to take action against Kablammy or the devs due to loss of self.

Content

Despite Haven being a closed system, Residents will not hold Kablammy accountable for any damaging or suspect game content. In fact, Residents are wholly responsible for our mistakes, because why not?

Patches

Due to necessary patches to keep Haven up-to-date, Kablammy reserves the right, at our sole discretion, to modify or replace these Terms at any time. We will make an attempt to notify all Residents of any changes but, let's face it, there's nothing you can do about it.

Contact Us

If you have any questions about these Terms of Service, a knowledgeable, around-the-clock staff can be reached by pressing the green Help button in-game. These ~~low-wage~~ treasured ~~peons~~ team members can't really access your account information in any beneficial way, but they work off the best scripts and probably speak English.

Lore

A Brief History of the Nine

The first sentients to spawn from the primordial ooze of Haven were the titans. They parted from the land in a violent tumult and became kings of the wild and all-powerful gods in their own right. To this end they wrought sons and daughters from the elements themselves: churning rock, roiling rivers, gushing wind, and fueling fires.

The kindred clans that grew learned to idolize the great titans of yore, not legends or figureheads but real, physical masters. Scores of errant folk pledged their loyalties for growing power and thus, too, became masters of the land, even as animals and others sprouted around them.

The Nine did not conquer nature so much as they were nature itself. And for an enduring great age, none would equal their might.

The Cleansing of the Old Gods

Man is nothing if not ambitious. Where the errant folk would cower and serve, mankind boldly swept through the wilderness and made it their own: carving rock, channeling ocean, harnessing wind, and mastering fire. Haven was being tamed in short order.

The titans of yore were not so easily cowed. They thrashed wildly against these incursions. The territories of the Nine were terrible places in this time of upheaval. But the clerics of man discovered the secret of the old giants. They were immortal, but they could be caged.

The Scourge and the Crusades

Once the nine great cities of man were founded, Haven became a prosperous and dutiful land. No victory, however, is permanent. The errant folk fought to reclaim the wild. Great goblins generals rose from their ranks and militarized the people. Savage wars followed.

An order of knights congregated to stop this new Scourge and protect the people. Roving bands of knights dispatched themselves to the deepest pockets of the wild to cleanse the land. These crusaders drove back their feral enemy, though heavy losses were incurred. Today, their successes and sacrifices guarantee safety for all mankind.

Haven User Guide

ATTRIBUTES

STRENGTH

Raw power.

Affects health points, endurance, and damage output.

Tested when attempting feats of power.

AGILITY

Speed and nimbleness.

Affects dodge rank and move/attack speed.

Tested when attempting feats of quickness.

CRAFT

Inherent handiness.

Affects build durability and output.

Tested when attempting feats of invention.

ESSENCE

Magical Affinity.

Affects spirit points and spell power.

Tested when attempting feats of magic.

STRIKE

Physical attack rating.

Affects chance to hit.

DODGE

Physical defense rating.

Affects chance to avoid hit.

HEALTH

Points representing life force. Slowly regenerates naturally when at home.

SPIRIT

Points that can be spent on active skills and in place of stamina. Slowly regenerates naturally.

CLASSES

A starting player chooses a single Core Class from 4 base disciplines. This defines the two Consort Classes (neighbors) as well as the Opposition Class.

SOLDIER

A natural combatant, soldiers are trained in a multitude of weapons and fighting styles. They're the hunters and knights, often relying on physical force to achieve their ends. An offensive class, soldiers shun the esoteric mystics.

Primary Attribute: Strength

ARTISAN

A heavily equipped defender and craftsman, artisans provide invaluable reinforcement to groups. They're the smiths and engineers, often relying on building strong communities for support. A defensive class, builders strive against the subterfuge of explorers.

Primary Attribute: Craft

MYSTIC

A powerful specialist, mystics cast a range of spells in any number of disciplines. They're the magicians and healers, often relying on superiority through supernatural means. An offensive class, mystics abhor the banality of soldiers.

Primary Attribute: Essence

EXPLORER

A furtive wildcard, explorers use speed and smarts to achieve their goals behind the scenes. They're the spies and adventurers, often nomadic and flexible. A support class, explorers work outside the order built by artisans.

Primary Attribute: Agility

SKILLS

Skills are specific techniques that are unlocked and purchased through game progression (Ex. sniper shot, rallying aura, fireball, healing, building)

SELECTION

Skills are available for "purchase" with skill points dependent on several factors:

- Class Options
- Level Availability
- Skill Tree Access
- Quest Rewards

CLASS OPTIONS

Classes offer differing skill set opportunities.

Soldier - weapons, hand-to-hand combat, tactical skills

Builder - defense buffs, tool building, urban skills

Mystic - spells, healing, spiritual skills

Scout - sneaking, first aid, wildlife skills

A starting Core Class will contain the major skills but minor skills can be purchased in Consort Classes (although not all Consort Skills will be available). Opposition Class skills are unavailable.

LEVEL AVAILABILITY

New skills become available at certain level thresholds. It is just a matter of leveling to unlock them.

SKILL TREE ACCESS

Any skill that can be purchased outright (in the above two categories) is a root skill. However, many skills are arranged into trees. Purchasing and/or leveling a root skill, for example, may unlock a branch of skills for future purchase. Those branch skills may further unlock others. This means some skills are only accessible after mastering others.

QUEST REWARDS

Almost anything in AO can be awarded on completion of special quests. Skills are no exception.

PROGRESSION

Most skills are purchased once and done, but weapon skills have levels. Spending a point will raise general expertise with the weapon (damage, hit chance, etc.). It will also allow individual weapon skills to be upgraded. A specialized weapon skill cannot be upgraded to a level higher than the general weapon skill.

PROFICIENCIES

Proficiencies are minor skills that improve through practice and research. They do not cost spirit and aren't limited by timers. Some proficiencies are learnable by everyone, but most of them are core class abilities. In general, attempting certain activities enough will activate a proficiency, which the player can improve by repeating the activity. Certain research items can also gift proficiency advances.

Proficiencies have 3 levels of knowledge:

FLEDGLING

Player has very limited experience in the area, enough to know to attempt it but not enough to be very successful. The proficiency performed is sometimes, and with mixed success.

SKILLED

Player is familiar with the basics of the activity and can repeatedly perform it at adequate levels. This can be a handy bonus in times of need. The proficiency performed is usually moderately successful, especially under simple circumstances.

EXPERT

Through extensive research and uses, the player has surpassed most others in the area of knowledge and can perform the activity with a level of precision that will impress others. The proficiency performed is usually successful, executed at a high level, even under duress.

DEATH

The following items occur upon death:

Respawn at home with a 4 hour forced lockdown (grounded). Can read emails, but no emails out.

Random **Equipment is dropped** (not all). Can be **Salvaged** by players and immediately returned to player at home. (Having friends is good.)

Level is zeroed out to minimum XP, but no level drop. Current level points are unassigned.

Party disbanded so cannot speak until regrouped.

About the Author

I'm Domino Finn: game-developer-turned-fantasy-author, media rebel, and product of my generation. (The fun is back, oh yessiree. It's the 2600 from Atari.)

Afterlife Online will be back. Join my reader group (http://dominofinn.com/newsletter/) to get the first word on sequels, cover reveals, and other DLC.

Help Reboot level up. Please leave a review where you made your purchase, even if it's only a line or two.

Finally, don't forget to keep in touch. You can contact me, connect on social media, and see my complete book catalog at DominoFinn.com.

Made in the USA
Columbia, SC
12 December 2017